The Double

TWO VERSIONS

The Double

TWO VERSIONS

Fyodor Dostoevsky

Translated from the Russian
by Evelyn Harden

ARDIS PUBLISHERS
WOODSTOCK & NEW YORK

This edition first published in the United States in 2004 by
Ardis Publishers
Woodstock & New York

WOODSTOCK:
One Overlook Drive
Woodstock, NY 12498
[for individual orders, bulk and special sales, contact our Woodstock office]

NEW YORK:
141 Wooster Street
New York, NY 10012

Ardis Publishers is an imprint of Peter Mayer Publishers, Inc.
www.ardisbooks.com

Library of Congress Cataloging-in-Publication Data

Dostoevsky, Fyodor, 1821-1881
The double.
Translation of the original 1846 version of *Dvoinik* and a later revision.
I. Harden, Evelyn J. II. Title.
PG3326.D8   1984   891.73'3   84-20385

Printed in Canada
ISBN 0-88233-757-2
3 5 7 9 8 6 4 2

To my son, Edgar

CONTENTS

Translator's Introduction

I.

Except for a few fragmentary drafts dating from the early 1860s, there are no extant manuscripts of *The Double*. They were probably destroyed in part by Dostoevsky (along with the manuscripts for other earlier works) before his arrest in late April 1849 as a member of the Petrashevsky circle and in part by the Third Section, which confiscated his papers when arresting him.[1]

Dostoevsky began to work on *The Double* in the summer of 1845, probably in Revel, where he arrived on June 9 to spend the summer with the family of his brother, Mikhail.[2] A letter to Mikhail, written just after Dostoevsky's return to Petersburg and dated the end of August-beginning of September, shows that during the summer Dostoevsky had made his brother familiar with Mr. Golyadkin. In the letter Dostoevsky calls himself "a real Golyadkin" and promises to begin working again the next day on the tale, which he had abandoned toward the end of his stay in Revel; he justifies his slowness in taking it up again by saying: "Golyadkin has gained because of my spleen. Two ideas and one new situation were born."[3] His work on it was resumed in September 1845.[4] He wrote another letter to Mikhail on October 8, 1845, humorously using the speech formulas of Mr. Golyadkin Senior and saying that he anticipated finishing it around November 15; he told Mikhail that Belinsky was urging him to finish it and "had already spread the word about it all over the literary world and had practically concluded an advance sale to Kraevsky."[5] His letter of November 16 to Mikhail showed, however, that Golyadkin was still not finished but absolutely had to be by the 25th.[6] Dostoevsky had high hopes for its success: "Golyadkin is coming out superbly; it's going to be my masterpiece."[7]

Early in December 1845 Dostoevsky read the beginning chapters of his tale to a gathering at Belinsky's. Ivan Turgenev left when the reading was only half over. Dostoevsky described the evening many

ix

years later, in November 1877, in *The Diary of a Writer:* " . . .I think it was in early December—Belinsky insisted that I read two or three chapters of this tale at his house. For this purpose he even arranged an evening gathering (which he almost never did) and invited his closest friends. Ivan Sergeevich Turgenev was there, I remember. He listened to only half of what I read, praised it and left. He was in an awful hurry to get somewhere. Belinsky liked the three or four chapters which I read very much (although they didn't deserve it). But Belinsky didn't know the end of the tale and was under the spell of the charm of *Poor Folk.*"[8]

The Double was actually finished on January 28, 1846, four days before the issue of *Notes of the Fatherland* in which it was to appear came out.[9] On February 1, the day of its appearance, Dostoevsky wrote Mikhail: "Golyadkin is coming out today. Four days ago I was still writing it . . . Golyadkin is ten times better than *Poor Folk.* Our bunch says that after *Dead Souls* there's never been anything like it in Russia, that it's a work of genius and how they do go on! What hopes they all place in me! Really, I couldn't have had greater success with Golyadkin. You will like it better than I don't know what! You will like it even better than *Dead Souls,* that I know."[10]

In his review of *The Petersburg Collection* which had come out in January 1846 and contained *Poor Folk,* Belinsky had written: "In this issue of *Notes of the Fatherland* the Russian public will read yet another novel by Mr. Dostoevsky called *The Double.* It is more than enough to convince them that no person of ordinary talent begins his career with works of *this* kind."[11]

But the critical response to the tale, some of which is given here, was in general negative. L. V. Brant, writing in *The Northern Bee* for 28 February 1846, said:

> One cannot imagine anything more colorless, monotonous, or boring than the endlessly drawn out, mortally exhausting story of the unentertaining "adventures of Mr. Golyadkin," who, from the very beginning to the very end of the tale, is deranged, incessantly makes blunders and does foolish things that are not funny and not moving, despite all the author's efforts to depict them as such in his pretensions to some 'deep,' abstruse humor. There is no end to the wordiness— heavyhanded, annoying, irksome, to the repetitions, to the circumlocutions for one and the same thought, for one and the same words which the author has come to like so much. We sincerely pity the young man who so falsely understands art and has obviously been made confused by the literary 'coterie' which for reasons of its own claims that he is a genius.[12]

S. P. Shevyryov wrote in *The Muscovite* (No. 2, 1846):

> ...We do not understand how the author of *Poor Folk*, a tale that is nevertheless remarkable, could write *The Double*... It is a sin against artistic conscience, without which there cannot be true talent. At the start one is constantly greeting familiar figures from Gogol: now Chichikov, now the Nose, now Petrushka, now the turkey cock in the shape of a samovar, now Selifan; but the reading of the entire tale, if you really feel like reading it to the end, has the effect on you of a most unpleasant and boring nightmare after a rich supper ... Woe to a talent if it binds itself to the rush proofs of a journal and printing presses extract tales from it. Then only nightmares can be born, not poetic creations. Mr. Dostoevsky will understand us if his talent is true."[13]

K. S. Aksakov wrote in *The Petersburg Collection* in 1847:

> In this tale we now see not the influence of Gogol, but an imitation of him ... In it Mr. Dostoevsky constantly mimics Gogol and frequently imitates him to such a degree that what comes out is no longer imitation, but borrowing ... In speaking of Mr. Dostoevsky's tale *The Double*, one can repeat the words which his Mr. Golyadkin often repeats: "Dear, it's bad, bad! Dear, it's bad, bad! Dear, my case is pretty bad now! Oh, dear, so that's the turn my case has taken now!" Yes, indeed, it's bad and it's taken a bad turn. If it were not for Mr. Dostoevsky's first tale, we would have no patience whatsoever to read his second; but we did it out of obligation, wishing to find something in his tale, and we found nothing; it is so boring that we put the book down many times and came back to it again and forced ourselves to read it through. Of course, judging by the first tale we hardly expected that the second would be like this. Where is the talent that we saw in the first tale? Or did it last only for the one? It wasn't for long that Dostoevsky flattered our hopes; he has quickly shown what he is."[14]

A. A. Grigorev wrote in *The Finnish Messenger* (No. 9, 1846):

> *The Double*, in our humanly imperfect opinion, is a work that is pathological and therapeutic but by no means literary: it is a story of madness, analyzed, it is true, to the extreme, but, nevertheless, as repulsive as a dead body. Furthermore, after reading *The Double* we unwittingly thought that if the author goes any further along this path he is fated to play in our literature the role that Hoffmann plays in German literature ... Mr. Dostoevsky has immersed himself in the analysis of the life of civil servants to such an extent that boring, naked reality is now beginning to take on for him the form of a delirium close to madness. Alas! one involuntarily recalls the idea of Gogol's "The Portrait!" ...[15]

Responding in February 1846 to the attacks on *The Double* in *The Northern Bee*,[16] Belinsky said of Dostoevsky's first two efforts: "Many would consider it a glorious and brilliant thing even to conclude their careers with these works." In the March 1846 issue of *Notes of the Fatherland* Belinsky included lengthier laudatory remarks about *The Double* in his extended review of *The Petersburg Collection:*

> Being the person of unusual talent that he is, the author in no way repeated himself in his second work—and it depicts a completely new world. The hero of the novel, Mr. Golyadkin, is one of those touchy people, crazy for self-esteem, who are so frequently to be encountered in the lower and middle strata of our society. It constantly seems to him that he is being insulted by words, looks and gestures, that intrigues are being plotted against him everywhere and attempts being made to undermine him. What makes this all the more funny is that his status, his rank, his job, his brains, his abilities are absolutely incapable of arousing envy towards him in anyone. He's not bright and not stupid, not rich and not poor, is very good and has a character that is soft to the point of being weak; and he could live on this earth not at all badly; but the morbid touchiness and suspiciousness of his character is the dark demon of his life, who is fated to make a hell of his existence. If one looks more closely about oneself, how many Mr. Golyadkins one will see, poor and rich, dumb and smart! Mr. Golyadkin is in ecstasies over his sole virtue, which consists in the fact that he goes about without a mask, that he is not one who intrigues, that he acts openly and takes the direct route. Even at the very beginning of the novel it doesn't take much to guess from his conversation with the doctor, Krestyan Ivanovich, that Mr. Golyadkin is mentally deranged. And so, the hero of the novel is a madman! A bold idea and executed by the author with astonishing artistry!... Everyone to whom the secrets of art are accessible will see from the first glance that in *The Double* there is even more creative talent and greater depth of thought than in *Poor Folk*.[17]

Belinsky then parried the public's attacks on the longwindedness and resultant boringness of *The Double,* a fault which he attributed to the limitations placed on Dostoevsky's enormous talent by immaturity and inexperience. He saw the story's essential flaw in the fact that almost all the characters speak almost alike, but he felt that he would not change anything in the tale. He said:

> If the author of *The Double* were to place a pen in our hands and give us the unconditional right to remove from the manuscript of his *The Double* everything that should seem to us to be longwinded and superfluous, we would not raise our hand against a single thing because every single thing in this novel is the height of perfection. But the fact of the matter is that there are far too many such magnificent things in *The Double,* and the same thing over and over again, no matter how magnificent it may be, both wearies and bores ...[18] In general *The Double* bears the stamp of an enormous and powerful talent, but one still young

and inexperienced: this is the source of all its flaws, but it is the source of all its merits as well. The one and the other are so closely linked that if the author should now take it into his head to rework *The Double* completely in order to leave in it only its beauty and remove all flaws, we are certain he would ruin it. The author narrates the adventures of his hero from himself, but totally in his /the hero's— EJH/ language and using his ideas: this, on the one hand, shows a wealth of humor in his talent, an infinitely powerful ability to perceive objectively the phenomena of life, an ability, so to speak, to put himself inside the skin of another creature completely alien to him; but, on the other hand, this very same thing has made many incidents in the novel unclear. For instance, every reader has an absolute right not to understand and not to guess that Mr. Golyadkin is composing the letters of Vakhrameyev and of Mr. Golyadkin Junior to him in his own deranged imagination and even that Golyadkin Junior's external resemblance to him is not so great and so striking as it has seemed to him in his deranged imagination, and in general not every reader will quickly guess Golyadkin's madness. These are all flaws, even though they are closely linked with the good points and the beauty of the whole work. There is only one essential flaw in this novel: almost all the people, no matter how masterfully their characters are sketched, speak an almost identical language. There is nothing further to point out.[19]

K. S. Aksakov's attacks on *The Double* moved Belinsky to respond again early in 1847 in defense of Dostoevsky.[20] In his "Contemporary Notes" Belinsky attacked on logical grounds the idea that the critics' excessive praise of Dostoevsky's first novel so went to his head that it made him ruin his second: this was impossible because the criticism of *Poor Folk* appeared a month after *The Double* was published. More important, however, was Belinsky's attack on what he deemed an outmoded idea: that criticism can kill talent by praising and berating it. No writer of talent, he felt, can be killed in this way because "he always remains true to his poetic instinct, sometimes even when his mental convictions are telling him otherwise."[21]

At the same time, in his January 1847 article "A Look at Russian Literature of 1846" Belinsky gave his final evaluation of *The Double*. Acknowledging that *The Double* had had no success with the public, Belinsky repeated his earlier idea about the basic cause of this lack of success:

> In *The Double* the author has demonstrated enormous creative power; the character of the hero belongs among the most profound, the boldest and the truest conceptions that Russian literature can boast; there is an infinitude of intelligence and truth in this work, and of artistic craftsmanship as well; but along with these things there is a terrible inability here to master and to handle in an economical way the abundance of one's powers. All the things that in *Poor Folk* were the

excusable flaws of a first effort appear in *The Double* as monstrous flaws, and all of this consists in one thing: in the inability of a talent with all-too-rich powers to establish a wise sense of measure as well as determine limits for the artistic development of his idea.[22]

But whereas he had earlier stated that nothing should be excised because everything was the height of perfection, Belinsky now advised Dostoevsky to cut *The Double* by a third, even if it meant throwing out good material.[23] In fact, he praised Dostoevsky for having already cut a wonderful scene out of *The Double* because he had felt that it was too long.[24] Belinsky must have heard this scene when Dostoevsky read several chapters from the as yet unfinished work in early December 1845.[25].

He now also indicated that another essential flaw of the story was its fantastic aspect, by which he meant those incidents in *The Double* which are the result of Golyadkin's deranged mind but which it is difficult to distinguish from reality. That is, he was taking up a topic he had already broached in his review of *The Petersburg Collection* for 1846: that Golyadkin's madness and incidents stemming from it were not necessarily understood by all readers. At that time he had pointed out as well that great talents write for both the connoisseur and the ordinary reader and had prophesied Dostoevsky's ultimate greatness.[26] Now he cuttingly said:

In our day the fantastic can have a place only in madhouses, not in literature, and be the domain of doctors, not of poets. For all these reasons the worth of *The Double* has been measured only by a few art dilettantes for whom literary works are the object not of enjoyment alone, but of study as well. The public, however, consists not of dilettantes, but of ordinary readers who read only what directly appeals to them, without giving themselves an account of why it is not to their taste. A work which appeals to connoisseurs but not to the majority may have its merits; but a truly good work is one that appeals to both parties, or, at least, while appealing to the first is also read by the second: after all, Gogol didn't appeal to everyone, but everyone read him...[27]

The change in tone was exacerbated by Belinsky's deep disappointment in Dostoevsky's third story, "Mr. Prokharchin,"[28] which he discussed in the same review, praising Gogol as the greater talent whom the "great talent," Dostoevsky, "would find it extremely useful to take as an example."[29]

On April 1, 1846, in a letter to Mikhail, Dostoevsky responded humorously to his readers' simultaneous annoyance with him and their inability to put the book down:

> But here's what's repugnant and distressing: our bunch, Belinsky and all the rest, are unhappy with me because of Golyadkin. The first impression was one of uncontrolled ecstasy, talk, noise, rumors. The second was one of criticism, namely, absolutely everybody, that is, our bunch and the entire reading public, found Golyadkin so boring and limp, so longwinded that it's impossible to read. But the most comical thing of all is that everyone is mad at me because it's longwinded and every single one of them is reading and rereading it like crazy. And one of our bunch does nothing else except read one chapter a day so as not to wear himself out, and smacks his lips with pleasure. Other members of the public cry that it's absolutely impossible, that it's stupid both to write such things and to publish them; others cry out that they were the models for it, while from some I've heard such compliments that I'm ashamed to repeat them.[30]

But he also spoke of his own despair and misgivings about *The Double:*

> As for me, for a certain time I even fell into despair. I have a terrible fault: boundless pride and ambition. The idea that I had not lived up to expectations and had ruined a thing that could have been a great work killed me. I couldn't stand Golyadkin. A lot of it was written in haste and in a state of exhaustion. The first half is better than the second. Alongside brilliant pages there's lousy stuff, garbage; it turns your stomach; you don't feel like reading it. And this is what made life hell for a time, and I fell sick with grief.[31]

At the end of October 1846 he wrote Mikhail that he was writing another tale, but that in order to live "I am trying to make up my mind to publish *Poor Folk* and a reworked version of *The Double* as separate books. I won't, for instance, put Part I and Part 2 on them. It will simply be *Poor Folk* separately and *The Double* likewise—all that I have done in the course of the year."[32] This plan was not realized, however; Dostoevsky put it off until the following fall, explaining in his letter to Mikhail of November 26, 1846: "By then the public will be better acquainted with me and my position will be clearer."[33] According to his letter of December 17 to Mikhail, he expected to spend the summer in Revel again and "revise my old stuff and prepare an edition for the fall."[34]

In a letter to Mikhail dated January-February 1847 he sounded a positive note about *The Double:*

I hear on the quiet (and from many people) such rumors about Golyadkin that it's awful. Some say outright that this work is a *wonder* and not understood. That it will play a fearsome role in the future, that if I had written just Golyadkin I would have done enough, and that for others it's more interesting than Dumas. But, oh, has my pride been frazzled. But brother! How pleasant it is to be understood.[35]

Dostoevsky wrote his brother again in April 1847 about publishing a "reworked" version of *The Double* "at my own expense, and maybe then my fate will look brighter."[36] Dostoevsky's arrest, in April 1849, however, kept him from carrying out his plan and he did not take it up again until the fall of 1859, when he returned from exile in Siberia.[37] In a letter written to Mikhail on October 1, 1859 from Tver, where Dostoevsky had taken up residence on his return to European Russia, he described a project he had for publishing an edition of his works and said he wished to include in it "a completely reworked version of *The Double*."[38] Explaining how he would proceed with the publication of the edition, Dostoevsky spoke with exhilaration about *The Double* and its importance:

> Meanwhile towards the middle of December I'll send you (or come with it myself) the reworked version of *The Double*. Believe me, brother, that this reworked version, equipped with an introduction, will be worth *a new novel*. They will see at last what *The Double* is! I hope to do even more than get them interested. In short, I'm challenging them all to do battle (and finally if I don't put *The Double* right now, when will I put it right? Why should I lose a first-rate idea, a type of supreme social importance that I was the first to discover and of whom I was the herald?)[39]

But on October 9 Dostoevsky wrote Mikhail: "*The Double* is not being included; I'll publish it later, *if it's successful,* separately, after revising it completely and giving it an introduction."[40] So the reworking of *The Double* was again put aside and was not included in the two-volume collected works published by Osnovsky, which appeared in 1860 in Moscow.[41]

Dostoevsky did not, however, abandon the idea, as the fragmentary rough drafts in two of his notebooks show. Notebook No. 1 for 1860-62 and Notebook No. 2 for 1862-64 contain drafts that keep returning to a limited but important number of new ideas and scenes for *The Double* and reworking them.[42] (A translation of these fragments follows that of the two redactions.)

Inasmuch as Dostoevsky's work on a new redaction, nearly fifteen years after the original story, coincided with his work as a journalist for

Time and *Epoch,* so-called "burning questions of the day" that were appearing in the press—natural sciences, atheism and nihilism—characterize the fragments as well (hydrogen and oxygen; "there no longer is a Supreme Being"; freedom, anarchy and irresponsibility without the "fathers") and distinguish them from the 1846 redaction. In addition, Dostoevsky introduces scenes that take place at Petrashevsky's and hark back to the forties and his own life. The fragments are linked to the journal redaction, however, through new episodes related to the old theme of Golyadkin Senior and Klara.

Golyadkin Junior figures in all three groups of episodes: in the fragments concerning "burning questions of the day," in the gatherings at Petrashevsky's and in the love intrigue. He remains true to his original character by seeming to be Golyadkin Senior's friend and trusted confidant (with the added role of advisor), but turning against him and betraying him. For example, Golyadkin Junior "begins to teach Senior how to conquer Klara," tells him he must be able to make a *bon mot,* helps him make one up, and then at a party, where Senior displays his awkwardness, cruelly divulges their intentions. At a gathering at Petrashevsky's which Senior and Junior attend, Junior makes speeches and they embrace. The next day when Senior attempts to tell Petrashevsky that Junior will inform, Petrashevsky, already forewarned by Junior, answers that he, Senior, is the informer.

Much of the material is dominated by the idea of the relationship to one's superiors as "fathers," an idea expressed in the journal redaction by Senior but now assigned to Junior; two of the four passsages marked NB by Dostoevsky elaborate on this idea, while a third passage, in which Junior views Senior's invitation to Klara to dance the polka as constituting a rebellion against society, could also be interpreted as a statement about the relationship to one's superiors as "fathers." "The most important psychological incident" in the work that Dostoevsky now calls a "poem" is Senior's constant recourse to Junior's advice and protection at the same time that he is intriguing against Junior.

Dostoevsky later wrote in Notebook No. 6 about Golyadkin Junior: "...my most important underground type (I hope I shall be forgiven this boast inasmuch as I have acknowledged the artistic failure of the type)."[43] The fragments of *The Double* in the notebooks for 1860-64: the forties (the Petrashevsky circle), the sixties (the "burning questions of the day"), Golyadkin Junior instructing Senior in the psychology of how to conquer Klara. *Notes from Underground* (1864): Part I (the hero in the 1860s), Part II (the hero in the 1840s), the underground man confessing[44] his psychology of how to conquer Liza. The connection is not far-fetched.

In the summer or fall of 1866, when he was preparing the third volume of a new edition of his works,[45] Dostoevsky finally reworked *The Double,* returning now to the journal redaction. The changes he made are discussed in section 4 of this Introduction.

In addition to calling Golyadkin Junior his "most important underground type," Dostoevsky pointed out the significance of *The Double* in introducing an important *word* into the Russian language and Russian literature. "I invented, or, to put it better, introduced only one word into the Russian language, and it caught on; everyone uses it: the verb 'to fade away' /stushevat'sya—EJH/[46] (in Golyadkin)," he noted in Notebook No. 6 for 1872-75.[47] He took this word up again in November 1877 in *The Diary of a Writer,* when he spoke of the reading at Belinsky's in December 1845, where he had used it:

> Well, it was right there, at that reading, that the word "to fade away," which later attained such wide usage, was used by me. Everyone has forgotten the tale—this it deserves—but they picked up the new word, made it a part of their vocabulary, and established it in literature.
>
> The word *stushevat'sya* means to disappear, to be obliterated, to be reduced, so to speak, *to nothing.* But to be obliterated not all at once, not by sinking into the earth loudly and ignominiously, but, so to speak, delicately, smoothly, imperceptibly sinking into nothingness. The way shading fades away in a drawing in a strip shaded with India ink, from black gradually to lighter and finally to complete white, *to nothing.* Probably in *The Double* this word was used by me aptly in those first three chapters which I read at Belinsky's, when depicting how an annoying and sly little man knew how to disappear from the stage opportunely (or something like that; I forget). I say this because the new word aroused no perplexity in the audience. On the contrary, it was immediately understood and taken note of. Belinsky interrupted me precisely in order to praise the expression. All of those who were listening then (all of them are still alive) also praised it. I remember very well that Ivan Sergeevich Turgenev also praised it (he has most likely forgotten now) . . . It caught on and entered literature, not right away but very gradually and imperceptibly . . .[48]

But he concluded this entry in *The Diary of a Writer* with the thought that the tale was a failure:

I failed absolutely with that tale, but the idea of it was quite clear, and I never adhered to anything in literature more serious than this idea. But I failed utterly with the form of this tale. I then revised it considerably, fifteen years later, for the then "Complete Collection" of my works; but even then I again became convinced that the thing was a total failure, and if I were to take up the idea now and state it anew, I would choose a completely different form; but in '46 I hadn't found this form and couldn't cope with the tale.[49]

II

The first redaction of *The Double,* consisting of fourteen chapters, was published in *Notes of the Fatherland,* No. 2 (1846). It bore the subtitle *The Adventures of Mr. Golyadkin,* which would immediately have evoked its link with Gogol's *The Adventures of Chichikov, or Dead Souls.* Dostoevsky's work, like Gogol's, depicted adventures experienced by its hero while attempting to fulfill his social ambitions, although in Chichikov's case it is a swindler's amassing of a fortune as the stepping stone to future marital and domestic bliss that is given prominence, while in *The Double* the clerk Golyadkin's interest lies rather in promotion and an advantageous marriage. Just as in writing *Poor Folk* Dostoevsky had chosen to give a humane treatment to the subject of "The Overcoat," so, in departing from a Gogolian model a second time with *The Double,* he again takes up the theme of human dignity, this time probing the question of the deformation of personality by a rigid civil service system, having as its result in the *unstable* personality the disintegration of the human being's self-esteem, the splitting of his personality, and his subsequent descent into total madness, requiring confinement. (It must be said, however, that Golyadkin's madness is caused by the bounds of the system only insofar as the system affects an already unstable personality that is going mad. No other character in the tale is affected in this way because no one else is unstable, or, should we say, alive. Only Golyadkin Senior is destroyed by the presence of Golyadkin Junior. The others see him, too, but because he is the *accepted* spectre of their own possible fate—replacement by another, as in the case of the deceased Semyon Ivanovich—they survive psychically.)

Moreover, Dostoevsky had offered further proof of the link with *Dead Souls* in the already quoted letter to his brother, Mikhail, written on February 1, 1846, the day of the tale's appearance in *Notes of the Fatherland:* "Golyadkin is ten times better than *Poor Folk.* Our bunch says that after *Dead Souls* there's never been anything like it in Russia, . . . You will like it better than I don't know what! You will like it even better than *Dead Souls,* that I know."

But *Dead Souls* had as it model Cervantes' *El Ingenioso Hidalgo Don Quijote de la Mancha.*[50] Chichikov is an inversion of Don Quixote in which "the noblest of heroes . . . is inverted into the basest of men."[51] And in the 1846 redaction of *The Double* Dostoevsky emphasized this link as well by imitating a technique used by Cervantes and placing at the beginning of each chapter a series of subheadings, syntactically similar to those of Cervantes, that mockingly outline the content of the chapter, without revealing details of plot. Compare Cervantes: "Chapter 1—Which tells of the quality and manner of life of the famous gentleman Don Quixote of La Mancha[52] (Capítulo primero—Que trata de la condición y ejercicio del famoso hidalgo don Quijote de La Mancha[53])"; Dostoevsky: "Chapter 1: Of how Titular Councilor Golyadkin awoke . . . (Glava 1: O tom, kak prosnulsya titulyarnyi sovetnik Golyadkin . . .)"[54] But whereas Cervantes characterized each chapter briefly, often in one sentence, Dostoevsky in almost every instance supplied a paragraph of several sentences. This can probably be accounted for by the difference of length in chapters: Cervantes' chapters are very short, while Dostoevsky's are relatively long.

Dostoevsky thus directed the reader to two models: one of moral depravity and the other of spiritual perfection,[55] and selecting neither extreme, created two unremarkable twin titular councilors as his heroes, a practical man and a madman, reducing their field of operation to Petersburg. He gave to Golyadkin Junior some of the qualities of Chichikov, following closely the inversion of Don Quixote created by Gogol: his exuberance, his ability to ingratiate himself and to charm others, his self-love, his hypocrisy, concealing "craftiness, treachery and dishonesty,"[56] his enterprising nature, his cowardice, made him, in short, rogue, rascal, villain, utter heel. In the case of Golyadkin Senior Dostoevsky created his own version of Don Quixote: he gave some of Don Quixote's qualities to Golyadkin Senior,[57] but treated them mockingly. Don Quixote's love of knight-errantry, with its practice of righting wrongs, is indeed dimly reflected in Golyadkin Senior's muddled statement to His Excellency that he "thought it was chivalrous." Don Quixote's love of "the most truthful books" of chivalry, which moves him to do good deeds, is parodied in Golyadkin Senior's attack on Klara's reading of pernicious sentimental love stories, which has induced her to ask him to rescue her. Nor ought one to forget that Senior's own reading is shallow: newspapers and journals, in which the Miscellany section has great attraction for him, and a few romantic tales. Don Quixote's knightly love for an idealized Dulcinea has its counterpart in Golyadkin Senior's invention of the idea that Klara loves him and wishes him to rescue her, which he does not want to do lest he lose his post. The purity and steadfastness of Don Quixote's love is mocked in Golyadkin Senior's offer of marriage to Karolina Ivanovna and his switching of allegiance to Klara; and in neither instance does Golyadkin speak of love. Don Quixote's strength of will and perseverance[58] is mocked in Golyadkin Senior's flagging will and inability to resolve what to Don Quixote's faithful squire, Sancho Panza, who tells the Squire of the Wood of how he loves Don Quixote and will never leave him, has his counterpart in Golyadkin Senior's rapscallion of a servant, Petrushka, who leaves him for a better post. And finally, but by no means exhausting the list, Dostoevsky endows his hero with the madness of "the maddest man in the world,"[59] of whom he wrote so movingly. Don Quixote, however, is returned to sanity and dies, still tended by the faithful, weeping Sancho and by his family and friends, while Golyadkin Senior becomes totally mad and, terrified and utterly alone, is driven to a madhouse accompanied only by his doctor, whom he now sees as a demon. Dostoevsky thus reduced the consummate rogue and the pure knight to a pair of mediocre twin clerks in the government service in Petersburg with their mediocre and limited demands for a post, or a promotion, or a profitable marriage, and made his tale a study of the deformation of personality caused by the lack of freedom in Russian life "to fulfill /one's/ Ego."[60]

Danilevsky, in comparing Don Quixote and Chichikov, spoke of the barrenness of Spanish and Russian life. "Don Quixote," he said, "turned out to be a living impersonation—rising to heroism—of the noblest spiritual qualities, for which a field for productive normal activity was lacking because of the emptiness of Spanish life ... in Cervantes' time a Spanish hero had no practical outlet. The realm of fantasy alone remained for him."[61] Chichikov he called the "hero of practical life ... deprived, on the one hand, of all idealism in his efforts ... on the other hand, unable to direct his activity towards something that is really practical and beneficial. This inability proceeds from the barrenness of Russian life, from its narrowness and its lack of freedom. Persons with a practical type of mind had to resort to ambitions that were purely personal, crudely egoistic, to the trickery of roguery, and to precisely that roguery connected with government offices which permeated all of Russian life."[62] Dostoevsky, in his fourth feuilleton, written on June 15, 1847, made his statement about the message of *The Double* when he took up the question of a person's "most natural necessity to become aware of, to embody and to fulfill his Ego in real life" and spoke of the stifling conditions of Russian life which destroy this "necessary egoism" and cause Russians to "have little sense of personal dignity,"[63] a lack of which leads to "psychic malformations."[64]

In 1866 Dostoevsky shortened the tale to thirteen chapters, combining chapters X and XI into one chapter. He replaced the subtitle *The Adventures of Mr. Golyadkin* with *A Poem of Petersburg* and removed the summarizing sentences at the beginning of each chapter. In this way the link between *The Double* and *Dead Souls* and *Don Quixote* was no longer made direct. The new subtitle now linked the work to Pushkin's poem *The Bronze Horseman,* with its theme of Petersburg, a city built on a swamp by decree of the same Peter the Great who established the Table of Ranks that stifled Golyadkin's life. *The Bronze Horseman* deals with the fate of the minor clerk, Evgeny, whose ambitions go no further than the security of job that would enable him to marry his Parasha. The drowning of his beloved as a result of one of the recurrent floods caused by the rising of the Neva River drives Evgeny insane and emboldens him to shake his fist at the monument to the man whose will was the source of all the benefits and disasters in the lives of Petersburg's inhabitants. Imagining, however, that the equestrian statue of Peter descends from its pedestal to pursue him, Evgeny runs for his life and from then on passes the monument meekly and submissively. Not long after he is found dead on one of the islands of the Neva. As traditionally interpreted, the poem deals with the conflict between the individual and the State,[65] and in this sense *The Double* belongs to *The Bronze Horseman* tradition. Moreover, just as in writing *Poor Folk* Dostoevsky set up Pushkin's compassionate attitude toward the clerk Samson Vyrin ("The Station Master") as the model to be emulated in contrast to Gogol's mocking attitude toward his clerk Akaky Akakievich ("The Overcoat"), so, in revising *The Double,* Dostoevsky again selected Pushkin's compassion for Evgeny over Gogol's satiric treatment of Chichikov, by making the links between *The Double* and *Dead Souls* and *Don Quixote* less obvious and establishing instead the link with *The Bronze Horseman.*

Early in chapter I the 1846 redaction contained a passage that continued the link with *Don Quixote:*

> The fact of the matter is that he very much liked sometimes to make himself the hero of a most ingenious novel, to entangle himself mentally in various intrigues and difficulties and, finally, to deliver himself from all unpleasantness with honor, eliminating all obstacles, conquering difficulties and magnanimously forgiving his enemies.

When Dostoevsky removed the subheadings, he also removed this passage. He removed as well in Golyadkin Senior's tirade against Klara (XIV: 1846) the reference to her as "moya siyatel'naya," a reference indicating her father's social ambitions for her, his intention to marry her to a count. I believe Dostoevsky removed these words because they hark back to the discussion between Sancho Panza and his wife about the fact that their daughter should be a countess, now that Sancho is to be the governor of an island. There are repeated references at this point in *Don Quixote* to "Your Ladyship," certainly a possible translation of "siyatel'naya," though I have rendered it as "little aristocrat." Dostoevsky left one overt reference to Spain in the Spanish serenade that Klara wants Golyadkin Senior to sing to her, but no one would be likely to use it to link *The Double* and *Don Quixote.*

However, he left many references to *Don Quixote* in his text. The reason seems to be that to remove them would have meant a major revision of *The Double.* For example, Don Quixote, at the beginning of his adventures, goes through the ceremony of keeping watch over his arms in the courtyard of the inn, where bright moonlight enables the spectators to see "every action of our new knight." Surely this is the inspiration for the scene near the end of *The Double* in which Golyadkin Senior hides behind the woodpile in Olsufi Ivanovich's courtyard and later is betrayed by the light from the windows which shows him up behind his woodpile to the guests. In chapter III of part I Don Quixote thinks he needs no money in his wanderings, but is told by the innkeeper that knights-errant carry money and a chest of ointments to heal their wounds. His modern counterpart, Golyadkin Senior, lovingly counts his money and takes it with him as he sallies forth; his doctor gives him a prescription which, when filled, consists of a vial of medicine for his psychic wounds. *Don Quixote* is filled with references to the age in which he lives: "our age and ... these our calamitous times," "our depraved age" and "I was born in the Age of Iron to restore in it the Golden Age." To this we must compare Golyadkin Senior's many statements about "the times in which we live" and "our industrial age." In chapter V of part I Don Quixote, the hero claiming to be people he cannot possibly be, on being told that he is not these people, says, "I know who I am," while Golyadkin Senior disclaims being himself: "It's not me." Don Quixote frequently speaks of enchantment and enchanters, who change what he sees, e.g., an army into sheep. Golyadkin Senior speaks several times of enchantment and magic: he says the behavior of others is such that someone must have cast a spell over everyone today; in the scene in which he is asked to pay for eleven pasties he asks himself whether some kind of wizardry is being practiced on him; he says that if a magician were to give him a chance to cut off a finger in order to make Junior disappear, he would agree. In *Don Quixote* there is a discussion of the use of the word "whoreson" as a form of praise. Compare to this the scene in which Golyadkin Senior tells the drunken Petrushka that the word "rogue," with which he addresses Petrushka, is not an insult. In the opening paragraph of chapter XLV in part II the narrator asks in high-flown language to be granted the ability to describe scrupulously Sancho's government, while in chapter IV of *The Double* the narrator, using a device called paralipsis, dwells at length in similar manner on Klara's birthday party. Nor should we forget that whereas Don Quixote (chapter XXII of part I) defies the king by freeing a group of convicts going "to serve the king in the galleys," stating as his reason that they "are being taken to their destination by force and not by their own free will," Golyadkin Senior looks upon his superiors as "fathers" (in the fragments the idea becomes his pitiful obsession—"How can one be without a father? I can't be without having someone who is like a father to me"). This is by no means the extent of the parallels, which are also lost through the deletion of the subheadings.

III

In addition to the now invisible ties with *Don Quixote*, *The Double* contains other ties, for example, with works by Gogol other than *Dead Souls*.[66] "The Diary of a Madman," the story of a poor clerk who falls in love with His Excellency's daughter, loses out to a rival who is richer and higher in rank and goes mad, comes immediately to mind. The correspondence between two poodles in Gogol's tale is replaced by Dostoevsky with Mr. Golyadkin Senior's exchange of invented letters with human beings, amounting to an exchange of self-derogation and self-defense. Poprishchin imagines in his madness that he is the King of Spain; Golyadkin Senior, going off to the madhouse, looks back at the Kingdom of Berendeyev, as the ultimate to which he aspired socially and from whose light he is cast out permanently into the exterior darkness (which is predicted on page one, where he wakes and knows that he is "not in some faroff kingdom").

"The Nose," in which the hero, Kovalyov, loses his nose, expects social ostracism for being different from others, is distressed to encounter the nose uniformed and of a higher rank than himself, but to his joy finds it back on his face one day, has as its theme the loss of social status that results from the loss of normalcy, from no longer being ordinary. In chapter I of *The Double* Mr. Golyadkin, like Kovalyov, examines his face in a mirror and, while he finds nothing missing, considers the disaster which would occur should he find, for example, a pimple. Mr. Golyadkin Senior's response to Junior's brazenness in chapter VIII: "I don't know, my dear sir, . . . how to explain to you now the strangeness of your behavior to me" is reminiscent of Kovalyov's remark to his nose.

"The Overcoat," in which the hero gets justice only beyond the grave, has its echoes in *The Double* as well, in the scene in which Mr. Golyadkin Junior, having requested permission from His Excellency to speak to Mr. Golyadkin Senior, addresses him in a manner similar to that in which the Important Person addressed Akaky Akakievich.

The scene from "The Story of How Ivan Ivanovich Quarreled with Ivan Nikiforovich" in which the two Ivans are pushed together for a reconciliation finds its parallel in the scene in the final chapter of *The Double* in which the two Mr. Golyadkins are brought together at Olsufi Ivanovich's.

There are also stylistic features which are Gogolian. For example, the description of the boiling samovar in chapter I is in Gogol's style. The reference to Mr. Golyadkin Junior as "extremely amiable in all respects" echoes, of course, *Dead Souls* and "the lady agreeable in all respects." The description of the ball at the beginning of chapter IV is similar in style to Gogol's comic descriptions and should be compared to the description of the party at the governor's in chapter I of the first volume of *Dead Souls*.[67] Gogol's ironic tones can be heard in Golyadkin's conversation with Petrushka about a coach in chapter I and are a reminder of the opening scenes of Gogol's *The Marriage*.[68] The servant bawling out the Ukrainian name, "the Bassavryukovs," is also reminiscent of early Gogol.

Pushkin's *The Bronze Horseman* can be detected in *The Double*—in the second paragraph of chapter V, the chapter in which the double appears, Mr. Golyadkin Senior is described in a manner much like Evgeny, running with "all his might as if fleeing a pursuer."

The idea of a "rag-person" appears in Lazhechnikov's *House of Ice,* which Dostoevsky liked very much and from which he may have taken the idea, turning it into a generalized expression of the fate of a downtrodden and humiliated person, suffering as a result of the loss of his rights as a human being.[69]

The influence of E. T. A. Hoffmann's stories on *The Double* has also been shown.[70]

Another likely influence is that of Greek mythology and tragedy. An excellent paper by one of my students entitled "Mythology and Violence: Unseen Elements in *The Idiot,*" which attempts to reappraise the figure of Myshkin as a Dionysus rather than a Christ figure and "to show that selected incidents and characters in *The Idiot* are illustrative of Rene Girard's theory of violence and sacrifice,"[71] led me to Girard's *Violence and the Sacred.*[72] What is interesting is that in *Violence and the Sacred* Girard makes mention of *The Double* in the chapter "From Mimetic Desire to the Monstrous Double," saying: "To my knowledge only Dostoevsky, both in his early novel 'The Double' and in the masterpieces of his maturity has set forth in concrete terms the elements of reciprocity at work in the proliferation of monsters."[73] I believe the topic deserves serious investigation.

IV

If we now try to characterize the differences between the redactions of 1846 and 1866 chapter by chapter, we see that chapters I-VII contain very few changes, VIII-IX contain more differences but no shifting of material, and X-XIV (X-XIII) contain changes which entail extensive shifts of material and cuts.

For example, in chapter I Dostoevsky cut out in the 1866 redaction a section containing the already cited passage about Mr. Golyadkin as the hero of an ingenious novel, because he was removing traces of references to *Don Quixote.* Two other cuts removed repetitious phrases. He also changed "mucky green" to "mucky greenish" and qualified "painted table," making it "red painted table."

In chapter II the very few differences between the two redactions consist chiefly of changes in punctuation. Dostoevsky also removed a few words, such as "my" and "his" and "but." He also removed repetitions, for example, when Krestyan Ivanovich's name appears twice in one sentence in direct address, or, when Krestyan Ivanovich says: "I did explain to you, I did explain to you last time . . ." He added a few words, such as "cleared his throat," and he changed some, such as "ispravit'" to "popravit'," which does not affect their translation.

In chapters III and IV Dostoevsky mainly cut repetitions. In chapter IV he added "he also wanted to dance with Klara Olsufyevna," an authorial comment.

In chapter V he made one cut, which is an authorial comment explaining the meaning of Mr. Golyadkin's condition: "He understood at last that he was utterly losing his presence of mind, that he was falling into an abyss."

In 1866 the first half of chapter VI had several cuts made in it, ranging from two to seven lines long. Deletions were made primarily of repetitious material, sometimes of material that gets too far ahead of the story, and of material that develops Golyadkin's suspicions concerning Petrushka.

In chapter VII, too, cuts are made chiefly in material referring to Petrushka and the fact that he knows everything.

In chapter VIII repetitious phrases and words were cut, as was a passage about Petrushka. However, Mr. Golyadkin's ranting and raving was dwelt on at greater length, as was his stupor. Again, as in chapter V, an authorial comment on his condition was removed: "The reality of the matter was at last killing Mr. Golyadkin."

In chapter IX Dostoevsky made cuts of the following kind: part of Mr. Golyadkin's ravings and repetitions such as "horn of arrogance" was deleted, as were statements that he must act, the question of whether his situation was reprehensible, Petrushka's involvement, Petrushka's drunkenness, Mr. Golyadkin Senior's self-teasing when he waits before opening the letter, his remarks about people, masks and impostorship. There were changes of individual words as well.

For the remaining chapters, which underwent more complex changes, a plot summary must be supplied. In chapter X (1846) Mr. Golyadkin wakes up, thinks of his situation, his dreams, his situation again, wakes up completely, discovers the door is locked and rushes back to bed to see whether he is dreaming or awake, thinks in great detail about his situation, dresses, lets himself out with another key, leaves for the office, changes his mind, and comes back home, where he writes a second letter to Vakhrameyev and a note to Golyadkin Junior. He then heads for the office again, pondering along the way that he needlessly wrote the letter and note and contemplating a style of writing that would have been more suitable. He arrives at his office building, talks down below with Ostafyev and Pisarenko, the copyists (another instance of the idea of replacement of one person by another), sees Mr. Golyadkin Junior go out on an assignment and return, and decides to go upstairs to his office.

In chapter XI (1846) it is dusk when Mr. Golyadkin Senior arrives at his office. His colleagues all treat him in a strange manner and form a circle around him. Suddenly Mr. Golyadkin Junior appears. He is very friendly to everyone except Mr. Golyadkin Senior. After accidentally shaking his hand, he wipes off his fingers, insulting Mr. Golyadkin Senior. He smoothes away the momentary disfavor of the other clerks by making a successful joke at Mr. Golyadkin Senior's expense. Mr. Golyadkin Senior tries to see His Excellency. Anton Antonovich tells him that the abominable deeds perpetrated by him against two ladies and against Mr. Golyadkin Junior have been made known and that he will hear of it officially that day. Mr. Golyadkin Senior says that he is not a freethinker and tries to blame Petrushka, but Anton Antonovich has no time for him. The guard gives Mr. Golyadkin Senior a letter from Vakhrameyev, which Mr. Golyadkin Senior puts into his pocket. The entire staff leaves work. Mr. Golyadkin Senior rushes out in pursuit of Mr. Golyadkin Junior.

In 1866 Dostoevsky combined the 1846 chapters X and XI to form chapter X. He changes the material from X (1846) substantially at the beginning of the chapter. Thus, Mr. Golyadkin wakes, thinks of his dreams and his situation, and wakes up completely. He discovers the door is locked, dresses, writes a very brief note to Mr. Golyadkin Junior, lets himself out with another key, and goes to the office. He talks down below to Ostafyev and Pisarenko, the copyists, sees Mr. Golyadkin Junior go out on an assignment and return, and decides to go upstairs to the office, too. By removing the second letter to Vakhrameyev, Dostoevsky deemphasized the theme of the impostor-usurper (Otrepyev). He also cut this reference out of the brief note to Mr. Golyadkin Junior which was retained in 1866. In addition he removed the theme of whether Mr. Golyadkin Senior is awake or asleep, as well as an allusion to chivalry, which was a link to the theme of Don Quixote. The material from XI (1846) which went into X (1866) remained essentially unchanged, except for the passage about freethinking and Petrushka's drunkenness and unreliability, which was deleted in chapter X (1866).

Chapter XII (1846) became chapter XI (1866). In XII (1846) Mr. Golyadkin Senior catches hold of Mr. Golyadkin Junior as he is getting into a carriage and persuades him to go into a coffee house to talk, which they do at length. During the conversation Mr. Golyadkin Junior's brazenness, familiarity, insulting behavior, and aggressiveness are depicted in detail. He wipes the fingers Mr. Golyadkin Senior has touched in shaking hands, as in chapter X (1846). He then runs away from Mr. Golyadkin Senior into the next room and soon after out of the coffee house. He gets into a droshky, but Mr. Golyadkin succeeds in getting in as well. Mr. Golyadkin Senior falls out as the carriage enters Olsufi Ivanovich's courtyard. Mr. Golyadkin Junior goes to see Olsufi Ivanovich while Mr. Golyadkin Senior runs away, en route knocking over two peasant women selling their wares. He runs into an eating establishment to read Vakhrameyev's letter, which he has just felt in his pocket. Vakhrameyev's letter is important because it takes up Mr. Golyadkin Senior's bad reputation and poor behavior toward Karolina Ivanovna. Impostorship is raised in this letter in answer to Mr. Golyadkin Senior's mention of it in his second letter to Vakhrameyev (X—1846). Karolina Ivanovna's connections, described at length, consist mostly of relatives, including an uncle who is the apothecary from whom Mr. Golyadkin gets his medicine; they also include Krestyan Ivanovich Rutenshpits. Having read Vakhrameyev's letter, Mr. Golyadkin Senior comes to and realizes how disreputable he looks. He then discovers the vial of medicine in his pocket and comes to the conclusion that it is poison and part of a plot devised by the Germans in Vakhrameyev's letter to murder him. He runs out of the eating establishment and goes home, where he meets the office guard, Mikheyev, with an official communication announcing that Mr. Golyadkin Senior has been relieved of his duties. Petrushka shows him another letter, this one from Klara Olsufyevna, begging him to rescue her. It, too, contains references to impostors and the text shows very clearly that Mr. Golyadkin Senior composed it because it is permeated with his particular commonplaces of speech style. Her letter concludes the chapter.

When Dostoevsky revised XII (1846) and made it XI (1866), he did the following: Mr. Golyadkin Senior catches Mr. Golyadkin Junior as he is getting into a carriage and persuades him to go into a coffee house to talk, which they do more briefly than in XII (1846). Mr. Golyadkin Junior's response to the idea about twins, for example, is limited to one sentence only. He then wipes the fingers Mr. Golyadkin Senior has touched in shaking his hand. He runs away from Mr. Golyadkin Senior into the next room and then out of the coffee house. He gets into a droshky, but Mr. Golyadkin Senior succeeds in getting in as well. Mr. Golyadkin Senior falls out as the carriage enters Olsufi Ivanovich's courtyard. Mr. Golyadkin Junior goes to see Olsufi Ivanovich, while Mr. Golyadkin Senior runs away, en route knocking over two peasant women selling their wares. He runs into an eating establishment to read a letter given him by the copyist that morning, which he has just felt in his pocket. It is from Klara Olsufyevna, who begs him to rescue her. It is shorter than in XII (1846) and contains no references to impostors. It also contains fewer of Mr. Golyadkin Senior's speech formulae, but enough to identify him still as author. Having read it, Mr. Golyadkin Senior comes to and realizes how disreputable he looks. He then discovers the vial of medicine in his pocket. It is not clear what the words he speaks when he pulls it out mean: a line like "Medicines are sold in the same apothecary shop" has no meaning and seems to have been an oversight on Dostoevsky's part, left in when he removed Vakhrameyev's letter. Nor does Mr. Golyadkin Senior actually say it is poison. He runs out and goes home, where he meets the office guard with a letter announcing that Mr. Golyadkin Senior has been relieved of his duties.

Chapter XIII (1846) became chapter XII (1866). In XIII (1846) Mr. Golyadkin Senior's condition after reading Klara Olsufyevna's letter is described. Mr. Golyadkin Senior and Petrushka discuss Petrushka's departure and Mr. Golyadkin Senior's elopement. Petrushka goes downstairs to bargain for a fox cloak for Klara Olsufyevna. Mr. Golyadkin Senior leaves his apartment. On the street he engages in a long, irate monologue addressed to Klara Olsufyevna, blaming her upbringing for her present immorality. He hires a cabbie for his elopement and goes to the home of his superior, whom he could not get to see at the office. He is admitted and after some discussion among the guests, who include his doctor, he is told that his case will be looked into and that he will be shown out. But he stays to complain against Mr.

Golyadkin Junior and is removed by his superior's servants and accompanied to the door by Mr. Golyadkin Junior. They exchange insults. He runs out, gets into his carriage and drives off.

Chapter XII (1866) is almost identical. The remarks about Mr. Golyadkin Senior's reaction to Klara Olsufyevna's letter are deleted because the previous chapter, XI (1866), did not conclude with her letter. One full speech of Mr. Golyadkin Senior's—in which he speaks further of Petrushka's awareness of his elopement—is deleted, as is a speech of Petrushka's—in which he speaks of the need to serve a good person.

Chapter XIV (1846) became chapter XIII (1866). In XIV (1846) Mr. Golyadkin Senior hides behind a woodpile in Olsufi Ivanovich's courtyard, waiting for Klara Olsufyevna. His cabbie comes to find him and receives the news that they will depart soon. Mr. Golyadkin Senior again launches into a tirade against the absent Klara Olsufyevna and tells her what their married life would be like and how unsuitable he is for her. The cabbie comes again and this time is paid and dismissed. Mr. Golyadkin Senior runs away from the courtyard, but then decides to return to his woodpile. He realizes he is not totally shielded by it and is visible to Olsufi Ivanovich's guests. Mr. Golyadkin Junior comes out and takes him inside, where the apartment is overflowing with guests. A kind of court is set up to judge him, consisting of Olsufi Ivanovich, Klara Olsufyevna, Vladimir Semyonovich, Andrei Fillipovich. Mr. Golyadkin Senior and Mr. Golyadkin Junior are brought together and the former receives the latter's Judas kiss. Suddenly Krestyan Ivanovich enters. Mr. Golyadkin is terrified. He is dragged out by Krestyan Ivanovich to a waiting carriage, which they both enter. Mr. Golyadkin Junior runs along beside it and finally disappears. No conversation takes place between Krestyan Ivanovich and Mr. Golyadkin Senior. Mr. Golyadkin Senior sinks into forgetfulness, then wakes to see a pair of fiery eyes. They come closer and closer. He feels as though a monster is poised, ready to grab hold of him, that this is not the same Krestyan Ivanovich that he knew before. He simply waits for something to happen to him. At this point the narrator announces that the story of Mr. Golyadkin's adventures is over.

In chapter XIII (1866) Dostoevsky changed the ending. When Mr. Golyadkin Senior comes to in the carriage, he does not lean against Krestyan Ivanovich. He sits alone and notices the landscape, which is described briefly. No snow is falling. Suddenly he notices the two fiery eyes looking at him and feels that this is a different, terrible Krestyan Ivanovich. He tries to appease Krestyan Ivanovich by saying that he seems to be all right. But Krestyan Ivanovich sternly announces to him in an indirect manner that he is on his way to a madhouse, by telling him what services will be supplied to him. He tells Mr. Golyadkin Senior that he is, however, not worthy of receiving them and makes him feel guilty. Mr. Golyadkin Senior screeches and grabs his head, for he has had a premonition of this. Thus, the fantastic and spooky ending is replaced by a more realistic and cruel one, one more in keeping with the preceding tone and style of the tale, and the final line with the word "adventures of Mr. Golyadkin" is removed in keeping with the removal of the subtitle. The conversation makes it clear that Mr. Golyadkin Senior is going to a madhouse and that the doctor, in reinforcing Mr. Golyadkin Senior's feelings that he does not deserve even the little he will be given, has become totally unsympathetic. The fact that the closing sentence consists of one of Mr. Golyadkin Senior's refrains is appropriate. Why, however, does Krestyan Ivanovich, who spoke perfect Russian (although he had the foreigner's difficulty in understanding some sayings) when he received his patient in chapter II, suddenly at the end clearly become a German speaking broken Russian? Dostoevsky removed Vakhrameyev's letter with its list of Germans supporting the abused Karolina Ivanovna, but reverts to his xenophobia here by making this demonic and cruel character, who in Mr. Golyadkin's eyes is another Krestyan Ivanovich, not the former one, cease to speak perfect Russian and betray his German origins.[74] The idea of two Krestyan Ivanoviches is as well another instance of the impostor.

To sum up, the differences between the redactions of 1846 and 1866 may be characterized as follows: (1) features which indicated the literary tradition to which the work belonged were deleted, and it was assigned to another literary tradition; (2) the number of chapters was reduced from fourteen to thirteen, by extensively cutting chapter X and combining it with chapter XI; (3) wordiness and repetitiveness were cut by reducing dialogues and monologues in size and cutting the correspondence between Golyadkin Senior and Vakhrameyev from two letters to one; (4) passages having to do with xenophobia and Golyadkin Senior's resultant fear of being poisoned were shortened and made much more obscure; (5) the theme of whether Golyadkin Senior was awake or asleep was shortened; (6) the theme of the impostor-usurper was made less obvious; (7) punctuation was changed; (8) the second half of the tale, especially chapters X, XII, and XIV underwent extensive change; (9) the ending was changed.

V

The layout of the translation requires an explanation. It was decided that the two redactions would not be reproduced separately in their entirety. The beginning of each redaction is given on facing pages, 1846 on the left, 1866 on the right, so that Dostoevsky's use of subheadings in the 1846 version would be clear. After this, the 1866 redaction continues as the basic text, and where the 1846 version differs from it these differences are given in italics in brackets. This procedure is followed in chapters I through IX, because they do not differ greatly in the two redactions. Starting with chapter X, the translations of the two redactions are presented separately, because they differ considerably from each other. The 1866 redaction of chapters X-XIII is presented first, followed by the 1846 redaction of chapters X-XIV. Because of the extent of these differences, it has not been possible to keep the two translations parallel.

Some punctuation has been changed in the interest of clarity and to suit English usage. Thus, even when the punctuation differs in the two Russian redactions, such differences may not be distinguished or acknowledged in the English versions.

I have tried to translate recurring words and expressions identically each time they appear so that the reader will become aware of Mr. Golyadkin Senior's style of thought and speech. In this way it becomes clear, I believe, that Mr. Golyadkin has to be the author of the letter from Klara Olsufyevna, as it is couched in terms that he constantly uses.

I wish to thank Irina Reid for her graciousness in spending many hours discussing the manuscript with me. I would also like to thank Robert Allen, Igor Grabar, Simon Karlinsky and Edward Kasinec for kindly answering my letters about the translation of certain terms, some technical. I am grateful to the Dean of Arts at Simon Fraser University for defraying some of the typing expenses. I wish also to express my deep gratitude to Bobette Grant for her competence, humor and patience in typing the manuscript.

Evelyn Jasiulko Harden

Notes

1. F. M. Dostoevsky, *Polnoe sobranie sochinenii (Complete Works),* 30 volumes, vol. 1 (Leningrad, 1972), p. 457. The present translation of both redactions of *The Double* is based on this volume (pp. 109-229 and pp. 334-431). This edition will henceforth be referred to as *PSS*.

2. Ibid., p. 482.

3. Ibid., p. 483; F. M. Dostoevsky, *Pis'ma (Letters),* edited and annotated by A. S. Dolinin, 4 volumes, vol. 1 (Moscow, 1928), p. 80. The description of Dostoevsky's feelings on arriving back in Petersburg, his arrival at his apartment, etc. (pp. 79-80) remind one greatly of details in *The Double.*

All translations of Russian material cited in the Introduction are my own.

4. *PSS,* vol. 1, p. 483.

5. Ibid., p. 43; Dolinin, vol. 1, pp. 81-82.

6. *PSS,* vol. 1, p. 483; Dolinin, vol. 1, p. 83.

7. *PSS,* vol. 1, p. 483; Dolinin, vol. 1, p. 85.

8. *PSS,* vol. 1, p. 483; *PSS,* vol. 26, pp. 65-66; *The Diary of a Writer,* trans. and annotated by Boris Brasol (New York, 1954), p. 883.

9. *PSS,* vol. 1, p. 483.

10. *PSS,* vol. 1, p. 483; Dolinin, vol. 1, p. 87.

11. *PSS,* vol. 1, p. 489; V. G. Belinsky, *Polnoe sobranie sochinenii (Complete Works),* 13 volumes, vol. 9 (Moscow, 1955), p. 476.

12. *PSS,* vol. 1, p. 490.

13. Ibid., pp. 490-91.

14. Ibid., p. 491.

15. Ibid.

16. *PSS,* vol. 1, p.489; Belinsky, vol. 9, p. 493.

17. *PSS,* vol. 1, p. 489-90; Belinsky, vol. 9, pp. 563-64.

18. Belinsky, vol. 9, p. 564.

19. *PSS,* vol. 1, p. 490; Belinsky, vol. 9, p. 565.

20. *PSS,* vol. 1, p. 492.

21. Belinsky, vol. 10, p. 98.

22. *PSS,* vol. 1, p. 492; Belinsky, vol. 10, p. 40.

23. *PSS,* vol. 1, p. 492; Belinsky, vol. 10, p. 41.

24. Belinsky, vol. 10, p. 41.

25. Ibid., p. 434.

26. *PSS,* vol. 1, p. 492; Belinsky, vol. 9, p. 566.

27. Ibid., p. 41.

28. *PSS,* vol. 1, p. 492; Dolinin, vol. 1, pp. 41-42.

29. Belinsky, vol. 10, p. 42.

30. *PSS,* vol. 1, p. 484; Dolinin, vol. 1, pp. 88-89.

31. *PSS,* vol. 1, p. 484; Dolinin, vol. 1, p. 89.

32. Dolinin, vol. 1, p. 100.

33. Ibid., p. 102.

34. Ibid., p. 104.

35. *PSS,* vol. 1, p. 484; Dolinin, vol. 1, p. 108.

36. *PSS,* vol. 1, p. 484; Dolinin, vol. 1, p. 109.

37. *PSS,* vol. 1, p. 484.

38. *PSS,* vol. 1, p. 484; Dolinin, vol. 1, p. 256.

39. Dolinin, vol. 1, p. 257.

40. *PSS,* vol. 1, p. 484; Dolinin, vol. 2, p. 606.

41. *PSS,* vol. 1, p. 484.

42. *Neizdannyi Dostoevskii,* eds. I. Zil'bershtein and L. Rozenblium, *Literaturnoe nasledstvo,* vol. 83 (Moscow, 1971), pp. 136-40, 178-79; *PSS,* vol. 1, p. 432-436; *The Unpublished Dostoevsky,* 3 volumes, ed. Carl Proffer, vol. 1 (Ardis, 1973), pp. 14-16 and 45-46. There are discrepancies between the versions in *Neizdannyi Dostoevskii* and *PSS.*

43. *Neizdannyi Dostoevskii,* pp. 310-11; *PSS,* vol. 1, p. 489; *The Unpublished Dostoevsky,* vol. 2 (Ardis, 1975), p. 28.

44. Dostoevsky also considered *The Double* to be a confession. He had written Mikhail in January-February 1847 that *Netochka Nezvanova* was "going to be a confession, like *Golyadkin,* but in a different tone and genre" (Dolinin, vol. 1, p. 108).

45. *PSS,* vol. 1, p. 485.

46. The verb has the technical meaning of "to pass gradually and imperceptibly, by means of the process of shading, from dark to light," and thence the meaning "to vanish," "to fade away," "to efface oneself," "to play a modest or a background role."

47. *Neizdannyi Dostoevskii,* p. 310; *PSS,* vol. 1, p. 489; *The Unpublished Dostoevsky,* vol. 2, p. 28.

48. *PSS,* vol. 26, p. 66; Brasol, pp. 883-884. It has been pointed out that Dostoevsky had to have read four chapters at Belinsky's, as the word "stushevat'sya" appears in chapter IV of *The Double (PSS,* vol. 26, p. 385), that Turgenev could not have left when the reading was only half over and still praised the use of the word because it appears in chapter IV (Ibid.), and that the word was used in Pushkin's time with the same meaning in conversational speech (Ibid., p. 384). But Dostoevsky was writing thirty-two years after the fact.

49. *PSS,* vol. 26, p. 65; Brasol, p. 883.

50. Pushkin, in giving Gogol the plot for *Dead Souls,* a plot he had intended to use himself and base on *Don Quixote,* spoke of Cervantes, urging Gogol to emulate the Spanish author in writing a long work to establish his place in Russian literature (Ludmilla B. Turkevich, *Cervantes in Russia* New York, 1975, pp. 44-45). Gogol himself alluded to *Don Quixote* in the last third of *Dead Souls* (Ibid., p. 53), thus showing his "sustained awareness of Cervantes and his hero" (Ibid., pp. 53-54).

51. Ibid., p. x.

52. Miguel de Cervantes Saavedra, *Don Quixote of La Mancha,* translated and with an introduction by Walter Starkie (New York, 1964), p. v.

53. Miguel de Cervantes Saavedra, *El Ingenioso Hidalgo Don Quijote de La Mancha* (Buenos Aires—Mexico, 1945), p. 19.

54. *PSS,* vol. 1, p. 334.

55. Turkevich, p. 50.

56. Ibid.

57. Turkevich sees Golyadkin as a quixotic figure, but does not develop the idea (p. 120).

58. Ibid., p. 51.

59. Ibid., p. 116; *PSS,* vol. 26, p. 25; Brasol, p. 836. Turkevich writes "Cervantes was the first novelist to create an abnormal individual as his hero" and Dostoevsky was "his most gifted counterpart" (p. 115).

60. Joseph Frank, *Dostoevsky: The Seeds of Revolt, 1821-1849* (Princeton, N.J., 1976), p. 233; *PSS,* vol. 18, p. 31;David Magarshack,*Dostoevsky's Occasional Writings* (New York, 1963), p. 33.

61. Turkevich, pp. 51-52.

62. Ibid., p. 52.

63. Frank, pp. 232-33; *PSS,* vol. 18, p. 31; Magarshack, p. 33.

64. Frank, p. 233.

65. For a different interpretation see Richard Gregg, "The Nature of Nature and the Nature of Eugene in *The Bronze Horseman," Slavic and East European Journal* 21, No. 2 (1977), pp. 167-79.

66. Many detailed analyses have been written of the influence of Gogol on Dostoevsky. See Priscilla Meyer and Stephen Rudy, eds., *Dostoevsky and Gogol* (Ardis, 1979) for a translation of some of them as well as an excellent introduction.

67. *PSS,* vol. 1, p. 486.

68. Ibid.

69. Ibid., p. 487.

70. Charles Passage, *Dostoevski the Adapter* (Chapel Hill, N.C., 1954), pp. 14-37.

71. Torsten Kehler, "Mythology and Violence: Unseen Elements in *The Idiot,"* unpublished paper.

72. Rene Girard, *Violence and the Sacred* (Baltimore, 1977).

73. Ibid., p. 161.

74. At this point reading the analysis of German character in Dostoevsky's fourth feuilleton might be helpful. *PSS,* vol. 26, pp. 29-34; Magarshack, pp. 29-38.

The Double

The Double
The Adventures of Mr. Golyadkin

(The Journal Redaction of 1846)

I

Of how Titular Councilor Golyadkin awoke. Of how he fitted himself out and set off for the place where his path lay. Of how Mr. Golyadkin justified himself in his own eyes and how he then drew up the rule that it is best of all to act boldly and with a frankness not devoid of nobility. Of where, finally, Mr. Golyadkin paid a visit to.

It was a little before eight in the morning when Titular Councilor Yakov Petrovich Golyadkin awoke after a long sleep, yawned, stretched and finally opened his eyes fully. For some two minutes, however, he lay motionless on his bed, like a person who is not yet absolutely certain whether he has awakened or is still asleep, whether everything that is happening around him now is taking place in a waking state and in reality or whether it is a continuation of his confused and drowsy dreams. Soon, however, Mr. Golyadkin's feelings began to take in their accustomed, everyday impressions more clearly and distinctly. The mucky green, soot-begrimed, dusty walls of his little room, his mahogany bureau, the imitation mahogany chairs, painted table, oilcloth-covered ottoman of a reddish color with tiny green flowers and, finally, his clothing, hastily taken off the night before and tossed in a heap on the ottoman, gazed at him familiarly. Finally, the gray autumn day, dull and dirty, peered into his room through the dim windowpane so angrily and with

The Double
A Poem of Petersburg

(The Redaction of 1866)

I

It was a little before eight in the morning when Titular Councilor[1] Yakov Petrovich Golyadkin awoke after a long sleep, yawned, stretched and finally opened his eyes fully. For some two minutes, however, he lay motionless on his bed, like a person who is not yet absolutely certain whether he has awakened or is still asleep, whether everything that is happening around him now is taking place in a waking state and in reality or whether it is a continuation of his confused and drowsy dreams. Soon, however, Mr. Golyadkin's senses began to take in their accustomed, everyday impressions more clearly and distinctly. The mucky greenish, soot-begrimed, dusty walls of his little room, his mahogany bureau, the imitation mahogany chairs, red painted table, oilcloth-covered ottoman of a reddish color with tiny green flowers and, finally, his clothing, hastily taken off the night before and tossed in a heap on the ottoman, gazed at him familiarly. Finally, the gray autumn day, dull and dirty, peered into his room through the dim windowpane so angrily and with

3

The Double

such a sour grimace that Mr. Golyadkin could in no way doubt
any longer that he was not in some far-off kingdom but in the
city of Petersburg, in the capital, on Shestilavochnaya Street,
on the fourth floor of an extremely large apartment complex,
in his own apartment. On making such an important discovery,
Mr. Golyadkin closed his eyes with a shudder, as if he regretted
having wakened from his recent sleep and wished to bring it
back for a brief moment. But a moment later he leapt out of
bed in a single bound, very likely because he had finally hit
upon the idea about which his scattered and distracted thoughts
had been revolving till that moment in a disorderly way. Upon
jumping out of bed, he immediately ran over to a small round
mirror standing on the bureau. Although the sleepy, weaksighted
and rather bald figure reflected in the mirror was so insignificant
that at first glance it would have called absolutely nobody's
particular attention to itself, its owner was obviously completely
satisfied with all that he saw in the mirror. "A fine thing it would
be," said Mr. Golyadkin under his breath, "a fine thing it would
be, if I were lacking something today, if, for example, something
had gone wrong, some strange pimple had popped out or some
other unpleasantness had occurred; for the time being things
aren't bad, though; for the time being everything is going
well." Very glad that everything was going well, Mr. Golyadkin
put the mirror back in its place, and, despite the fact that he was
barefoot and had on the outfit in which he was wont to go to
sleep, ran to the window and with great interest began to search
out something in the courtyard, on which the windows of his
apartment faced. Evidently, what he found in the courtyard
also satisfied him completely; his face lit up with a complacent
smile. Then, having looked first, however, behind the partition
into his servant, Petrushka's, cubbyhole and assured himself
that Petrushka was not there, he went on tiptoe over to the
table, opened a drawer in it, felt around in the very back corner
of this drawer, finally took a worn green billfold out from under
some old yellowed papers and other junk, opened it carefully,
and cautiously and delightedly peeked into its most remote
secret compartment. Very likely, the packet of green, grey,
blue, red, and various multicolored banknotes gazed back at

4

Mr. Golyadkin extremely affably and approvingly; with a beaming face he placed the open billfold in front of him on the table and heartily rubbed his hands together in token of the greatest pleasure. Finally he took it out, his comforting packet of banknotes, and, for the hundredth time since just yesterday, began to count it again, carefully rubbing each note between his thumb and index finger. "Seven hundred fifty rubles in notes!"[2] he finally finished counting in a low voice. "Seven hundred fifty rubles . . . a goodly sum! This is a pleasant sum," he continued in a shaking voice rendered somewhat weak by pleasure, gripping the packet in his hands and smiling significantly; "this is an extremely pleasant sum! A pleasant sum for anyone! I'd like to see the person now to whom this sum would be an insignificant sum! Such a sum can take a person far . . ." [*Delete:* " *Add: I'd be curious to know where this sum could take me, for example," concluded Mr. Golyadkin, "if I should, for example, just like that, for whatever reasons, suddenly, for whatever cause, retire and thus be left without any income?" Upon asking himself such an important question, Mr. Golyadkin fell to musing. We shall note here, appropriately, one small peculiarity in Mr. Golyadkin's character. The fact of the matter is that he very much liked sometimes to make certain romantic suppositions about himself; he liked sometimes to make himself the hero of a most ingenious novel, to entangle himself mentally in various intrigues and difficulties and, finally, to deliver himself from all unpleasantness with honor, eliminating all obstacles, conquering difficulties and magnanimously forgiving his enemies. Waking from his musings, Mr. Golyadkin, with a serious and significant mien, put his money into the billfold, the billfold into the table in its former place and glanced at the clock. The clock was getting ready to strike. It was exactly eight.*]

"But what *is* this?" thought Mr. Golyadkin; "where *is* Petrushka?" Still in the same outfit, he again took a look behind the partition. Again there was no sign of Petrushka behind the partition, and only a samovar placed there on the floor fussed, fumed, and lost its temper, threatening continually to boil over, and rapidly and excitedly babbled something in its queer language, burring and lisping to Mr. Golyadkin; very likely it was saying, "Do take me, good people, for I have absolutely finished boiling and am ready."

5

"Damn him!" thought Mr. Golyadkin. "That lazy rogue can drive a person mad ultimately; where is he gadding about?" Seething with righteous indignation, he went into the hallway, which consisted of a small corridor at the end of which was the door into the entranceway, opened this door a crack and saw his servant surrounded by a considerable crowd of all kinds of domestic and other riff-raff. Petrushka was recounting something, the others were listening. Evidently, neither the subject of the conversation nor the conversation itself appealed to Mr. Golyadkin. He called Petrushka at once and returned to the room quite displeased and even upset. "That rogue is ready to betray a person for less than a penny, especially his master," he thought to himself, "and he *has* betrayed me; he most certainly has betrayed me; I'm ready to wager that he has betrayed me for less than a penny. Well? . . ."

"They've brought the livery, sir."

"Put it on and come here."

After putting on the livery, Petrushka, grinning foolishly, went into his master's room. He was gotten up as oddly as could be. He had on an extremely shabby green footman's livery with gold braid that was coming off, evidently made for a person a good two feet taller than he. He held a hat trimmed with the same gold braid and with green feathers as well, while at his side he had a footman's sword in a leather scabbard.

Finally, to complete the picture, Petrushka, following his favorite custom of always going about half-dressed, was now, too, barefoot. Mr. Golyadkin looked Petrushka over and was evidently pleased. The livery had obviously been hired for some solemn occasion. It was noticeable besides that during the inspection Petrushka looked at his master with strange expectation and followed his every move with unusual curiosity, which extremely embarrassed Mr. Golyadkin.

"Well, what about the carriage?"

"The carriage has also arrived."

"For the whole day?"

"For the whole day. Twenty-five rubles in notes."

"Did they bring the boots, too?"

"They brought the boots, too."

"Blockhead! Can't say, 'They brought the boots, too, sir'. Give them here."

Having indicated his pleasure that the boots fitted well, Mr. Golyadkin asked for some tea and expressed his wish to wash and shave. He shaved himself extremely carefully and washed himself in the same manner, swallowed his tea hurriedly and set about his major and final robing process: he put on almost perfectly new trousers; then a shirtfront with bronze buttons and a vest with extremely bright and pleasant little flowers; around his neck he tied a multicolored silk tie and, finally, pulled on the jacket of his civil service uniform, also fairly new and carefully brushed. While dressing, he looked lovingly at his boots several times, lifted now one foot, now the other, admired the style and continually whispered something to himself under his breath, from time to time winking with an expressive grimace at what was going on in his mind. That morning, however, Mr. Golyadkin was extremely absentminded, for he hardly noticed the grins and grimaces at his expense from Petrushka, who was helping him dress. Finally, having done everything that had to be done and gotten completely dressed, Mr. Golyadkin put his billfold into his pocket, took a last admiring look at Petrushka, who had put on his boots and was thus also completely ready, and noting that everything had now been done and that there was nothing more to wait for, ran bustling down his stairway, with slight trepidation in his heart. A light blue hired coach with some sort of coat-of-arms on it thundered up to the steps. Petrushka, exchanging winks with the driver and some idle onlookers, helped his master into the coach; in a strange voice and barely restraining his idiotic laughter, he shouted: "Drive off!" and leapt onto the rear footboard, and the whole kit and caboodle, rattling and thundering, ringing and creaking, drove off to Nevsky Prospect. No sooner had the light blue coach driven out the gate than Mr. Golyadkin convulsively rubbed his hands together and broke into quiet, inaudible laughter, like a person of merry nature who has succeeded in playing a wonderful trick and is utterly delighted with it. But immediately after the fit of merriment the laughter gave way to a strange worried expression on Mr.

Golyadkin's face. Despite the fact that the weather was damp
and dull, he lowered both windows of the coach and carefully
began to examine the passersby to the right and to the left,
immediately putting on an expression of decorum and gravity
as soon as he noticed that anyone was looking at him. At the
turn from Liteynaya Street into Nevsky Prospect, he shuddered
from a very unpleasant sensation, and, wincing like a poor soul
on whose corn someone has just accidentally trod, hastily, and
even fearfully, huddled into the darkest corner of his coach.
The fact of the matter was that he had encountered two
colleagues, two young clerks from the same department as the
one in which he himself worked. These clerks, so it seemed to
Mr. Golyadkin, were, for their part, also in a state of extreme
bewilderment, having thus encountered their colleague; one
of them even pointed to Mr. Golyadkin. It even seemed to Mr.
Golyadkin that the other one called him loudly by name,
which, it goes without saying, was extremely improper on the
street. Our hero kept quiet and did not respond. "How
childish!" he began to reason to himself. "Well, what's so odd?
A person in a coach; the person has to be in a coach and so he
has engaged a coach. Utter rubbish! I know them—just boys
who still need to be thrashed! All they'd like to do is play pitch
and toss while pulling down a salary and gad about; that's what
they're interested in. I'd tell them all a thing or two, but..." Mr.
Golyadkin broke off and sat stockstill. A lively pair of Kazan
horses, extremely familiar to Mr. Golyadkin and harnessed to a
smart droshky, was rapidly gaining on his coach from the right.
The gentleman sitting in the droshky, inadvertently catching
sight of the face of Mr. Golyadkin, who had quite unwarily
stuck his head out the window of the coach, was evidently also
taken aback by such an unexpected encounter and, bending
out as far as he could, began with the greatest curiosity and
interest to peer into that corner of the coach where our hero
was attempting to hide himself. The gentleman in the droshky
was Andrei Filippovich, the division chief in the same place
where Mr. Golyadkin served as assistant to his section head. Mr.
Golyadkin, seeing that Andrei Filippovich had unmistakably
recognized him, that he was staring, and that it was absolutely

impossible to hide himself, blushed to his ears. "Shall I bow or
not? Shall I respond or not? Shall I admit that it's me or not?"
thought our hero in indescribable anguish; "or shall I pretend
that it's not me but someone else, who strikingly resembles me,
and look unconcerned? It's really not me, it isn't, and that's
that!" said Mr. Golyadkin, removing his hat before Andrei
Fillippovich and not taking his eyes off him. "I'm . . . I'm fine,"
he forced himself to whisper; "I'm quite all right; it's not me at
all, Andrei Filippovich; it's not me at all, it isn't, and that's
that." Soon, however, the droshky passed the coach and the
magnetic power of the division chief's gaze [*Add: finally*] ceased
[*Add: to exert a hold on Mr. Golyadkin*]. However, he continued to
blush, smile and mutter something to himself . . . "I was a fool not
to respond," he thought finally; "I should simply have said, boldly
and with a frankness not devoid of nobility, 'There it is, Andrei
Filippovich; I've also been invited to dinner and that's that!' "
Then, suddenly remembering that he had made a fool of
himself, our hero blushed a fiery red, scowled and threw a
terrible and defiant glance into a front corner of the coach, a
glance intended to reduce all his enemies instantaneously to
ashes. At last, in a burst of inspiration he suddenly pulled the
cord tied to the coachman's elbow, stopped the coach and
ordered him to turn back into Liteynaya Street. The fact of the
matter is that Mr. Golyadkin felt the need, very likely for the
sake of his own tranquillity, to tell something most interesting
to his doctor, Krestyan Ivanovich, immediately. And although
he had become acquainted with Krestyan Ivanovich only very
recently, that is, he had only visited him once, the previous
week, as a result of certain problems, after all a doctor, as they
say, is like a confessor; it would be foolish to conceal oneself
from him, while to know a patient is his duty. "Will it be all
right, though?" continued our hero, emerging from the carriage
at the entrance to a five-story house on Liteynaya Street, before
which he had ordered the driver to stop his coach; "will it be
all right? Will it be the proper thing? Will it be an appropriate
time? Well, but why not?" he continued, climbing the stairs
and trying to catch his breath and restrain the thumping of his
heart, which had the habit of thumping on other people's

stairways; "why not? After all, I'm coming about my own business and there's nothing reprehensible in that . . . [*Add: it doesn't seem to me there is.*] It would be foolish to conceal oneself. I'll just pretend that I didn't come for any special reason, that I just chanced to drive by . . . And he'll see that that's just the way it should be."

Reasoning thus, Mr. Golyadkin climbed the stairs to the second floor and stopped before Apartment No. 5, on the door of which there was a handsome brass plate with "Krestyan Ivanovich Rutenshpits, Doctor of Medicine and Surgery" on it. Standing there, our hero hastened to plant a presentable, unconcerned expression, not without a certain affability, on his countenance and got ready to give a tug to the bell-pull. Once ready to give a tug to the bell-pull, he immediately and quite appropriately reasoned that it might be better to come tomorrow and that for the moment there was no urgency [*Add: , none at all.*]. But because Mr. Golyadkin suddenly heard someone's footsteps on the stairs, he immediately reversed his new decision, and at the same time, moreover with the most resolute look, rang Krestyan Ivanovich's doorbell.

II

*[Add: Of how Mr. Golyadkin went in to see Krestyan
Ivanovich. Of what exactly he discussed with him; how he
then shed some tears; how he next clearly demonstrated that he
possessed certain, even certain extremely important, virtues
necessary in practical life, and that certain people sometimes
know how to serve up an egg mixed with ground hempseeds, as
the saying goes; how, finally, he asked permission to withdraw
and having asked it departed, leaving Krestyan Ivanovich
amazed. Mr. Golyadkin's opinion of Krestyan Ivanovich.]*

Doctor of Medicine and Surgery, Krestyan Ivanovich
Rutenshpits, an extremely hale though already elderly man,
endowed with thick greying eyebrows and sidewhiskers, with
an expressive, flashing glance, by the sole means of which,
evidently, he banished all ailments, and, finally, with an
important decoration, was sitting that morning in his office, in
his comfortable armchair, drinking coffee brought to him by
his wife's own hand, smoking a cigar and from time to time
writing out prescriptions for his patients. After prescribing a
vial of medicine for a little old man suffering from hemorrhoids
and seeing the ailing little old man out by the side door,
Krestyan Ivanovich sat down to await his next appointment. In
walked Mr. Golyadkin.
    Evidently, Krestyan Ivanovich did not in the least expect
or wish to see Mr. Golyadkin before him, for he suddenly
became embarrassed for an instant and involuntarily exhibited
a strange, one might even say, displeased expression on his
face. Inasmuch as Mr. Golyadkin, for his part, almost always
flagged inopportunely and lost his presence of mind at those
moments when he had to assail someone about his own

personal affairs, so now, too, not having prepared the opening sentence, which was for him in such instances a genuine stumbling block, he became extremely embarrassed, muttered something—it seemed to be an apology—and, at a loss what to do next, took a chair and sat down. But, remembering that he had seated himself without being invited to do so, he immediately sensed his lack of decorum and hastened to correct his mistake, which had resulted from an ignorance of high society and of good breeding, by quickly getting up from the place which he had occupied without invitation. Then, coming to his senses and dimly noting that he had done two foolish things at once, he decided without delay upon a third, that is, he started to try to give a justification of himself, muttered something with a smile, blushed, became embarrassed, lapsed into a significant silence and finally sat down once and for all and did not get up any more; instead, to be on the safe side, he armed himself with that very same defiant look which had the unusual power of enabling Mr. Golyadkin's imagination to reduce to ashes and utterly rout his enemies. Moreover, this look fully expressed Mr. Golyadkin's independence, that is, it said clearly that Mr. Golyadkin was feeling just fine, that he went his own way like everyone else and that, in any case, other people's concerns had nothing to do with him. Krestyan Ivanovich coughed, cleared his throat, [*Delete: cleared his throat,*] evidently as a sign of his approval of and consent to all this, and fixed a critical, inquiring eye on Mr. Golyadkin.

"Krestyan Ivanovich," began Mr. Golyadkin with a smile, "I've come to trouble you a second time and now make bold a second time to ask your indulgence . . ." Mr. Golyadkin was obviously having difficulty in finding the words.

"Hm . . . yes!" uttered Krestyan Ivanovich, letting a stream of smoke out of his mouth and putting the cigar down on the table, "but you must follow instructions; I did explain to you [*Add: , I did explain to you last time*] that your course of treatment must consist of a change in your habits . . . You need to amuse yourself, for example; you must visit your friends and acquaintances, and at the same time you mustn't be an enemy of the bottle; you must keep jolly company as well."

Mr. Golyadkin, continuing to smile, hastened to note that it seemed to him he was like everyone else, that he was his own master, that he had his amusements like everyone else... that he could, of course, go to the theatre because he also, like everyone else, had the means, that during the day he was at work, while in the evening he was at home, that he was quite all right; he even noted in passing at this point that he was, as far as he could see, no worse than anyone else, that he lived at home, in his own apartment, and that, finally, he had Petrushka. At this point, Mr. Golyadkin faltered.

"Hm, no, such a regime is wrong, and not at all what I was meaning to ask you about. I am interested in knowing in general whether you are really fond of jolly company, whether you spend your time in a jolly fashion... Well, are you leading a melancholy or a jolly kind of life now?"

"Krestyan Ivanovich, I..."

"Hm... I'm saying," the doctor interrupted, "that you must make a radical change in your entire way of living and in a certain sense you must remake your character." (Krestyan Ivanovich strongly stressed the word "remake" and paused for a moment with a highly significant look.) "You must not avoid a jolly life; you must go to theatres and to a club and, in any case, you must not be an enemy of the bottle. It's not right to sit at home... you absolutely must not sit at home."

"I like peace and quiet, Krestyan Ivanovich," said Mr. Golyadkin, throwing a significant look at Krestyan Ivanovich and obviously searching for the words that would give the most fortuitous expression to his thought. "In the apartment there are only Petrushka and I... I mean my servant, Krestyan Ivanovich. I mean, Krestyan Ivanovich, that I go my way, my separate way, Krestyan Ivanovich. I keep to myself and, as far as I can see, am not dependent on anyone. I also go out for walks, Krestyan Ivanovich."

"What's that?... Yes! But right now there can't be any pleasure in walking. The weather is extremely bad."

"Yes, sir, Krestyan Ivanovich. I may be a quiet man, Krestyan Ivanovich, as I think I have already had the honor of explaining to you, but my path goes a separate way, Krestyan

Ivanovich. The road of life is broad... I mean... what I mean, Krestyan Ivanovich... Forgive me, Krestyan Ivanovich, I do not have a gift for fine words."

"Hm... you were saying..."

"I was saying that you must forgive me, Krestyan Ivanovich, for not having, as far as I can see, a gift for fine words," said Mr. Golyadkin in a half-offended tone, losing his thread a bit and becoming confused. "In this respect, Krestyan Ivanovich, I am not like other people," he added with a kind of odd smile, "and I don't know how to talk a lot; I haven't learned how to create a fine style. But to make up for it, Krestyan Ivanovich, I am a man of action; to make up for it, I am a man of action, Krestyan Ivanovich!"

"Hm... what's that?... you're a man of action?" responded Krestyan Ivanovich. Then for a moment silence ensued. The doctor looked somewhat strangely and incredulously at Mr. Golyadkin. Mr. Golyadkin in turn also glanced rather incredulously at the doctor from the corner of his eye.

"Krestyan Ivanovich, I..." Mr. Golyadkin went on in his former tone, a bit exasperated and taken aback by Krestyan Ivanovich's extreme persistence, "I like peace, Krestyan Ivanovich, not the hubbub of society. There, I was saying, in society, Krestyan Ivanovich, you have to know how to bow and scrape... (Mr. Golyadkin hereupon gave a little scrape of his foot along the floor); there they expect it, sir, and they also expect puns... you have to know how to make scented compliments, sir ... that's what they expect there. But I haven't learned that, Krestyan Ivanovich; I haven't learned all those sly tricks. There wasn't time [*Add:*, *Krestyan Ivanovich.*]. I am a simple and uncomplicated man, and have no affected polish. On this issue, Krestyan Ivanovich, I lay down my arms. I surrender, speaking in this sense." All of this Mr. Golyadkin uttered, of course, with a look that clearly gave one to understand that our hero did not at all regret that he was surrendering in this sense or that he had not learned sly tricks but that he even felt the exact opposite. Krestyan Ivanovich, as he listened to him, looked down with an extremely unpleasant grimace and seemed to be having a

presentiment of something. After Mr. Golyadkin's tirade there
ensued a rather prolonged and significant silence.

"You seem to have strayed from the subject a bit,"
Krestyan Ivanovich said finally in a low voice. "I have to admit
I couldn't altogether understand you."

'I don't have a gift for fine words, Krestyan Ivanovich. I
have already had the honor of informing you, Krestyan Ivanovich,
that I do not have a gift for fine words," said Mr. Golyadkin, this
time in a harsh and resolute tone.

"Hm . . ."

"Krestyan Ivanovich!" Mr. Golyadkin began again, in a
voice quiet but full of significance, in a somewhat solemn vein
and dwelling on every point. "Krestyan Ivanovich! When I
came in here, I began with apologies. Now I repeat what I said
before and again ask your indulgence for a time. I have nothing
to hide from you, Krestyan Ivanovich. I'm a little man; you
know that yourself. But fortunately I don't regret that I'm a
little man. Quite the contrary, Krestyan Ivanovich, and to be
perfectly frank, I'm even proud of the fact that I'm not a big
man, but a little one. I'm not an intriguer—and I'm proud of
that, too. I don't operate on the sly but openly, without guile;
and although I too could cause harm, ever so much harm, and
even know whom to harm and how to do it, Krestyan Ivanovich,
I don't want to sully myself and in this sense I wash my hands of
it. In this sense, I say, I wash them of it, Krestyan Ivanovich!"
For an instant Mr. Golyadkin lapsed expressively into silence.
He had been speaking with mild animation.

"I make my way, Krestyan Ivanovich," our hero went on,
"directly and openly and without deviousness because I scorn it
and I leave it to others. I don't try to humiliate those who,
perhaps, are better than you and I . . . that is, I mean, than they
and I, Krestyan Ivanovich; I didn't mean you. [*Delete: ; I didn't
mean you. Add: , than they and I.*] I don't like things half-hinted. I
don't like worthless two-faced people. I have an aversion to
slander and gossip. I put a mask on only to go to a masquerade; I
don't go around in one in front of people every day. I shall
merely ask you, Krestyan Ivanovich, how would you go about
taking revenge on your enemy, your worst enemy, the one you

15

considered the worst?" concluded Mr. Golyadkin, casting a defiant glance at Krestyan Ivanovich.

Although Mr. Golyadkin had uttered all this as distinctly and clearly as could be, with assurance, weighing his words and calculating their likely effect, nevertheless he was now looking at Krestyan Ivanovich with uneasiness, with great uneasiness, with extreme uneasiness. He now became all attention and timidly, with vexed and anguished impatience, awaited Krestyan Ivanovich's reply. But to Mr. Golyadkin's amazement and utter dismay, Krestyan Ivanovich muttered something under his breath, then pulled his armchair up to his desk and rather drily but nevertheless politely announced to him something to the effect that his time was valuable, that he somehow did not altogether understand, that nevertheless he was ready to help in whatever way he could within his power but that everything beyond that and not relating to him he would not touch. Hereupon he took his pen, drew a sheet of paper toward him, cut a small piece from it the size of a prescription form and announced that he would immediately prescribe what was necessary.

"No, sir, it's not necessary, Krestyan Ivanovich! No, sir, it's not at all necessary!" uttered Mr. Golyadkin, getting up from his seat and seizing Krestyan Ivanovich's right hand. "It's not at all what's needed in this instance, Krestyan Ivanovich..."

But while Mr. Golyadkin was saying all this, a strange change came over him. His grey eyes flashed somewhat strangely, his lips began to quiver, all his muscles and all his facial features began to twitch and move. He was trembling all over. Having delivered his first gesture and stopped Krestyan Ivanovich's hand, Mr. Golyadkin now stood motionless, as though he had no faith in himself and was awaiting an inspiration to further action.

Then a rather strange scene occurred.

Somewhat taken aback, Krestyan Ivanovich seemed for an instant to be stuck to his chair and, losing his presence of mind, gazed wide-eyed at Mr. Golyadkin, who was looking at him in the same way. Finally Krestyan Ivanovich got up, holding on slightly to one lapel of Mr. Golyadkin's jacket. For several seconds they both stood this way, motionless and not taking their eyes off one another. Then, and in an unusually strange way moreover, Mr. Golyadkin's second gesture was delivered. His lips began to tremble, his chin began to quiver, and our hero quite unexpectedly burst into tears. Sobbing, shaking his head and striking his breast with his right hand, while also clutching one lapel of Krestyan Ivanovich's informal garb with his left, he tried to speak and to explain something then and there, but was unable to say a word. At last Krestyan Ivanovich recovered from his astonishment.

"Enough, calm yourself, sit down!" he uttered at last, trying to seat Mr. Golyadkin in an armchair.

"I have enemies, Krestyan Ivanovich, I have enemies; I have evil enemies, who have sworn to ruin me . . ." replied Mr. Golyadkin in a frightened whisper.

"Come now, that's enough. What enemies? There's no need to mention your enemies! No need whatsoever. Sit down; sit down," continued Krestyan Ivanovich, finally seating Mr. Golyadkin in the armchair.

Mr. Golyadkin finally settled down, not taking his eyes off Krestyan Ivanovich. Krestyan Ivanovich, with an extremely displeased look, began to pace back and forth from one corner of his office to the other. A long silence ensued.

"I am grateful to you, Krestyan Ivanovich, extremely grateful, and I feel keenly all that you have just done for me [*Add:, Krestyan Ivanovich.*]. To my dying day I won't forget your kindness, Krestyan Ivanovich," said Mr. Golyadkin at last, getting up from the chair with an offended look.

"Enough, enough! I tell you, enough!" Krestyan Ivanovich responded rather sternly to Mr. Golyadkin's display, seating him once again. "Well, what is it? Tell me what it is now that's so unpleasant," continued Krestyan Ivanovich, "and what enemies are you talking about? What's bothering you?"

"No, Krestyan Ivanovich, we'd better leave this now," replied Mr. Golyadkin, looking down at the floor. "We'd better put all this aside, for a while . . . till another time, Krestyan Ivanovich, till a more opportune time, when everything will be revealed, and the mask will fall from certain faces, and certain things will be disclosed. But now, for the time being, that is, after what has happened between us . . . you yourself will agree, Krestyan Ivanovich . . . Permit me to wish you a good morning, Krestyan Ivanovich," said Mr. Golyadkin, getting up this time resolutely and seriously and seizing his hat.

"Ah, well . . . as you wish . . . hm . . ." (A momentary silence ensued.) "I, for my part, you know, am ready to do whatever I can . . . and sincerely wish you well."

"I understand you, Krestyan Ivanovich; I understand; I understand you perfectly now . . . In any case, excuse me for having disturbed you, Krestyan Ivanovich."

"Hm . . . No, that's not what I meant. However, as you wish. Continue the medication as before . . ." [*Delete: Continue the medication as before . . ." Add: The medication is the same as before. Continue . . ."*]

"I shall continue the medication as you say, Krestyan Ivanovich; I shall continue it and I shall get it at the same apothecary shop . . . These days, Krestyan Ivanovich, being an apothecary is an important thing . . ."

"What? In what sense do you mean that?"

"In the most ordinary sense, Krestyan Ivanovich. I mean that's how the world is nowadays . . ."

"Hm . . ."

"And that every boy, not only the apothecary's, turns up his nose these days at a decent person."

"Hm . . . Just how do you understand that?"

"I am speaking, Krestyan Ivanovich, of a certain person . . . of our mutual acquaintance, Krestyan Ivanovich; say, for example, of Vladimir Semyonovich . . ."

"Ah!"

"Yes, Krestyan Ivanovich. And I know certain people, Krestyan Ivanovich, who don't adhere to the general opinion so much that they can't sometimes speak the truth."

"Ah! . . . Just how is that?"

"Oh, just so, sir. That, however, is beside the point. They know sometimes how to serve up an egg mixed with ground hempseeds."

"What? To serve up what?"

"To serve up an egg mixed with ground hempseeds, Krestyan Ivanovich. That's a Russian saying. They know sometimes just the perfect way to congratulate someone, for example. There are such people, Krestyan Ivanovich."

"To congratulate?"

"Yes, sir, to congratulate, Krestyan Ivanovich, as one of my close acquaintances did recently . . ."

"One of your close acquaintances . . . Ah! What happened?" said Krestyan Ivanovich, looking attentively at Mr. Golyadkin.

"Yes, sir, one of my close acquaintances congratulated another also extremely close acquaintance, and what's more, a friend, as they say, a dearest friend, on his promotion, on his receiving the rank of Collegiate Assessor.[3] This is how it happened. 'I am deeply happy,' he says, 'of the opportunity to tender you my congratulations, Vladimir Semyonovich, my *sincere* congratulations on receiving a promotion. And I am all the more glad because today, as the whole world knows, there aren't any more fortune-telling grandmothers.'" Hereupon Mr. Golyadkin nodded his head slyly, and, screwing up his eyes, looked at Krestyan Ivanovich . . .

"Hm . . . That's what he said . . ."

"That's what he said, Krestyan Ivanovich, that's what he said, and at the same time he also looked at Andrei Filippovich, at the uncle of our precious Vladimir Semyonovich. And what is it to me, Krestyan Ivanovich, that he's been made a Collegiate Assessor? Really, what is it to me? And he wants to get married and his mother's milk, pardon the expression, not yet dry on his lips. That's just what I said. 'There you are, Vladimir Semyonovich,' I said. Now I've said it all. Do permit me to leave."

"Hm . . ."

"Yes, Krestyan Ivanovich, do permit me, I say, to leave now. And then, to kill two birds with one stone and have done with,—as I cut down that young man with the remark about grandmothers—I turned also to Klara Olsufyevna (this was the day before yesterday at Olsufi Ivanovich's)—and she had just finished singing a tender romance—I said, 'You have been so kind as to sing the romance tenderly but those who are listening to you aren't doing it with a pure heart.' And I am clearly hinting by this, you understand, Krestyan Ivanovich, I am clearly hinting by this that they are not seeking after her now but have an ulterior motive . . ."

"Ah! Well, and what did he say? . . ."

"He looked as though he'd bitten into a lemon, as the saying goes, Krestyan Ivanovich."

"Hm . . ."

"Yes, sir, Krestyan Ivanovich. I said to the old man himself as well,—'Olsufi Ivanovich,' I said, 'I know how much I owe you. I value to the full the acts of kindness with which you've showered me almost since my childhood years. But open your eyes, Olsufi Ivanovich,' I said. 'Look about you. I myself conduct the matter frankly and openly, Olsufi Ivanovich.'"

"Ah, so!"

"Yes, Krestyan Ivanovich. Just so . . ."

"And what did he say?"

"What indeed, Krestyan Ivanovich! He hemmed and hawed, and said one thing and another, and 'I know you,' and that His Excellency was a benevolent person—and off he went and on and on . . . But what of it? He's really gone dotty from old age, as they say."

"Ah! So that's how it is now!"

"Yes, Krestyan Ivanovich. And that's how we all are! Poor little old thing! He's [*Delete: Poor little old thing! He's Add: The poor little old thing is*] staring into the grave, has the odor of incense about him, as they say. But when some old wives' gossip gets started, he's right there to listen to it. They just can't do without him . . ."

"Gossip, you say?"

"Yes, Krestyan Ivanovich, they started some gossip. Our bear had a hand in it, too, and so did his precious nephew. They joined up with the old ladies, of course, and cooked up the affair. What do you think? What do you suppose they thought up in order to do a person in? . . ."

"To do a person in?"

"Yes, Krestyan Ivanovich, to do a person in, to do a person in morally. They spread . . . I'm still talking about my close acquaintance . . ."

20

Krestyan Ivanovich nodded.

"They spread a rumor about him . . . I confess to you I am even ashamed to speak of it, Krestyan Ivanovich . . ."

"Hm . . ."

"They spread a rumor that he's signed his name to a promise of marriage when he's already engaged . . . And what do you think, Krestyan Ivanovich, to whom?"

"Really?"

"To a cook, to a disreputable German woman from whom he takes his dinners. Instead of paying his debts, he's offering her his hand."

"'That's what they're saying?"

"Can you believe it, Krestyan Ivanovich? A German, a base, vile, shameless German, Karolina Ivanovna, if you know . . ."

"I confess, for my part . . ."

"I understand you, Krestyan Ivanovich, I understand and for my part I sense it . . ."

"Tell me, please, where are you living now?"

"Where am I living now, Krestyan Ivanovich?"

"Yes . . . I mean . . ., you used to live before, I think . . ."

"I used to live, Krestyan Ivanovich; I used to live; I did use to live before. How could I not live!" replied Mr. Golyadkin, accompanying his words with a little laugh and somewhat embarrassing Krestyan Ivanovich with his reply.

"No, you took it the wrong way. I meant for my part . . ."

"I also meant, Krestyan Ivanovich, for my part, I also meant . . .," continued Mr. Golyadin, laughing. "However, [*Delete:* "*However, Add:* "*But*] I have taken up far too much of your time, [*Add: however,*] Krestyan Ivanovich. You will, I hope, permit me now . . . to wish you a good morning . . ."

"Hm . . ."

"Yes, Krestyan Ivanovich, I understand you; I understand you perfectly now," said our hero, showing off a bit before Krestyan Ivanovich. "And so, permit me to wish you a good morning . . ."*

---

*The last sentence of dialogue appears as a separate paragraph in the 1846 version [EJH].

Here our hero bowed, scraping his foot, and went out of the room, leaving Krestyan Ivanovich in a state of extreme amazement. As he descended the doctor's stairway he smiled and gleefully rubbed his hands together. On the front step, after taking a breath of fresh air, he felt free and was actually even ready to acknowledge himself the happiest of mortals and then set off straight for the office—when suddenly his coach thundered up to the entrance. He glanced at it and recalled everything. Petrushka was already opening the coach door. A strange and extremely unpleasant sensation took hold of Mr. Golyadkin. It was as if he had blushed for an instant. Something pricked him. He was just about to put his foot on the step of the coach, when suddenly he turned and looked at Krestyan Ivanovich's windows. Just as he thought! Krestyan Ivanovich was standing at one of the windows, stroking his sidewhiskers with his right hand and looking rather curiously at our hero.

"That doctor is stupid," thought Mr. Golyadkin, ensconcing himself in the [*Delete: the Add: his*] coach, "extremely stupid. Perhaps he does do a good job of treating his patients, but all the same . . . he's as stupid as a block of wood." Mr. Golyadkin settled himself, Petrushka shouted: "Drive off!"—and the coach drove off again to Nevsky Prospect.

III

[Add: Of exactly how many rubles Mr. Golyadkin contracted to pay and how many he spent. What he then demonstrated to his two colleagues. What constitutes the private and what the official life of Mr. Golyadkin. Of how, finally, Mr. Golyadkin preferred to dine sans façon, as they say among respectable people, and how it all finally ended.]

That entire morning was spent by Mr. Golyadkin in a frightful bustle of activity. On reaching Nevsky Prospect our hero ordered the driver to stop at the Shopping Arcade. Jumping out of his carriage, he ran into the arcade, accompanied by Petrushka, and went straight to a shop which sold articles of silver and gold. It was clear just from Mr. Golyadkin's look that he was burdened with concerns and had a frightful pile of business to conduct. After transacting for a complete dinner and tea service costing some one thousand five hundred rubles in notes, and also managing to get a cigar case of fanciful shape and a complete silver shaving set included in the same price, and after inquiring the price, finally, of one or two other knickknacks which were in their way useful and pleasant, Mr. Golyadkin concluded with a promise to drop in tomorrow without fail or even send today for his purchases, took down the number of the shop and, after attentively hearing out the merchant, who was asking for a small deposit, promised that a small deposit would be given in due course. After which he hurriedly took leave of the bewildered merchant and went on along the arcade, followed by a whole flock of assistants, glancing back at Petrushka every moment and carefully seeking out some new shop. On the way he ran into a moneychanging shop and exchanged all his large bills for smaller ones, and although he lost in the transaction, he nevertheless exchanged them and his billfold grew significantly fatter, which evidently afforded him extreme pleasure. At last he stopped at a shop selling various materials for ladies. After transacting again for goods costing a notable sum, here too Mr. Golyadkin promised the merchant that he would come by without fail, took down the number of the shop and to the question of a small deposit again repeated that a small deposit too would be given in due course. Then he called in at several more shops; in all of them he transacted purchases, inquired the price of various knick-knacks, sometimes argued for a long time with the merchants, left the shop and returned three times—in a word, he evinced an unusual amount of activity. From the Shopping Arcade our hero set off for a well-known furniture shop, where he transacted for furniture for six rooms, regarded with pleasure a fashionable and extremely fanciful ladies' dressing table in the latest style and, having assured the merchant that he would send for everything without fail, left the store, as was his wont, with the promise of a small deposit. Then he went to one or two other places and transacted for a few other things. In a word there was evidently no end to his concerns. Finally all of this seemed to start annoying Mr. Golyadkin greatly. God knows why, but pangs of conscience even began to torment him for no apparent reason. Not for anything in the world would he have agreed now to encounter, for example, Andrei Filippovich or even Krestyan Ivanovich. Finally the city clocks struck three in the afternoon. When Mr. Golyadkin got back into the coach once and for all, of all the acquisitions made by him that morning there actually turned out to be only a pair of gloves and a bottle of scent for one and a half rubles in notes. Since it was still rather early for Mr. Golyadkin, he ordered his driver to stop alongside a well-known restaurant on Nevsky Prospect of which he had hitherto known only through hearsay, got out of the coach and ran in to have a bite to eat, rest and wait it out until a certain time.

After having had a bite to eat the way a person does when he has before him the prospect of a sumptuous dinner party, that is, after having had a little snack in order, as they say, to stave off the pangs, and having drunk a shot of vodka, Mr. Golyadkin seated himself in an armchair, and after having unassumingly looked about, peacefully settled down with a certain skinny little national newspaper. After reading a few lines, he got up, looked at himself in the mirror, put his clothing to rights and smoothed his hair. Next he went over to the window and looked to see whether his coach was there . . . then he sat down again and took up the newspaper. It was evident that our hero was in a state of extreme agitation. Glancing at his watch and seeing that it was only just a quarter past three, consequently, that he still had to wait a good while, and at the same time reasoning that it was ill-mannered to just sit there, Mr. Golyadkin ordered that he be brought some chocolate for which, by the way, he had no great desire at the present time. After drinking the chocolate and noting that the time had passed a bit, he went out to pay his bill. Suddenly someone clapped him on the shoulder.

He turned around and saw before him two of his colleagues, the very ones he had encountered that morning on [*Delete: on Add: in*] Liteynaya Street—fellows still extremely young in years and junior in rank. Our hero's relationship to them was neither this nor that, neither friendship nor open hostility. Of course, decorum was observed on both sides; but further intimacy did not and, moreover, could not exist. An encounter at the present time was extremely unpleasant for Mr. Golyadkin. He frowned slightly and for a moment became embarrassed.

"Yakov Petrovich! Yakov Petrovich!" twittered both collegiate registrars,[4] "you here? For what . . ."

"Ah! It's you, gentlemen!" Mr. Golyadkin interrupted hastily, becoming a bit disconcerted and scandalized by the amazement of the clerks and also by the familiarity of their manner, but nevertheless, against his will putting on a show of familiarity and hale fellow well met. "You've deserted, gentlemen, heh-heh-heh! . . ." Next, in order to maintain his dignity and to patronize the departmental youth, with whom he was always within proper bounds, he even tried to pat one of the young men on the shoulder, but in this instance familiarity did not

25

lend itself to Mr. Golyadkin and instead of a proper and familiar gesture something completely different resulted.

"Well, now, is our bear at work? . . ."

"Who's that, Yakov Petrovich?"

"Why, the bear. As if you don't know whom they call the bear? . . ." Mr. Golyadkin gave a laugh and turned to the cashier for his change. "I'm speaking of Andrei Filippovich, gentlemen," he continued, finishing with the cashier and turning now to the clerks with an extremely serious look. Both collegiate registrars winked significantly at one another.

"He's still at work and was asking for you, Yakov Petrovich," replied one of them.

"He is, eh! In that case let him stay there, gentlemen. And he was asking for me, eh?"

"He was, Yakov Petrovich. But what is this, you, [*Add: Yakov Petrovich,*] all perfumed and pomaded, a regular dandy? . . ."

"Yes, gentlemen, that's so! Enough . . ." replied Mr. Golyadkin, looking away and smiling strainedly. Seeing that Mr. Golyadkin was smiling, the clerks roared with laughter. Mr. Golyadkin became somewhat sullen.

[*Add: "But still, Yakov Petrovich? . . ."*]

"I'll tell you, gentlemen, as your friend," said our hero after a brief silence, as though (so be it) having resolved to disclose something to the clerks; "you, gentlemen, all know me, but up to now you have known only one aspect of me. No one can be reproached for it and in part, I confess, I myself have been to blame."

Mr. Golyadkin pressed his lips together tightly and glanced significantly at the clerks. The clerks again winked at one another.

"Up to now, gentlemen, you have not known me. [*Delete: not known me. Add: known me only in part and not completely...*] To give an explanation of myself here and now would not be altogether appropriate. I shall tell you only a couple of things casually in passing. There are people, gentlemen, who do not like devious ways and wear masks only for a masquerade. There are people who do not see a direct human purpose in the adroit ability to bow and scrape. There are also such people, gentlemen, as will

26

not say that they are happy and living life to the full when, for example, their trousers fit them well. There are, finally, people who do not like to jump and whirl about to no purpose, to play up to other people and lick their boots, and most of all, gentlemen, to stick their noses in where they are not at all asked to... I have said just about everything, gentlemen; now do permit me to leave..."

Mr. Golyadkin stopped. Since the collegiate registrars had now had their fill, both of them suddenly, in an extremely impolite manner, burst into side-splitting laughter. Mr. Golyadkin blushed a fiery red.

"Laugh, gentlemen, laugh while you can! You will live and learn," he said with a feeling of offended dignity, taking his hat and retreating to the door.

"But I will say further, gentlemen," he added, turning for the last time to the collegiate registrars, "I will say further [*Add:*, *gentlemen*]—both of you are here face to face with me. Here, gentlemen, are my rules: if a thing doesn't succeed—I don't give in; if it does succeed—I stand firm, and in any case I don't undermine anyone. I'm not an intriguer—and I'm proud of it. I wouldn't be any good as a diplomat. They say besides, gentlemen, that the bird flies itself to the hunter. It's the truth, and I'm ready to admit it: but who here is the hunter and who the bird? That is indeed the question, gentlemen!"

Mr. Golyadkin fell eloquently silent and with a most significant mien, that is, raising his eyebrows and pressing his lips together as tightly as can be, he took leave of his fellow clerks and then went out, leaving them in a state of extreme amazement.

"Where do you wish to go?" asked Petrushka rather sternly, for he had probably gotten annoyed with hanging about in the cold. "Where do you wish to go?" he asked Mr. Golyadkin, meeting the [*Delete: the Add: his*] terrible, all-annihiliating glance [*Add:*, *that same glance*] with which our hero had already twice equipped himself that morning and to which he now had recourse for the third time, as he went down the stairs.

"To the Izmaylovsky Bridge."

"To the Izmaylovsky Bridge! Drive off!"

"Dinner won't start at their place till after four or even at five," thought Mr. Golyadkin; "isn't it too early now? But after all, I can even go a bit early; and what's more it's a family dinner. I can just go sans façon, as they say among respectable people. Why shouldn't I be able to go sans façon? Our bear also said that everything would be sans façon, and therefore I also..." So thought Mr. Golyadkin; but meanwhile his agitation continued to increase. It was evident that he was preparing for something extremely troublesome, to say the least, was whispering to himself, gesticulating with his right hand, glancing incessantly out the windows of the coach, so that, looking at Mr. Golyadkin now, really no one would have said that he was getting ready to dine well, without ceremony, and what's more in his own family circle—sans façon, as they say among respectable people. At last, right at the Izmaylovsky Bridge Mr. Golyadkin pointed to a house; the coach thundered through the gates and stopped at the entrance of the right façade. Noticing the figure of a woman in a window on the second floor, Mr. Golyadkin blew her a kiss. However, he did not know himself what he was doing because he was absolutely more dead than alive at that moment. He emerged from the coach pale and distracted; he went up the steps of the front entrance, took off his hat, automatically straightened his clothing and, though feeling a slight trembling in his knees, started up the stairway.

"Is Olsufi Ivanovich at home?" he asked the servant who opened the door.

"At home, sir; that is, no, sir, he is not at home, sir."

"What? What do you mean, my dear fellow? [*Add: He's home.*] I—I've come to dinner, old chap. Why, you know me, don't you?"

Of course I do, sir. I've been told not to admit you, sir."

"You... you, old chap... you must be mistaken, old chap. It's me. [*Add: You see that it's me.*] I've been invited, old chap. I've come to dinner," said Mr. Golyadkin, taking off his overcoat and displaying the obvious intention of heading for the inner rooms.

"Excuse me, sir; you mustn't, sir. I've been told not to admit you, sir. I have been told to refuse you entrance, sir. That's how it is!"

Mr. Golyadkin turned pale. At that very moment the door to the inner rooms opened, and in came Gerasimych, Olsufi Ivanovich's old butler.

"This gentleman here wants to go in, Yemelyan Gerasimovich, but I . . ."

"But you are a fool, Alekseyich. Off with you into the rooms, and send that scoundrel Semyonych here. You mustn't, sir," he said politely but firmly, addressing Mr. Golyadkin. "It's quite impossible, sir. He asks to be excused, sir. He cannot receive you, sir."

"And is that how he put it, that he cannot receive me?" asked Mr. Golyadkin hesitantly. "Excuse my asking, Gerasimych. But why is it quite impossible?"

"It's quite impossible, sir. I announced you, sir. He said, 'Ask him to excuse me.' He can't receive you, sir, he said."

"But why? How can this be? How . . . [Add: Gerasimych . . . I . . .]"

"Excuse me; excuse me! . . ."

"Ah, well, indeed, that's a different matter—[Delete: that's a different matter— Add: it's a different matter,] if he asks to be excused. Still, [Delete: Still, Add: But still,] excuse me, Gerasimych; how can this be, Gerasimych?"

"Excuse me, excuse me!" objected Gerasimych, pushing Mr. Golyadkin aside most firmly with his hand and making way for two gentlemen who were at that very instant coming into the entrance hall. The gentlemen arriving were Andrei Filippovich and his nephew, Vladimir Semyonovich. Both of them looked at Mr. Golyadkin in bewilderment. Andrei Filippovich was about to say something, but Mr. Golyadkin had already made up his mind. He was already leaving Olsufi Ivanovich's entrance hall, eyes lowered, blushing, smiling, with an utterly embarrassed countenance.

"I'll come by later, Gerasimych. I shall explain myself. I hope all this will be explained without delay in good time," he said, speaking partly on the threshold and partly on the stairs. [*Delete:* . *Add:* . . .]

"Yakov Petrovich, Yakov Petrovich! . . ." came the voice of Andrei Filippovich, who had followed after Mr. Golyadkin.

Mr. Golyadkin was then already on the first landing. He turned around quickly to Andrei Filippovich.

"What can I do for you, Andrei Filippovich?" he asked in a rather firm tone.

"What is the matter with you, Yakov Petrovich? What does this mean? . . ."

"Nothing, Andrei Filippovich, sir. I'm here on my own business. This is my private life, Andrei Filippovich."

[*Delete previous paragraph. Add: "Nothing, Andrei Filippovich. I'm fine. I'm here on my own business. This is my private life, Andrei Filippovich, this is my private life."*]

"What's that, sir?"

"I'm saying, Andrei Filippovich, that this is my private life and that, as far as I can see, one cannot find anything reprehensible in it concerning my official relations."

"What! Concerning your official . . . [*Add: What?* . . .] What is the matter with you, sir?"

"Nothing, Andrei Filippovich, absolutely nothing. A brazen miss, nothing more . . ."

"What! . . . What?!" Andrei Filippovich [*Add: almost*] became flustered in amazement. Mr. Golyadkin, who up until that point had been conversing from the bottom of the stairway with Andrei Filippovich, looked as though he was ready to leap straight into his face; seeing that the head of division had become somewhat confused, he took, almost unbeknownst to himself, a step forward. Andrei Filippovich drew back. Mr. Golyadkin went up another step and yet another. Andrei Filippovich looked about uneasily. All of a sudden Mr. Golyadkin went quickly up the stairway. Even more quickly Andrei Filippovich leapt into the room and slammed the door behind him. Mr. Golyadkin was left alone. Everything went dark before his eyes. He was completely bewildered and stood now in a state of muddled hesitation, as if recalling some equally muddled event that had occurred quite recently.

"Dear, dear!" he whispered, smiling with effort. In the meantime on the stairway below could be heard the voices and footsteps of probably other guests who had been invited by Olsufi Ivanovich. Mr. Golyadkin came somewhat to his senses, hastily turned up his raccoon collar, muffling himself in it as much as he could—and began to go down the stairs with small tottering steps, hurrying and stumbling. He felt within him a kind of weakening and numbness. His embarrassment was so intense that, after coming out onto the front steps, he did not even wait for the [*Delete: the Add: his*] coach to draw up but went straight across the muddy courtyard to his vehicle. When he had reached his vehicle and was preparing to climb into it, Mr. Golyadkin mentally wished he might sink into the earth or at least hide himself in a mousehole together with the [*Delete: the Add: his*] coach. It seemed to him that everyone in Olsufi Ivanovich's house was staring at him now from every window. He knew that he would absolutely die right there on the spot if he should turn around.

"What are you laughing at, you blockhead?" he burst out at Petrushka, who was about to help him into the coach.

"And why should I laugh? I'm not doing anything. Where shall we go now?"

"Head for home. Go . . ."

"Head for home!" shouted Petrushka, perching himself on the footboard.

"He's got a voice like a crow!" thought Mr. Golyadkin. Meanwhile the coach had already driven rather far beyond the Izmaylovsky Bridge. Suddenly our hero pulled the cord with all his might and shouted to his driver to turn back immediately. The driver turned the horses around and two minutes later drove into Olsufi Ivanovich's courtyard again.

"Never mind, you fool, never mind! Go back!" Mr. Golyadkin shouted. And it was as if the driver had been expecting such an order: without [*Delete: : without Add:. Without*] making any objection or stopping at the entrance, he circled the entire courtyard and again drove out onto the street.

Mr. Golyadkin did not go home. Instead, after they passed the Semyonovsky Bridge he ordered the driver to turn into a sidestreet and stop at an eating establishment with a rather modest exterior. Getting out of the coach, our hero paid the driver what he owed him and thus rid himself finally of his vehicle. He ordered Petrushka to go home and await his return, while he went into the eating establishment, took a private room and ordered dinner to be served to him. He felt extremely sick, while his head was in a state of utter disorder and chaos. For a long time he paced the room in agitation. Finally he sat down on a chair, propped his forehead on his hands and began trying with all his might to review and resolve a few things with respect to his present situation.

IV

[Add: Exactly what kind of dinner and what kind of ball were being given by State Councilor[5] Berendeyev. Something about the usefulness of back stairways. Of how Mr. Golyadkin shows that he is acquainted with the former French Minister, Villèle. Mr. Golyadkin's opinion about the Jesuits. Of how Mr. Golyadkin, helped by the Jesuits, finally attains his end; how he then seeks his rightful social status and strives to earn the approbation of the host. How, on this appropriate occasion, he recalls hairless heads and Arab emirs. The polka and the conclusion of this absolutely plausible chapter.]

The day, the festive birthday of Klara Olsufyevna, only daughter of State Councilor Berendeyev, Mr. Golyadkin's one-time benefactor—a day marked by a splendid, magnificent dinner party, such a dinner party as had not been seen for a long time within the apartment walls of civil servants at the Izmaylovsky Bridge and thereabouts—by a dinner party which resembled more a kind of Balthazar's feast than a dinner party—which evoked something Babylonian with respect to its brilliance, luxury and propriety, with Clicquot champagne, with oysters and the fruits of Yeliseyev's and Milyutin's shops, with every kind of fatted calf and all the ranks of civil service—this festive day, marked by such a festive dinner party, concluded with a splendid ball, a small, intimate, family ball but nevertheless splendid with respect to taste, refinement and propriety. Of course, I completely agree, such balls do take place, but *[Add: they take place rarely, extremely]* rarely. Such balls, resembling, rather, joyous family occasions than balls, can only be given in such houses as, for example, the house of State Councilor Berendeyev. I shall go even further and say: I doubt even that such balls can be given in the houses of all State Councilors. Oh, if only I were a poet!—of course, at least such as Homer or Pushkin; with any less talent one couldn't butt in—I would unfailingly depict for you in brilliant colors and with a generous brush, oh, readers! all of that gala day. Nay, I would begin my poem with the dinner party; I would lay particular emphasis on that striking and at the same time solemn moment when the first congratulatory cup was raised in honor of the queen of the festivities. I would depict for you, first of all, those guests plunged into respectful silence and expectation, resembling more the eloquence of Demosthenes than silence. I would depict for you next Andrei Filippovich, as the eldest of the guests, having even a certain right to first place, adorned with grey hair and with the decorations appropriate to his grey hair, who rose from his place and raised above his head the congratulatory goblet of sparkling wine—a wine brought from a distant kingdom for the express purpose of accompanying such moments—a wine resembling more divine nectar than wine. I would depict for you the guests and the happy parents of the queen of the festivities, who also raised their goblets after Andrei Filippovich and fixed their eyes, full of expectation, upon him. I would depict for you how that frequently mentioned Andrei Filippovich, shedding first a tear into the goblet, delivered his congratulations and his wish, proposed a toast and drank to the health . . . But, I confess and confess fully that I would be unable to depict all the exaltation of that moment when the queen of the festivities herself, Klara Olsufyevna, blushing like a spring rose with the glow of bliss and modesty, sank from fullness of feeling into the arms of her tender mother, how her tender mother was moved to tears and how at this her father himself, the venerable old man and State Councilor, Olsufi Ivanovich, deprived of the use of his legs through long service and rewarded by fate for such diligence with a bit of capital, a little house, some small estates and a beauty of a daughter, began to sob—began to sob like a child and declared through his tears that His Excellency was a beneficent man. I would be unable, yes, I would simply be unable to depict for you either the general heartfelt enthusiasm

34

which followed immediately upon that moment—an enthusiasm clearly expressed even in the behavior of one young Collegiate Registrar (who at that instant resembled more a State Councilor than a Collegiate Registrar), who was also moved to tears in listening to Andrei Filippovich. In his turn, Andrei Filippovich at that solemn moment did not at all resemble a Collegiate Councilor[6] and chief of division in a certain department,—no, he seemed something else . . . I just do not know exactly what, but not a Collegiate Councilor. [*Add: No!*] He was more exalted! Finally . . . Oh! Why do I not possess the secret of elevated, powerful style, of solemn style for depicting all those wonderful and edifying moments of human life, which seem intentionally arranged as proof of how virtue sometimes triumphs over treachery, freethinking, vice and envy! I shall say nothing, but shall silently—which will be better than any eloquence—point out to you that fortunate young man, entering his twenty-sixth spring, Valdimir Semyonovich, Andrei Filippovich's nephew, who in his turn rose from his place, who in his turn proposed a toast and on whom were fixed the weeping eyes of the parents of the queen of the festivities, the proud eyes of Andrei Filippovich, the shy eyes of the queen of the festivities herself, the enraptured eyes of the guests and even the decorously envious eyes of certain young colleagues of this splendid young man. I shall say nothing, although I cannot help noting that everything about this young man—who resembled more an old man than a young one, speaking in a manner intended to be complimentary to him—everything, from his blooming cheeks to the very rank of Collegiate Assessor which he bore, all of it at that solemn moment almost seemed to say, 'It is to these lofty heights that good conduct can lead a man!' I shall not describe how, finally, Anton Antonovich Setochkin, the section head of a certain department, a colleague of Andrei Filippovich and a former colleague of Olsufi Ivanovich, as well as an old friend of the family and the godfather of Klara Olsufyevna,—a little old man, with snow-white hair, proposing in his turn a toast, crowed like a cock and recited some merry verses; how he, through such a proper obliviousness to propriety, if one may express oneself thus, set the entire company laughing till they

35

cried and how Klara Olsufyevna herself, at her parents' bidding, kissed him for such merriment and affability. I shall say only that finally the guests, who after such a dinner party naturally must have felt they were relatives and brothers to one another, got up [*Add: at last*] from the table; how then the little old man and the solid and sedate people, after a brief [*Delete: brief Add: certain amount of*] time spent in friendly conversation and even in the exchange of some, it goes without saying, extremely decorous and affable confidences, staidly passed into another room and, not wasting golden time but dividing up into groups of players, sat down with a feeling of their own worth at tables covered with green baize; how the ladies, settling themselves in the drawing room, all suddenly became unusually affable and began to converse about various dress materials; how finally, the most worthy host himself, deprived of the use of his legs through faithful and true service and rewarded for it by all that has already been mentioned above, began to walk about on crutches among his guests, supported by Vladimir Semyonovich and Klara Olsufyevna, and how suddenly also becoming unusually affable, he decided to improvise a small modest ball regardless of the expense; how for this purpose an efficient young man (the very one who at dinner had resembled a State Councilor more than a young man) was sent off to get musicians; how then the musicians, numbering eleven in all, arrived, and how, finally, exactly at half past eight, the inviting strains of a French quadrille sounded, followed by various other dances... It goes without saying that my pen is too weak, flagging and dull for a proper description of the ball improvised by the singular affability of the greyhaired host. Besides, how, I will ask, how can I, a modest narrator of the adventures of Mr. Golyadkin, extremely curious as they are in their own way—how can I depict this unusual and seemly assemblage of beauty, brilliance, decorum,, gaiety, affable solidity and solid affability, frolicsomeness, joy, all the mirth and laughter of all those officials' ladies, resembling rather fays than ladies—speaking in a manner intended to be complimentary to them—with their pink and white shoulders and visages, with their airy figures, with their nimbly twinkling homeopathic—to put it in elevated style—little feet? How will I depict to you, finally, their cavaliers, those brilliant officials, merry ones and solid ones, young ones and sedate ones, joyful ones and decorously lacklustre ones, some smoking a pipe during the intervals between dances in a small remote green room and others not smoking a pipe during the intervals—cavaliers, bearing, each and every one, a becoming rank and surname, cavaliers deeply imbued with a sense of the elegant and a sense of their own worth, cavaliers speaking with the ladies for the most part in French, and if in Russian, then using only the most well-bred expressions, paying compliments and making utterances of profound meaning—cavaliers, possibly only in the smoking room permitting themselves certain amiable deviations from well-bred language, certain phrases of friendly and amiable familiarity, such as these, for example: "Well, you old so-and-so, Petka, you really were cutting a fancy polka!" or "Well, you old so-and-so, Vasya, you really gave your partner a hard time!" All this, as I have already had the honor of explaining to you above, oh, readers! my pen is incapable of depicting, and therefore I keep silent. Let us rather return to Mr. Golyadkin, the one true hero of our extremely plausible tale.

The fact of the matter is that he now finds himself in an extremely strange position, to say the least. He, ladies and gentlemen, is also here, that is, not at the ball but almost at the ball; he, ladies and gentlemen, is fine; even though he is going his own way, still at this moment he is standing on a path not altogether direct; he is standing now—it's even a strange thing to say—he is standing now in the entranceway on the back stairs of Olsufi Ivanovich's apartment. But it doesn't matter that he is standing here; he's all right. He, ladies and gentlemen, is standing in a corner, lodged in a small space which, although it is not especially warm, is, nevertheless, especially dark, partly hidden by an enormous wardrobe and old screens, among all sorts of trash, rubbish and junk, remaining concealed until the opportune moment and meanwhile simply watching the progress of things as an outside observer. He, ladies and gentlemen, is only watching now; after all, he, ladies and gentlemen, can also go in... and why not do so? He has only to take a step, and

in he will go, and do so with the greatest agility. Just now—
standing, by the way, for more than two hours already in the
cold between the cupboard and the screens, among the rubbish,
trash, and junk—he was quoting, for his own justification, a
phrase by the French Minister, Villèle (of blessed memory),
who said: "Everything comes in due course, if only one has the
gumption to wait it out." Mr. Golyadkin had found this phrase
once [*Add: in some book,*] in a book on a completely extraneous
subject, but now he very appropriately recalled it. The phrase,
in the first place, was most appropriate for his present situation,
while, in the second place, what doesn't come into the head of a
person waiting out a happy ending to his situation for almost
three whole hours in an entranceway in the darkness and in the
cold? Having quoted most appropriately, as has already been
said, the phrase of the former French Minister Villèle, Mr.
Golyadkin thereupon, for reasons [*Add: , however,*] unknown,
recalled also the former Turkish Vizier, Martsimiris, as well as
the margrave's beautiful wife, Luisa, both of whose story he had
also once read in some book. Then he recalled that the Jesuits
even made it their rule to consider all means justified as long as
the end could be achieved. Raising his own hopes a bit with
such a historical point, Mr. Golyadkin said to himself, he said,
'Why speak of the Jesuits?'; he said that the Jesuits were to a
man the greatest fools, that he would outdo them, that if only
for even a minute the pantry (that room the door of which
opened directly into the entranceway and onto the back
staircase, where Mr. Golyadkin was now to be found) were to be
free of traffic, then he, Jesuits or not, would betake himself—
[*Delete: —*] and go straight through, first from the pantry into
the room where tea was served, then into that room where they
were now playing cards, and then straight into the ballroom,
where they were now dancing the polka. And he would go
through, he would absolutely, without fail, go through, he
would go through without looking at anything, he would slip
through—and that would be that and no one would notice; and
once there he would know what to do. Thus it is in this kind of
situation, ladies and gentlemen, that we now find the hero of
our completely plausible story, although, however, it is difficult

to explain just what was happening to him right then. For the fact of the matter is that he knew how to get as far as the stairway and to the entranceway, for, he said, 'Why not get that far? Everyone gets that far.' But he did not dare to push on any further; he clearly did not dare to do that... not because there was something he did not dare to do, but just because he did not want to, because he would rather be unnoticed. And so there he is, ladies and gentlemen, waiting it out now unnoticed, and waiting it out unnoticed exactly two and a half hours. And why not wait it out? Why, Villèle waited it out. "But what does Villèle have to do with it!" thought Mr. Golyadkin. "Why bring him in? And what if I were now to, you know ... [*Add: push my way in, just so ...*] go ahead and push my way in? ... Oh, you, you're just a nonentity, you are!" said Mr. Golyadkin, pinching his benumbed cheek with his benumbed fingers; "what a fool you are; what a poor beggar you are; what a Poor Beggar name you have!..."[7] However, these endearing statements addressed to his own person at that moment were only by the way, made in passing and without any obvious purpose. He was about to thrust his way in and had moved forward; the moment had come; the pantry had emptied out and there was no one in it. Mr. Golyadkin saw all this through a small window. Two steps and he found himself at the door and had already begun to open it. "Shall I go in or not? Well, shall I or not? I will go in ... after all, why shouldn't I? He who dares can go where he will!" Having thus bolstered himself up, our hero suddenly and quite unexpectedly retreated behind the screens. "No," he thought; "what if someone comes in? [*Add: What if they do?*] There, that's just what's happened; they've come in; now why did I let the moment slip by when there was no one in there? I should just [*Add: go on and push my way in...*] go on and push my way in! ... No, why push one's way in when one has a character like mine! Oh, what a despicable trait! I've become chicken-hearted. To be chicken-hearted is my way, and that's all there is to it! To make a mess is always my way; no question about it. Well, do just go on standing here [*Add: now*] like a blockhead! I wish I were home now drinking a cup of tea ... [*Add: I'd really love to have a cup.*] It would be so pleasant to have a cup. If I come home late

39

Petrushka will probably grumble. Maybe I should go home? The hell with all this! I'm going in and that's that!" Having thus resolved his situation, Mr. Golyadkin quickly moved forward, as if someone had touched a spring in him; just two steps and he found himself in the pantry; he discarded his overcoat, took off his hat, hastily shoved it all into a corner, put his clothing to rights and smoothed his hair; then . . . then he moved into the room where tea was served; from this room he whisked into still another room, and slipped almost undetected among the excited card players; then . . . then . . . At this point, Mr. Golyadkin became oblivious to everything that was going on around him and, like a bolt out of the blue, appeared right smack in the ballroom.

As luck would have it, at that point no one was dancing. The ladies were promenading about the room in picturesque groups. The men were gathering in small groups or whisking about the rooms, engaging the ladies to dance. Mr. Golyadkin noticed none of this. He saw only Klara Olsufyevna, alongside her Andrei Filippovich, then Vladimir Semyonovich, and two or three officers, and two or three young men, also extremely interesting, who, as one could tell at first sight, were showing some promise or had already demonstrated it . . . He also saw one or two other people. Or no. He no longer saw anyone or looked at anyone . . . but propelled by that very same spring by means of which he had catapulted into someone's ball uninvited, he took a step forward, then another, and still another; in passing he stumbled against a councilor and stomped on his foot; incidentally, he had already stepped on the gown of a dignified old lady and torn it somewhat; he jostled a servant carrying a tray, jostled someone else as well, and without noticing all of this or, rather, noticing it but at the same time not looking at anyone and continuing to make his way forward, he suddenly found himself standing before Klara Olsufyevna herself. Without any doubt, he would not have blinked an eye and would have felt the greatest pleasure, if the earth had opened up beneath his feet at that moment and swallowed him; but what is done cannot be undone . . . indeed in no wise can it be undone. What ought he to do now? If you don't succeed, stand firm, and if you do succeed, don't give in. Mr. Golyadkin, of course, was no intriguer and no expert at bowing and scraping... That's simply how it was. Moreover, the Jesuits had also somehow gotten mixed up in this... However, they were not the ones who interested Mr. Golyadkin! All those who were moving about, making a hubbub, talking, laughing, suddenly, as if at the wave of a hand, fell silent and little by little gathered in a crowd around Mr. Golyadkin. Mr. Golyadkin, however, seemed to hear nothing and see nothing; he could not look... not for anything in the world could he look; he looked down at the floor and just stood that way, promising himself, however, in passing, that, word of honor, he would somehow or other shoot himself that night. After giving his word of honor, Mr. Golyadkin mentally said to himself: "Here goes!"—and suddenly to his own very great amazement quite unexpectedly began to speak.

Mr. Golyadkin began with congratulations and polite good wishes. The congratulations went well; but over the good wishes our hero faltered. He had felt that if he once faltered everything would immediately go to the devil. And that is what happened—he faltered and got stuck... got stuck and blushed; blushed and became flustered; became flustered and raised his eyes; raised his eyes and looked around; looked around and— and froze... Everyone was standing there, everyone was silent, everyone was expectant; a little way off a whisper arose; a little closer to him a loud laugh burst out. Mr. Golyadkin cast a humble, embarrassed glance at Andrei Filippovich. Andrei Filippovich answered Mr. Golyadkin with the kind of look that, if our hero had not already been totally and completely annihilated, would have without fail annihilated him again—if that were only possible. The silence continued.

"This is concerned more with personal matters and with my private life, Andrei Filippovich," Mr. Golyadkin, more dead than alive, uttered in a barely audible voice. "This is not an official matter, Andrei Filippovich..."

"Have shame, sir, have shame!" uttered Andrei Filippovich in a low voice, with an indescribable air of indignation. He uttered this, took Klara Olsufyevna by the arm and turned away from Mr. Golyadkin.

"I have nothing to be ashamed of, Andrei Filippovich," answered Mr. Golyadkin also in a low voice, directing his unfortunate gaze all around, feeling embarrassed and trying therefore to seek out in the perplexed crowd his rightful social position.

"Why, it's nothing, it's nothing, ladies and gentlemen! Well, and what of it? Why, this could happen to anyone," whispered Mr. Golyadkin, moving away little by little from the spot where he had been standing and trying to get through the crowd surrounding him. They made a path for him. Our hero somehow passed between the two rows of curious and perplexed observers. Fate was drawing him along. Mr. Golyadkin himself felt this, that it was fate that was drawing him along. Of course, he would have given a great deal for the opportunity of finding himself now, without a breach of decorum, back at his former spot in the entranceway next to the back stairway; but, as this was decidedly impossible, he began to try to slip away somewhere into a corner and to just stand there—modestly, in a seemly manner, apart, bothering no one, not calling any special attention to himself, but at the same time earning the approbation of the guests and of the host. However, Mr. Golyadkin felt as if something were eroding him, as if he were wavering, falling. At last he made his way to a corner and stood in it like a rather indifferent outside observer, resting his hands on the backs of two chairs, thus totally claiming them, and trying as far as possible to cast a cheerful glance at those guests of Olsufi Ivanovich who had formed a group around him. Closest of all to him stood an officer, a tall and handsome fellow, beside whom Mr. Golyadkin felt he was a mere insect.

"These two chairs, lieutenant, are reserved: one for Klara Olsufyevna and the other for Princess Chevchekhanova, who is dancing here; I'm holding them for them now, lieutenant," uttered Mr. Golyadkin breathlessly, turning an imploring gaze at the lieutenant. The lieutenant silently turned away, with a devastating smile. Having suffered a defeat in one quarter, our hero made an attempt to seek his good fortune elsewhere and turned directly to a grave-looking councilor wearing an important cross around his neck. But the councilor meted out to him such a cold look that Mr. Golyadkin clearly felt that he had suddenly been doused with a bucket of cold water. Mr. Golyadkin fell silent. He decided that it was better to keep quiet, not to begin a conversation, to show that he was all right, that he was like everyone else and that his position, at least as far as he could see, was also a seemly one. With this purpose in mind, he fixed his gaze on the cuffs of his jacket, then raised his eyes and glued them on a gentleman with an extremely dignified countenance. "That gentleman is wearing a wig," thought Mr. Golyadkin, "and if the wig were to be removed, there would be a bald head, as bare as the palm of my hand." Upon making such an important discovery, Mr. Golyadkin recalled the Arab emirs, who, if one were to remove from their heads the green turbans which they wear as a sign of their kinship with the Prophet Mohammed, would also be left with bare, hairless heads. Then, and probably because of the peculiar concatenation of ideas about Turks in his head, Mr. Golyadkin moved on to Turkish slippers and hereupon recalled incidentally that Andrei Filippovich wore shoes that resembled slippers rather than shoes. It was clear that Mr. Golyadkin had in part come to terms with his situation. "Now if that chandelier," the thought flashed through Mr. Golyadkin's mind, "if that chandelier should fall from its place now and onto the company, I would immediately rush to save Klara Olsufyevna. After saving her, I would say to her: 'Don't worry, young lady; it's nothing, young lady; I am your saviour.' Then . . ." Here Mr Golyadkin gave a sidelong glance, searching out Klara Olsufyevna, and caught sight of Gerasimych, Olsufi Ivanovich's old butler. Gerasimych, with the most concerned, the most officially solemn look was making his way directly towards him. Mr. Golyadkin shuddered and screwed up his face because of some unaccountable and at the same time most unpleasant sensation. He looked around automatically. He was thinking of somehow easily, secretly sidling away from any trouble, of just suddenly disappearing out of sight, that is, of acting as if he were not at all to blame, as if he had nothing at all to do with the matter.

However, before our hero could manage to come to any decision, Gerasimych was already standing before him.

"You see, Gerasimych," said our hero, turning to Gerasimych with an attempt at a smile; "you [*Add: "know what? You*] just go and tell them—you see there, the candle there in the candelabra, Gerasimych—it's going to fall this minute; so you, you know, tell them to fix it; it really is going to fall right this minute, Gerasimych . . ."

"The candle, sir? No, sir. The candle is standing up straight, sir. But there's someone asking for you, sir."

"Just who is it that's asking for me, Gerasimych?"

"Why, I really don't know, sir, who exactly, sir. Someone's servant, sir. He said, 'Is Yakov Petrovich Golyadkin here? Call him out,' he said; 'it's an extremely important and urgent matter . . .' That's how it is, sir."

"No, Gerasimych, you are mistaken; in this instance, you are mistaken, Gerasimych."

"Hardly, sir."

"No, Gerasimych, not hardly; there's no hardly about it, Gerasimych. No one is asking for me, Gerasimych; there isn't anyone to ask for me. And I am at home here, that is, in my place, Gerasimych."

Mr. Golyadkin paused for breath and looked around. Just as he thought! Everyone in the ballroom, everyone was all eyes and all ears in solemn expectation. The men were crowding closer and listening in. Farther off the ladies were anxiously whispering among themselves. The host himself had appeared at an extremely short distance from Mr. Golyadkin, and, although from his appearance one could not tell that he too in turn was playing a direct and firsthand part in Mr. Golyadkin's affairs, for all of this was being done in a delicate way, nevertheless all of this was making the hero of our tale clearly feel that the decisive moment had come for him. Mr. Golyadkin clearly saw that the time for the daring stroke had come, the time for heaping shame upon his enemies. Mr. Golyadkin was in a state of agitation. Mr. Golyadkin felt a certain inspiration, and in a trembling, solemn voice began again, addressing the waiting Gerasimych:

"No, my friend, no one is asking for me. You are mistaken. I shall go further and say that you were mistaken this morning, too, when you were assuring me... making so bold as to assure me, I say, (Mr. Golyadkin raised his voice), that Olsufi Ivanovich, who has been my benefactor for longer than I can remember, who has, in a certain sense, been like a father to me, had shown me the door of his house at a moment when his paternal heart was full of festive, familial joy." (Mr. Golyadkin looked about well satisfied with himself, but deeply moved. Tears appeared on his eyelashes.) "I repeat, my friend," concluded our hero, "you were mistaken; you were cruelly and unpardonably mistaken..."

The moment was one of triumph. Mr. Golyadkin felt that the effect he had produced was exactly right. Mr. Golyadkin stood modestly lowering his eyes and awaiting Olsufi Ivanovich's embrace. Agitation and bewilderment were noticeable in the guests. Even the unshakeable and terrible Gerasimych stuttered over the words "Hardly, sir" ... when suddenly the merciless orchestra for no apparent reason struck up a polka. All was lost; all was scattered to the four winds. Mr. Golyadkin shuddered; Gerasimych staggered back; the entire ballroom began to billow like the sea and Vladimir Semyonovich was already flying along with Klara Olsufyevna, leading the dance, followed by the handsome lieutenant and the Princess Chevchekhanova. With curiosity and delight the spectators jostled one another to catch a glimpse of those dancing the polka—an interesting, new, fashionable dance which was the latest thing. Mr. Golyadkin was forgotten for a time. But, suddenly everyone became agitated and perturbed, and began bustling about; the music stopped ... a strange thing had occurred. Wearied by the dance, Klara Olsufyevna, barely able to catch her breath from exhaustion, her cheeks burning and her breast heaving, had finally fallen into an armchair, totally worn out. All hearts had gone out to the charming enchantress; everyone, vying with one another, was rushing to greet her and thank her for the pleasure she had given them—when suddenly before her appeared Mr. Golyadkin. Mr. Golyadkin was pale and extremely unsettled; he also seemed to be exhausted; he could barely walk. For some reason he was smiling. He was holding out his hand beseechingly. Klara Olsufyevna, in her amazement, did not manage to pull her hand away in time and rose mechanically at Mr. Golyadkin's invitation. Mr. Golyadkin staggered forward, once, then a second time, then he raised his foot, then somehow bowed and scraped it, then somehow stamped it, then tripped... he too wished to dance with Klara Olsufyevna. [*Delete: he too wished to dance with Klara Olsufyevna.*] Klara Olsufyevna screamed. Everyone rushed to free her hand from Mr. Golyadkin's and immediately our hero was pushed almost ten paces away by the crowd. Around him too a circle gathered. There were squeals and shrieks from two old ladies whom Mr. Golyadkin had almost knocked over in his retreat. The commotion was terrible; everyone was asking questions, everyone was shouting, everyone was arguing. The orchestra had fallen silent. Our hero stood fidgeting in his circle and absent-mindedly, half-smiling, muttering something to himself, to the effect that "And why shouldn't he?" and that the polka, at least as far as he could see, was a new and very interesting dance created to amuse the ladies... but [*Delete: but Add: But*] that as things had taken such a turn, he was ready to consent. But no one seemed to be asking for Mr. Golyadkin's consent. Our hero felt that suddenly someone's hand fell on his arm, that another hand rested lightly on his back, that he was being directed with special care in a certain direction. Finally he noticed that he was headed straight for the door. Mr. Golyadkin wanted to say something, to do something... But no, he no longer wanted anything. He was just laughing mechanically in answer. At last he felt that his overcoat was being put on him, that his hat had been clapped on down over his eyes, that finally he found himself in the entranceway, in the darkness and in the cold, and at last on the stairway. Finally, he tripped; it seemed to him that he was falling into an abyss; he wanted to cry out—and suddenly found himself in the courtyard. A gust of fresh air struck him; he stopped for a moment. At that instant the strains of the orchestra, which had struck up again, reached him. Mr. Golyadkin suddenly recalled everything; all his diminished powers seemed to be restored again. He darted from the spot on which he had up until then been standing as though rooted to it, and rushed headlong out of the courtyard, somewhere, into the open, to freedom, anywhere . . .

V

[Add: A perfectly inexplicable occurrence]

All the towers of Petersburg that had clocks which strike the hour were sounding exactly midnight when Mr. Golyadkin, beside himself, ran out onto the Fontanka embankment, close to the Izmaylovsky Bridge, fleeing from his enemies, from persecution, from the hail of slights that had been delivered to him, from the shrieks of the alarmed old women, from the moaning and groaning of the ladies and from the annihilating looks of Andrei Filippovich. Mr. Golyadkin had been annihilated—annihilated totally—in the full sense of the word, and if he still maintained the ability to run it was only through some miracle, a miracle in which he himself finally refused to believe. The night was terrible, a November night—wet, foggy, rainy, snowy, pregnant with flus, colds, cold sores, sore throats, fevers of all kinds and sorts—in a word, with all the gifts of a Petersburg November. The wind howled in the deserted streets, raising the black water of the Fontanka above the mooring rings and brazenly pushing against the gaunt street lamps along the embankment; and they in turn accompanied its howling with a thin, piercing creak that comprised the ceaseless, whining, rattling concert so familiar to every inhabitant of Petersburg. Rain and snow were falling together. The streams of rain water, driven by the wind, were spraying almost horizontally, as if from a fire hose, and pricked and whipped the face of the unfortunate Mr. Golyadkin like thousands of pins and needles. In the hush of the night, broken only by the distant rumbling of coaches, the howling of the wind and the creaking of the street lamps, there dolefully sounded the lashing and gurgling of water running down from all the roofs, porches, gutters and ledges onto the granite of the pavement. There was not a soul anywhere; moreover, it seemed that there could not be at such an hour and in such weather. And so, only Mr. Golyadkin, alone with his despair, trotted then along the Fontanka pavement with his usual small and rapid step, hurrying to get as quickly as possible to his Shestilavochnaya Street, to his fourth floor and to his apartment.

Although the snow, the rain and everything nameless that appears when a blizzard rages and fog builds up under a November Petersburg sky, all suddenly attacked Mr. Golyadkin, already annihilated by misfortune, showing him no mercy or respite, penetrating to his bones, gluing his eyelids together, gusting from all sides, driving him from his path and out of his senses, although all of this overturned on Mr. Golyadkin in one fell swoop, as if having deliberately communicated and conspired with his enemies to give a rousing finale to his day, evening and night, nevertheless Mr. Golyadkin remained almost insensible to this final proof of hounding by fate: so powerfully had everything that had happened to him several minutes ago at State Councilor Berendeyev's shaken and staggered him! If at this point some impartial outside observer had glanced just slightly, from the corner of his eye, at the melancholy gait of Mr. Golyadkin, he would immediately have been filled with a sense of all the terrible horror of his misfortunes and would undoubtedly have said that Mr. Golyadkin looked now as if he wanted to hide somewhere from himself, as if he wanted to run away somewhere from himself. Yes! That was exactly how it was. We shall go further and say: Mr. Golyadkin not only wished now to run away from himself, but even to be completely annihilated, to cease to exist, to turn to dust. At that moment he was oblivious to everything around him, uncomprehending of everything that was happening around him, and looked as though none of the unpleasantness of the stormy night, not the long walk, nor the rain, nor the snow, nor the wind, nor all the cruel bad weather really existed for him. The galosh which had come loose from the boot on Mr. Golyadkin's right foot remained where it was in the slush and snow, on the pavement of the Fontanka, and Mr. Golyadkin did not think of going back for it nor indeed notice its loss. He was so dazed that several times, suddenly, regardless of what was around him, he stood stockstill in the middle of the pavement, totally absorbed by the idea of his recent terrible downfall; at those moments he would die and disappear; then suddenly he would tear himself from the spot like a madman and run and run without looking back, as if fleeing from a pursuer and from some even more terrible misfortune . . . Truly, his situation was appalling! . . . Finally, his strength exhausted, Mr. Golyadkin stopped, leaned on the railing of the embankment in the pose of a person who has suddenly and quite unexpectedly had a nosebleed, and began to stare into the murky, dark waters of the Fontanka. It is impossible to say just how much time he spent thus engaged. All that can be said is that at that instant Mr. Golyadkin had reached a point of such despair, was so harried, so tormented, so exhausted and so utterly dispirited that he had forgotten about everything: about the Izmaylovsky Bridge and Shesti-lavochnaya Street, and his present situation . . . Indeed, what of it? He really did not care; the thing was over and done with; the decision had been signed and sealed; what did it matter to him? . . . Suddenly . . . suddenly he shuddered all over and involuntarily leapt aside a couple of paces. With a feeling of inexplicable anxiety he began to look around, but there was no one there, nothing out of the ordinary had happened; but nevertheless . . . nevertheless it seemed to him that just then, that very minute, someone had been standing there, near him, alongside him, also leaning his elbows on the railing of the embankment, and—strange though it was!—had even said something to him, said something quickly, abruptly, not altogether intelligibly, but about something closely concerning him. "What is this? Have I dreamed this up?" said Mr. Golyadkin, looking about once more. "But where am I standing? . . . Dear, dear!" he concluded, shaking his head; but meanwhile with an uneasy, anguished feeling, even with fear, he began to peer into the murky, wet distance, straining his vision and trying his utmost to penetrate with his nearsighted eyes the wet tract stretching out before him. However, there was nothing new; nothing out of the ordinary struck Mr. Golyadkin's eye.

Everything seemed to be in order, was as it should be, that is, the snow was falling even more heavily and thickly and in bigger flakes; at a distance of twenty paces nothing was visible; the street lamps creaked even more piercingly than before, and the wind seemed to wail its melancholy song even more sadly and plaintively, like a persistent beggar beseeching a copper for food. "Dear, dear! What is wrong with me?" Mr. Golyadkin repeated, setting off on his way again and continuing to look around slightly. But meanwhile some new sensation echoed through all of Mr. Golyadkin's being: it was not exactly anguish or fear... a feverish trembling went through him. The moment was unbearably unpleasant! "Oh, it's nothing," he uttered, to give himself courage. "Oh, it's nothing; perhaps this is nothing at all and a blot on no one's honor. Perhaps this is how it had to be," he continued, not understanding himself what he was saying. "Perhaps it will all turn out for the best ultimately and there won't be anything to complain about and everyone will be vindicated." Speaking thus and easing his heart with words, Mr. Golyadkin shook himself off a bit, shook off the snowflakes that had piled up in a thick layer on his hat, his collar, his overcoat, his cravat, his boots, and on everything—but still he could not repulse or shake off the strange feeling, his strange, vague anguish. Somewhere far off a cannon sounded. "What weather!" thought our hero. "Hark! Does that mean there's going to be a flood? You can see the water has risen too high." Mr. Golyadkin had no sooner said or thought this than he saw ahead of him a passerby coming towards him, also, probably, like him, on some belated errand [*Add: or other*]. It would seem to be a trifling, fortuitous thing. But, for some unknown reason, Mr. Golyadkin became confused and even frightened; he became a bit flustered. Not that he was afraid that this was a person with evil intentions, but just that perhaps . . . "Why, who knows who he may be, this belated traveller," flashed through Mr. Golyadkin's mind. "Perhaps he's the same as everyone else; perhaps he isn't and his main reason for being here is not that he doesn't have a purpose, but that he does; he will cross my path and bother me." Perhaps, however, Mr. Golyadkin did not exactly think this, but only momentarily sensed something like it, which was very unpleasant. Indeed, there was no time to think and to sense. The passerby was now just a couple of paces away. Mr. Golyadkin, as was ever his wont, immediately hastened to assume an utterly special air—an air which clearly expressed that he, Golyadkin, was going his own way, that he was fine, that the way was broad enough for everyone and that after all he, Golyadkin, was not bothering anyone. Suddenly he stopped dead, as though struck by lightning, and then rapidly swung around in the direction of the passerby, who had just barely gone past him—swung around as if he had been jerked from behind, as if the wind had turned him like a weathervane. The passerby was rapidly disappearing into the snowstorm. He, too, was walking hastily; he, too, was dressed like Mr. Golyadkin and muffled from head to foot and just like him, his footsteps tapping, was mincing along the pavement of the Fontanka with a rapid, small step, in a faint trot. "What - what is this?" whispered Mr. Golyadkin, smiling uncertainly; [*Add: but*] still, he shuddered all over. A chill ran down his spine. Meanwhile the passerby had disappeared completely... Even his footsteps could no longer be heard. But Mr. Golyadkin continued to stand there and look after him. However, at last he gradually came to his senses. "Why, whatever is this?" he thought with annoyance. "Have I actually gone out of my mind or something?" He turned and went his way, hastening and shortening his step more and more and doing his best now not to think of anything at all. To this end he even closed his eyes finally. Suddenly, through the howling of the wind and the noise of the storm, the sound of someone's footsteps very close by again reached his ears. He shuddered and opened his eyes. Up ahead once more, some twenty paces away, appeared a small dark figure rapidly approaching him. The small figure was hurrying, rushing, hastening. The distance between them was rapidly diminishing. Mr. Golyadkin could now even see his new belated companion distinctly; he made him out and gave a cry of amazement and horror. His legs gave way beneath him. It was that same familiar passerby, whom, some ten minutes before, he had let go past him, and who suddenly, quite unexpectedly, now appeared again before him.

But it was not this marvel alone that struck Mr. Golyadkin. Mr. Golyadkin was so struck that he stopped, cried out, tried to say something, and set off to catch up with the stranger, even shouted something to him, probably wishing to stop him as quickly as possible. The stranger actually did stop—[*Delete:* — *Add:* ,] some ten paces from Mr. Golyadkin, so that the light of a nearby street lamp fell on his entire figure; he stopped, turned around to Mr. Golyadkin, and with an impatient and anxious look waited to hear what he would say. "Excuse me; perhaps I am mistaken," uttered our hero in a trembling voice. The stranger turned away silently, annoyed, and rapidly went his way, as if hastening to make up the two seconds he had wasted on Mr. Golyadkin. As for Mr. Golyadkin, all his nerves were shattered, his knees gave way and became weak, and with a moan he sat down on a curbstone. Indeed, there really was cause for feeling such confusion. The fact of the matter is that this stranger seemed to him now somehow familiar. This in itself would have been nothing. But he recognized, almost completely recognized this person now. He had frequently seen him, this person, had seen him somewhere, quite recently even. Where could it have been? Could it have been yesterday? However, once again the fact that Mr. Golyadkin had seen him frequently was not the main thing. Moreover, there was nothing really special about this person. This person at first glance absolutely did not elicit anyone's special attention. He was a person like any other, decent, it goes without saying, like all other decent people, and perhaps even had some rather significant qualities; in [*Delete:* ; in *Add:* . In] a word, he was a person in his own right. Mr. Golyadkin did not harbor either hatred or enmity or even the slightest hostility toward this person; quite the contrary, it would seem. But nevertheless (and this was precisely the point), but nevertheless, not for any treasure in the world would he have desired to encounter him and especially to encounter him as he had now, for example. We shall go further and say: Mr. Golyadkin knew this person quite well; he even knew this person's name and his surname. But nevertheless, not for anything, and, once again, not for any treasure in the world would he have wished to utter his name, would he have agreed to acknowledge that his name was such-and-such, that his patronymic was such-and-such and such-and-such his surname. Whether Mr. Golyadkin's bewilderment lasted a long time or a short time, just whether he sat on the curbstone for a long time, I cannot say, but coming somewhat to his senses at last, he suddenly began to run without looking back, using what strength he still had; it took his breath away; twice he stumbled and almost fell, and given this circumstance Mr. Golyadkin's other boot became orphaned, also abandoned by its galosh. At last Mr. Golyadkin slackened his pace somewhat in order to catch his breath, hastily glanced around and saw that he had already run, without noticing it, his entire route along the Fontanka, had crossed the Anichkov Bridge, traversed a part of Nevsky Prospect, and was now standing at the turn into Liteynaya Street. Mr. Golyadkin turned into Liteynaya Street. His situation at that instant resembled that of a person standing on the edge of a terrifying precipice, when the earth beneath him is breaking up, has already given way, already moved, sways for the last time, collapses and drags him into the abyss; meanwhile, the poor unfortunate lacks the strength, the firmness of will, to jump back, to avert his eyes from the yawning abyss. The abyss draws him and he finally jumps into it himself, himself hastening the moment of his own destruction. Mr. Golyadkin knew, felt and was absolutely sure that along the way something else bad would certainly happen to him, that some further unpleasantness would burst upon him, that, for example, he would again meet his stranger. But, oddly enough, he even desired this encounter, considered it unavoidable, and asked only that all of this would end as quickly as possible, that his situation would somehow be resolved, but as quickly as possible. Meanwhile, he ran on and on, and was literally being propelled by some external force, for he felt throughout his entire being a kind of weakness and numbness. He could not think about anything, although his thoughts caught at everything, like the blackthorn. [*Add: He understood at last that he was losing his presence of mind utterly, that he was falling into an abyss.*] A lost little dog, all wet and worn out with shivering, attached itself to Mr. Golyadkin and also ran along sidling up to him, hurriedly, tail tucked under and ears flattened, glancing at him now and then timidly and perceptively. Some distant, already long-forgotten idea—a recollection of some event that had occurred a long time ago—now came into his head, pounded in his head like a hammer, annoying him and refusing to leave him. "Oh, dear, that nasty little dog!" whispered Mr. Golyadkin, not understanding himself what he was saying. Finally he caught sight of his stranger at the turn into Italyanskaya Street. Only now the stranger was no longer walking towards him, but was going in the same direction as he, and was running, too, several steps ahead of him. At last they entered Shestilavochnaya Street. Mr. Golyadkin caught his breath. The stranger stopped right in front of the very house in which Mr. Golyadkin lived. The ring of the bell could be heard and at almost the same time the scrape of the iron bolt. The gate opened, the stranger stooped, whisked inside, then disappeared. At almost the very same instant Mr. Golyadkin also arrived and like an arrow flew in through the gate. Ignoring the grumbling janitor, breathless, he ran into the courtyard and immediately caught sight of his interesting companion, who had for a moment been lost to view. The stranger became visible for a moment at the entrance to the stairway which led to Mr. Golyadkin's apartment. Mr. Golyadkin rushed after him. The stairway was dark, damp and dirty. On every landing there was heaped an enormous amount of every kind of junk belonging to the tenants, so that a stranger, an inexperienced person, finding himself on this stairway when it was dark, would have been forced to travel it half an hour, at the risk of breaking his legs and cursing the stairway together with his acquaintances who had taken such inconvenient lodgings. But Mr. Golyadkin's companion seemed to know the place, seemed to be at home. He ran lightly up the stairs, without any problem and with a perfect knowledge of the surroundings. Mr. Golyadkin had almost overtaken him; some two or three times the hem of the stranger's overcoat even struck him on the nose. His heart was sinking. The mysterious person stopped right before the door of Mr. Golyadkin's apartment, knocked, and (this, by the way, would have astonished Mr. Golyadkin at any other time) Petrushka, as if he had been sitting up waiting, immediately opened the door and followed with a candle in his hands after the person who had entered. Beside himself, the hero of our tale ran into his quarters. Without taking off his overcoat and hat, he went along the brief corridor and, as if thunderstruck, stopped on the threshold of his room. All of Mr. Golyadkin's premonitions had come true, absolutely. Everything that he had feared and foreseen had actually come to pass now. His breathing stopped. His head began to spin. The stranger was sitting before him, on his very bed, also in an overcoat and hat, smiling slightly, squinting a bit, and nodding to him in a friendly manner. Mr. Golyadkin wanted to cry out, but could not; to protest in some way, but did not have the strength to. His hair stood on end and he sat down on the spot, insensible with horror. And, indeed, he had good reason. Mr. Golyadkin had [*Add: at last*] fully recognized his nocturnal friend. His nocturnal friend was none other than he himself, Mr. Golyadkin himself, another Mr. Golyadkin, but exactly like him, in a word, what is called his double in every respect. . . . .

VI

[*Add*: *Of how Mr. Golyadkin attempts to explain the inexplicable occurrence and how at last to some extent explains it. Mr. Golyadkin's decision. Something about Siamese twins. Of how Mr. Golyadkin almost becomes reconciled with Siamese twins and agrees, by the way, that Krylov is a great fable writer. The encounter and the embarrassing situation of Mr. Golyadkin.*]

The next day, at exactly eight o'clock, Mr. Golyadkin awoke on his bed. At once all the unusual things of the previous day and the entire incredible, wild night, with its almost impossible adventures, presented themselves simultaneously to his imagination and memory, down to the last terrifying detail. Such fierce, fiendish malice on the part of his enemies and especially the most recent proof of this malice turned Mr. Golyadkin's heart to ice. But at the same time it was all so strange, incomprehensible, wild, seemed so impossible, that it was really difficult to give credence to this whole affair. Mr. Golyadkin would even have been ready himself to acknowledge it all a vain delusion, a momentary disorder of the imagination, an obscuring of the mind, had he not fortunately known through bitter experience to what lengths malice can sometimes drive a person, to what lengths the ferocity of an enemy, seeking to avenge his honor and self-esteem, can sometimes go. Moreover, Mr. Golyadkin's heavy limbs, his dazed head, his aching back and vicious cold bore powerful witness to and upheld the total likelihood of yesterday's nocturnal walk and, to some extent, of everything else that had occurred during that walk. And what is more, finally, Mr. Golyadkin had known for a very long time now that something was being concocted by those people there, [*Add: that something evil was being concocted,*] that those people there had someone else in with them. [*Add: It was clear and certain that all this was not a dream and not a state of delirium.*] But [*Add: , still,*] what of it? After pondering it well, Mr. Golyadkin decided to hold his tongue, to resign himself and not to protest about this matter for the time being. [*Add: For his part he was firmly convinced of the utter certitude of the matter; what he did not know was from just whose direction the blow was coming. "And God only knows," he thought, "why, if one looks at it this way, then who knows? Perhaps it's really nothing.*] "[*Delete: "*] For maybe what they had in mind was just to frighten me a bit, but when they see that I don't mind, I'm not protesting, but am resigning myself completely and bearing it [*Delete: it Add: both my shame and grief*] with humility, then they will back off, they will back off themselves, and what's more they will back off first." [*Delete: " Add: Perhaps—who knows—perhaps they even wish me well. It will pass! It may be that I am attacking good people!"* Mr. Golyadkin pondered his situation thus and in any case resolved to await the consequences humbly, and in due course, later, when, for example, danger would threaten too much, only then perhaps would he go to His Excellency.*]

These then were the kinds of thoughts that were in Mr. Golyadkin's mind when, stretching himself in his bed and slowly and carefully straightening out his tired limbs, he waited for Petrushka to make his customary appearance in the room. He had already been waiting fifteen minutes. He could hear that sluggard Petrushka pottering about with the samovar behind the partition, but still he could not bring himself to call him. We shall go further and say: Mr. Golyadkin was even somewhat afraid now of a confrontation with Petrushka. "Why, God knows," he thought, "why, God knows how that rogue looks at this entire matter now. He says absolutely nothing but he's a crafty one." [*Add: Mr. Golyadkin even had a secret, remote suspicion that right here was where he must seek the key and the solution to the riddle.*] At last the door creaked and Petrushka appeared with a tray in his hands. Mr. Golyadkin gave a timid sidelong glance, waiting impatiently to see what would happen, waiting [*Delete: to see what would happen, waiting*] to see whether he would finally say something about a certain occurrence. But

Petrushka said nothing; on the contrary, he was somehow more uncommunicative, sterner and angrier than usual. He was looking at everything sullenly, without raising his eyes. In general it was obvious that he was extremely displeased about something. He did not so much as glance at his master, which, let it be said in passing, somewhat wounded Mr. Golyadkin. He placed everything he had brought on the table, turned and without a word went off behind his partition. "He knows, he knows, he knows all about everything, that good-for-nothing!" grumbled Mr. Golyadkin, as he set about having his tea. [*Add:* *"I ought to interrogate him thoroughly and worm a thing or two out of him. I should begin with something remote from the subject, in a subtle way, and make him blurt it out. He's stubborn, the scoundrel . . . but what if I do it in a nice way? Just flatter him a bit first—that's the way—and only then go on to interrogate him."*] But still our hero did not interrogate his servant about anything whatsoever, although Petrushka came into the room several times after that for various reasons. Mr. Golyadkin was in a most anxious frame of mind. [*Add:* *"If only all of this would be resolved quickly," he thought; "no matter how it goes, just let all this mess be resolved as quickly as possible."*] He was also terrified to go to the office. He had a strong premonition that it was precisely there that something was wrong. "So you'll go," he thought, "but suppose you encounter some problem? Wouldn't it be better to be patient now? Wouldn't it be better to wait now? As for them, let them do as they wish. But today I ought to wait here, gather my strength, put myself to rights, ponder this whole matter well, and then I could seize the moment and surprise them all like a bolt from the blue, while I myself would act as if there was nothing wrong." While pondering thus, Mr. Golyadkin smoked pipe after pipe. Time was flying; it was already almost half past nine. "Why, it's half past nine already," thought Mr. Golyadkin, "and too late to make an appearance. Besides, I'm sick; of course, I'm sick; I'm really sick. Who is to say I'm not? What do I care! And if they [*Delete:* *And if they* *Add:* *So let them*] send somebody to check up; so let the inspector come. What do I care, really? Why, my back aches; I have a cough and a cold. And lastly I just can't go, not at all, because of this weather. I could become sick and then I'd

probably die. Nowadays the death-rate is particularly high..."
It was with such arguments that Mr. Golyadkin finally assuaged
his conscience completely and found self-justification beforehand for the dressing down which he expected from Andrei
Filippovich for being remiss in his work. In general, in all such
circumstances our hero very much liked to justify himself in his
own eyes by means of his various irrefutable arguments and
thus to assuage his conscience completely. And so, having now
assuaged his conscience completely, he took up his pipe, filled
it and had no sooner begun to really puff on it than he quickly
leapt up from the ottoman, threw the pipe aside, washed
himself vigorously, shaved, smoothed his hair, pulled on his
uniform jacket and everything else, seized some papers and
flew off to the office.

Mr. Golyadkin entered his division timidly, in trembling
anticipation of something extremely bad, an anticipation
which, though unconscious and vague, was at the same time
[*Add: highly*] unpleasant. He sat down timidly at his customary
place next to the head of section, Anton Antonovich Setochkin.
Without looking at anything, without letting himself be distracted
by anything, he buried himself in the contents of the papers
lying before him. He had resolved and promised himself that he
would avoid all he could everything provocative, everything
capable of strongly compromising him, such as: indiscreet
questions, anyone's jokes and unsuitable references to all the
circumstances of the previous evening. He had even resolved
that he would avoid all the usual amenities with his colleagues,
that is, inquiries about their health and so forth. [*Add: Nevertheless, Mr. Golyadkin knew and clearly understood that his affairs
were going badly and that his case had been lost. This was why a deep
inner anxiety would not leave him for even a moment, but sent its poisonous
roots more and more deeply into his soul and grew greater and greater,
so that no matter how much he struggled to do so, he could not at all
get down to his usual manner of working, that is, to put aside his concern
about everything extraneous and bend over, in the manner required,
without raising his head from his desk, and tranquilly, for five hours or
more, move his pen along the paper.*] But it was evident also [*Delete:
But it was evident also Add: It was evident*] that he could not go on in

this way, that it was impossible to. His anxiety and ignorance of something that intimately affected him always tormented him more than the thing that was actually affecting him. And this is why, despite the fact that he had promised himself not to become involved in anything, no matter what was going on, and to avoid everything, no matter what it was, Mr. Golyadkin would from time to time raise his head very slightly in a stealthy manner and furtively glance to each side, to the right and to the left; he would peep at the countenances of his colleagues and try to deduce from them whether there was something new and special relating to him and being concealed from him with some bad motives in mind. He supposed that there was a necessary connection between all that had happened to him the day before and everything that now surrounded him. [*Delete:* . *Add: ; he tried to disentangle mentally all the knots of his doubts, to puzzle out and fathom the whole intrigue and all the various stratagems surrounding him.*] Finally, in his anguish, he began to wish that everything would just be resolved as quickly as possible—somehow—even if it should end in misfortune. No matter! [*Add: If it would just happen as quickly as possible.*] Then and there fate took hold of Mr. Golyadkin. No sooner had he wished than his doubts were suddenly dispelled, but in the strangest and most unexpected manner.

The door of the other room suddenly creaked faintly and timidly as if to say that the person entering was extremely unimportant, and someone's figure, extremely familiar indeed to Mr. Golyadkin, came and stood shyly before the very same desk at which our hero was occupying a place. Our hero did not raise his head. No, he had descried this figure only casually, with the slightest glance, but he already knew everything, understood everything down to the slightest detail. He burned with shame and buried his wretched head in a paper for exactly the same purpose as an ostrich, pursued by a hunter, hides its head in the burning sand. The new arrival bowed to Andrei Filippovich and then an officially kind voice was heard, the sort that superiors in places of work everywhere use in speaking to new subordinates. "Sit down right here," said Andrei Filippovich, pointing out Anton Antonovich's desk to the new man; "right here opposite Mr. Golyadkin, and we'll get some work for you to do right away." Andrei Filippovich ended by making a rapid and decorously authoritative gesture to the new arrival, and then immediately delved into the contents of various papers from a pile which lay before him.

Mr. Golyadkin finally raised his eyes, and if he did not faint it was only because from the first he had had a premonition of the whole business, because from the first he had been forewarned about everything, having guessed in his heart who the newcomer was. Mr. Golyadkin's first move was to look quickly about—to see whether there was any sound of whispering, whether there was any sort of office joke being made about this, whether someone's face had twisted in amazement, whether, finally, someone had fallen under a desk in fright. But to Mr. Golyadkin's great astonishment nothing of the sort could be detected in anyone. The conduct of his companions and colleagues struck Mr. Golyadkin. It seemed beyond the bounds of common sense. Mr. Golyadkin even became frightened at such an unusual silence. The fact of its existence spoke for itself; it was a strange, shocking, wild business. There *was* reason to react. All this, of course, only flashed through Mr. Golyadkin's mind. He himself felt as though he were roasting over a slow fire. And there was indeed reason to feel so. [*Add: The truth of everything that Mr. Golyadkin was feeling was being completely upheld by the circumstances of the present moment.*] The one who was now sitting opposite Mr. Golyadkin was Mr. Golyadkin's terror, was Mr. Golyadkin's shame, was Mr. Golyadkin's nightmare of the day before, in a word, was Mr. Golyadkin himself, not the Mr. Golyadkin who was now sitting on his chair with his mouth wide open and his pen frozen in his hand; not the one who served as assistant to his head of section; not the one who liked to efface himself and fade into the crowd; not the one, finally, whose gait clearly said: "Don't touch me, and I won't touch you" or "Don't touch me, for I'm not hurting you"; no, this was a different Mr. Golyadkin, completely different but at the same time absolutely identical to the first one, of the same height, the same build, dressed the same, with the same bald spot, in a word, nothing, absolutely nothing had been overlooked to make an absolute likeness, so that if one were to take them and place them side by side, no one, absolutely no one, would have taken it upon himself to determine just who was the real Golyadkin and who the counterfeit, who the old and who the new, who the original and who the copy.

Our hero, if a comparison is possible, was now in the position of a person at whose expense some prankster was amusing himself, furtively focussing a burning glass on him as a joke. "Whatever is this? Is it a dream, or not?" he [*Delete: he*] thought [*Add: Mr. Golyadkin*]. "Is it real, or a continuation of yesterday's business? But how can it be? By what right is all this taking place? Who has permitted such a clerk? Who gave the directive for it? Am I sleeping? Am I daydreaming?" Mr. Golyadkin tried to pinch himself, and even tried to take a decision to pinch someone else... No, it was not a dream, and that was that. [*Add: He and he himself was sitting before himself, as though a mirror had been placed before him.*] Mr. Golyadkin felt the sweat pouring from him. He felt that something unprecedented and hitherto unheard of and therefore, to crown his misfortune, indecent, was happening to him, for Mr. Golyadkin understood and sensed all the disadvantage of being the first example of this kind of lampoon. He even began, finally, to doubt his own existence, and although he had been prepared for everything in advance and had himself wished that his doubts would somehow be dispelled, still the very nature of the circumstances did indeed warrant surprise. Anguish oppressed and tormented him. At times he would become totally deprived of both his reason and memory. Coming to his senses after such a moment, he would notice that he was moving the pen over the paper mechanically and unconsciously. Having no confidence in himself, he was starting to check over everything he had written—and understanding nothing. At last the other Mr. Golyadkin, who had until now been sitting there sedately and quietly, rose and disappeared through the door into another division on some matter. Mr. Golyadkin looked around—there was nothing; all was quiet. Only the scratching of pens, the rustle of turning sheets of paper and the talking in the corners somewhat further removed from Andrei Filippovich's seat was audible. Mr. Golyadkin glanced at Anton Antonovich, and since, in all probability, our hero's countenance reflected utterly his present situation and was in harmony with the entire purport of the matter, and consequently was, in a certain respect, very remarkable, the good Anton Antonovich, laying his pen aside, inquired with unusual sympathy after Mr. Golyadkin's health.

"I'm all right, thank God, Anton Antonovich," uttered Mr. Golyadkin, stuttering; "I'm perfectly well, Anton Antonovich; I'm fine now, Anton Antonovich," he added uncertainly, not yet completely trusting Anton Antonovich, whose name he was mentioning so frequently.

"Ah! And I thought you were not well. No wonder, though. It could be! Right now, in particular, there are constantly all sorts of infections about. You know . . ."

"Yes, Anton Antonovich, I know that all sorts of infections are about . . . But, Anton Antonovich, that's not why I . . ." continued Mr. Golyadkin, staring at Anton Antonovich. "You see, Anton Antonovich, I don't even know how to tell you, that is, I mean, from what angle to approach this matter, Anton Antonovich . . ."

"What's that, sir? I . . . you know . . . I must confess to you, I don't follow you very well. You . . . know, explain yourself in greater detail, in what respect you feel ill at ease here," said Anton Antonovich, himself feeling somewhat ill at ease, on seeing that tears had actually come into Mr. Golyadkin's eyes.

"I really . . . here, Anton Antonovich . . . there's a clerk here, Anton Antonovich . . ."

"Well, sir! I still don't understand."

"I mean, Anton Antonovich, that there's a new clerk here."

"Yes, sir; there is, sir. With the same surname as you."

"What?" cried Mr. Golyadkin.

"I said he has the same surname as you. He's also Golyadkin. Can he be your brother?"

"No, sir, Anton Antonovich. I . . ."

"Hm! Do tell. And I thought he must be a close relative of yours. You know, there's a certain family resemblance."

Mr. Golyadkin was struck with amazement and for a while left speechless. To treat so lightly such a shocking, unprecedented thing, a thing really rare of its kind, a thing which would have amazed even the most uninterested observer, to [*Delete:*, *to Add:* . *To*] speak of a family resemblance when it was like looking into a mirror!

"You know what I advise you, Yakov Petrovich," continued Anton Antonovich. "You go see a doctor and get his advice. You know, you somehow *look* quite unwell. Your eyes particularly . . . you know, they have a sort of peculiar expression."

"No, sir, Anton Antonovich. I, of course, feel . . . I keep wanting to ask—who is this clerk?"

"Well, sir?"

"That is, haven't you noticed something peculiar about him, Anton Antonovich . . . something markedly significant?"

"Which is?"

"That is, I mean, Anton Antonovich, such a striking resemblance to someone, for example, that is, to me, for example. You spoke just now of a family resemblance, Anton Antonovich. [*Add:* *You just mentioned it.*] You made the remark casually . . . Do you know, sometimes such twins do occur, that is, exactly alike, like two peas in a pod, so that you can't distinguish them? Well, that's what I'm talking about, sir."

"Yes, sir," said Anton Antonovich, thinking it over a bit and seeming to be struck for the first time by the thought of such an occurrence. "Yes, sir! Absolutely, sir. The resemblance is indeed striking and you're perfectly right in saying it—one really could take you for one another," he continued, his eyes getting bigger and bigger. "And you know, Yakov Petrovich, it's even a wondrous resemblance, a fantastic one, as they sometimes say, that is, it's absolutely the way you . . . Did you notice, Yakov Petrovich? I even wanted to ask you for an explanation myself. Yes, I must confess I didn't pay proper attention at first. It's a wonder, really a wonder! And do you know, Yakov Petrovich, you probably weren't born here, were you, I'd venture to say?"

"No, sir."

"He's also not from these parts. Perhaps he's from the same parts as you. May I make so bold as to inquire where your mother lived for the greater part of her life?"

"You said . . . you said, Anton Antonovich, that he's not from these parts?"

"No, sir, not from these parts. Yes, indeed, how odd it is," continued the talkative Anton Antonovich, for whom the opportunity to chatter a bit about something was a real treat. "It really does stir your curiosity; for how often you could go by him, brush against him, bump into him, and not notice. [*Add: It could be an elephant, as they say, and you wouldn't notice it, Yakov Petrovich.*] However, don't you be embarrassed. [*Add: Don't you be embarrassed by these particular circumstances.*] These things happen. It's . . . do you know . . . let me tell you something; the very same thing happened to my aunt on my mother's side. Before she died she also saw her double . . ."

"No, sir, I—excuse me for interrupting you, Anton Antonovich—I would like to find out, Anton Antonovich . . . what about this clerk? That is, how does he come to be here?"

"Why, in place of Semyon Ivanovich, who died. To fill the vacancy. A vacancy occurred and so they gave it to him [*Add: now*]. Yes, indeed, that goodhearted, poor soul, Semyon Ivanovich, left three children, they say, each younger than the next. His widow threw herself at the feet of His Excellency. They say, however, that she's concealing something. She has money, but she's concealing it . . ."

"No, sir, I . . . I'm still asking [*Add: you*] about that other matter, Anton Antonovich."

"Which is? Why, yes! But why are you so interested in it? I'm telling you: don't you be embarrassed. This is all to some extent just a passing thing. What of it? After all, you're not involved. The Lord God Himself has arranged it this way. This is His will and it's a sin to murmur against it. His profound wisdom is evident in it. And you, Yakov Petrovich, as far as I can see, are not in the least to blame. There are so many wonders in the world! Mother Nature is bountiful. But you won't be asked to answer for this. You won't have to answer for it. Why, as an apropos example, you have heard, I expect, of, what do they . . .

what do they call them? Oh, yes, Siamese twins. Their backs are attached to one another and they live like that, and eat and sleep together. People say they get big money."

"Excuse me, Anton Antonovich . . ."

"I get your drift; I do! Yes! But what of it? It's nothing! I'm telling you, as far as I can see, there is nothing to be embarrassed about. What of it? He's a clerk just like any other. He seems to be a capable person. He says his name is Golyadkin. Not from these parts, he says. A Titular Councilor. He spoke with His Excellency personally."

"Oh, and how did it go, sir?"

"It was all right, sir. They say he stated his case adequately, presented his arguments. 'It's this way, Your Excellency; I don't have a fortune and I wish to serve, and I'd be especially flattered to serve under your direction . . .' Well, and all that one should say, you know; he expressed it all very cleverly. Must be a smart person. But, of course, he did come with a recommendation. After all, you can't get anywhere without one . . ."

"Well, sir, from whom was it, sir? . . . That is, I mean, just who has stuck his finger into this shameless business?"

"Yes, sir. They say it's a good recommendation. His Excellency, they say, had a laugh over it with Andrei Filippovich."

"Had a laugh over it with Andrei Filippovich?"

"Yes, sir. He just smiled and said all right, and probably, and that for his part he had nothing against it, as long as he performed his job faithfully . . ."

"Well, sir. Do go on, sir. You're cheering me up somewhat, Anton Antonovich. I beg you, do go on, sir."

"Excuse me, once again I don't quite . . . Well, sir. Yes, sir. Well, now, it's nothing, sir. A simple matter. I'm telling you, don't you be embarrassed. And there's nothing shady about it . . ."

"No, sir. I, that is, I want to ask you, Anton Antonovich, did His Excellency not add anything further . . . about me, for example?"

"But, of course! Yes, sir! Well, no, nothing. You can feel perfectly at ease. You know, it's . . . of course, it goes without

69

saying, it's a rather striking occurrence and at first . . . why, take me, for example; at first I almost didn't notice it. I really don't know why I didn't notice it until you pointed it out to me. But nevertheless you can feel perfectly at ease. He didn't say anything in particular, anything at all," added the kind Anton Antonovich, getting up from his chair.

"And so, Anton Antonovich, I . . ."

"Ah, do excuse me, sir. As it is I've been chattering away about nothing, when here's a piece of important and urgent business. I must take care of it."

"Anton Antonovich!" Andrei Filippovich's politely summoning voice rang out. "His Excellency has been asking for you." [*Delete: ." Add: . . ."*]

"At once, at once, Andrei Filippovich. I'm coming at once, sir." And taking up a small pile of papers, Anton Antonovich flew first to Andrei Filippovich and then to His Excellency's office.

"So that's the way it is," thought Mr. Golyadkin to himself. "So that's the kind of game that's being played here! So that's the way the wind is blowing here now . . . Not bad. So things have taken a most pleasant turn," [*Delete: ," Add: . Marvelous, and that's that!*"] said our hero to himself, rubbing his hands together and in his joy oblivious to the feel of the chair beneath him. "[*Add: So that's how it is!*] So our situation is quite an ordinary one. So it turns out to be just a trifle; it all comes to nothing. Indeed, no one knows anything and not a peep out of them, the blackguards, sitting and doing their work. Marvelous, marvelous! I like a good person, always have, and am always ready to respect him . . . Still, after all, it may be risky, when you think of it; that Anton Antonovich . . . one is afraid to trust him: his hair is too grey and he's rather shaky on his legs—he's so old. However, the most wonderful and most important thing is that His Excellency didn't say anything and let it go. That's good! I approve! Only what's Andrei Filippovich butting in for with his laughs? What business is it of his? Slippery old customer! Always in my way, always trying to run across a person's path like a black cat, always working at cross purposes and trying to spite you, trying to spite you and working at cross purposes . . ."

Mr. Golyadkin looked around again and his hopes were again renewed. Nevertheless, he felt that a distant thought, some bad thought, was still troubling him. It even crossed his mind to get into the good graces of the clerks somehow, to take the initiative and even (for example, on leaving work or by approaching them as if on an office matter) hint in the midst of the conversation that, 'Well, gentlemen, this is the way it is, such a striking resemblance, a strange occurrence, a lampoon'— that is, to banter about himself and thus test the extent of the danger. "For, after all, still waters run dark and deep," our hero concluded mentally. However, Mr. Golyadkin only considered this. He thought better of it and caught himself in time. He understood that it would mean going too far. "That's you all over!" he said, to himself, tapping himself lightly on the forehead. "Now you'll be scintillating because you're overjoyed! What a righteous soul you are! No, you and I had better have patience, Yakov Petrovich; we'll wait and have patience!" Nevertheless, and as we have already pointed out, Mr. Golyadkin was renewed in perfect hope, as if he had risen from the dead. "It's nothing," he thought. "It's as if an enormous weight had been removed from my chest. Now that's something! 'And the little coffer opened simply by raising the lid.'[8] That Krylov was right; that Krylov was right . . . he knew his stuff; that Krylov was a slippery customer and a great fable writer! And as far as *this* one is concerned, let him have a post, let him work and prosper, as long as he doesn't bother anyone or meddle with them. Let him have a post—I consent and approve!"

But meanwhile the hours had been passing, they had flown and before anyone noticed it struck four. The office closed for the day. Andrei Filippovich reached for his hat and, as usual, everyone followed suit. Mr. Golyadkin lagged behind a bit, as long as he needed to, and deliberately left last—when all the others had already gone their separate ways. Out on the street he felt as if he were in paradise, so much so that he even felt the desire to go out of his way and take a stroll along Nevsky Prospect. "Now that's fate!" said our hero; "an unexpected turn in this whole affair. And the weather has cleared, and there's a fine frost and there are sleighs out. Now frost really suits a Russian. A Russian really gets on well with frost! I do like the Russian. There's both a light snow and new-fallen snow, as a hunter would say. Oh, to catch a rabbit when the first snow has fallen! Ho-ho! Ah, well, it doesn't matter!"

This is how Mr. Golyadkin's rapture gave expression to itself, but nevertheless something kept troubling his mind. It was not exactly anguish, but at moments something so gnawed at his heart that Mr. Golyadkin did not know where to find relief. "However, let's wait a day and see and then we'll go ahead and rejoice. But what ever is the matter? Well, we'll think it through and see. Well, let's think it through, my young friend; well, let's think it through. Well, a person just like you, in the first place, absolutely like you. Well, and so what of it? If he's the same kind of person, should I cry? What is it to me? I'm not a party to it. I don't care, and that's that! He's made up his mind to do it and that's that! Let him have a post! Well, what a marvel and what a strange thing; they say that Siamese twins... Well, but why bring them in, the Siamese ones? So they are twins, but after all even great people have sometimes looked like eccentrics. We even know from history that the great Suvorov crowed like a cock... Well, but he did all that because of politics. And great generals... but, indeed, what of generals? I go my own way, and that's that, and I don't care about anybody else, and in my innocence I scorn my enemy; I'm not an intriguer and I'm proud of that. I'm irreproachable, straightforward, neat, pleasant and without malice..."

Suddenly Mr. Golyadkin fell silent, stopped short, and began shaking like a leaf; he even closed his eyes for an instant. Hoping, however, that the object causing his fright was merely an illusion, he opened his eyes at last and timidly glanced out of the corner of his eye to the right. No, it was not an illusion!... Alongside him minced his matinal acquaintance, smiling, peering into his face, and, it seemed, waiting for a chance to begin a conversation. The conversation, however, did not commence. They both walked along thus some fifty paces. Mr. Golyadkin sought to bundle himself up as much as possible, to bury himself in his overcoat, and to pull his hat down over his eyes as far as it would go. To crown the insult, even his friend's overcoat and hat were just like his, as if they had that moment been taken off Mr. Golyadkin's back.

"Sir," uttered our hero at last, attempting to speak almost in a whisper and not looking at his friend, "we are, I think, going separate ways... I am even certain of it," he said, after a brief silence. "I am certain at last that you have understood my meaning completely," he added rather sternly in conclusion.

"I would like," said Mr. Golyadkin's friend at last, "I would like... You will, I trust, be so magnanimous as to forgive me . . . I do not know to whom to turn here . . . My circumstances—I hope that you will forgive my boldness; it even seemed to me that you were motivated by compassion to take an interest in me this morning. For my part, from the first glance I felt drawn to you; I . . ." At this point Mr. Golyadkin mentally wished that his new colleague would be swallowed up by the earth. "If I could dare to hope, Yakov Petrovich, that you would be so indulgent as to hear me out . . ."

"We . . . Here we . . . we . . . we'd better go to my place," answered Mr. Golyadkin. "We'll cross over now to the other side of Nevsky Prospect. It will be more convenient for us there, and then we'll go by way of a little sidestreet... It would be better if we took a little sidestreet. [*Add: It's closer if we take a little sidestreet . . .*]"

"Yes, sir. If you wish, let's take a little sidestreet, sir," Mr. Golyadkin's meek companion said timidly, as if hinting by the tone of his answer that who was he to question it and that in his situation he was ready to be satisfied even with going by way of a little sidestreet. As for Mr. Golyadkin, he had absolutely no idea what was happening to him. He did not trust himself. He had not yet recovered from his amazement.

VII

[*Add: The two Mister Golyadkins. Of how they discussed various matters. Of how one Mr. Golyadkin wept, while the other composed verses. Mr. Golyadkin finds that he is utterly happy and promises himself to conduct himself well in future. Mr. Golyadkin Junior's opinion about a friendly roof over one's head. Mr. Golyadkin Senior protests and restores the somewhat sullied reputation of the Prophet Mohammed. Petrushka's unseemly conduct. Of how Mr. Golyadkin Senior finally goes off to sleep.*]

He recovered somewhat on the stairway and at the entrance to his apartment. "Oh, I'm a regular fool!" he upbraided himself mentally. "And where am I taking him? [*Add: And what will he say to me?*] I'm putting a noose around my own neck. And what will Petrushka think, when he sees us together? What will that scoundrel dare to think now? He *is* suspicious..." But it was too late to regret it now. Mr. Golyadkin knocked, the door opened, and Petrushka began to help the guest and the master off with their overcoats. Mr. Golyadkin looked casually at Petrushka, just cast a cursory glance at him, trying to penetrate his countenance and guess his thoughts. But to his very great astonishment he saw that his servant was not at all surprised but, on the contrary, even seemed to be expecting something of the sort. Of course, he was scowling and looking away and seemed to be getting ready to devour someone. [*Add: "A joke is a joke," thought our hero.*] "Can someone have cast a spell over them all today?" thought our hero. [*Delete: " thought our hero.*] "[*Delete: "*] Some fiend has visited them! There certainly has to be something peculiar in everyone [*Delete: everyone Add: all these people*] today. [*Add: Why, the rogue is only pretending; he's simply pretending. He knows; he knows everything!*] Damn it, what torture!" Continuing to think and ponder thus, Mr. Golyadkin conducted the [*Delete: the Add: his*] guest into his room and humbly invited him to sit down. The guest was, to all appearances, extremely embarrassed. He felt very timid, meekly watched his host's every move, caught his glances and from them seemed to be trying to guess his thoughts. Something humiliated, beaten down and intimidated expressed itself in all his gestures, so that he, if you will permit the comparison, rather resembled at that moment a person who, for want of clothing of his own, has donned another's: the sleeves ride up, the waist is almost up around his neck, and he constantly either straightens the too short vest on himself or sidles away and avoids you, or strives to hide himself somewhere, or peers into everyone's eyes and listens intently to determine whether people are not perhaps talking about his circumstances, laughing at him, feeling ashamed of him; and the person blushes, and the person loses his presence of mind, and his self-esteem suffers . . . Mr. Golyadkin had placed his hat on the window sill; as a result of a careless movement the hat fell on the floor. The guest immediately rushed to pick it up, dusted it all off, carefully placed it back in the spot where it had been and put his own on the floor, next to a chair on the very edge of which he meekly placed himself. This trivial occurrence opened Mr. Golyadkin's eyes somewhat. He understood that his guest was in very straitened circumstances and therefore ceased to trouble himself further about how to begin, leaving it all, as was right and proper, to the guest himself. The guest, for his part, also did not begin; whether he felt timid, whether he was a bit ashamed, whether out of courtesy he was waiting for his host to begin was not clear and was difficult to fathom. At that moment Petrushka entered. He stopped in the doorway and fixed his eyes in the direction completely opposite to where both the guest and his master were sitting.

"Do you wish me to order two dinners?" he uttered carelessly, in a husky voice.

"I, I don't know . . . You, yes, my good fellow, order two dinners."

Petrushka left. Mr. Golyadkin glanced at his guest. The guest blushed to his ears. Mr. Golyadkin was a kind-hearted person and, therefore, out of the kindness of his heart he immediately formulated a theory: "A poor man," he thought, "and besides he's held his post for only one day; probably has suffered in his time. Perhaps the only thing he has to his name is his decent clothing, but nothing to buy dinner with. Ah, poor soul, how beaten down he is! Well, it doesn't matter. To some extent it's even better . . ."

"Excuse me that I . . ." began Mr. Golyadkin, "by the way, permit to know whom I am addressing?"

"I . . . I'm . . . Yakov Petrovich," his guest almost whispered, as if ashamed and shy, as if begging pardon that he too was called Yakov Petrovich.

"Yakov Petrovich!" repeated our hero, unable to conceal his confusion.

"Yes, sir, just so, sir . . . I'm your namesake, sir," answered Mr. Golyadkin's meek guest, making so bold as to smile and say something a bit humorous. But he immediately shrank back, assuming a most serious and, indeed, embarrassed air, upon noticing that his host was in no laughing mood.

"You . . . do permit me to ask you what the occasion of this honor is . . ."

"Knowing of your magnanimity and your virtues," his guest interrupted quickly but in a timid voice, rising slightly from his chair, "[*Add: knowing of your virtues,*] I have made so bold as to turn to you and beseech your . . . acquaintance and patronage . . .," concluded his guest, obviously having difficulty in finding his expressions and choosing words which were not too flattering and degrading so that he would not compromise his own self-esteem, but which were also not too bold or smacking of an unseemly attempt to imply that they were equals. In general it can be said that Mr. Golyadkin's guest conducted himself like a noble beggar in a mended coat with a passport in his pocket attesting to his noble birth who has not yet had enough practice in holding out his hand properly.

"You embarrass me," answered Mr. Golyadkin, looking over himself, his walls and his guest, "in just what way could I be

77

... that is, I mean, in exactly what respect can I be of service to you?"

"I felt drawn to you at first sight, Yakov Petrovich, and, be so magnanimous as to forgive me, I placed my hopes in you—I made so bold as to place my hopes, Yakov Petrovich. I... I'm utterly lost here, Yakov Petrovich; I'm poor. I've suffered terribly, Yakov Petrovich, and I'm still new here. On learning that you, with the usual, innate qualities of your splendid heart, had the same surname as I..."

Mr. Golyadkin frowned.

"The same surname as I do and are from the same region as me, I resolved to turn to you and give you an account of my straitened situation."

"Very well, sir; very well. I really don't know what to say to you," answered Mr. Golyadkin in an embarrassed voice; "after dinner we'll have a little talk..."

The guest bowed. Dinner arrived. Petrushka laid the table—and guest and host set about surfeiting themselves. Dinner did not last long. They both hurried—the host because he was not in his usual element and felt ashamed besides that the dinner was a poor one; he was ashamed partly because he wished [*Delete: wished Add: wanted*] to give the guest a good meal and partly because he wished to show that he did not live like a beggar. For his part the guest was in a state of very great confusion and extremely embarrassed. After having once taken a piece of bread and eaten it, he was afraid to stretch his hand out for another piece; he was ashamed to take the best tidbits and made assurances constantly that he was not at all hungry, that the dinner was excellent, and that he, for his part, was completely satisfied with it and would remember it till his dying day. When the meal was over, Mr. Golyadkin lit up his pipe and proferred the guest another, which was kept for friends. They both sat down opposite one another and the guest began to relate his adventures.

Mr. Golyadkin Junior's tale lasted some three or four hours. The story of his adventures was, however, comprised of the most trivial and the most paltry, if one may say so, incidents. It was a story of service somewhere in a lawcourt in

the provinces, of procurators and presidents, of certain chancery
intrigues, of the corruption of soul of one of the chief clerks, of
an inspector, of a sudden change of superior, of how Mr.
Golyadkin the Second had suffered though completely innocent;
of his aged aunt, Pelageya Semyonovna; of how, through the
various intrigues of his enemies, he had lost his post and had
come to Petersburg on foot; of how he had languished and led a
wretched life here in Petersburg; of how for a long time he had
fruitlessly sought a post, gone through all his money, spent his
last cent on food, practically lived in the street, had eaten stale
bread and drunk it down with his tears, slept on the bare floor
and, finally, of how some kindhearted person had undertaken
to intercede for him, had given him a recommendation and had
magnanimously obtained a new post for him. Mr. Golyadkin's
guest wept while recounting this and wiped his tears with a dark
blue checkered handkerchief greatly resembling a piece of
oilcloth. He concluded by opening his heart completely to Mr.
Golyadkin and confessed that for the time being he not only
had nothing to live on or to set himself up with decently, but
also had nothing with which to buy proper clothing; he
concluded by saying that he could not even scrape together
enough for some used boots and that he had borrowed his
uniform from someone for a short time.

Mr. Golyadkin was moved, was truly touched. Moreover,
even though his guest's story was a most trivial one, every word
of this story fell on Mr. Golyadkin's heart like manna from
Heaven. The fact of the matter is that Mr. Golyadkin was
beginning to forget his recent misgivings; he permitted his
heart to feel freedom and joy and, finally, mentally consigned
himself to the category of fool. Everything was so natural! Was
there really any reason to be so distressed and to sound such an
alarm?! Well, there was, there really was one delicate circumstance, but after all it didn't matter. It couldn't sully a person,
put a blot on his self-esteem and ruin his career when the
person was not to blame, when nature herself was involved
here. Moreover, the guest was asking for patronage, the guest
was weeping, the guest was blaming fate, seemed so unpreten-
tious, so without malice and guile, so pitiful and insignificant,

and seemed now himself ashamed, though perhaps for a different reason, of the strange resemblance between his face and that of his host. He was conducting himself in a manner as trustworthy as could be, was trying so hard to please his host and looked the way a person looks when he has pangs of conscience and feels guilty before another person. If, for example, the conversation turned on some dubious point, the guest immediately agreed with Mr. Golyadkin's opinion. And if, accidentally, he somehow ran counter in his opinion to that of Mr. Golyadkin and then noticed his lapse, he would immediately correct his speech, explain himself and quickly make it known that he understood everything in exactly the same manner as his host, thought as he did and looked at everything with exactly the same eyes as he did. In a word, the guest was making every possible effort to make up to Mr. Golyadkin, and Mr. Golyadkin finally decided that his guest must be a most amiable person in every respect. Meanwhile, tea was served; it was after eight. Mr. Golyadkin was in a splendid frame of mind; he brightened up, warmed up, gradually let himself go and finally entered into a very animated and diverting conversation with his guest. Mr. Golyadkin, when in high spirits, liked sometimes to relate interesting bits of information. And so it was now. He related to his guest much about the capital, about its diversions and charms, about the theater, about the clubs, about Bryulov's latest painting; about how two Englishmen came from England to Petersburg expressly to have a look at the iron fencing of the Summer Garden and immediately upon having done this left for home again; about work, about Olsufi Ivanovich and about Andrei Filippovich; about the fact that Russia was hour by hour moving toward perfection and that here Philology flourishes today; about an anecdote which he had recently read in *The Northern Bee,* and how in India there is a boa constrictor of unusual strength; finally, about Baron Brambeus, etc. In a word, Mr. Golyadkin was perfectly content; in the first place, because he felt completely at ease; in the second place, because he not only did not fear his enemies but was even ready now to challenge them all to the most decisive battle; in the third place, because he himself was granting patronage, and, finally, doing a good deed. He was aware, however, in his heart that he was still not altogether happy at that moment, that there was still something worrisome, though only slightly worrisome, lodged there inside him, and that it was gnawing at his heart even now. His recollection of last evening at Olsufi Ivanovich's tormented him sorely. He would have given a great deal now if some of the previous day's events had not occurred. "Still, after all, it doesn't matter!" our hero concluded finally and firmly resolved in his heart henceforth to conduct himself well and not make such blunders again. As Mr. Golyadkin had now let himself go altogether and had suddenly become almost completely happy, he even took it into his head to play the hedonist a bit. Rum was brought in by Petrushka and a punch was made. Guest and host drained a glass each and then a second. The guest turned out to be even more amiable than before, and for his part gave more than one proof of his straightforwardness and happy character, energetically partook of Mr. Golyadkin's pleasure, seemed to take joy only in his joy and looked upon him as his true and only benefactor. Taking up a pen and a small sheet of paper, he asked Mr. Golyadkin not to look at what he was going to write, and then, when he had finished, himself showed his host what he had written. It turned out to be a quatrain, written rather sentimentally, but in a splendid style and hand, and evidently was the composition of the amiable guest himself. The verses were as follows:

> Though thou shouldst forget me quite,
> I shall e'er remember thee;
> We know not what may be in life—
> So, I pray, remember me.

With tears in his eyes Mr. Golyadkin embraced his guest and, deeply and utterly touched at last, made his guest privy to certain of his own secrets and private matters, in speaking of which great emphasis was placed on Andrei Filippovich and on Klara Olsufyevna. "Why, yes, Yakov Petrovich, you and I will get along after all," said our hero to his guest. "You and I,

Yakov Petrovich, are [*Delete: are Add: will get along; we're*] going
to get along like a fish in water, like blood brothers. We're
going to be crafty, old friend; we'll be crafty together. We're
going to carry on our own intrigue to spite them... just to spite
them we'll carry on our own intrigue. As [*Delete: As Add: You and
I are as one now, but as*] for them, don't you trust any of them. For I
know you, Yakov Petrovich, and I understand your character.
Why, you would tell them absolutely everything, you righteous
soul! You keep away from all of them, brother." The guest was
in complete agreement, thanked Mr. Golyadkin and at last also
shed a few tears. "You know, Yasha," continued Mr. Golyadkin
in a trembling and weak voice, "Yasha, you come and move in
with me for a time or move in for good. We'll get along. What
do you think of that, brother, eh? And don't you be embarrassed
and don't complain that such a strange situation exists between
us now. It's a sin to complain, brother; [*Add: resign yourself and be
humble;*] this is nature! But mother nature is generous, so there,
brother Yasha! I love you; I love you like a brother, I say. And
you and I are going to be crafty, Yasha, and for our part we're
going to dig a hole under them and get the better of them." The
consumption of punch finally reached three and four glasses
each, and then Mr. Goldyakin began to experience two sensa-
tions: one—that he was unusually happy, and the other—that
he could no longer stay on his feet [*Add: and was swaying.*]. The
guest was, of course, invited to spend the night. A bed was
somehow put together from two rows of chairs. Mr. Golyadkin
Junior announced that under a friendly roof one can sleep
sweetly even on the bare floor, that for his part he could fall
asleep wherever necessary with humility and gratefulness, that
he was in paradise now and that, finally, he had experienced
many misfortunes and much grief in his time, had seen
everything, endured all things, and—who knows what the
future holds?—perhaps he would have to endure still more. Mr.
Golyadkin Senior protested against this and began to argue
that one had to place one's hope in God. The guest agreed
completely and said that there was, of course, no one like God.
Here Mr. Golyadkin Senior noted that the Turks are in a certain
respect right in invoking the name of God even in their sleep.

Then, while not agreeing with certain scholars in certain aspersions cast by them on the Turkish prophet Mohammed, and acknowledging him to be a great politician of his kind, Mr. Golyadkin changed the subject to a highly interesting description of an Algerian barbershop about which he had read in some issue of a journal in the miscellany section. Guest and host laughed much at the naiveté of the Turks, but could not help expressing due amazement at their fanaticism, aroused by opium . . . The guest began at last to undress, and Mr. Golyadkin went out behind the partition, partly out of the kindness of his heart for, "Perhaps," he thought, "he doesn't have a decent shirt to his name," and he didn't want to embarrass a person who had suffered enough already, and partly to reassure himself as far as possible about Petrushka, to test him, to cheer up, if possible, and to be kind to this person [*Add: , just so,*] so that now everyone would be happy and no bad feelings would remain. It must be noted that Petrushka continued to make Mr. Golyadkin feel a bit embarrassed.

"You go to bed now, Pyotr," said Mr. Golyadkin meekly, entering his servant's quarters. "You go to bed now and tomorrow at eight o'clock wake me up. Do you understand, Petrushka?"

Mr. Golyadkin spoke unusually softly and kindly. But Petrushka said nothing. At that point he was fussing about by his bed and did not even turn around to his master, which he should have done, however, out of simple respect for him.

"Did you hear me, Pyotr?" Mr. Golyadkin continued. "You go to bed now, and tomorrow, Petrusha, you wake me up at eight o'clock. Understand?"

"All right, I know already. What is this?" Petrushka muttered to himself.

"Well, that's fine, Petrusha. I'm just saying this so that you will feel at ease and happy. Here we all are now happy—and you should also feel at ease and happy. And now I wish you good night. Go to sleep, Petrusha, go to sleep. We all have to labor . . . You know, brother, don't go thinking anything . . ."

Mr. Golyadkin began but stopped. "Won't it be too much?" he thought. "Have I gone too far? It's always that way. I always go too far." Our hero left Petrushka's quarters greatly annoyed with himself. Moreover, he was somewhat offended by Petrushka's rudeness and stubbornness. "Try being nice to a rascal; the master is doing the rascal an honor and he doesn't sense it," thought Mr. Golyadkin. "However, such is the base tendency of all that ilk!" Staggering somewhat, he returned to his room and, seeing that his [*Delete: his Add: the*] guest had [*Add: now*] quite settled down, he sat down for a moment on the guest's bed. "Come now, Yasha, confess," he began in a whisper, bobbing his head; "why, you rascal, you've wronged me, haven't you? After all, my namesake, you know, um..." he continued, twitting his guest in a rather familiar way. Finally, after taking leave of him in a friendly manner, Mr. Golyadkin headed for bed. The guest meanwhile began to snore. Mr. Golyadkin in turn began to get into his bed; in the meantime, laughing now and then, he whispered to himself: "Why, you are drunk today, my dear Yakov Petrovich; what a rascal you are, what a poor beggar you are, what a Poor Beggar name you have!! Well, why are you overcome with joy? After all, tomorrow you'll pay for it, you sniveling thing, you. What am I going to do with you?" Here a rather strange sensation echoed through all of Mr. Golyadkin's being, something resembling doubt or contrition. "I really let myself go," he thought, "for now there's a noise in my head and I'm drunk. Couldn't resist, simpleton that you are! Babbled absolute nonsense when you were going to be crafty, you rascal. Of course, forgiving and forgetting is the prime virtue, but still things are bad! I see that!" Here Mr. Golyadkin got up, took the candle and went on tiptoe to have another look at his sleeping guest. He stood over him for a long time, lost in thought. "An unpleasant picture! A travesty, an utter travesty, and that's that!"

Finally Mr. Golyadkin settled down. There was a noise, a crackling, a ringing in his head. He began to sink more and more deeply into sleep . . . he made an effort to think of something, to remember something extremely interesting, to resolve something extremely important, some delicate matter—but could not. Sleep descended upon his wretched head and he

dropped off the way people usually do when they are un-
accustomed to drinking and suddenly consume five glasses of
punch at some friendly evening gathering.

VIII

*[Add: Of what happened to Mr. Golyadkin upon awakening.
Of how Mr. Golyadkin became somewhat fainthearted. The
encounter of both Mr. Golyadkins. How one Mr. Golyadkin
shows off before the other Mr. Golyadkin. Mr. Golyadkin
Junior's fiendish betrayal. Mr. Golyadkin Junior's impropriety
and ignorance. Mr. Golyadkin Junior's disgraceful behavior.
Mr. Golyadkin Senior's opinion of rags, feelings of self-esteem
and reputations. Of how this chapter ends.]*

As usual the next day Mr. Golyadkin awoke at eight
o'clock. On awakening he immediately recalled all the events
of the previous evening—recalled them and frowned. "Dear,
what a fool I made [*Delete: what a fool I made Add: I did make such a
fool*] of myself yesterday!" he thought, raising himself up a bit in
his bed and glancing at his guest's bed. But how great was his
astonishment when he saw that not only the guest but even the
bed on which the guest had been sleeping were not in the room!
"What is this?" Mr. Golyadkin almost shrieked. "What can
have happened? What does this new occurrence mean?" While
Mr. Golyadkin gazed perplexedly at the empty place with his
mouth open, the door creaked and Petrushka entered with the
tea tray. "Where is he, where is he?" uttered our hero in a
barely audible voice, pointing his finger at the place which had
been assigned to the guest the previous night. Petrushka at first
said nothing in response; he did not even look at his master, but
turned his eyes to the corner at the right, thus forcing Mr.
Golyadkin to glance into the corner at the right as well.
However, after some silence Petrushka answered in a rather
hoarse and rude voice that his master was not at home.

"You fool; why, *I* am your master, Petrushka," uttered Mr. Golyadkin in a broken voice, looking intently at his servant.

Petrushka did not answer but gave Mr. Golyadkin such a look that the latter blushed to his ears—a look of insulting reproach, resembling downright abuse. Mr. Golyadkin's heart fell, as they say. At last Petrushka announced that *the other one* had been gone for some hour and a half now and [*Delete: and Add: , that he*] had not wanted to wait. [*Delete: . Add: , and that he had promised to meet with him in due course for a chat and have it out once and for all.*] Of course, the answer was probable and plausible. It was evident that Petrushka was not lying, that his insulting look and the words *the other one* which he had used were only the result of the whole notorious and infamous occurrence. [*Delete: Add: ; that, finally, Petrushka was, somehow, within his rights in speaking and acting thus and that one must not hold a grudge against him or give him a sound scolding because of it; consequently, on this score Mr. Golyadkin could obviously remain absolutely calm.*] But still he understood, though only vaguely, that something was wrong and that fate had yet another surprise in store for him, and a not altogether pleasant one. "All right, we shall see," he thought; "we shall see; we shall get to the bottom of all this in due course . . . Oh, dear God!" he moaned in conclusion, now in a completely different voice, "and why did I go and invite him; for what purpose did I do all that? Why, truly I'm putting my neck into their scurvy noose myself; I'm tying the noose with my own hands. Oh, where are your brains; where are they? Why, you can't keep from babbling utter nonsense, like some child, some office clerk, like some worthless creature with no rank, a spineless creature, some rotten rag; what a gossip you are, what an old woman! . . . Oh, saints above! And he wrote verses, the rascal, and declared his love for me! Now, how could I manage it, you know . . . How could I show him the door in a polite way, the rascal, if he comes back? Of course, there are many different ways of saying it and doing it . . . I could say: 'This is the way it is, given my limited salary' . . . or intimidate him somehow, by saying, 'After taking into consideration such and such and such and such, I am forced to make plain' . . ."

that he must pay for half of the room and board and in advance. Hm! No, damn it, no! That will be damaging to me. It's not delicate enough. Perhaps I can [*Delete: can Add: could*] do it this way: go and suggest to Petrushka that he should annoy him somehow, offend him somehow, [*Add: that he should*] insult him [*Add: sometimes*], and get rid of him in this way? I'd like to set them all against one another . . . No, damn it, no! That's dangerous, and again, if one looks at it from such a point of view, why, it's really bad! Really bad! But then suppose he doesn't come? Won't that be bad, too? [*Delete: Won't that be bad, too? Add: What will happen then?*] I babbled a lot of nonsense last night! . . . Oh, it's bad, bad! Dear me, my situation is really quite bad! Oh, what a fool I am, a damned fool! You can't cram what you ought into your head; you can't beat reason into it! Well, and suppose he comes [*Delete: comes Add: doesn't come*], and refuses? Oh, God, let him come! I'd be so terribly happy, if he would come. I'd give a lot to have him come . . ." Thus reasoned Mr. Golyadkin, gulping his tea and glancing incessantly at the clock on the wall. "It's a quarter to nine now. Time to go. Something is going to happen, but what? I'd love to know what exactly lies behind all this— the purpose, the drift and what the various stratagems are. It would be good to find out just what all these people are driving at and what their first step will be . . ." Mr. Golyadkin could bear it no longer. He threw down his partially smoked pipe, dressed and set out for work, wishing to expose the danger, if possible, and to ascertain everything firsthand. And there was danger. This he knew— that there was danger. "And now we shall . . . get to the bottom of it," said Mr. Golyadkin, taking off his overcoat and galoshes in the anteroom. "Now we'll get to the bottom of this entire business right away." Having thus resolved to take action, our hero put his clothing to rights, assumed a proper and official air and was just about to pass into the next room, when, suddenly, right in the doorway, his acquaintance of the day before, his friend and comrade, ran into him. Mr. Golyadkin Junior seemed not to notice Mr. Golyadkin Senior, although they had encountered one another practically nose to nose. Mr. Golyadkin Junior seemed to be busy; he was rushing off somewhere; he was out of

89

breath. He had such an official, such a businesslike expression that it seemed as if everyone could read on his face: "on a special assignment . . ."

"Ah, it's you, Yakov Petrovich!" said our hero, seizing his guest of the day before by the arm.

"Later, later, excuse me, you can tell me later!" shouted Mr. Golyadkin Junior, rushing forward. [*Delete: . Add: . . .*]

"But excuse me. I believe you wanted, Yakov Petrovich, you know, sir . . ."

"What, sir? Explain it quickly, sir." Here Mr. Golyadkin's guest of the day before stopped as though reluctantly forcing himself to and placed his ear right up to Mr. Golyadkin's nose.

"I must tell you, Yakov Petrovich, that I am amazed at the reception . . . a reception which, evidently, I could not at all have expected."

"There is an appropriate form for everything, sir. Go see His Excellency's secretary and then address yourself, as is proper, to the office supervisor. Do you have a petition? . . ."

"You . . . I don't know, Yakov Petrovich! You simply amaze me, Yakov Petrovich! Either you really don't recognize me or you are joking due to the inherent joviality of your character."

"Ah, it's you!" said Mr. Golyadkin Junior, as if he had only now recognized Mr. Golyadkin Senior. "So, is it you? [*Add: Well, I'm very glad that it's you!*] Well, now, did you rest well?" Hereupon Mr. Golyadkin Junior, smiling slightly, smiling officially and formally—although not at all the way he should have done (for, after all, in any case he owed a debt of gratitude to Mr. Golyadkin Senior)—and so, smiling officially and formally, added that for his part he was extremely happy that Mr. Golyadkin had had a good rest. Then he bowed slightly, took a few mincing steps in place, glanced to the right, to the left, then lowered his eyes to the ground, set his aim for the side door, and whispering rapidly that he was on a special assignment, whisked into the next room. And that was the last that was seen [*Delete: was seen Add: our hero saw*] of him.

"Now that's a fine thing! . . ." whispered our hero, dumbfounded for a moment. "Now that's a fine thing! So that's the sort of thing that's going on here! . . ." At this point Mr. Golyadkin felt that for some reason he had goose bumps all over. "However," he continued to himself, making his way to his own division, "however, after all, I have been talking about such a situation for a long time now. I've had a premonition for a long time now that he was on a special assignment. Why, I was saying just yesterday that this person was surely being used on some special assignment . . . [*Add: Still, what is all this? . . . If one reasons this way, it comes out as a not altogether unusual thing. In the first place there is probably some misunderstanding here, while in the second place, why, the same thing is happening to everyone; perhaps the same thing will happen to everyone . . .*]"

"Have you finished copying the document you were working on yesterday, Yakov Petrovich?" Anton Antonovich Setochkin said, when Mr. Golyadkin had seated himself beside him. "Do you have it here?"

"It's here," whispered Mr. Golyadkin, giving his head of section a rather flustered look.

"That's just fine, sir. I mention it because Andrei Filippovich has asked for it twice now. His Excellency will be wanting it any minute . . ."

"Yes, sir. It's finished, sir . . ."

"Well then, that's fine, sir."

"I have always, I believe, performed my duties properly, Anton Antonovich, and I take pains with the work assigned to me by my superiors, and do it diligently."

"Yes, sir. But what do you mean by that, sir?"

"I don't mean anything, Anton Antonovich, sir. I only want to explain, Anton Antonovich, that I . . . that is, I wanted to express that sometimes, in seeking their revolting daily bread, ill-will and envy spare no one, sir . . ."

"Excuse me, I don't altogether get your meaning. That is, what person are you alluding to now?" [*Delete: are you alluding to now?" Add: are you, by the turn of meaning of your words, making reference to now?"*]

"That is, I only meant, Anton Antonovich, that I take the direct route and scorn to take a roundabout route, that I am not one who intrigues and that, if I may be permitted to say so, I can be quite justly proud of it . . ."

"Yes, sir. Just so, sir, and, to my mind at least, your reasoning is totally justified. But do permit me to point out to you, Yakov Petrovich, that in good society making personal remarks is not altogether permissible, sir. What is said behind my back, I, for example, am ready to put up with, because who isn't abused behind his back! But to my face—if you please, [*Add: but*] I, my good sir, for example, will not permit anyone to be impertinent with me to my face. I, my good sir, have grown grey in the government [*Delete: the government*] service [*Add: to the Tsar*] and in my old age will not permit anyone, sir, to be impertinent with me to my face . . ."

"No, sir, Anton Antonovich . . . I . . . [*Delete: I . . .*] you, you see, Anton Antonovich, you seem not to have altogether comprehended me, Anton Antonovich, sir. [*Delete: . Add: , in the meaning of my words.*] While I, for pity's sake, Anton Antonovich, I, for my part, can only deem it an honor, sir . . ."

"Well, then, I beg your pardon, too, sir. We were schooled in the old manner, sir. And it's too late for us to learn your ways, newfangled ways. We would seem to have had sufficient wit to serve our country up to now. As you yourself know, my good sir, I have a decoration for twenty [*Delete: twenty Add: twenty-five*] years of unblemished service, sir . . ."

"I am aware of it, Anton Antonovich; for my part I am fully aware of all of this, sir. But it's not that [*Delete: that Add: myself*] I was speaking of, sir. I was speaking about a mask, Anton Antonovich, sir . . ."

"About a mask, sir?"

"That is, again you . . . I fear that here too you will take the meaning the wrong way, that is the meaning of my words, as you yourself put it, Anton Antonovich. I am only developing the theme, that is, I am putting forth the idea, Anton Antonovich, that people wearing masks have ceased to be uncommon and that nowadays it's difficult to recognize the person under the mask, sir . . ."

"Well, sir, you know, sir, it's really not so difficult as all that, sir. Sometimes it's even rather easy, sir; sometimes you don't have to look very far, sir."

"No, sir. You know, sir, I am saying, Anton Antonovich, sir, I am saying about myself, that I, for example, put on a mask only when there is a need for it, that is, solely for a carnival and for occasions of merrymaking, speaking in the literal sense, but that I do not wear a mask before other people every day, speaking in the other, more figurative sense, sir. That's what I meant, Anton Antonovich."

"Yes, well, let's leave all this for the moment. Besides I don't have time, sir," said Anton Antonovich, getting up from his seat and gathering together some papers to report on them to His Excellency. "Your affair, I imagine, will be cleared up in due course before long. You will see yourself whom you should reproach and whom you should accuse, and therefore I humbly beseech you to spare me any further private explanations and opinions that are an impediment to our work, sir . . ."

"No, sir, Anton Antonovich, I . . ." paling slightly, Mr. Golyadkin began, addressing the departing figure of Anton Antonovich; "Anton Antonovich, I didn't mean that at all, sir. What on earth is going on?" our hero, left alone, continued now to himself. "Which way is the wind blowing here and what does this new twist mean? [*Add: My dear God! Can it be that I'm asleep? . . .*]" At the same time as our dazed and half-dead hero was preparing to resolve this new [*Add: and rather interesting*] problem, a noise was heard in the next room, an energetic movement was unmistakably made, the door opened, and Andrei Filippovich, who had just before that betaken himself to His Excellency's room on office matters, appeared out of breath in the doorway and called for Mr. Golyadkin. Knowing the reason why and not wishing to make Andrei Filippovich wait, Mr. Golyadkin leapt up from his seat and, as was proper, immediately began to bustle about energetically, preparing and putting in final order the documents which had been asked for, and himself preparing to follow the documents and Andrei Filippovich into His Excellency's office. Suddenly, and practically from under the arm of Andrei Filippovich, who was standing right in the doorway at that moment, Mr. Golyadkin Junior whisked into the room, bustling, breathless, exhausted by his duties, with a grave and decidedly official air, and rushed up to Mr. Golyadkin Senior, who was least of all expecting such a sally . . .

"The papers, Yakov Petrovich, the papers . . . His Excellency has been pleased to ask whether you have them ready?" twittered Mr. Golyadkin Senior's friend hurriedly in a low voice. "Andrei Filippovich is waiting for you . . ."

"I don't need you to tell me he is waiting," said Mr. Golyadkin, also hurriedly and in a whisper.

"No, Yakov Petrovich, I didn't mean that; I didn't mean that at all, Yakov Petrovich. I sympathize, Yakov Petrovich, and I am prompted by heartfelt concern. [*Delete*: . *Add*: . . .]"

"Which I most humbly beseech you to spare me. Excuse me; excuse me, sir . . ."

"You will, of course, put them in a folder, Yakov Petrovich, and put a marker in at the third page. Allow me, Yakov Petrovich . . ."

"No, you allow me . . ."

"But there's an ink blot here, Yakov Petrovich. [*Delete*: . *Add*: , an ink blot.] Have you noticed the ink blot? . . ."

At this point Andrei Filippovich called Mr. Golyadkin a second time.

"Right away, Andrei Filippovich. I just have a bit more to do here . . . My dear sir, do you understand plain Russian?"

"It would be best to take it out with a penknife, Yakov Petrovich. You'd better leave it to me. You'd better not touch it yourself, Yakov Petrovich, but leave it to me. [*Delete*: . *Add*: and] I can partly take it out with my penknife . . ."

Andrei Filippovich called Mr. Golyadkin a third time.

"Why, for pity's sake, where is the blot? There really doesn't seem to be any blot here at all."

"It's a huge blot. Here it is! Here, if you please, here's where I saw it. Here, if you please . . . you just allow me, Yakov Petrovich; [*Delete*: ; *Add*: , you just allow me.] I can partly take it out with a penknife. I'm doing it out of concern, Yakov Petrovich, and [*Delete*: , and *Add*: ; I'm doing it] with the penknife out of the goodness of my heart . . . [*Add*: you just allow me;] there we are; there, and that's that . . ."

At this point, and completely unexpectedly, Mr. Golyadkin
Junior overpowered Mr. Golyadkin Senior in the momentary
struggle that had arisen between them and, in any case totally
against Mr. Golyadkin Senior's will, suddenly, without rhyme
or reason, took possession of the document which their
superior had demanded and, instead of scraping it with his
penknife out of the goodness of his heart, as he had perfidiously
assured Mr. Golyadkin Senior he would, quickly rolled it up,
shoved it under his arm, in two leaps was by the side of Andrei
Filippovich, who had not noticed any of his tricks, and flew into
the director's office with him. Mr. Golyadkin Senior stood
rooted to the spot, holding the penknife in his hands, as if
getting ready to scrape something with it . . . [*Delete:* . .]

Our hero did not yet completely understand his new
situation. He had not yet come to his senses. He had felt the
blow, but he thought that there was no particular purpose in it.
[*Delete:* . Add: , and meanwhile whispered to himself: "Right away,
Andrei Filippovich; I'll be right there. I'm just about ready . . ." However,
in an instant he understood, even though he understood rather vaguely and
even though he continued to think that there was no particular purpose in
it, that it was nothing . . .*] In terrible, indescribable anguish he
finally tore himself from the spot and rushed straight for the
director's office, beseeching heaven along the way, however,
that everything would somehow turn out for the best, would
have happened for no particular purpose, and would be all
right . . . In the room just before the director's office he ran
straight into Andrei Filippovich and his namesake. Both of
them were already coming back; Mr. Golyadkin stepped aside.
Andrei Filippovich was talking jovially and smiling. Mr. Golyadkin Senior's namesake was also smiling, fawning, walking with
mincing steps at a respectful distance from Andrei Filippovich
and whispering something in his ear with an elated air, to which
Andrei Filippovich was responding by nodding his head in a
benign manner. In a flash our hero understood the entire state
of affairs. The fact of the matter was that his work (as he found
out later) had almost surpassed His Excellency's expectations
and had, in fact, been ready right on time. His Excellency had
been highly pleased. It was even said that His Excellency had

said "Thank you" to Mr. Golyadkin Junior, a heartfelt "thank you"; he [*Delete:* ; *he Add:* , *and*] had said that he would keep it in mind when an opportunity arose and that he would be sure not to forget... Of course, the first thing Mr. Golyadkin had to do was to protest, to protest with all his might, to do his utmost. Almost beside himself and pale as death, he rushed up to Andrei Filippovich. But Andrei Filippovich, on hearing that Mr. Golyadkin's business was personal, [*Add: firmly*] refused to listen, remarking firmly [*Delete: firmly*] that he did not have a moment to spare even for his own concerns.

The dryness of his tone and the sharpness of his refusal struck Mr. Golyadkin forcefully. [*Add: "It's nothing; it seems to be nothing," he thought.*] "It [*Delete: "It Add: "But it*] would be better if I approached it from a somewhat different angle... I'd better go to Anton Antonovich." To Mr. Golyadkin's misfortune Anton Antonovich also turned out not to be available: he, too, was busy somewhere with something. "So, he had a reason when he asked to be spared explanations and opinions!" thought our hero. "That's what he was driving at—the slippery old customer! [*Add: Still, this too is, after all, nothing.*] In that case I simply must make so bold as to petition His Excellency."

Still pale and feeling that his head was in a state of complete disorder, sorely perplexed as to just what he ought to resolve to do, Mr. Golyadkin sat down on a chair. [*Add: The reality of this situation was absolutely killing Mr. Golyadkin.*] "It would have been far better if all of this had happened for no particular purpose," he kept thinking [*Delete: kept thinking Add: thought*] to himself. "Indeed, such a shady affair was even altogether incredible. It is, in the first place, nonsense, and in the second place it cannot happen. It probably just seemed to me somehow that it happened, or something different from what actually happened took place; or, I suppose, it was I myself who went... and somehow I took myself for someone else completely... in a word, this whole business is absolutely impossible."

Mr. Golyadkin had no sooner decided that this whole business was absolutely impossible than suddenly Mr. Golyadkin Junior flew into the room with papers in both hands and under his arms. After uttering a few brief necessary words to Andrei Filippovich in passing, exchanging a few words with one or two others, pleasantries with some others, banter with still others, Mr. Golyadkin Junior, obviously having no time to waste, now seemed to be preparing to leave the room, but to Mr. Golyadkin Senior's good fortune he stopped right in the doorway and started to speak in passing to two or three young clerks who happened to be standing there. Mr. Golyadkin Senior rushed over to him. No sooner had Mr. Golyadkin Junior seen Mr. Golyadkin Senior's move than he immediately began to look about with great anxiety to see where he could slip out the fastest. But our hero was already gripping the sleeves of his guest of the day before. The clerks surrounding the two titular councilors moved back and waited with curiosity to see what would happen. The senior Titular Councilor understood only too well that good opinion was not now on his side; he understood only too well that they were intriguing against him: it was all the more necessary now to stand up for himself. The moment was decisive.

"Well, sir?" uttered Mr. Golyadkin Junior, looking rather insolently at Mr. Golyadkin Senior.

Mr. Golyadkin Senior was scarcely breathing.

"I don't know, my dear sir," he began, "how to explain to you now the strangeness of your behavior to me."

"Well, sir. Do continue, sir." Here Mr. Golyadkin Junior looked around and winked at the clerks surrounding them, as if to let them know that the comedy was about to begin.

"The insolence and shamelessness of your mode of behavior toward me, my dear sir, in the present instance reveal your true nature even more . . . than any words of mine could. Don't rely too much on the game you're playing. It's a rather poor one . . ."

"Well, Yakov Petrovich, do [*Delete: do*] tell me now, what sort of night did you have?" answered [*Add: Mr.*] Golyadkin Junior, looking Mr. Golyadkin Senior straight in the eye.

"You, my dear sir, are forgetting yourself," said the Titular Councilor, utterly taken aback and barely feeling the floor beneath his feet. "I trust that you will change your tone . . ."

"Duckie!!" uttered Mr. Golyadkin Junior, making a rather improper grimace at Mr. Golyadkin Senior and suddenly, totally unexpectedly, under the pretext of an affectionate gesture, pinched his rather plump right cheek. Our hero blushed a fiery red. No sooner had Mr. Golyadkin Senior's friend perceived that his opponent, shaking all over, speechless with fury, red as a boiled lobster, and, finally, driven to the breaking point, might even resolve upon a formal attack, than he immediately and in the most shameless manner, in his turn, forestalled him. After patting him a few times more on the cheek, tickling him a few times more, playing with him thus for a few seconds more, as he stood motionless and mad with rage, to the great amusement of the young men surrounding them, Mr. Golyadkin Junior, with a shamelessness that would make the heart indignant, finally rapped Mr. Golyadkin Senior smartly on his protruding belly and with a most venomous and broadly insinuating smile, said to him: "[*Add: You said,* '] You're a tricky one, you are, brother Yakov Petrovich; you're a tricky one! You and I are going to be crafty, Yakov Petrovich, crafty [*Add:* ']." Then, before our hero could in the slightest recover from the last attack, Mr. Golyadkin Junior (giving first just a little smile to the spectators surrounding them) suddenly assumed a most busy, most businesslike, and most official air, looked down at the ground, drew himself in, scrunched himself up, and quickly uttering "on a special assignment," gave a flick of his short little leg and darted into the adjoining room. Our hero could not believe his eyes and was still in no condition to come to his senses . . .

At last he did come to his senses. Realizing in an instant that he was finished, that he had been annihilated, in a manner of speaking, that he had besmirched himself and sullied his reputation, that he had been ridiculed and humiliated in the presence of outsiders, that he had been perfidiously defiled by the one whom only yesterday he had considered his best and most trustworthy friend, that, finally, he had failed utterly, Mr. Golyadkin gave chase to his enemy. At that very instant he tried not to think any more of those who had been witness to his humiliation. "They are all part of a conspiracy," he said to himself; "one supports the other and one sets the other against me." However, after taking a dozen steps, our hero saw clearly that all pursuit was empty and vain and therefore he turned back. "You won't get away," he thought; "you'll be put away in good time; you'll be punished for all the unhappiness you've caused." With fierce coldbloodedness and with the most energetic determination Mr. Golyadkin got to his chair and sat down on it. "You won't get away!" he said again. It was now no longer a question of any passive defense: the fume of decisive, offensive warfare was in the air, and anyone who saw Mr. Golyadkin at that moment when, blushing and barely restraining his agitation, he plunged his pen into the inkwell, and saw with what fury he began to write on the paper, could have decided beforehand that things could not be allowed to pass thus and could not end in some simple womanish way. In the depths of his soul he had made a decision and in the depths of his heart he had sworn to carry it out. But in truth he still did not quite know how to proceed, or rather, he did not at all know. But it did not matter; it was nothing! "But in this day and age one gets nowhere by means of imposture and shamelessness, my dear sir. Imposture and shamelessness, my dear sir, do not lead to good, but to the noose. Only Grishka Otrepyev, my dear sir, won through imposture, by deceiving a blind people, but not for long." This last occurrence notwithstanding, Mr. Golyadkin decided to wait until the mask should fall from certain persons and a few things be revealed. For this to happen it was necessary, in the first place, that office hours should end as soon as possible, and until then our hero decided to undertake nothing. Then, when office hours ended, he would take a certain measure. Then he would know how to proceed, having taken this measure, how to arrange his plan of action in order to smash the horn of arrogance and crush the serpent gnawing the dust in contempt of its impotence. What Mr. Golyadkin could not do was permit himself to be filthied, like a rag on which people wipe their dirty boots. He could not agree to this, particularly in the present instance. If it were not for this last humiliation, our hero, perhaps, would even have resolved to restrain himself; perhaps he would have resolved to keep silent, submit and not protest too stubbornly; he would just have argued a bit, would have insisted a bit on certain claims, would have proved that he was within his rights, then would have retreated a bit, then, perhaps, would have retreated a bit more, then would have agreed altogether, then, and particularly when the opposing side would have solemnly acknowledged that he was within his rights, then, perhaps, he would even have become reconciled completely, he would even have been somewhat moved, perhaps even—who knows—a new friendship might have come into being, a firm, warm friendship on an even broader basis than that of the previous evening, so that this friendship might, finally, have so totally eclipsed the unpleasantness of the rather unseemly resemblance between these two persons that both titular councilors would have been utterly happy and would have lived, finally, to be a hundred and so forth. To be perfectly frank, Mr. Golyadkin was even beginning to regret somewhat [*Add: , even to regret strongly,*] that he had stood up for himself and for his rights and had thereupon been the recipient of unpleasantness because of it. "If he would give in," thought Mr. Golyadkin, "if he would say that it was a joke, I would forgive him. I would forgive him even more, if only he would admit it out loud. But I will not allow myself to be filthied like a rag. And if I have not allowed people unlike him to sully me, all the more will I not allow this corrupt person to attempt it. I am not a rag. I, my dear sir, am not a rag!" In a word, our hero had made up his mind. "You yourself, you, my dear sir, are guilty!" He had made up his mind to protest, and to protest with all his might, to the utmost. That was the kind of person he was! He could in no way consent to let himself be insulted, still less could he permit himself to be filthied like a rag, and, finally, least of all could he permit a completely corrupt person to do it. We are not disputing, however; we are not disputing. Perhaps, if someone wanted to, if, for example, someone really felt like turning Mr. Golyadkin into a rag, he would have turned him into one; he would have turned him into one without opposition and with impunity (Mr. Golyadkin himself sometimes felt this) and there would have emerged a rag and not Mr. Golyadkin—just so, a nasty, filthy rag would have emerged; but this rag would not have been a simple one; this rag would have had self-esteem; this would have been a rag with life in it and feeling; even though it would have had timid self-esteem and timid feelings deep within its filthy folds, still it would have had feelings . . .

The hours dragged on incredibly slowly; at last it struck four. Not long after, everyone got up and, following their superiors, set out for home. Mr. Golyadkin mingled with the crowd; his eye did not slumber and did not lose sight of its object. At last our hero saw his friend run up to the attendants who were giving out the overcoats, and, as was his vile wont, stand fawning before them in anticipation of his. The decisive moment had come. Somehow Mr. Golyadkin squeezed through the crowd and, not wishing to lag behind, also tried to get his overcoat. But an overcoat was handed first to Mr. Golyadkin's cohort and friend, because here too he had managed in his own fashion to get into their good graces, make up to them, whisper in their ear and act despicably.

Donning his overcoat, Mr. Golyadkin Junior glanced ironically at Mr. Golyadkin Senior, thus spiting him openly and brazenly. Then, with his accustomed effrontery, he looked around, minced about among the clerks for a last farewell— probably to leave a pleasing impression— made a remark to one, whispered about something with another, respectfully fell all over a third, addressed a smile to a fourth, gave his hand to a fifth, and jovially whisked down the stairs. Mr. Golyadkin Senior followed and, to his indescribable delight, caught up with him on the last step and seized him by the collar of his overcoat. Mr. Golyadkin Junior seemed somewhat frightened and looked about nonplussed.

"What do you mean by this?" he whispered at last to Mr. Golyadkin in a weak voice.

"Sir, if you are a gentleman, I trust you will recall our friendly relationship of yesterday," uttered our hero.

"Ah, yes. Well, now. Did you have a good rest, sir?"

For a moment rage rendered Mr. Golyadkin Senior incapable of speech.

101

"I did have a good rest, sir... But do permit me to tell you, my dear sir, that the game you're playing is extremely complicated..."

"Who says so? It's my enemies who say that," curtly answered the self-styled Mr. Golyadkin, at the same time unexpectedly freeing himself from the weak grasp of the real Mr. Golyadkin. Having freed himself, he rushed down the stairway, looked about, caught sight of a cabman, ran up to him, got into the droshky and in one instant disappeared from Mr. Golyadkin Senior's sight. In despair and abandoned by all, the Titular Councilor looked about, but there was no other cabman. He tried to run but his legs were giving way beneath him. With a downcast countenance, his mouth open, huddled up and feeling utterly destroyed, he leaned weakly against a lamp post and remained thus for several minutes in the middle of the pavement. All seemed [*Delete: All seemed Add: Everything seemed to have dumped on Mr. Golyadkin at once; all seemed*] lost for Mr. Golyadkin...

IX

[*Add: Mr. Golyadkin's decision. Mr. Golyadkin's various pronouncements, primarily about twins and about various scoundrels existing on this earth. How Mr. Golyadkin consumes eleven pasties and finds in this occurrence nothing disparaging to his reputation. Mr. Golyadkin's letter to a person notorious for his disgraceful behavior and slanderous bent. Of how Mr. Golyadkin then ran, wearied and went to sleep. How he then awoke and demonstrated to Petrushka that he, Petrushka, was a rogue in the honorable sense of this word. Mr. Golyadkin's correspondence and final decision.*]

Apparently everything, and even nature itself, had taken up arms against Mr. Golyadkin, but he was still on his feet and unconquered; he felt it—that he was unconquered. He was ready to do battle. He rubbed his hands together with such feeling and such energy when he came to his senses after his initial amazement that now just from Mr. Golyadkin's air one could conclude that he would not concede. [*Delete: . Add: , that he would in no wise concede, that in his words, "If, my dear sir, you do not wish to proceed in a delicate manner, then we shall take drastic measures. That's how it is, sir. That's just how it is, my dear sir!" Mr. Golyadkin even felt that it was his duty to rise up with all his might against the misfortune that was threatening, to smash the horn of arrogance and to put to shame unseemly malevolence.*] However, danger was imminent, was apparent; Mr. Golyadkin felt this, too; but how was he to tackle it, this danger? That was the question. For one instant the thought even flashed through Mr. Golyadkin's head: "Should I leave all this as it is; should I simply back off? Well, what of it? Why, it's nothing. I shall stand apart, as though it isn't me," thought Mr. Golyadkin. "I shall let everything pass.

It's not me and that's that. He is also separate, and perhaps he'll back off. He'll fawn a bit, the scoundrel; he'll fawn a bit, hang around for a while, and then he'll back off. That's how it will be! I shall succeed by dint of humility. Now, where is the danger? Why, what danger is there? I'd like anyone to show me where the danger lies in this situation. A trifling matter! An ordinary matter! . . ." Here Mr. Golyadkin stopped short. The words died on his lips; he even cursed himself for having had this thought; he then and there found himself guilty of being despicable and cowardly for having had this thought; however, his cause had still not advanced a single step. He felt that coming to a decision about something at the present moment was an absolute necessity for him; he even felt that he would give a great deal to anyone who could tell him just what he had to come to a decision about. After all, how was he to figure it out? Moreover, there wasn't time to figure it out. [*Add: All he knew was that he could not remain like this, not at all, absolutely not, in no way was it possible; he absolutely had to do something.*] In any case, in order not to waste time [*Add: , in order not to waste his precious time*], he took a cab and rushed home. "[*Add: No, brother," he thought to himself, "now, brother, the worst has come.*] Well? How do you feel now?" he thought to himself. "[*Delete: " he thought to himself. "*] How do you feel now, if you please, Yakov Petrovich? What will you do? What will you do now, you scoundrel, you, you rascal, you! You've brought yourself to this and now you're weeping, and now you're sniveling!" Mr. Golyadkin taunted himself thus, bouncing up and down in his cabman's jolting carriage. Taunting himself thus and pouring salt into his wounds at that moment gave some deep pleasure, almost even a voluptuous pleasure, to Mr. Golyadkin. "Well," he thought, "if some magician should come along now, or if it should happen in some official manner, and they should say: 'Give up a finger of your right hand, Golyadkin, and we'll be quits. There won't be another Golyadkin and you will be happy [*Add: , Golyadkin*], only you'll be minus a finger—I would give up my finger; I absolutely would; I'd give it up without blinking an eye. Oh, damn it all!" shouted the Titular Councilor finally in despair. "Why all this? Why did all this have to happen, just this, this very thing, as if something else couldn't have happened instead! And everything was fine at first. Everyone was satisfied and happy. But no, this had to happen! Talking won't get you anywhere, though. I must act." [*Delete:* . *Add:* , *he concluded, climbing the stairs to his apartment.* "*I must act, and to be perfectly frank at last, I must act more forcefully and more ruthlessly, so, in a direct, open and noble manner . . .*"]

And so, having almost come to a decision about something, Mr. Golyadkin, on entering his apartment, immediately seized his pipe and, sucking on it with all his might and sending out puffs of smoke to the right and to the left, began to pace back and forth across the room in a state of extreme agitation. Meanwhile Petrushka began to set the table. At last Mr. Golyadkin made up his mind completely, suddenly threw down his pipe, pulled on his overcoat, said he would not dine at home and rushed out of his apartment. On the stairway a breathless Petrushka caught up with him, holding the hat he had forgotten. Mr. Golyadkin took the hat and wanted in passing to make some excuses to Petrushka so that Petrushka should not go thinking anything in particular—he wanted to say: "Well, that's odd; I forgot my hat" and so forth—but as Petrushka did not so much as look at him and went away immediately, Mr. Golyadkin, without further explanations, put on his hat, ran down the stairs, and, repeating over and over that everything would perhaps be for the best and that the matter would work out somehow, though he nevertheless felt a chill all over his body right down to the soles of his feet, emerged into the street, took a cab and flew off to see Andrei Filippovich. "Wouldn't it be better to come tomorrow, though?" thought Mr. Golyadkin, seizing the bell-pull by the door of Andrei Filippovich's apartment. "And besides, what in particular shall I say? There's nothing particular about it. This matter is so insignificant; why, ultimately, it is, really insignificant and trifling, that is, almost a trifling matter . . . Yes, that's how it is, this whole thing, this situation . . ." Suddenly Mr. Golyadkin pulled the bell. The bell rang. Someone's footsteps could be heard inside . . . At that point Mr. Golyadkin even cursed himself, partly for his hastiness and audacity. The recent unpleasant events, which Mr. Golyadkin had almost forgotten about in doing his work, and the disagreement with Andrei Filippovich then and there came back into his mind. But it was too late now to flee: the door opened. To Mr. Golyadkin's good fortune he was informed that Andrei Filippovich had not returned from the office and that he was not dining at home. "I know where he's dining; he's dining near the Izmaylovsky Bridge," thought our hero and was terribly overjoyed. To the servant's question of "What message shall I give?", he said, "I . . . my good man . . . it's all right; I will come back later, my good man," and, even feeling somewhat heartened, ran down the stairs. Emerging onto the street, he decided to let the carriage go and settled with the cabman. Even when the cabman asked for a bit extra, saying, "I waited for a long time, sir, and didn't spare the horse for Your Worship," he gave him a extra five kopeks, what's more gave it very readily; he then set out on foot.

"This really is the sort of thing," thought Mr. Golyadkin, "that just can't be left this way. [*Delete:* . *Add:* , *not at all. It's been decided that it can't and there's nothing further to be said about it.*] However, if you reason thus, if you reason sensibly, then what is there here really to trouble myself about? Well, yes, still, I shall keep on speaking of it: why should I trouble myself? Why should I toil, struggle, be tormented, kill myself? First of all, the deed is done, and can't be undone . . . indeed it can't! Let's argue it this way: a person makes his appearance; a person makes his appearance with adequate letters of recommendation, which say he's a capable clerk, well-behaved, but poor, and he has suffered various unpleasantness—been in some scrapes—well, but then poverty is no crime; this has nothing to do with me. Well, really now, what is this nonsense? Why, it so happened, it was so arranged, it was so arranged by nature itself that a man resembles another man like two peas in a pod, that he is an exact copy of the other man; is that any reason not to give him a job in the office? If it's a matter of fate, if it's a matter of fate alone, if only blind fortune is to blame for this, should he now be filthied like a rag, should he now be refused a post? Where, after that, would one find justice? He's a poor, downtrodden, intimidated person. One's heart aches for him;

compassion demands that he be cared for! Yes! I declare! Fine
thing it would be if our superiors reasoned as I do, unruly fellow
that I am! What a noggin I have, indeed! I'm as stupid
sometimes as a dozen fools put together! No, no! They did well,
and thanks should go to them for being charitable to the poor
wretch . . . Well now, let's suppose, for the sake of example,
that we are twins, that we were simply born like that, that we are
twin brothers, and that's that. That's the way it is! Well, what of
it? Well, nothing of it! All the clerks can be made to get used to
it . . . and any outsider entering our department would certainly
not find anything unseemly and offensive in such a situation.
There's even something touching about it. What a thought!
Divine Providence created two absolutely identical persons,
and beneficent superiors, seeing that it was Divine Providence,
gave refuge to the two twins. "It would, of course," continued
Mr. Golyadkin, taking a breath and lowering his voice somewhat,
"it would, of course . . . it would, of course, have been better if
there had been none of this [*Add:* , *if everything had remained as
before and there had been nothing touching,*] touching business,
[*Delete: touching business,*] and if there had been no twins either . . .
Damn it all! And what need was there for it? What need was
there that was so special and so urgently pressing?! My dear
God! [*Add: Still though, is it reprehensible? Now, is it reprehensible?
Does it, after all, besmirch anyone's honor? Well, then it's nothing; well,
then everything is fine; well, then everything is as it was before and
everyone should keep quiet . . . and be pleased by that . . . and they should
not say anything . . . and should not contradict at all . . .*] Oh, what a
mess this is! And look at the kind of character he has; he has
such a wanton, nasty disposition; he's such a scoundrel, so
frivolous, a suckup, a lickspittle; what a Poor Beggar he is!
Perhaps he'll conduct himself badly yet and sully my name, the
villain. And I have to keep an eye on him now and court him!
Oh, what a nuisance! Still, what of it? It doesn't matter! So, he's
a scoundrel; so let him be a scoundrel; the other, to make up for
it, is an honest man. Well, then he will be a scoundrel, while I
shall be an honest man, and they will say that that Golyadkin
there is a scoundrel; take no notice of him and don't confuse
him with the other one; but this Golyadkin here is honest,

virtuous, meek, forgiving, utterly reliable in his work and deserving of promotion. There you have it! All right then . . . but suppose, you know . . . Suppose they, you know . . . go and confuse us! Why, he is capable of anything! Oh, dear God! . . . And he'll pass himself off as another person; he'll take his place—he's such a scoundrel—he'll pass himself off as if the other person was a rag, a rag. Oh, dear God! What a disaster this is! . . ."

Reasoning and lamenting thus, Mr. Golyadkin ran along, taking no notice of the way and almost unaware of where he was going. He came to his senses on Nevsky Prospect and then only because he collided with some passerby so neatly and so squarely that he saw stars. Without raising his head Mr. Golyadkin mumbled an apology and only when the passerby, after grunting something not very flattering, had moved a considerable distance away did he raise his nose and look about to see where he was and how he had gotten there. After looking about and noticing that he was right beside the restaurant in which he had spent some time getting himself ready for the dinner party at Olsufi Ivanovich's, our hero suddenly began to feel rumbles and gurgles in his stomach, recalled that he had not dined, that there was no dinner party awaiting him anywhere, and therefore, not wasting his precious time, ran up the stairs, to [*Delete: to Add: into*] the restaurant to grab a quick bite of something and avoid delay by doing it as fast as he could. And although everything in the restaurant was expensive, still that little circumstance did not stop Mr. Golyadkin this time. Moreover, there was no time to pause over such trifles now. In the brightly lit room at the counter, on which lay a diverse heap of all that is required for a snack by respectable people, stood quite a dense crowd of customers. The man at the counter was hard pressed to pour, serve, receive payment, and give change. Mr. Golyadkin waited his turn and when it came he modestly stretched his hand toward a pasty. After retiring to a corner, turning his back to the other people, and eating with gusto, he returned to the man at the counter, placed the dish on the table, and, knowing the price, took out a ten-kopek piece and put the coin on the counter, catching the man's eye, as if to say, "Here's the money—one pasty," and so forth.

"That'll be one ruble, ten kopeks," said the man, straining the words through his teeth.

Mr. Golyadkin was duly astonished.

"What's that you say? . . . I . . . I believe I've only had one pasty."

"You've had eleven," retorted the man with certainty.

"You . . . so it seems to me . . . you seem to be mistaken . . . I really had only one pasty, I think."

"I counted them. You had eleven. Since you've had them, you must pay for them. We don't give anything away free."

Mr. Golyadkin was stunned. "What is this? Some kind of wizardry being practiced on me?" he thought. Meanwhile, the man awaited Mr. Golyadkin's decision; people had gathered around Mr. Golyadkin; Mr. Golyadkin was about to dig into his pocket for a silver ruble to settle up immediately and avoid any further unpleasantness. "Well, if it's eleven, then it's eleven," he thought, reddening like a boiled lobster; "well, what's so terrible about eating eleven pasties? Why, a person was hungry and so he ate eleven pasties. So, let him eat to his heart's content. Why, there's nothing in it to be surprised at or laugh at . . ." Suddenly it was as if Mr. Golyadkin had experienced a sharp twinge. He raised his eyes—and instantaneously understood the mystery, understood the wizardry entirely; all difficulties were immediately dispelled . . . In the doorway of the neighboring room, almost directly behind the counterman's back and facing Mr. Golyadkin, in the doorway which, however, our hero had taken up until then for a mirror, stood a small man—stood he, stood Mr. Golyadkin himself, not the old Mr. Golyadkin, not the hero of our tale, but the other Mr. Golyadkin, the new Mr. Golyadkin. The other Mr. Golyadkin was apparently in excellent spirits. He was smiling at Mr. Golyadkin the First, nodding his head to him, winking at him, shuffling his feet slightly, and looking as if—the least little thing and he would disappear, go into the neighboring room and there probably take a back exit and that would be the last they would see of him . . . and all pursuit would be vain. [*Delete*: . *Add*: —*as if he were saying, "Do stop concerning yourself about me, sir, and that's that."*] In his hands was the last piece of the tenth pasty which, before Mr. Golyadkin's very eyes, he dispatched into his mouth, smacking his lips with pleasure. [*Delete:* . *Add:* , *and almost saying, "Pasties paid for somebody else are good!"*] "He did pass himself off as me, the scoundrel!" thought Mr. Golyadkin, burning with shame; "he wasn't ashamed that other people were around! Do they see him? No one seems to notice him . . ." Mr. Golyadkin threw down the silver ruble as if he had burnt all his fingers with it and, without noticing the counterman's archly insolent smile, a smile of triumph and quiet authority, he forced his way through the crowd and rushed out without a backward glance. "I'm grateful that at least he didn't totally compromise anyone!" thought the senior Mr. Golyadkin. "I'm grateful to the rascal, to both him and fate, that everything turned out all right. The counterman was rude, that's all. But what of it—after all he was within his rights! I owed a ruble ten, so he was within his rights. [*Add: Otherwise, I could have reported him for . . .*] 'We don't give anyone anything free!' he said. He could at least have been a bit more polite, the good-for-nothing! . . ."

Mr. Golyadkin was saying all this as he went down the stairs to the entrance. However, on the last step he stopped dead and suddenly blushed so hard that tears even came to his eyes from his attack of wounded self-esteem. After standing for half a minute like a post, he suddenly stamped his foot with determination, leapt from the entranceway into the street in a single bound and without a backward glance, gasping for breath, feeling no weariness, rushed home, to Shestilavochnaya Street. Once home, without taking off even his outer clothing despite his habit of being casual when at home, and without even taking up his pipe first, he immediately settled himself on the ottoman, pulled the inkwell towards him, took a pen, got a sheet of letter paper and set about penning the following epistle with a hand trembling from inner agitation:

Dear Yakov Petrovich,
    Sir!

I would in no wise have taken up my pen, did not my circumstances and you yourself, my dear sir, compel me to do so. Believe me that necessity alone has forced me to enter into such discussions with you and therefore I beseech you above all else to consider this measure of mine not as a deliberately intended attempt, my dear sir, to bring insult to you, but as the necessary consequence of the circumstances now binding us together.

"It seems to be all right, proper, polite, though not without force and firmness . . . There doesn't seem to be anything in it for him to be offended by. Besides, I'm within my rights," thought Mr. Golyadkin, reading over what he had written.

Your unexpected and strange appearance, my dear sir, on a stormy night, after the rude and unseemly deed perpetrated against me by my enemies, whose names I do not speak out of contempt for them, was the seed of all the misunderstanding which exists between us at the present time. Moreover, your obstinate desire, my dear sir, to stand your own ground and forcibly enter into the circle of my existence and of all my relationships in practical life exceeds even the bounds required by common courtesy and by common social custom. I think there is no point in mentioning here your filching, my dear sir, of my papers and of my own good name for the purpose of currying favor with our superiors— a favor unmerited by you. Nor is there any point either in mentioning here your deliberate and insulting evasion of the explanations required on this occasion. Finally, to leave nothing out, I do not make mention here either of your most recent, strange, one might say incomprehensible, deed perpetrated against me in the coffee house. Far be it from me to lament my needless expenditure of a silver ruble; however, I cannot help but manifest all my indignation at the recollection of your blatant encroachment, [*Add: my dear*] sir, upon my honor and what is more in the presence of several persons who, although not personal acquaintances of mine, were nevertheless extremely well-bred . . .

"Am I not going too far?" thought Mr. Golyadkin. "Won't it be too much? Won't it be too offensive—that remark about being well-bred, for example? . . . Well, it doesn't matter! I have to show him my firmness of character. However, to soften things I can just flatter him a bit and butter him up at the end. Anyway, we'll see."

But I would not undertake, my dear sir, to weary you with my letter, were I not firmly confident that the nobility of your deepest feelings and your open, direct character will indicate to you the means for rectifying all omissions and restoring all to its former state.

In perfect trust I make bold to rest assured that you will not take my letter amiss and that at the same time you will not refuse to explain yourself precisely and unmistakably in this matter in a letter entrusted to my servant.

In anticipation, I have the honor to be, dear sir [*Delete: dear sir,*]

[*Add: Dear sir,*] Your most humble servant,

Ya. Golyadkin.

"Well, all's well now. The deed is done, even as far as being put in writing. But who is to blame? He is himself to blame; he brings a person to the point where he must demand something in writing. But I am within my rights . . ."

After reading over the letter for the last time, Mr. Golyadkin folded it, sealed it and called Petrushka. Petrushka appeared, as was his wont, with sleepy-looking eyes and extremely angry at something.

"Here, old chap, you take this letter . . . understand?"

Petrushka said nothing.

"Take it and deliver it to the office. There you are to look for the person on duty, for Provincial Secretary[9] Vakhrameyev. Vakhrameyev is on duty today. Do you understand that?"

"Yes, I do."

"Yes, I do! Can't you say: 'Yes, I do, sir'? Ask for the clerk Vakhrameyev and say to him, 'This is the way it is,' say, 'my master has charged me to deliver his compliments and most humbly asks that you check in our office address book and find out where Titular Councilor Golyadkin lives.' "

Petrushka remained silent and it seemed to Mr. Golyadkin that he smiled.

"Well, so now, Pyotr, you will ask him for the address and find out where the new clerk Golyadkin lives."

"All right."

"Ask for the address and take this letter to that address. Understand?"

"I understand."

"If, when you are there . . . I mean there, at the place to which you will take the letter . . . the gentleman to whom you will give this letter, that Golyadkin . . . Why are you laughing, you dolt?"

"But why should I be laughing? What's it to me? I'm not doing anything, sir. It's not for the likes of me to laugh . . ."

"Well, so then . . . if that gentleman should ask 'How is your master, how is he?' If he says, you know . . . well, if he tries to worm anything out of you, you just say nothing and answer, 'My master is fine and asks for an answer from you in writing.' Understand?"

"I understand, sir."

"Well, so then, you say, 'My master,' you say, say, 'He's fine,' you say, 'and in good health, and is getting ready right now,' you say, 'to pay a visit to someone. And,' you say, 'he asks for an answer from you in writing.' Understand?"

"I understand, sir."

"Go on, then."

"Indeed, how one has to labor with this dolt as well! He laughs, and that's all. Why is he laughing? I've come to grief. Thus have I come to grief! However, perhaps it will all turn out for the best... That rogue will undoubtedly gad about now for a couple of hours. He'll disappear somewhere yet. You can't send him anywhere. Oh, what a disaster!... What disaster has befallen me!..."

Feeling thus the full extent of his misfortune, our hero resolved to play a passive role for two hours while waiting for Petrushka.

For about an hour he walked about the room, smoked, then abandoned his pipe and sat down with a book, then lay down on the ottoman, then took up his pipe once more, then began to move quickly about the room again. He tried to think things over but was absolutely unable to think about anything. At last the agony of being passive reached its climax and Mr. Golyadkin made up his mind to take a step. "Petrushka won't come for another hour," he thought. "I can leave the key with the janitor, and in the meantime I myself will, uh... investigate the matter; I'll investigate the matter on my own." Losing no time and hastening to investigate the matter, Mr. Golyadkin took his hat, went out of the room, locked his apartment, stopped by at the janitor's, handed over the key to him along with ten kopeks—Mr. Golyadkin had of late become unusually generous—and set out for where he had to go. First Mr. Golyadkin set out on foot for the Izmaylovsky Bridge. It took about half an hour to walk there. On reaching the goal of his journey, he went directly into the courtyard of the house with which he was familiar and glanced at the windows of the apartment of State Councilor Berendeyev. Except for three windows hung with red curtains the rest were all dark. "Olsufi Ivanovich probably has no guests today," thought Mr. Golyadkin. "They're probably home all by themselves now." Our hero stood in the courtyard for a while, trying now to make up his mind about something. But apparently a decision was not fated to take place. Mr. Golyadkin dismissed the idea with a wave of his hand and went back out to the street. "No, I shouldn't have come here. What is there for me to do here? . . . I'd better go now, uh . . . and investigate the matter in person." Upon taking such a decision, Mr. Golyadkin set out for his office. He had a long way to go; in addition, it was terribly muddy and wet snow was falling in very thick flakes. But for our hero there seemed to be no difficulties at that moment. He got thoroughly soaked, it's true, and also became quite spattered with mud, "but that's nothing as long as the goal is reached." And indeed, Mr. Golyadkin was now approaching his goal. The dark mass of the enormous government building loomed visible in the distance. "Stop!" he thought. "Where am I going and what am I going to do once I'm there? Suppose I do find out where he lives, but in the meantime Petrushka has most likely returned already and brought me the answer. I'm only wasting my precious time for nothing. I've already wasted my time for nothing. Well, it doesn't matter. This can all still be remedied. However, should I perhaps drop in and see Vakhrameyev? But, no! I can do it later . . . Oh, dear! There was no need to go out at all! But, no, that's the kind of character I have! Such a knack that whether I do have to or whether I don't have to, I'm everlastingly trying somehow to rush ahead . . . Hm . . . what time is it, anyway? It must be nine already. Petrushka may come and not find me in. I was an absolute fool to go out . . . Oh, dear, it really is a troublesome business!"

Sincerely acknowledging in this way that he had been an absolute fool, our hero ran back to Shestilavochnaya Street. He arrived weary and exhausted. Furthermore, he learned from the janitor that it hadn't entered Petrushka's head to come home yet. "There now! I've already had a premonition of this," thought our hero, "and meanwhile it's nine o'clock. Oh, dear, what a scoundrel he is! Everlastingly getting drunk somewhere! Dear God! Oh, what a day it's been my unfortunate lot to have!" Reflecting and lamenting thus, Mr. Golyadkin unlocked his apartment, got a light, undressed completely, smoked a pipe, and, exhausted, weary, defeated, hungry, lay down on the ottoman to wait for Petrushka. The candle burned dimly, snuff forming on the wick; its light flickered on the walls . . . Mr.

Golyadkin gazed and gazed and thought and thought and finally fell sound asleep.

It was late when he awoke. The candle had burned down almost completely, was smoking and ready to go out altogether at that moment. Mr. Golyadkin leapt up, came alive and remembered everything, absolutely everything. Behind the partition Petrushka's heavy snoring could be heard. Mr. Golyadkin rushed to the window—not a light anywhere. He opened the small pane—it was quiet. The city seemed devoid of life; it was sleeping. It must have been about two or three o'clock; just so: the clock behind the partition strained and struck two. Mr. Golyadkin rushed behind the partition.

Somehow, but only after prolonged effort, he shook Petrushka awake and succeeded in getting him to sit up on the bed. In that time the candle went out altogether. Some ten minutes passed before Mr. Golyadkin succeeded in finding another candle and lighting it. In that time Petrushka had succeeded in falling asleep again. "What a villain you are! What a scoundrel you are!" said Mr. Golyadkin, shaking him awake once more. "Will you get up? Will you wake up?" After half an hour of effort, Mr. Golyadkin did succeed, however, in rousing his servant completely and dragging him out from behind the partition. Only then did our hero see that Petrushka was, as the saying goes, dead drunk and hardly able to stand on his legs.

"You good-for-nothing, you!" shouted Mr. Golyadkin. "You villain, you! You've done me in! Lord, where can he have gotten rid of that letter? Oh, my God, why, what if it . . . And why did I write it? I just had to go and write it! I let myself get carried away by my self-esteem! Nincompoop! And this is where my self-esteem has landed me. There's your self-esteem, you scoundrel, you, there's your self-esteem! . . . Well, you! What have you done with the letter, you villain, you? To whom did you give it? . . ."

"I didn't give anybody any letter; and I didn't have any letter . . . so there!"

Mr. Golyadkin wrung his hands in despair.

"You listen, Pyotr . . . you listen; you listen to me . . ."

"I'm listening . . ."

116

"Where did you go? Answer . . ."

"Where did I go . . . I went to see good people! What do I care!"

"Oh, dear God! Where did you go first? Were you at the office? . . . You listen, Pyotr. Maybe you're drunk?"

"Me drunk? May I be rooted to the spot this very moment, I haven't had any . . . any . . . anything. So there . . ."

"No, no, it doesn't matter that you're drunk . . . I just asked. It's all right that you're drunk. I didn't mean anything, Petrusha; I didn't mean anything . . . Perhaps you've just forgotten for a while, but you'll remember everything. Come now, try to remember. Were you at Vakhrameyev's, the clerk's? Were you or weren't you?"

"I wasn't there and there was no such clerk. May I be . . ."

"No, no, Pyotr! No, Petrusha. Why, I don't mind. After all, you see I don't mind. Why, whatever is the matter? Why, it's cold outside and damp. And so a person has had a bit to drink. Why, it's nothing . . . [*Delete:* . .] I'm not angry. I had something to drink myself today, old chap . . . Come on, now; try to remember, old chap: were you at the clerk Vakhrameyev's?"

"Now, how was it? Oh, yes, this is the way it was; yes, honest to God, I was there; may I be . . ."

"Why, that's fine, Petrusha; it's fine that you've been there. You see, I'm not angry . . . Well, well," continued our hero, trying to placate his servant even more, clapping him on the shoulder and smiling at him. "Well, you villain, you've had a wee drop . . . had a drop for ten kopeks, have you? What a [*Add: great*] rogue you are! Well, it's all right. Why, you see that I'm not angry . . . I'm not angry, old chap, I'm not angry . . ."

"No, I'm not a rogue. Have it your own way, sir . . . I only dropped in to see some good people, but I'm not a rogue, and I've never been a rogue . . ."

"Of course not, no, Petrusha! You listen, Pyotr. Why, I didn't mean anything. Why, I'm not berating you by calling you a rogue. I'm only saying it to comfort you. I'm speaking of it in the honorable sense. Why, this is flattering to some people, Petrusha, if you say to them that they are a slippery customer, or a crafty fellow, and that they know what's what and won't let

117

anyone fool them. Some people like this... [*Delete*: .. *Add*: *It flatters them. It's in the honorable sense that I am calling you a rogue...*] Come, come, it's nothing! Come, now, you just tell me, [*Add*: *now, you just tell me,*] Petrusha, frankly and openly, as you would a friend... well, were you at the clerk Vakhrameyev's and did he give you the address?"

"Yes, he gave me the address; he gave me the address, too. A nice clerk! 'And your master,' he says, 'is a nice man, a very nice man,' he says. 'I,' he says, 'tell him,' he says, 'give my regards,' he says, 'to your master; thank him and tell him that I,' he says, 'like him; there,' he says, 'how I do respect your master! Because,' he says, 'you, your master,' he says, 'Petrusha, is a nice man,' he says, 'and you,' he says, 'are also a nice man, Petrushka,—there...'"

"Oh, dear God! And what of the address, the address, Judas that you are?" The last words Mr. Golyadkin uttered almost in a whisper.

"The address, too ... he gave me the address, too. [*Delete*: . *Add*: *; he did also give me the address.*]"

"He did? Well, just where does he live, Golyadkin, the clerk Golyadkin, the Titular Councilor?"

"'You will find Golyadkin,' he says, 'on Shestilavochnaya Street. Now, when you enter,' he says, 'Shestilavochnaya, go to the right, up the stairs to the fourth floor. That's where,' he says, 'you'll find Golyadkin...'"

"You fraud, you!" shouted our hero, finally losing his patience. "You villain, you! Why, that's me! Why, it's me you're talking about! But there's another Golyadkin; I'm speaking of the other one, you fraud, you!"

"Well, have it your own way! What do I care! Have it your own way! So there!"

"But what of the letter, the letter..."

"What letter? There wasn't any letter and I didn't see any letter."

"But what did you do with it—you rogue, you?!"

"I delivered it; I delivered the letter. 'Give my regards,' he says; 'thank him. Your master,' he says, 'is nice. Give my regards,' he says, 'to your master...'"

"But who said that? Was it Golyadkin who said it?"

Petrushka said nothing for a moment and then grinned broadly, looking straight into his master's eyes.

"Listen, you, you villain, you!" began Mr. Golyadkin, choking and becoming flustered with rage; "what have you done to me? You tell me what you've done to me! You have done me in, you scoundrel, you! You've put me in an impossible position, you Judas, you!"

"Well, have it your own way now! What do I care?" said Petrushka firmly, withdrawing behind the partition.

"Come here, come here, you villain, you! . . ."

"No, I won't come to you now; I won't come at all. What do I care! I'll go to good people . . . Good people live honestly. Good people live without fakery and never have doubles . . ."

Mr. Golyadkin's hands and feet turned to ice and his breathing became labored . . .

"Yes, sir," continued Petrushka, "they never have doubles; [*Add: they live honestly;*] they aren't an offense to God and honest people . . ."

"You good-for-nothing, you're drunk! You sleep now, you villain, you! And tomorrow you'll get it," uttered Mr. Golyadkin in a barely audible voice. As for Petrushka, he mumbled something more; then he could be heard getting heavily into his bed so that it creaked. He gave a long drawn out yawn, stretched, and finally started to snore, sunk in the sleep of the just, as the saying goes. Mr. Golyadkin was more dead than alive. Petrushka's behavior, his highly strange allusions, which were at the same time so distant that there was consequently no reason to be angry, the moreso as a drunken person was speaking, and finally, the whole nasty turn that the matter had taken—all this had completely shaken [*Add: Mr.*] Golyadkin. [*Delete: . Add: , by showing him clearly what deep roots slander, treachery, intrigue and informing had put down and, finally, how much ground a person known for his unseemly bent had gained in the opinion of private persons and even more in public opinion. And the evidence of it was Petrushka and the tone that had been communicated to that villain by Mr. Golyadkin's ill-wishers.*] "What on earth possessed me to rake him over the coals in the middle of the night?" said our hero, trembling all over from a morbid sensation. "What on earth pushed me to get involved with a drunken person? What sense can you expect from a drunken person? Everything he says is a lie. What was it, though, that he was alluding to, that villain? Oh, dear God! And why did I write all those letters? My own murderer, that's what I am! Self-destructive creature that I am! I couldn't keep still! I had to babble nonsense! And what for? I'm perishing; I resemble a rag, but, oh, no, still I have to bring my self-esteem into it. 'My honor is suffering,' I say; 'I must save my honor,' I say! Self-destructive creature that I am!" [*Delete: "* *Add: And what a bent there is in all that ilk; what an inclination there is in that villain! He sees that a person has stumbled, that a person has put his foot into it, that a person is caught in a morass up to his ears, and so he immediately sets out to spite him: he says, 'You're caught in a morass, so just for that, here's something else for you into the bargain', and he piques the person, and cuts the person to the quick!... No compassion whatsoever! And me, what about me? What a nasty bent there is in me! A vile little nature!... And I really needed so to save my honor—it really was urgent! And I'm ready to assume ties with a drunken person! As if even a five-year-old child doesn't know that a drunken person insists on lying and committing crudities. And he commits them because he is drunk, because a drunken person has this vile tendency to commit crudities, because according to human nature it has to be just this way and not some other. Consequently, in one respect he's right; consequently, he's right in all respects, and there's no being offended by it. One ought to be offended, however, at that fool who's ready to assume ties with a drunken person. That's how, in justice and in truth, it should be! He's had a lot to drink, so he starts being crude. That's how it has to be. A person insists on this; this is his nature, and for this I am not to blame—that's how it is!..."*]

So[*] spoke Mr. Golyadkin, sitting on his ottoman and not daring to move out of fear. Suddenly his eyes became fixed on an object which attracted his attention completely. In terror— was not the object which had attracted his attention an illusion, a trick of the imagination?—he stretched his hand out to it, with hope, with timidity, with indescribable curiosity... No, it was not a trick of the imagination! Not an illusion! A letter,

---

* In the 1846 version this is not a new paragraph [EJH].

really a letter, without any doubt a letter, and addressed to him... Mr. Golyadkin took the letter from the table. His heart was pounding furiously. "That rogue probably brought it," he thought, "and put it here and then forgot it; that's probably how it all happened; that probably is just how it all happened... [*Add: How ever did it get here, though? Who could have...? Who could have written the letter to me like this?... I'd give a great deal to find out just what's in this letter, to simply find out, to find out without reading it!... Lord, Lord!..."* Mr. Golyadkin put the letter aside for the time being, pulled out his handkerchief and mopped the perspiration which had appeared on his brow. Then... then he folded his arms and for a long time whispered something to himself with unusual ardor; then, unable to restrain his impatience any longer, he broke the seal, turned the page and read the signature.]" The letter was from the clerk Vakhrameyev, Mr. Golyadkin's young colleague and onetime friend. "I had a premonition of all this, though," thought our hero, "[*Delete:, " Add: . "I certainly had a premonition of all this yesterday,*] and I also had a premonition of everything that is going to be in the letter now... [*Add: What of it? It's all one! It's the chance I knew I was taking ... Well!... It doesn't matter..."* Mr. Golyadkin began to read.]" The letter was as follows:

> Dear Yakov Petrovich,
>   Sir!
> Your servant is drunk and there's no getting any sense out of him. For this reason I prefer to answer in writing. I hasten to inform you that the commission with which you have entrusted me, which consists in transmitting a letter to a certain person whom you know, I agree to carry out with all faithfulness and exactness. This same person, who is very well known to you and who has now taken the place of a friend to me, whose name I do not utter here (because I do not wish to blacken needlessly the reputation of a completely innocent person), is lodging with us in the apartment of Karolina Ivanovna, in the very same room where earlier, during your stay with us, the travelling infantry officer from Tambov was lodged.

However, one can always find this person in the company of honest and sincere people, which is more than can be said for some [*Add: people*]. I intend to sever my ties with you as of this day; we cannot remain on a friendly footing and preserve the former harmonious aspect of our camaraderie, and therefore I beg you, my dear sir, immediately on the receipt of this frank letter of mine, to send me the two rubles you owe me for the razors of foreign make which were sold to you by me, if you deign to recall, seven months ago on credit, while you were still lodging with us at Karolina Ivanovna's, [*Add: a woman*] whom I respect with all my heart. I take this action because you, according to the stories of intelligent persons, have lost your self-esteem and reputation and have become dangerous to the morality of innocent and untainted persons; for certain people do not live according to truth and, moreover, their words are falsehood and their good intentions suspect. One can always and everywhere find people capable of rebuffing the wrong done to Karolina Ivanovna, who has ever been irreproachable in her conduct, in the second place is an honest woman and moreover a spinster, not young in years but nevertheless of a good foreign family—which several persons have asked me to note in this letter of mine in passing, and I speak for myself, too. But in any case you will know all in good time if you do not know it already, for you have made yourself notorious, according to the stories of intelligent persons, in every corner of the [*Delete: the Add: our populous*] capital and, thus, may already have obtained pertinent information about yourself, [*Add: my dear*] sir, in many places. In [*Delete: In Add: And in*] concluding this letter of mine, I must inform you, my dear sir, that a certain person whom you know, whose name I do not mention here out of certain noble considerations, is greatly respected by highminded persons; moreover, he is of a jovial and

122

pleasant temperament, successful both at work and among all sober-minded people, true to his word and in friendship true and does not wrong behind their backs those with whom to their faces he is on friendly terms.

In any case I remain
Your humble servant
N. Vakhrameyev

P.S. Get rid of your servant. He is a drunkard and brings you, in all probability, much trouble. Take instead Yevstafi, who used to work for us and is right now without a position. Your present servant is not only a drunkard, but a thief as well, because last week he sold a pound of sugar, in pieces, to Karolina Ivanovna at a reduced price, which, in my opinion, he could not have done except by robbing you in a cunning manner, little by little and at various times. I write this to you, wishing you well despite the fact that some people know only how to offend and deceive everyone, mainly those who are honest and of good character; moreover, they revile them behind their backs and represent them as contrary to what they really are solely out of envy and because they cannot say that they are as good themselves.

V.

After reading Vakhrameyev's letter, our hero remained immobile on his ottoman for a long time. Some new light was breaking through all the dim and mysterious haze which had been surrounding him for two days now. Our hero was partly beginning to understand... He was about to try to get up from the ottoman and walk up and down the room once or twice to refresh himself, somehow collect his scattered thoughts, focus them on a certain subject, and then, after putting himself straight somewhat, to ponder his situation in a mature manner. [*Delete* . *Add:* , *to resolve firmly and without fail to do something and to act in accordance with this resolve.*] But no sooner did he attempt to

123

get up than he fell back again onto the ottoman, feeble and weak. "Of course, I had a premonition of all this; [*Add: I agree that it had to be this way; it absolutely had to be that I should have a premonition of all this; but,*] still, how did he come to write that and what is the direct meaning of these words? Suppose I do know the meaning, but where will this lead? [*Add: My dear God! Where will all this lead?*] If he [*Delete: he Add: they*] had said straight out, 'This is just the way it is; [*Delete: ; Add: , and*] this is required and that is required,' I would have done it. [*Delete: . Add: , and I would have done something to please them, and the whole affair would have taken a turn for the better, and everyone would have been satisfied and happy.*] The twists and turns this business is taking—it's so unpleasant! Oh, if only tomorrow would come and I could get down to the matter! Now I know what to do. [*Delete . Add: ; I know very well just what I have to do now.*] 'This is the way it is,' I'll say; 'I agree to the arguments'. I will not sell my honor, but, you know . . . perhaps; how did he, that certain person, that obnoxious personage, get involved in this though? And just why did he get involved in it? Oh, if only tomorrow would come! Until then they'll give me a bad name; they're intriguing; they're trying to spite me! The most important thing is not to waste time but, for instance, to at least write a letter now and just mention thus and such and say I agree to thus and such. And send it off tomorrow as soon as it's daylight and go myself a bit earlier, you know, . . . and have a go at them from another angle and forestall them, the dear fellows . . . They'll give me a bad name and that's it!"

Mr. Golyadkin drew a piece of paper towards him, took a pen and wrote the following epistle in answer to the letter of Provincial Secretary Vakhrameyev:

Dear Nestor Ignatyevich,
    Sir!
It was with deeply sorrowful amazement that I read the insulting letter you wrote me, for I see clearly that under the name of certain unseemly persons and certain people with false good intentions you mean me. It is with genuine grief that I see how quickly, successfully and extensively slander has

spread its roots to the detriment of my prosperity, my honor and my good name. And what is all the more saddening and offensive is that even honest people with a truly noble turn of mind and, most important of all, endowed with frank and open natures, are abandoning the interests of honorable people and attaching themselves and the best qualities of their hearts to pernicious putrefaction, which unfortunately has multiplied greatly and with extreme insidiousness in the difficult and immoral times in which we live. [*Add: I am speaking in general; as far as particular persons are concerned, I consider it superfluous to mention them here, although I deem it my sacred duty to caution inexperienced and untainted innocence against pernicious monsters endowed with poisonous breath, who falsely and insincerely have taken on human form and, with an effrontery that makes the soul indignant, are passing themselves off as other persons, these latter complete outsiders living openly and nobly, taking the direct way, without a mask, with an undisguised face, scorning crooked ways and intrigues and justly proud of it.*] In conclusion I shall say that my debt of two silver rubles which you mention I consider it my sacred duty to return to you in its entirety.

As far as concerns your allusions, my dear sir, to a certain person of the female sex, to the intentions, calculations and various designs of that person, why, I shall tell you, my dear sir, that I have only dimly and vaguely comprehended all these allusions. Permit me, my dear sir, to preserve unsullied the noble turn of my mind and my honest name. But in any case I am prepared to condescend to an explanation personally, preferring the fidelity of personal contact over the written word, and, moreover, I am prepared to enter into various peaceable, and, of course, mutual, terms of agreement. To this end I beg you, my dear sir, to convey to that person my readiness to make a personal concession and, moreover, to request her to appoint the time and place of meeting. I found it galling, my dear sir, to read your allusions to my having insulted you, betrayed our pristine friendship and spoken badly of you. I ascribe all this to the misunderstanding, base calumny, envy and ill will of those whom I can justly call my most bitter enemies. But they probably do not know that innocence takes its strength from its very innocence, that the shamelessness, the brazenness, and the heart-perturbing familiarity of some persons will, sooner or later, earn for itself the stigma of universal contempt and that these persons will perish solely through their own lack of decency and through the corruptness of their hearts. In conclusion I beg you, my dear sir, to convey to these persons that their strange pretentions and ignoble and fantastic desire to oust others from the places these others occupy by their very existence in this world, and to supplant them, are worthy of amazement, contempt, pity, and, moreover, of the madhouse; that, furthermore, such attitudes are strictly prohibited by law which, in my opinion, is absolutely just, for everyone should be satisfied with his own place. Everything has its limits, and if this is a joke, then it is not in good taste. I shall go further and say: it is absolutely immoral, for I make bold to assure you, my dear sir, that my ideas, set forth above, concerning *one's place*, are purely moral.

In any case, I have the honor to remain

Your humble servant

Ya. Golyadkin.

X

1866 Redaction

In general one might say that the events of the previous day had shaken Mr. Golyadkin to the core. Our hero slept extremely badly, that is, he could in no wise fall completely asleep for even five minutes; it was as if some joker had sprinkled cut-up bristles into his bed. He spent the entire night in a sort of half-sleeping, half-waking state, tossing and turning from side to side, moaning and groaning, falling asleep for one moment and waking up again the next, and all this was accompanied by a kind of strange anguish, dim recollections, hideous apparitions— in a word, by everything unpleasant that one can possibly imagine . . . Now the figure of Andrei Filippovich would appear before him in a kind of strange, mysterious half-light—a dry figure, an angry figure, with a cold, harsh look and a coldly civil reprimand... And no sooner would Mr. Golyadkin begin to approach Andrei Filippovich to justify himself before him somehow, in this way or that, and to prove to him that he was not at all the way his enemies painted him, that he was like this or like that, and even possessed, above and beyond his usual innate qualities, this one and that one, than thereupon a certain person notorious for his unseemly inclinations would appear and he would forthwith by some means most perturbing to the soul destroy all of Mr. Golyadkin's intended undertakings; he would thereupon, almost before Mr. Golyadkin's very eyes, thoroughly blacken his reputation, trample his self-esteem in the mud and then forthwith take his place at work and in society. Or else Mr. Golyadkin's head would smart from some rap on it, recently acquired and humiliatingly accepted, received either socially or somehow in the line of duty, against which rap it was difficult to protest . . . And as Mr. Golyadkin was about to start puzzling over just why it was difficult to protest even against such a rap, this very thought about the rap would imperceptibly flow into some other form, into the form of a certain petty or rather considerably base deed seen, heard or recently committed by him, and frequently committed not even on base grounds and not even from some base motive, but just so—sometimes, for example, by chance—out of delicacy, another time because of his own complete helplessness, or, finally, because . . . because, in a word, well, Mr. Golyadkin knew very well *why*! Hereupon Mr. Golyadkin would blush in his sleep and, suppressing his blushes, would mutter to himself, saying that there, for example, one might have shown firmness of character, one might have shown considerably greater firmness of character in that instance . . . and then he would conclude by saying, "What is firmness of character? . . . Why mention it now? . . ." But what would enrage and irritate Mr. Golyadkin most of all was the fact that hereupon and without fail at such a moment, whether summoned or not, there would appear a person notorious for his disgraceful and slanderous inclinations and he would also— despite the fact that the affair now seemed notorious—he would also, thereupon, mutter with an unseemly smile, "What does firmness of character have to do with it? What firmness of character you and I will have, Yakov Petrovich!" Or else Mr. Golyadkin would dream that he was in a splendid company, famous for the wit and breeding of all the persons comprising it; that he, Mr. Golyadkin, in his turn had distinguished himself by his amiability and wit, that everyone had come to like him, even certain of his enemies who were there had come to like him, which was very pleasant for Mr. Golyadkin; that everyone acknowledged his superiority and that, finally, Mr. Golyadkin himself overheard with pleasure as his host, taking several guests aside, thereupon praised him, Mr. Golyadkin . . . and suddenly, for no reason at all, again there appeared a person notorious for his evil intentions and bestial impulses, in the form of Mr. Golyadkin Junior, and thereupon, forthwith, in an instant, solely by having made his appearance, Golyadkin

Junior destroyed all the triumph and all the glory of Mr.
Golyadkin Senior, overshadowed Golyadkin Senior, trampled
Golyadkin Senior in the mud and, finally, clearly demonstrated
that Golyadkin Senior, who was also the real Golyadkin, was
not at all the real one but a counterfeit, and that *he* was the real
one; that, finally, Golyadkin Senior was not at all what he
seemed, but a so-and-so, and consequently should not and did
not have the right to be in the society of persons who were well-
intentioned and well-bred. And all of this happened so quickly
that Mr. Golyadkin Senior did not even have time to open his
mouth before everyone went over completely to the disgraceful
and counterfeit Mr. Golyadkin and with the deepest scorn
renounced him, the real and innocent Mr. Golyadkin. There
was not one person whose opinion the bestial Mr. Golyadkin
would not have altered in an instant to his own way of thinking.
There was not one person, even the most insignificant of the
entire company, whom the worthless and false Mr. Golyadkin
would not fawn over in his own, most saccharine manner, not
one person with whom he would not attempt to ingratiate
himself in his own way, not one person before whom he would
not burn, according to his wont, the most pleasant and sweet-
smelling incense, so that the person who was enveloped in its
smoke would simply sniff and sneeze till the tears came, in
token of his supreme pleasure. And the main thing was that all
this would happen in an instant: the swiftness of the suspect and
worthless Mr. Golyadkin's progress was astonishing! He would
hardly succeed, for example, in currying favor with one person,
in getting into his good graces, than before you could blink an
eye, he would already be attempting to do so with another. He
would quietly work away currying favor with another, gain
from him a smile of good will, give a flick of his short little,
round little, though rather clumsy little leg, and there he would
be with a third; and now he is making advances to the third,
fawning over him in a friendly manner; one has not even had
time to open one's mouth, one has not even had time to be
amazed, when already he is with a fourth and already on those
same terms with the fourth; horrors—witchcraft and nothing
else! And everyone is glad to see him, and everyone likes

him, and everyone exalts him, and everyone proclaims in chorus that the amiability and satiric bent of his mind is by far superior to the amiability and satiric bent of the real Mr. Golyadkin's mind, and they thereby put to shame the real and innocent Mr. Golyadkin, and reject the truthloving Mr. Golyadkin, and now they are rudely pushing the well-intentioned Mr. Golyadkin and delivering raps to the real Mr. Golyadkin, so well-known for his love of his neighbor! . . . In anguish, terror, and rage, the much-suffering Mr. Golyadkin ran out onto the street and began trying to hire a cab, so that he could fly straight to His Excellency's or, if not there, then at least to Andrei Filippovich's, but—horrors! The cabman would in no wise agree to take Mr. Golyadkin, saying, "Sir, we cannot take two people who look exactly alike; Your Worship, a good man strives to live honestly, not just any old way, and he never has a double." In an outburst of shame, the completely honest Mr. Golyadkin would look around and really assure himself, with his own eyes, that the cabmen and Petrushka, who was conspiring with them, were all indeed right; for the corrupt Mr. Golyadkin would, in fact, be there close beside him, and in accordance with his base traits of character, would even at this point, even at this critical moment, undeniably be preparing to do something utterly unseemly and not at all indicative of the particular nobility of character that is usually acquired in the course of one's upbringing—a nobility which at every convenient opportunity the repulsive Mr. Golyadkin the Second lauded himself for having. Beside himself with shame and despair, the ruined though completely legitimate Mr. Golyadkin fled blindly, giving himself up to the will of fate, regardless of where it might lead him; but with every step he took, with every thud of his foot against the granite of the pavement there would spring up, out of the ground, an exact likeness of the repulsive Mr. Golyadkin with his corruptness of heart. And all of these exact likenesses, immediately upon making their appearance, began running one after the other and stretched out in a long chain like a string of geese, waddling after Mr. Golyadkin Senior, so that there was nowhere to escape to from these exact likenesses; so that Mr. Golyadkin, who was in every way possible deserving of pity, was breathless with fear; so that finally a terrible host of exact likenesses had sprung into being; so that the entire capital was clogged with exact likenesses and a policeman, seeing such a breach of propriety, was forced to take all of these exact likenesses by the scruff of the neck and imprison them in a police booth that happened to be just beside him . . . Frozen and numb with fear, our hero was waking up, and, frozen and numb with fear, he was feeling that his waking hours were hardly more cheerful . . . He felt oppressed and tormented . . . An anguish that seemed as though someone were consuming his heart out of his breast began to come over him . . .

Finally Mr. Golyadkin could bear it no longer. "It shall not be!" he shouted, raising himself up in bed with determination and waking up altogether after this exclamation.

The day was evidently well under way. It was unusually bright in the room; the sun's rays filtered densely through the frost-covered panes and spilled profusely about the room, which astonished Mr. Golyadkin more than a little; for after all it was only at noon that the sun peeped into his room in its normal round; there had almost never been such exceptions in the course of the heavenly body before, at least not insofar as Mr. Golyadkin himself could recall. Our hero had no sooner marvelled at this than the wall clock behind the partition began to whir as if it were going to strike. "Ah, there it goes!" thought Mr. Golyadkin and anxiously and apprehensively prepared to listen . . . But to Mr. Golyadkin's utter and final frustration, his clock strained itself and struck only once. "What's going on here?" our hero cried, jumping out of bed altogether. Without dressing, just as he was, he rushed behind the partition, not believing his ears. The clock really did say one. Mr. Golyadkin glanced at Petrushka's bed, but there wasn't even the least hint of Petrushka anywhere in the room: his bed had evidently been made up for some time now and left; his shoes were also gone— an unmistakeable sign that Petrushka really was not home. Mr. Golyadkin rushed to the door; it was locked. "Why, where can Petrushka be?" he continued in a whisper, overcome with intense excitement and feeling a rather considerable trembling in all his limbs . . . Suddenly a thought flashed through his mind

. . . Mr. Golyadkin rushed to his desk, surveyed it, and rummaged about—just as he thought: his letter of the day before to Vakhrameyev was not there . . . Petrushka was also nowhere behind the partition; it said one on the wall clock, while in Vakhrameyev's letter of the day before some new points had been introduced which, though they had at first glance been extremely obscure, had now become perfectly clear. Finally, Petrushka, too—Petrushka had obviously been bribed! Yes, yes, that was it!

"So that's where the main plot was being hatched!" cried Mr. Golyadkin, striking his forehead and opening his eyes wider and wider. "So, it's in the den of that stingy German that all the main forces of darkness are hiding now! So, it must be that she was only creating a strategic diversion when she directed me to the Izmailovsky Bridge; she was distracting my attention; she was confusing me (the good-for-nothing witch!) and that's how she was undermining me!!! Yes, that's it! If only one looks at the matter from this aspect, then that's exactly how it all is! And the appearance of that utter heel can also be explained completely now: so it's all connected. They've been keeping him in reserve for a long time now, getting him ready and saving him for a rainy day. Why, that's how it is now, how it has all turned out! That's how it has all been resolved! Ah, well, it doesn't matter! No time has been lost so far! . . ." At this point Mr. Golyadkin recalled with horror that it was already going on two. "What if they have succeeded by now in . . ." A groan escaped from his breast . . . "But, of course not; they're lying; they haven't succeeded—we'll see . . ." Somehow he got dressed, seized a piece of paper and a pen and scribbled the following epistle:

Dear Yakov Petrovich,
Sir!
Either you or I, but not the two of us! And therefore I am declaring to you that your strange, ludicrous and at the same time impossible desire to seem to be my twin and to pass yourself off as such will only lead to your utter dishonor and defeat. And

therefore I beg you, for the sake of your own good, to withdraw and make way for people who are truly honorable and well-intentioned. If not, I am prepared to decide on the most extreme measures. I lay down my pen and wait . . . However, I remain ready to render service or—satisfaction.

Ya. Golyadkin

Our hero rubbed his hands together energetically when he had finished the note. Then, pulling on his overcoat and putting on his hat, he unlocked his apartment with another, spare key and set out for the office. He went as far as the office, but could not resolve whether to enter; actually, by now it was too late; Mr. Golyadkin's watch showed half past two. Suddenly an apparently extremely trivial occurrence dispelled certain of Mr. Golyadkin's doubts: from behind the corner of the office building a breathless and red-faced figure suddenly appeared and with a stealthy, ratlike gait darted up the entrance steps and then immediately into the vestibule. It was the copyist, Ostafyev, a person very well known to Mr. Golyadkin, a person who was quite useful and ready to do anything for ten kopeks. Knowing Ostafyev's weak spot and realizing that after an absence due to most urgent business he had probably become even more avid than before for ten-kopek coins, our hero determined not to begrudge them and immediately darted up the entrance steps and then also into the vestibule after Ostafyev, called to him, and with a mysterious air invited him to step over into a secluded corner behind an enormous iron stove. Once there our hero began to interrogate him.

"Well, now, my friend, how are things, you know . . . do you understand what I mean? . . ."

"At your service, Your Worship; I wish Your Worship good health."

"All right, my friend, all right; but I shall show my gratitude to you, dear friend. Well, look now, how is it, my friend?"

"What is it that you would like to ask about, sir?" Here Ostafyev put his hand up to his mouth, which had inadvertently fallen open, and tried to close it somewhat.

"Well, I, look, my friend, I, you know... now don't you go thinking anything... Well, now, is Andrei Filippovich here?..."

"He's here, sir."

"And are the clerks here?"

"Yes, the clerks too, sir, as they should be, sir."

"And His Excellency, too?"

"Yes, His Excellency too, sir." Here the copyist once more put his hand up to close his mouth, which had again fallen open, and looked at Mr. Golyadkin somewhat curiously and strangely. At least so it seemed to our hero.

"And there's nothing special, my friend?"

"No, sir; not at all, sir."

"Have you heard anything about me, my friend? Any little thing, eh? Just maybe, my friend; do you understand what I mean?"

"No, sir, nothing yet." Here the copyist again put his hand up to close his mouth and again looked somewhat strangely at Mr. Golyadkin. The fact of the matter is that now our hero was trying to penetrate Ostafyev's countenance, to read something in it, to see whether he wasn't hiding something. And actually, it seemed as if he was hiding something; the fact of the matter is that somehow Ostafyev was becoming more and more rude and cold and was now less sympathetic to Mr. Golyadkin's interests than he had been at the start of their conversation. "He is partly within his rights," thought Mr. Golyadkin. "After all, what am I to him? Perhaps he has already received something from the other side, and that's why he has been absent due to most urgent business. And so I'll take a chance and give him something . . ." Mr. Golyadkin realized that the time for handing out ten-kopek pieces had come.

"Here, this is for you, dear friend . . ."

"I'm most deeply grateful to Your Worship."

"I'll give you even more."

"Yes, sir, Your Worship."

"I'll give you even more in just a moment and when this business is over I'll give you as much again. Understand?"

The copyist said nothing, stood at attention, and looked fixedly at Mr. Golyadkin.

"Well, tell me now: have you heard anything about me? . . ."

"So far it seems . . . you know, sir . . . so far there's nothing, sir." Ostafyev responded slowly and deliberately, also putting on, like Mr. Golyadkin, a somewhat mysterious air, wiggling his eyebrows slightly, looking at the ground, trying to find the right tone and, in a word, attempting with all his might to earn what had been promised him because he considered that what he had been given was already his and his in no uncertain terms.

"And hasn't anything been made known?"

"No, not yet, sir."

"But, listen . . . you know . . . perhaps it will be made known?"

"Later, of course, perhaps it will be made known, sir."

"It's bad!" thought our hero.

"Listen, here's some more, old chap."

"I'm most deeply grateful to Your Worship."

"Was Vakhrameyev here yesterday? . . ."

"He was, sir."

"And wasn't there someone else? . . . Try to remember, old chap."

The copyist searched his memory for a moment but could recall nothing appropriate.

"No, sir; there wasn't anyone else, sir."

"Hm!" Silence ensued.

"Listen, old chap, here's some more for you. Tell me everything down to the last detail."

"Yes, sir." Now Ostafyev stood there as meek as a lamb: this was what Mr. Golyadkin wanted.

"Explain to me now, old chap; what sort of a footing is he on?"

"All right, sir; a good one, sir," responded the copyist, staring wide-eyed at Mr. Golyadkin.

"What do you mean 'a good one'?"

"Just that, sir." Here Ostafyev wiggled his eyebrows significantly. However, he was decidedly coming to a dead end and did not know what else to say. "It's bad!" thought Mr. Golyadkin.

"Hasn't there been anything more concerning Vakhrameyev?"

"Why, no, everything is the same as it was, sir."

"Try and think."

"There is, they say, sir."

"Well, and what is it?"

Ostafyev put his hand up to his mouth.

"Isn't there a letter from there to me?"

"Today the guard, Mikheyev, went to Vakhrameyev's apartment, to his German landlady there, sir. So I'll go and ask, if you want."

"Be so kind, old chap, for God's sake! . . . I'm just . . . Don't you go thinking anything, old chap; I'm just asking. Go and make inquiries, old chap; find out whether they're cooking something up on my account. What is *he* doing? That's what I need to know. Now you find *that* out, dear friend, and I shall show my gratitude to you later, dear friend . . ."

"Yes, sir, Your Worship, and Ivan Semyonych sat in your place today, sir."

"Ivan Semyonych? Ah, yes! Really?"

"Andrei Filippovich told him to sit there, sir . . ."

"Really? For what reason? Find that out, old chap; for God's sake, find that out, old chap. Find it all out—and I shall show my gratitude to you, my dear fellow; that's what I need . . . But don't you go thinking anything, old chap . . ."

"Yes, sir, yes, sir. I'll come right back down here, sir. But, Your Worship, aren't you coming in today?"

"No, my friend. I just happened to come by; why, I just happened to; I only came to have a look, dear friend, but I shall show my gratitude to you later, my dear fellow."

"Yes, sir." The copyist ran quickly and eagerly up the stairs and Mr. Golyadkin was left alone.

"It's bad," he thought. "Dear, it's bad, bad! Oh, my case . . . is really pretty bad now! What was the meaning of it all? Just what did certain of that drunkard's allusions mean, for example, and who's doing is this? Ah! Now I know who's doing this is. Here's what's going on. They most likely found out and then they put him . . . But, why am I saying—*they* put? It was Andrei Filippovich who put him, put Ivan Semyonovich in my place. But why did he put him in my place and just what was his purpose in doing it? They probably found out . . . This is Vakhrameyev's work, I mean, not Vakhrameyev's—he's as stupid as a post, that Vakhrameyev. It's all of them who are working on his behalf and who have also put that scoundrel up to coming here for the same purpose. And the German complained, that one-eyed witch! I always suspected that all this intriguing had more to it than meets the eye and that there surely had to be something in all those old-wives' tales and that old-biddy gossip. I even told Krestyan Ivanovich as much; 'They've sworn to murder a person, speaking in the moral sense,' I said, 'and they've seized upon Karolina Ivanovna.' No, experts are at work here, it's obvious! The hand of a master is at work here, sir, and not Vakhrameyev's. I've already said Vakhrameyev is stupid, but this . . . Now I know who's working here on their behalf: that scoundrel, that imposter is! On the basis of this alone he makes his way, which also partly explains his success in high society. But actually it might be well to know what sort of footing he's on now . . . where does he stand with them? But why ever did they take on Ivan Semyonovich? What the devil did they need Ivan Semyonovich for? As if they couldn't find anyone else. Still, no matter who they put in my place, it would all have been just the same. All I know is that I have suspected that Ivan Semyonovich for a long time; I noticed a long time ago what he was like: such a nasty little old fellow, so vile—they say he lends money and charges interest rates as high as any Jew. But the bear is responsible for putting all this together. The bear is involved in this whole affair. That's how it started. It started at the Izmaylovsky Bridge; that's how it started . . ." Here Mr. Golyadkin puckered up his face as though he had bitten into a lemon, probably because he had recalled something highly unpleasant. "Well, it doesn't matter anyway!" he thought. "But here I am going on about my own affairs. Why doesn't Ostafyev come? He probably settled down to some work or got held up somehow. Why, to some extent it's even a good thing that I am carrying on an intrigue in this way and engaging in some undermining of my own. All I have to do is give Ostafyev ten kopeks and he's, you know . . . he's on my side. Only here's the point: is he really on my side? Perhaps the other side has been getting at him too . . . and they have an agreement with him and are carrying on an intrigue. Why, he has the look of a villain, the fraud, a veritable villain! He's hiding something, the rogue! 'No, nothing', he says, and 'I am most deeply', he says, 'grateful to you', he says, 'Your Worship.' What a villain you are!"

There was a noise . . . Mr. Golyadkin hunched himself up and leapt behind the stove. Someone came down the stairway and went out into the street. "Who would be leaving now?" our hero thought to himself. A moment later other footsteps could be heard . . . At this point Mr. Golyadkin could not restrain himself and poked just the tip of his nose ever so slightly out from behind his bulwark—poked it out and immediately pulled back as though someone had pricked it with a pin. This time you-know-who was going by, that is, the rogue, intriguer, and profligate was going by, with his usual vile small step, mincing along and throwing his feet out as though getting ready to kick someone. "Scoundrel!" uttered our hero to himself. However, Mr. Golyadkin could not help noticing that the scoundrel had under his arm an enormous green portfolio belonging to His Excellency. "There he goes again on a special assignment," thought Mr. Golyadkin, flushing, and hunching himself up even more than before in vexation. Hardly had Mr. Golyadkin Junior flashed by Mr. Golyadkin Senior without noticing him in the least than someone's footsteps were heard for the third time and this time Mr. Golyadkin guessed that these footsteps were the copyist's. Indeed, the sleeked-down figure of a copyist peeped in at him, behind the stove; it was not, however, Ostafyev's figure, but that of another copyist, Pisarenko by name. This astounded Mr. Golyadkin. "Why is it that he has let others in on the secret?" thought our hero. "What barbarians! They hold nothing sacred!"

"Well, what is it, my friend?" he uttered, turning to Pisarenko. "Who sent you, my friend? . . ."

"I've come, sir, on the matter of your business, sir. For the time being there isn't any news from anyone, sir. But if there is, we'll inform you, sir."

"What about Ostafyev? . . ."

"Oh, he can't come at all, Your Worship, sir. His Excellency has walked through the division twice already and I, too, have no time now."

"Thank you, my dear fellow, thank you . . . But just tell me . . ."

"Really and truly, I have no time, sir . . . He's constantly asking for us, sir . . . But if you would please to stand here a while longer, sir, then if there should be anything concerning your case, sir, then we'll inform you, sir . . ."

"No, my friend, you just tell me . . ."

"Excuse me, sir; I have no time, sir," said Pisarenko, pulling away from Mr. Golyadkin, who had grabbed hold of the front of his jacket. "I really can't. You be so kind as to stand here a while longer, sir, and we'll inform you."

"Just a moment, just a moment, my friend! Just a moment, dear friend! Now this is what I ask: here's a letter, my friend, and I'll show my gratitude to you, my dear fellow."

"Yes, sir."

"Try and give it to Mr. Golyadkin, my dear fellow."

"To Golyadkin?"

"Yes, my friend, to Mr. Golyadkin."

"All right, sir. As soon as I can get away, I'll deliver it, sir. And in the meantime you stand here. No one will see you here . . ."

"No, I . . . my friend, don't you go thinking . . . why, I'm not standing here so that no one will see me. But I'm not going to be here now, my friend . . . I'll be right there in the sidestreet. There's a coffee house there; and I shall be waiting there, and, if anything happens, you inform me about everything. Understand?"

"Fine, sir. Just let me go. I understand . . ."

"And I shall show my gratitude to you, my dear fellow!" Mr. Golyadkin shouted after Pisarenko, who had finally freed himself . . . "The scoundrel seemed to get ruder after a while," thought our hero, furtively coming out from behind the stove. "There's a further twist here. That's clear . . . At first it was one thing and another . . . Still, he really was in a hurry. Perhaps there *is* a great deal of work. And His Excellency has been through the division twice . . . What could be the occasion for that? . . . Ugh! Well, never mind! Still, perhaps it's nothing, but now we shall see . . ."

At this point Mr. Golyadkin was going to open the door and wanted to go out into the street, when suddenly at that very instant His Excellency's coach thundered up to the entrance. Mr. Golyadkin barely had time to recover from the shock when the coach door was opened from within, and the gentleman sitting inside jumped out onto the front steps. The passenger was none other than that same Mr. Golyadkin Junior who had left some ten minutes before. Mr. Golyadkin Senior recalled that the director's apartment was only a few steps away. "He's on a special assignment," our hero thought to himself. In the meantime Mr. Golyadkin Junior, after taking a bulging green portfolio and some other papers out of the coach and finally giving some instructions to the coachman, opened the door, almost hitting Mr. Golyadkin Senior with it and, deliberately taking no notice of him just to spite him, set off at a run up the office stairway. "It's bad!" thought Mr. Golyadkin; "Oh, dear, so that's the turn my case has taken now! Oh, dear God, look at him, will you!" Our hero stood motionless for half a minute longer; finally, he made up his mind. Not giving it much thought, but feeling a powerful trepidation in his heart and a trembling in all his limbs, he ran up the stairs after his friend.

"Ah! Here goes! What do I care? I'm not a party to this matter," he thought, taking off his hat, overcoat and galoshes in the anteroom.

When Mr. Golyadkin entered his division, dusk had already fallen completely. Neither Andrei Filippovich nor Anton Antonovich was in the room. They were both in the Director's office, handing in reports; the Director, as rumor had it, was in turn in a hurry to report to his superior. As a result of these circumstances and also because the dusk contributed to it and office hours were ending, some of the clerks, chiefly the younger ones, were, at the very moment that our hero entered, engaged in some form of idleness; they were gathering together, conversing, discussing and laughing, and some of the youngest ones, that is, some of those with the lowest rank, were even secretly and under cover of the general hubbub playing pitch-and-toss in a corner by the window. Cognizant of what constitutes proper behavior and feeling at the present moment a particular need to purchase and find favor, Mr. Golyadkin immediately went up to those with whom he was on better terms to wish them good day and so forth. But his colleagues responded somewhat strangely to Mr. Golyadkin's greeting. He was unpleasantly struck by a general coldness, dryness, one might even say, severity in their reception of him. No one shook hands with him. Some simply said, "Hello" and walked away; others merely nodded; a few simply turned away and pretended that they hadn't noticed anything; finally, some—and what was most offensive of all to Mr. Golyadkin, some of the young ones with the lowest ranks, boys who, as Mr. Golyadkin had rightly expressed himself concerning them, knew only how to play pitch-and-toss when the occasion arose and gad about—gradually surrounded Mr. Golyadkin, forming a group about him and almost cutting off his escape. All of them looked at him with a kind of insulting curiosity.

It was a bad sign. Mr. Golyadkin sensed this and was for his part prudently prepared to ignore it. Suddenly a quite unexpected occurrence completely finished Mr. Golyadkin, as they say, and made him utterly desolate.

In the small group of young colleagues surrounding him, suddenly and as if deliberately, at what was Mr. Golyadkin's most anguished moment, there appeared Mr. Golyadkin Junior, jovial as always, with a little smile as always, overvivacious, too, as always; in a word, playing pranks, cavorting about, fawning, guffawing, quick with his tongue and quick on his feet, as always, as before, just as he had been yesterday, for example, at a moment that had been most unpleasant for Mr. Golyadkin Senior. Grinning, whirling about, mincing along, with his little smile that so clearly said, "Good evening" to everyone, he pushed his way into the little group of clerks, shook this one's hand, clapped that one on the shoulder, lightly embraced another, explained to a fourth exactly on what business His Excellency had sent him, where he had gone, what he had done, what he had brought back with him; to a fifth and most likely his best friend he gave a smacking kiss right on the lips—in a word, everything was happening exactly as it had in Mr. Golyadkin Senior's dream. After cavorting his fill, dealing with each one in his own inimitable way, disposing them all favorably towards himself, whether he needed to or not, and sucking up to all of them to his heart's content, Mr. Golyadkin Junior suddenly, and probably by mistake, because he had failed up to that point to notice his oldest friend, held his hand out to Mr. Golyadkin Senior as well. Probably also by mistake, although, however, he had by no means failed to take full notice of the ignoble Mr. Golyadkin Junior, our hero thereupon eagerly seized the hand which had been extended to him so unexpectedly and shook it in the firmest and friendliest manner, shook it with a strange, totally unexpected inner stirring and a weepy feeling. Whether our hero was deceived by his unseemly enemy's first move, whether he was simply at a loss to know what to do, or whether he sensed and acknowledged in the depths of his soul the full extent of his helplessness is difficult to say. The fact remains that Mr. Golyadkin Senior, being of sound mind and body, did of his own free will and in the presence of witnesses, solemnly shake the hand of one whom he called his mortal enemy. But what was the amazement, frenzy and rage, what was the horror and shame of Mr. Golyadkin Senior, when his foe and mortal enemy, the ignoble Mr. Golyadkin Junior, on noticing the mistake of the persecuted, innocent person whom he had so perfidiously deceived, without shame, without feeling, without compassion or conscience, and with intolerable effrontery and crudity, suddenly tore his hand out of Mr. Golyadkin Senior's hand; as if that were not enough, he flicked his hand as though he had soiled it with something quite awful; as if that were not enough, he spat to one side, accompanying all this with the most insulting gesture; and as if that were not enough, he took out his handkerchief and thereupon, in the most excessive manner, wiped all of the fingers that had for a moment lain in Mr. Golyadkin Senior's hand. While doing this, Mr. Golyadkin Junior, as was his vile wont, deliberately looked about, making sure that everyone should see what he was doing, looked everyone in the eye, and obviously tried to convey to everyone all that was most unfavorable about Mr. Golyadkin. The behavior of the revolting Mr. Golyadkin Junior seemed to arouse the general indignation of the clerks surrounding them; even the flighty young people showed their displeasure. A grumbling and murmuring arose on all sides. The general stir could not fail to reach the ears of Mr. Golyadkin Senior; but suddenly an apropos little joke occurred to Mr. Golyadkin Junior and erupted from his lips, smashing and destroying our hero's last hopes and tipping the balance again in favor of his mortal and worthless enemy.

"This is our Russian Faublas, gentlemen; permit me to introduce the young Faublas," piped Mr. Golyadkin Junior, mincing and whirling about among the clerks with his customary brazenness, and pointing out to them the benumbed but infuriated real Mr. Golyadkin. "Let's give each other a kiss, duckie!" he continued with intolerable familiarity, moving toward the person he had so perfidiously insulted. The worthless Mr. Golyadkin Junior's little joke, it seems, found a ready response, the moreso since it contained an insidious allusion to an incident which evidently had already been made public and was known to everyone. Our hero felt the hand of his enemies heavy upon him. However, he had already made a resolve. With a burning look, pale face, and a fixed smile he somehow made his way out of the crowd and with uneven, quickened steps set his course straight for His Excellency's office. In the room just before it he was met by Andrei Filippovich, who had just emerged from seeing His Excellency, and although there was a sizeable number of all sorts of other persons in the room at that moment who were complete strangers to Mr. Golyadkin, still our hero did not wish to pay any attention to this fact. Directly, resolutely, boldly, almost surprised at himself and yet lauding himself inwardly for his boldness, losing no time, he assailed

Andrei Filippovich, who was quite amazed at such an unexpected assault.

"Ah! What do you . . . What do you want?" asked the division chief, not listening to the stammering Mr. Golyadkin.

"Andrei Filippovich, I . . . may I have a conversation with His Excellency, Andrei Filippovich, now, right now and in private?" uttered our hero, volubly and distinctly, while casting a most determined look at Andrei Filippovich.

"What, sir? Of course not, sir." Andrei Filippovich measured Mr. Golyadkin from head to foot with his glance.

"Andrei Filippovich, I'm saying all this because I am amazed that no one here unmasks the impostor and scoundrel."

"Wha-a-at, sir?"

"Scoundrel, Andrei Filippovich."

"And just whom are you pleased to speak of thus?"

"Of a certain person, Andrei Filippovich. I am alluding to a certain person, Andrei Filippovich; I am within my rights . . . I think, Andrei Filippovich, that our superiors should encourage such action," added Mr. Golyadkin, obviously beside himself; "Andrei Filippovich . . . you probably see yourself, Andrei Filippovich, that this noble action signifies that I have every good intention of accepting our superior as a father, Andrei Filippovich. 'I accept our beneficent superior as a father,' I say, 'and blindly entrust my fate to him. This is the way it is,' I say . . . 'that's how it is . . .' " Here Mr. Golyadkin's voice began to quaver, his face turned red, and two tears gathered on his eyelashes.

Andrei Filippovich was so astonished at what Mr. Golyadkin had said that he involuntarily took a couple steps back. Then he looked about uneasily . . . It is difficult to say how the matter would have ended . . . But suddenly the door of His Excellency's office opened and he himself emerged, accompanied by several other officials. Everyone in the room trailed after him. His Excellency called Andrei Filippovich and began to walk along with him, conversing about some matters of business. When everyone had moved off and left the room, Mr. Golyadkin came to his senses. Calming down, he took refuge under the wing of Anton Antonovich Setochkin, who in turn was hobbling along

144

behind everyone else and, so it seemed to Mr. Golyadkin, had a most severe and preoccupied look on his face. "I've just talked a lot of nonsense and made a mess again," he thought to himself; "well, it doesn't matter."

"I hope that at least you, Anton Antonovich, will agree to hear me out and understand my situation," he uttered quietly in a voice still trembling slightly from agitation. "Cast aside by everyone, I turn to you. I am still at a loss to understand what Andrei Filippovich's words meant, Anton Antonovich. Explain them to me, if you can . . ."

"Everything will be explained in good time, sir," answered Anton Antonovich severely and without haste, and, so it seemed to Mr. Golyadkin, with a look which clearly gave to understand that Anton Antonovich did not at all wish to continue the conversation. "You will shortly know everything, sir. This very day you will be officially informed of everything."

"What do you mean by officially, Anton Antonovich? Just why will it be officially, sir?" asked our hero timidly.

"It's not for you and me to reason why our superiors decide as they do, Yakov Petrovich."

"But why our superiors, Anton Antonovich," uttered Mr. Golyadkin, feeling even more timid, "why our superiors? I don't see why it's necessary to bother our superiors, Anton Antonovich . . . Perhaps you mean something to do with what happened yesterday, Anton Antonovich?"

"Oh, no, sir; not yesterday, sir; there's something else that leaves much to be desired where you're concerned, sir."

"What leaves much to be desired, Anton Antonovich? It seems to me, Anton Antonovich, there's nothing that leaves much to be desired where I'm concerned."

"And whom were you planning to be crafty with?" Anton Antonovich sharply cut short the absolutely dumbfounded Mr. Golyadkin. Mr. Golyadkin shuddered and turned white as a sheet.

"Of course, Anton Antonovich," he uttered in a barely audible voice, "if one heeds the voice of slander and listens to a person's enemies without hearing the justification offered by the other side, then, of course . . . of course, Anton Antonovich,

145

then a person can suffer for it, Anton Antonovich, suffer innocently and for nothing."

"Just so, sir; but what about that unseemly performance of yours that hurt the reputation of an honorable young lady from that beneficent, esteemed and well-known family that was so good to you?"

"What performance is that, Anton Antonovich?"

"Just so, sir; and as far as another young lady is concerned, who although poor is nevertheless of honest foreign extraction, you don't know what admirable deed you performed there either, sir?"

"Permit me, Anton Antonovich . . . do me the kindness, Anton Antonovich, of hearing me out . . ."

"And your perfidious behavior and slander of another person—your accusing another of what you are guilty of yourself? Eh? What do you call that?"

"I did not chase him out, Anton Antonovich," uttered our hero, all aflutter, "nor did I instruct Petrushka, that is, my servant, to do anything of the sort, sir . . . He ate my bread, Anton Antonovich; he enjoyed my hospitality," our hero added so expressively and with such deep feeling that his chin began to tremble slightly and the tears were ready to come again.

"You're just saying that, Yakov Petrovich, that he ate your bread," answered Anton Antonovich, grinning, and a slyness could be heard in his voice that made Mr. Golyadkin's heart ache.

"Permit me most humbly to ask you something else, Anton Antonovich: does His Excellency know all about this matter?"

"Of course, sir! But do let me go now, sir. I have no time for you now . . . This very day you'll find out about everything you need to know, sir."

"Stay just a minute longer, Anton Antonovich, for God's sake . . ."

"You can tell me later, sir . . ."

"No, Anton Antonovich, sir; I, sir . . . you see, sir . . . just listen, Anton Antonovich . . . This isn't at all freethinking on my

146

part, Anton Antonovich; I shun freethinking; I'm quite prepared for my part and have even expressed the idea that . . ."

"All right, sir, all right. I've already heard it, sir . . ."

"No, sir, you haven't heard it, Anton Antonovich. This is something else, Anton Antonovich. This is good, really good, and pleasant to hear . . . I have expressed, as I explained before, Anton Antonovich, the idea that Divine Providence created two absolutely identical beings, and that our beneficent superiors, seeing that it was Divine Providence, took the two twins to their bosom, sir. This is good, Anton Antonovich. You can see that this is very good, Anton Antonovich, and that I am far from being a freethinker. Our beneficent superior is like a father to me. 'This is the way it is,' I say 'our beneficent superior, and you, you know' . . . I say . . . 'a young man must have work' . . . Back me up, Anton Antonovich; intercede for me, Anton Antonovich . . . I don't mean anything, sir . . . Anton Antonovich, for God's sake, just one little word more . . . Anton Antonovich . . ."

But Anton Antonovich was already far away from Mr. Golyadkin . . . Our hero did not know where he was standing, what he was hearing, what he was doing, what had happened to him, and what more was going to happen to him—because everything he had heard and everything that had happened to him had so confused and shaken him.

With a beseeching look he sought out Anton Antonovich in the crowd of clerks in order to justify himself still further in his eyes and tell him something extremely well-intentioned and quite honorable and pleasant about himself . . . However, little by little, a new light was beginning to break through the confusion of Mr. Golyadkin's mind, a new and terrible light that revealed suddenly and at once an entire perspective of circumstances hitherto completely unknown and totally unsuspected . . . At that moment someone gave our utterly disconcerted hero a poke in the ribs. He looked around. Before him stood Pisarenko.

"A letter, Your Honor, sir."

"Ah! . . . You've already been there, my dear fellow?"

147

"No, it was brought here this morning at ten o'clock, sir. Sergey Mikheyev, the guard, brought it from Provincial Secretary Vakhrameyev's apartment, sir."

"All right, my friend, all right. I shall show my gratitude to you, my dear fellow."

Saying this, Mr. Golyadkin put the letter away in the side pocket of his jacket and buttoned it all the way up; then he looked around and, to his amazement, noticed that he was already in the vestibule among a little group of clerks that had clustered at the exit, for office hours had ended. Up until then Mr. Golyadkin had not only failed to notice this last circumstance, but had also failed to notice and could not remember how he had suddenly come to be wearing his overcoat and galoshes and to be holding his hat in his hands. All the clerks were standing motionless in respectful expectation. The fact of the matter is that His Excellency had stopped at the bottom of the stairs and while waiting for his carriage, which for some reason had been delayed, was carrying on a highly interesting conversation with two councilors and Andrei Filippovich. A short distance from the two councilors and Andrei Filippovich stood Anton Antonovich Setochkin and some other clerks, who, seeing that His Excellency was pleased to joke and laugh, were smiling broadly. The clerks clustered at the top of the stairs were also smiling and waiting for His Excellency to laugh again. The only one who was not smiling was Fedoseyich, the potbellied doorman, who stood stiffly at attention holding the door handle and awaiting with impatience that portion of his daily pleasure which consisted in suddenly flinging one half of the double doors wide open with a single sweep of his arm, and then bowing low and respectfully letting His Excellency pass. But the one who obviously was gladdest of all and felt the most pleasure was Mr. Golyadkin's unworthy and ignoble enemy. At that moment he even forgot all the clerks and even left off flitting and mincing about among them, as was his vile wont; he even forgot to take advantage of the opportunity to fawn over anyone at that moment. He was all eyes and ears, and scrunching himself up somewhat oddly—probably in order to hear better— never took his eyes off His Excellency; and only occasionally did his arms, legs and head give a barely noticeable twitch, betraying all the innermost, hidden stirrings of his soul.

"See how excited he is by it!" thought our hero; "he looks the favorite, the rogue! I'd like to know—what is it that makes him get on in well-bred society? No brains, no character, no education, no feeling; the rascal is lucky! Dear God! Why, how fast a person can get on, when you think of it, and ingratiate himself with everyone! And the man will go far; I give my oath that he'll go far, the rascal; he'll make it—the rascal is lucky! I'd also like to know—just what is it that he keeps whispering to them all? What sort of mysterious things is he concocting with all these people and what sort of secrets are they talking about? Dear God! If only I could . . . you know . . . and if only I could talk with them a bit, too . . . I'd say, 'This is the way it is' . . . perhaps I should ask him . . . I'd say, 'This is the way it is, but I won't do it any more'; I'd say, 'I'm to blame, but a young man, Your Excellency, has to work these days; I'm not at all embarrassed by my obscure situation.' That's how it is! I won't protest in any way either, but will bear everything with patience and humility—that's what I'll do! Is this really the way to proceed? . . . You'll never get through to him, the rascal; no words penetrate; you can't pound any sense into his unruly head . . . Still, we'll try. I may happen to find an opportune moment and then I'll try . . ."

Feeling in his agitation, anguish and confusion that he could not go on this way, that the decisive moment was approaching and that he simply had to come to an understanding with someone, our hero was about to begin moving gradually toward the spot where his unworthy and mysterious friend was standing; but just then His Excellency's long-awaited carriage came rumbling up to the entrance. Fedoseyich jerked open the door and, bowing as low as low could be, let His Excellency pass. All those who had been waiting at once surged to the exit and for a moment separated Mr. Golyadkin Senior from Mr. Golyadkin Junior. "You won't get away!" said our hero, forcing his way through the crowd and keeping his eyes pinned on his man. At last the crowd gave way. Our hero felt he was free and dashed off in pursuit of his foe.

XI

Mr. Golyadkin's breathing became labored. He sped as if on wings after his rapidly retreating foe. He felt within him the presence of enormous energy. However, despite the presence of this enormous energy, Mr. Golyadkin could be perfectly confident that at that moment even a mere mosquito, if only it had been able to live in Petersburg in such a season, could very easily have knocked him over with one wing. He felt furthermore that his strength had flagged and that he had become utterly weak, that he was being borne along by a completely separate and external force, that he was moving not of his own volition, but that, on the contrary, his legs were giving way beneath him and refusing to function. Still, it all might turn out for the best. "For the best—not for the best," thought Mr. Golyadkin, almost breathless from running so fast, "but that the case has been lost, of that there is not the slightest doubt now; that I am completely done for is certain and has been signed, sealed and delivered." Despite all this, it was as if our hero had been resurrected from the dead, had weathered the battle and seized the victory, when he succeeded in laying hold of the overcoat of his foe, who was already placing one foot on the step of a droshky, with the driver of which he had just contracted to be taken somewhere. "Sir! Sir!" he shouted to the ignoble Mr. Golyadkin Junior, whom he had finally overtaken. "Sir, I hope that you . . ."

"No, don't you go hoping for anything, please," Mr. Golyadkin's unfeeling foe answered evasively, standing with one foot on one step of the droshky and trying with all his might to land the other inside the carriage, but instead waving it vainly in the air; trying to maintain his equilibrium and at the same time trying with all his might to disengage his overcoat from the grasp of Mr. Golyadkin Senior who, for his part, had laid hold of it with all the means that nature had bestowed on him.

"Yakov Petrovich! Just ten minutes . . ."

"Excuse me, I haven't time, sir."

"You must agree, Yakov Petrovich . . . Please, Yakov Petrovich . . . For God's sake, Yakov Petrovich . . . This is the way it is—let's have it out . . . man to man . . . One little second, Yakov Petrovich! . . ."

"My dear boy, I don't have time," answered Mr. Golyadkin's falsely noble foe with uncivil familiarity disguised as goodheartedness. "Another time, believe me, I'll do it out of the goodness of my heart and with utmost sincerity, but now, I really just can't."

"Scoundrel!" thought our hero.

"Yakov Petrovich!" he cried in anguish, "I have never been your enemy. Malicious people have painted an unfair picture of me . . . For my part I am prepared . . . Yakov Petrovich, if you like, let's you and I go somewhere right now, shall we, Yakov Petrovich? . . . And there with utmost sincerity, as you so rightly said just now, and in direct and noble language . . . Let's go into that coffee house there; then everything will explain itself—yes, indeed, Yakov Petrovich! Then everything will surely explain itself . . ."

"Into the coffee house? Very well, sir. I have no objection. Let's go into the coffee house, but on one condition, my dear, and on one condition only, that there everything will explain itself. I say, 'This is the way it is, duckie,'" uttered Mr. Golyadkin Junior, climbing down from the droshky and shamelessly clapping our hero on the shoulder. "What a dear old chap you are. For you, Yakov Petrovich, I am prepared to go by way of a sidestreet (as you were once pleased to note so rightly, Yakov Petrovich). Why, you really are a rascal; you do what you will with a person!" continued Mr. Golyadkin's false friend with an easy smile, hovering about him and fawning over him.

The coffee house which both Mr. Golyadkins entered was located far from the main streets and was at that moment completely deserted. A rather fat German woman appeared at the counter the moment the bell sounded. Mr. Golyadkin and his unworthy foe went on into a second room, where a puffy-looking boy with cropped hair was fussing about near the stove with a bundle of kindling, trying to remake the fire that had gone out in it. At the request of Mr. Golyadkin Junior chocolate was served.

"She's a tasty morsel, all right," uttered Mr. Golyadkin Junior, winking roguishly at Mr. Golyadkin Senior.

Our hero blushed and said nothing.

"Oh, yes, I forgot; excuse me. I know your taste. We, sir, are partial to slender little German ladies. We, I say, you upright soul, Yakov Petrovich, are both partial to slender little German ladies who, however, have not yet lost all their charms. We rent apartments from them; we corrupt their morals; we give our hearts to them for beer soup and milk soup and give various written promises. That's what we do, isn't it? Oh, you Faublas, you, you traitor, you!"

In saying all this Mr. Golyadkin Junior was making a completely worthless but maliciously cunning allusion to a certain person of the female sex, and he was fawning over Mr. Golyadkin, smiling at him under the pretext of amiability, and thus falsely exhibiting cordiality toward him and joy at having met him. Noting, however, that Mr. Golyadkin Senior was by no means so stupid and so lacking in education and good manners as to believe him at once, the ignoble person resolved to change his tactics and conduct matters openly. Hereupon, having uttered his vile remarks, the false Mr. Golyadkin concluded by clapping the solid Mr. Golyadkin on the shoulder with a perturbing shamelessness and familiarity, and, not satisfied with this, set about making fun of him in a manner that was utterly unseemly in good society, namely, he intended to repeat his earlier vile gesture, that is, despite the resistance and faint cries of the perturbed Mr. Golyadkin Senior, to pinch his cheek. At the sight of such corruptness our hero's blood boiled but he held his tongue . . . that is, until an opportune moment should present itself.

"That is the talk of my enemies," he answered at last, in a quavering voice, prudently restraining himself. At the same time our hero looked back uneasily at the door. The fact of the

153

matter is that Mr. Golyadkin Junior was evidently in fine fettle and ready to engage in various pranks which were inadmissible in a public place and, generally speaking, not permitted by the laws of society, chiefly of well-bred society.

"Ah, well, in that case, have it your own way," Mr. Golyadkin Junior retorted seriously to Mr. Golyadkin Senior's thought, placing his empty cup, which he had drunk down with unseemly greediness, on the table. "Well, sir, there's no point in my spending much time with you . . . Well, sir, how are you getting on now, Yakov Petrovich?"

"There's only one thing I can say to you, Yakov Petrovich," answered our hero with composure and dignity; "I have never been your enemy."

"Hm . . . Well, and how is Petrushka getting on? What's his name? It *is* Petrushka, I believe? Why, yes! Well, how is he? Fine? Same as ever?"

"He is also the same as ever, Yakov Petrovich," answered the somewhat astonished Mr. Golyadkin Senior. "I don't know, Yakov Petrovich . . . for my part . . . that is, looking at things nobly and frankly, Yakov Petrovich, you must admit yourself, Yakov Petrovich . . ."

"Yes, sir. But you know yourself, Yakov Petrovich," answered Mr. Golyadkin Junior in a quiet and expressive voice, thus falsely portraying himself as sad, full of remorse and deserving of pity; "you know yourself, these are hard times we live in . . . I appeal to you, Yakov Petrovich; you're an intelligent man and will judge rightly," threw in Mr. Golyadkin Junior, basely flattering Mr. Golyadkin Senior. "Life is no picnic, you know yourself, Yakov Petrovich," concluded Mr. Golyadkin Junior significantly, pretending thus to be an intelligent and learned man capable of discussing lofty subjects.

"For my part, Yakov Petrovich," answered our hero animatedly, "for my part, scorning roundabout means and speaking boldly and frankly, using direct and noble language and placing the entire matter on an honorable level, I shall tell you, I can frankly and nobly affirm, Yakov Petrovich, that I am absolutely innocent and that, you know yourself, Yakov Petrovich, a mutual error—anything can happen—the world's judgment, the opinion of the servile mob . . . I am speaking frankly, Yakov Petrovich; anything can happen. I shall say further, Yakov Petrovich, if we judge thus, if we look at the matter from a noble and lofty point of view, then I shall say boldly, I shall say without false shame, Yakov Petrovich, that I shall even find it pleasant to disclose that I have been in error, I shall even find it pleasant to admit it. You know it yourself; you are an intelligent man and, what is more, an honorable one. Without shame, without false shame, I am ready to admit it . . ." concluded our hero with dignity and nobility.

"Destiny, fate! Yakov Petrovich . . . But let's put all this aside," uttered Mr. Golyadkin Junior with a sigh. "Let us rather use the brief moments of our encounter for a more profitable and pleasant conversation, as two colleagues should with one another . . . I really have not been able to say two words to you in all this time . . . It's not I who am to blame for this, Yakov Petrovich . . ."

"Nor I either," interrupted our hero heatedly, "nor I either! My heart tells me, Yakov Petrovich, that it's not I who am to blame for all this. Let us blame fate for all this, Yakov Petrovich," added Mr. Golyadkin Senior in a utterly conciliatory tone. His voice was gradually beginning to weaken and tremble.

"Well, now! How is your health in general?" said the errant one in a sweet voice.

"I have a bit of a cough," answered our hero even more sweetly.

"Take care of yourself. There are many infections going about now; you can easily catch tonsilitis and I, I confess to you, am already starting to bundle myself up in flannel."

"Yes, Yakov Petrovich, you can easily catch tonsilitis, sir . . . Yakov Petrovich!" uttered our hero after a modest silence. "Yakov Petrovich! I see that I was in error . . . I am touched by the recollection of those happy moments which we were able to spend together under my humble, but, I make so bold as to say, cordial roof . . ."

"In your letter, however, you wrote something else," uttered Mr. Golyadkin Junior somewhat reproachfully, and he was absolutely right (though only in this one respect was he absolutely right).

"Yakov Petrovich! I was in error... I see clearly now that I was in error in that unfortunate letter of mine, too. Yakov Petrovich, it pains me to look at you; Yakov Petrovich, you won't believe . . . Give me that letter so that I can tear it up before your very eyes, Yakov Petrovich, or if this is utterly impossible, then I beseech you to read it the other way round—quite the other way round, that is, with a deliberately friendly intent, giving the opposite sense to every word in my letter. I was in error. Forgive me, Yakov Petrovich, I was completely... I was sadly in error, Yakov Petrovich."

"You were saying?" asked Mr. Golyadkin Senior's perfidious friend rather absentmindedly and indifferently.

"I was saying that I have been completely in error, Yakov Petrovich, and that for my part, utterly without false shame, I . . ."

"Ah, well, all right! It's quite all right that you were in error," Mr. Golyadkin Junior answered rudely.

"I even had the idea," added our frank hero in a noble manner, completely oblivious to the terrible perfidy of his false friend, "I even had the idea of saying, 'Look, two absolutely identical persons were created . . .' "

"Ah! That's your idea!"

Hereupon Mr. Golyadkin Junior, notorious for his worthlessness, got up and grabbed his hat. Still failing to notice the ruse, Mr. Golyadkin Senior also got up, smiling ingenuously and nobly at his false friend and trying in his innocence to be nice to him, to reassure him and in this way to start up a new friendship . . .

"Goodbye, Your Excellency!" cried Mr. Golyadkin Junior suddenly. Our hero shuddered, noting in his enemy's face something almost bacchanalian, and, solely for the purpose of ridding himself of him, shoved into the extended hand of that immoral person two fingers of his own hand; but at this point . . . at this point Mr. Golyadkin Junior's shamelessness exceeded all bounds. Seizing the two fingers of Mr. Golyadkin Senior's hand and at first pressing them, the unworthy person thereupon, before Mr. Golyadkin's very eyes, resolved to repeat his shameless prank of that afternoon. The limit of human patience was exhausted . . .

He was already putting into his pocket the handkerchief with which he had wiped his fingers when Mr. Golyadkin Senior came to his senses and dashed after him into the next room, into which, as was his nasty habit, his irreconcilable enemy had already hastened to escape. As if nothing was wrong, he was standing at the counter eating pasties and with great composure, like a virtuous man, exchanging pleasantries with the German woman. "I mustn't—not in front of ladies," thought our hero and also went up to the counter, beside himself with agitation.

"No, she's really not bad-looking! What do you think?" Mr. Golyadkin Junior began his unseemly pranks again, probably counting on Mr. Golyadkin's endless patience. The fat German woman, for her part, looked at both her customers with inexpressive, vacant eyes, evidently not understanding any Russian, and smiled affably. Our hero blushed a fiery red at the words of the shameless Mr. Golyadkin Junior and, unable to restrain himself, flung himself at last upon him with the intention of tearing him to pieces and thus finishing him off once and for all; but Mr. Golyadkin Junior, as was his vile wont, was already far away: he had taken to his heels and was now at the entrance. It goes without saying that after the initial momentary stupor which naturally seized Mr. Golyadkin Senior, he came to his senses and dashed full speed after his insulter, who was already getting into the carriage, the driver of which had obviously agreed to wait for him. But at that very moment the fat German woman, witnessing the flight of the two customers, let out a scream and rang her little bell furiously. Our hero turned, almost on the wing, threw her the money for himself and for that shameless person who had not paid, without demanding any change, and, despite the fact that he had lost time, nevertheless succeeded, although once again only on the wing, in catching up with his foe. Hanging onto the splashboard of the droshky with every means bestowed on him by nature, our hero was borne along the street for some time, trying to clamber into the carriage, while Mr. Golyadkin Junior repulsed him with all his might. Meanwhile the driver, using whip and reins and foot and words, urged on his exhausted jade, which quite unexpectedly broke into a gallop, taking hold of the bit with its teeth and kicking out, as was its nasty habit, with its back legs at every third step. Finally our hero did succeed after all in clambering into the droshky, and sat back to back with the driver, and face to face with his foe, knee to knee with that shameless person, and with his right hand used every means to hang onto the extremely shabby fur collar on the overcoat of his corrupt and most bitter foe . . .

The enemies were borne along and for some time said nothing. Our hero could scarcely catch his breath; the road was utterly dreadful and he continually bounced up and down, in danger of breaking his neck. Moreover, his most bitter foe continued to refuse to acknowledge himself vanquished and was trying to topple his opponent into the mud. To crown all this unpleasantness, the weather was really terrible. The snow was coming down in large flakes and trying as hard as it could in every way to get inside the real Mr. Golyadkin's open overcoat. All around it was foggy and pitch dark. It was difficult to distinguish in what direction and along what streets they were rushing . . . It seemed to Mr. Golyadkin that something familiar was happening to him. For one instant he tried to recall whether he had had a presentiment of anything yesterday . . . in a dream, for example . . . Finally his anguish became utterly excruciating. He pressed against his merciless opponent and was going to shout . . . But his shout was already dying on his lips . . . There was a moment when Mr. Golyadkin forgot everything and decided that all of this was absolutely nothing and that it was happening just like that, somehow, in an inexplicable manner, and to protest it would be a superfluous and utterly wasted effort . . . But suddenly and almost at the same instant as our hero was coming to all these conclusions, a careless jolt put an entirely different complexion on the matter. Like a sack of flour Mr. Golyadkin fell off the droshky and rolled away somewhere, acknowledging quite rightly at the moment of his fall that he really had gotten angry most inopportunely. Jumping to his feet at last, he saw that they had arrived somewhere; the droshky was standing in the middle of some-one's courtyard, and our hero noticed from the first glance that it was the courtyard of the very house in which Olsufi Ivanovich had an apartment. At that very same instant he noticed that his friend was already making his way up the front steps and was probably going to Olsufi Ivanovich's. In his indescribable anguish he was going to rush to catch up with his foe, but luckily for him he wisely thought better of it in time. Not forgetting to settle with the cabman, Mr. Golyadkin rushed out into the street and began to run as fast as he could, somewhere, anywhere. The snow was coming down as before in large flakes; as before it was foggy, wet and dark. Our hero did not walk but flew, knocking over everyone in his path—peasant men and women and children—and himself in turn rebounding off peasant women and men and children. Around him and in his wake could be heard the sound of frightened voices, squealing and shouting . . . But Mr. Golyadkin seemed to have lost consciousness and refused to pay attention to anything... He came to his senses, however, at the Semyonovsky Bridge and then only because he had awkwardly managed somehow to bump into and knock down two peasant women with their street wares and at the same time to fall down himself. "It's nothing," thought Mr. Golyadkin; "all of this still has a very good chance of turning out for the best." And hereupon he put his hand into his pocket, wishing to make amends with a silver ruble for spilling the cakes, apples, peas and various other items. Suddenly a new light dawned on Mr. Golyadkin; in his pocket he felt the letter which the copyist had given him that morning. Recalling, however, that there was an eating establish-ment he knew nearby, he rushed into the eating establishment, lost no time in settling down at a table lit by a tallow candle and, paying no attention to anything nor listening to the waiter who had appeared to take his order, he broke the seal and began to read the following, which utterly staggered him:

Noble man, suffering for me and forever dear
to my heart!
I suffer, I perish—save me! A slanderer, an intriguer, a man notorious for his worthless tendencies

has ensnared me in his nets and I am undone! I have fallen! But he is repulsive to me, while you! . . . We have been kept apart, my letters to you have been intercepted—and all this has been done by an immoral person, taking advantage of his one good quality—his resemblance to you. In any case one can be ugly but still captivate with one's intellect, strong feelings and pleasing manners. . . I perish! I am being married off forcibly, and the one who intrigues in this most of all is my father, my benefactor and State Councilor, Olsufi Ivanovich, who probably desires to take over my place and my relationships in well-bred society. . . But I have made up my mind and am protesting with every means bestowed on me by nature. Await me in your coach today at exactly nine o'clock by the windows of Olsufi Ivanovich's apartment. We are giving a ball again and the handsome lieutenant will be there. I shall come out and we shall fly. Besides, there are other posts where one may still be of use to one's native land. In any case, remember, my friend, that innocence is strong by virtue of its innocence. Farewell. Wait at the entrance with the coach. I shall throw myself into the protection of your embracing arms at exactly two a.m.

> Yours till the grave,
> Klara Olsufyevna

After reading the letter, our hero remained for several minutes as if thunderstruck. Feeling terrible anguish and terrible agitation, white as a sheet, with the letter in his hands, he walked up and down the room several times; to crown his unfortunate situation, our hero was unaware that he was at that moment the object of special attention for everyone in the room. Probably the disorder of his dress, his uncontrolled agitation, his walking, or rather, running, his gesticulations with both hands, and perhaps his few enigmatic words absent-mindedly addressed to the air—all this probably spoke very badly for Mr. Golyadkin in the opinion of all the customers; and even the waiter was beginning to cast suspicious glances at him. Coming to his senses, our hero noticed that he was standing in the middle of the room and staring in an almost unseemly and impolite manner at an old man of very respectable appearance who, having dined and said some prayers before an icon, had settled himself in his seat again and had in turn riveted his eyes on Mr. Golyadkin. Our hero looked vaguely about him and noticed that everyone, absolutely everyone, was giving him the most ominous and suspicious looks. Suddenly a retired military man with a red collar on his uniform loudly requested "The Police Gazette." Mr. Golyadkin shuddered and blushed; he inadvertently lowered his eyes and saw that he was in clothing so disreputable that he would not wear it even at home let alone in a public place. His shoes, his trousers and his entire left side were completely covered with mud, his right footstrap was torn loose and his coat was even ripped in many places. In his unending anguish our hero went over to the table at which he had been reading and saw that the waiter was approaching him with a strange and brazenly insistent expression on his face. Utterly flustered and downcast, our hero began to examine the table at which he was now standing. On the table lay the dirty plates from someone's dinner, a soiled napkin, and a knife, fork and spoon which had just recently been used. "Why, who's been having dinner?" thought our hero. "Can it have been me? Well, anything is possible! I had dinner and didn't even notice it. What shall I do?" Raising his eyes, Mr. Golyadkin once again saw the waiter standing beside him and getting ready to say something to him.

"How much do I owe you, old chap?" asked our hero in a quavering voice.

Loud laughter resounded around Mr. Golyadkin; even the waiter gave a funny smile. Mr. Golyadkin realized that in this as well he had come off badly and had committed a terrible blunder. When he realized all this, he became so embarrassed that he was forced to reach into his pocket for his handkerchief, probably for the sake of having something to do instead of just standing there; but to his indescribable amazement and that of all those around him, instead of the handkerchief he pulled out a vial containing some kind of medicine which had been prescribed four days earlier by Krestyan Ivanovich. "The medicines are obtained at the same apothecary shop," flashed through Mr. Golyadkin's mind... Suddenly he shuddered and almost cried out in horror. New light was dawning... The dark, revolting, reddish liquid gleamed ominously before Mr. Golyadkin's eyes . . . The vial fell out of his hands and instantly shattered to pieces. Our hero cried out and leapt back a few steps from the spilled liquid... he was shaking in every limb and sweat was breaking out on his temples and brow. "My life must be in danger!" Meanwhile a stir and commotion arose in the room; everyone was surrounding Mr. Golyadkin; everyone was talking to Mr. Golyadkin. But our hero was mute and motionless, seeing nothing, hearing nothing, feeling nothing . . . At last, as though tearing himself from the spot, he dashed out of the eating establishment, shoved aside each and every one attempting to restrain him, fell almost senseless into the first droshky for hire that came along and flew off to his apartment.

In the entranceway of his apartment he met Mikheyev, the office guard, with an official envelope in his hands. "I know, my friend, I know everything," our exhausted hero answered in a weak, anguished voice; "it's the official..." The envelope did in fact contain an order to Mr. Golyadkin, signed by Andrei Filippovich, to turn over his duties to Ivan Semyonovich. Taking the envelope and giving the guard ten kopeks, Mr. Golyadkin entered his apartment and saw that Petrushka was getting all his odds and ends and all his things ready and gathering them in a pile, obviously with the intention of leaving Mr. Golyadkin and moving from his place to that of Karolina Ivanovna, who had enticed him into replacing Yevstafi.

XII

Petrushka entered with a swagger, his manner strangely casual and his mien boorishly triumphant. It was evident that he had gotten some idea into his head, that he felt himself to be completely within his rights, and that he looked like a complete outsider, that is, like someone else's servant, but certainly in no way like Mr. Golyadkin's former servant.

"Well, so you see, my dear fellow," began our hero, gasping for breath, "what time is it now, my dear fellow?"

Without a word Petrushka headed behind the partition, then returned and in a rather independent tone announced that it was nearly half past seven.

"That's fine, my dear fellow, that's fine. Well, you see, my dear fellow . . . permit me to tell you, my dear fellow, that everything seems to be over between us now."

Petrushka said nothing.

"Well, now that everything is over between us, tell me frankly now, tell me as you would a friend, where have you been, old chap?"

"Where have I been? With good people, sir."

"I know, my friend, I know. I've always been satisfied with you, my dear fellow, and I shall give you a reference . . . Well, what are you doing with them now?"

"What indeed, sir! You know yourself, sir. It's clear, sir, a good person doesn't teach you to do bad."

"I know, my dear fellow, I know. Nowadays good people are rare, my friend; treasure them, my friend. Well, and how are they?"

"You know how, sir . . . Only I can't serve you any longer now, sir; you must know that, sir."

"I know, my dear fellow, I know; I know your zeal and diligence; I've seen it all, my friend; I've noticed it. I respect you, my friend. I respect a good and honest person, even if he's a servant."

"Of course, I know, sir! Our kind, of course, as you yourself must know, sir, want to be where it's best. That's just the way it is, sir. I'm the same way! It's well known, sir, that one just can't get along without a good person, sir."

"Well, that's fine, old chap, that's fine; I sense it... Well, here's your money and your reference. Now let's kiss one another, old chap, and say goodbye... Well now, my dear fellow, I shall ask a favor of you, one last favor," said Mr. Golyadkin in a solemn tone. "You see, my dear fellow, all sorts of things can happen. Sorrow, my friend, lies in wait even in gilded palaces, and there is no escape from it. You know, my friend, it seems to me I've always been kind to you..."

Petrushka said nothing.

"It seems to me I've always been kind to you, my dear fellow... Well, how much linen do we have now, my dear fellow?"

"Why, everything's there, sir. Linen shirts six, sir; socks three pairs; four dickeys, sir; one jersey flannel; underwear two sets, sir. You know yourself that's all, sir. I haven't taken anything of yours, sir... I take care of my master's property, sir. I may have my moments, sir, you know... I know, sir... but that I should be guilty of that—never, sir; you know that yourself, sir..."

"I believe it, my friend, I believe it. That's not what I'm talking about, my friend, that's not what I'm talking about; you see, here's what, my friend..."

"I know, sir; I know it already, sir. Now when I was working for General Stolbnyakov, sir, he let me go because he was going away to Saratov... he had an estate there..."

"No, my friend, that's not what I'm talking about. I don't mean anything... don't you go thinking anything, my dear friend..."

"I know, sir. It's easy to slander people of our sort, sir. But I've given satisfaction everywhere, sir. Ministers, generals, senators, counts, sir. I've been with all of them, sir; at Prince Svinchatkin's, sir; at Pereborkin's, the colonel's, sir; at Nedo-

barov's, the general's. They visited us, too, sir, came out to the
estate, sir, to see our folks. You know, sir . . ."

"Yes, my friend, yes; fine, my friend, fine. And now I, too,
am going away, my friend . . . A different way lies before
everyone, my dear fellow, and no one knows what road he may
find himself on. Well, my friend, help me get dressed now; and
also lay out my uniform jacket . . . another pair of trousers,
sheets, blankets, pillows . . ."

"Do you wish everything to be tied up into a bundle, sir?"

"Yes, my friend, yes; why not into a bundle? . . . Who
knows what may happen to us? Well, and now, my dear fellow,
you go find me a coach . . ."

"A coach, sir? . . ."

"Yes, my friend, a coach, a really roomy one and for a
specific time. And don't you go thinking anything, my friend . . ."

"And do you mean to go far away, sir?"

"I don't know, my friend; that I also don't know. I think
you'd better put a down quilt in there as well. What do you
think, my friend? I am relying on you, my dear fellow . . ."

"You mean you're going away right now, sir?"

"Yes, my friend, yes! Something has come up . . . that's
how it is, my dear fellow, that's how it is . . ."

"I know, sir; the same thing happened to a lieutenant in
our regiment, sir; at a landowner's, sir . . . he carried her off,
sir . . ."

"Carried her off? . . . What do you mean? My dear fellow,
you . . ."

"Yes, sir; he carried her off, sir, and they were married at
another estate. Everything had been arranged in advance, sir.
There was a pursuit, sir. But the prince took their part at that
point, sir, the late prince, sir—well, and things were smoothed
over, sir . . ."

"They were married, but . . . how is it that you know, my
dear fellow? By what manner of means did you get to know, my
dear fellow?"

"Why, I just know, sir; what do think, sir! News flies
quickly, sir. We know everything, sir . . . It could happen to
anyone, of course. Only I shall tell you now, sir, permit me to say

it in my plain servant's way, sir, since it's come to that now, I'll
tell you, sir: you have an enemy; you have a rival, sir, a powerful
rival; so there you are, sir . . ."

"I know, my friend, I know; you know yourself, my dear
fellow. . . Well, then, I'm relying on you. What shall we do now,
my friend? What do you advise?"

"Here's what, sir. If you've chosen that way of doing
things, roughly speaking, sir, then you are going to have to buy
some things, sir—well, like sheets, pillows, another down quilt,
sir, for a double bed, sir, a good blanket, sir—why, right here at
our neighbor's downstairs, sir—she's a tradeswoman, sir—
there's a fine lady's fox cloak; you can have a look at it and buy
it; you can go downstairs and look at it right now, sir. It's just
what you'll need now, sir; a fine cloak, sir, satin, lined with fox,
sir . . ."

"Very well, my friend, very well. I agree, my friend. I'm
relying on you, I'm relying on you completely. Why not have a
cloak, too, my dear fellow . . . Only hurry, hurry! For God's
sake, hurry! I'll buy the cloak, too, only please hurry! It will
soon be eight! Hurry, for God's sake, my friend! Hasten, be
quick, my friend! . . ."

Petrushka dropped the bundle of linen, pillows, blankets,
sheets and odds and ends that he had been about to gather
together and tie up and rushed headlong out of the room. Mr.
Golyadkin meanwhile seized the letter once more—but he was
unable to read it. Clutching his wretched head with both hands,
he leaned against the wall in amazement. He was unable to
think about anything; he was unable to do anything either; he
didn't know himself what was happening to him. At last, seeing
that time was passing and that neither Petrushka nor the cloak
were making their appearance, Mr. Golyadkin decided to go
himself. Opening the door into the entranceway, he heard a
hubbub of conversation, arguing and gossiping below . . .
Several female neighbors were babbling, shouting, discussing
and dickering over something—Mr. Golyadkin already knew
exactly what it was about. Petrushka's voice was audible; then
there was the sound of footsteps. "Oh, my God! They'll drag
everybody and his brother into it!" groaned Mr. Golyadkin,

wringing his hands in despair and dashing back into his room.
Back in his room he fell almost senseless onto the ottoman,
face down on a cushion. For a minute he lay like this, then leapt
up and, not waiting for Petrushka, put on his galoshes, hat and
overcoat, grabbed his wallet and ran headlong down the stairs.
"I don't need anything, anything, my dear fellow! I'll do it
myself; I'll do it all myself. For the time being I have no need of
you and meanwhile perhaps this matter will turn out for the
best," Mr. Golyadkin muttered to Petrushka, meeting him on
the stairway. Then he ran out into the courtyard and was off; his
heart was fainting; he had not yet made up his mind . . . how to
proceed, what to do, and how to act at this critical moment . . .

"That's the question: dear God, how ought I to act? Why
did all this have to happen?" he cried out at last in despair,
hobbling along the street aimlessly and haphazardly; "why did
all this have to happen? Why, if it were not for this, for this very
thing, then everything would have been settled; at one go, with
a single stroke, a single, deft, energetic, firm stroke, it would
have been settled. I'd stake having my finger cut off that it
would have been settled! And I even know just how it would
have been settled. Here's how it would all have happened: I
would have gone and said, 'This is the way things are, but I, sir,
with your permission, could not care less'; I would have said,
'Things aren't done that way'; I would have said, 'Sir, my dear
sir, things are not done that way and you won't win us over by
imposture; an impostor, sir, is a person, you know—who is
worthless and of no use to his native land. Do you understand
that?' I would have said, 'Do you understand that, my dear sir?!'
That's how it would have happened . . . But no, on the other
hand, what am I saying? It's not at all like that, absolutely not . . .
What nonsense I'm talking, fool that I am, self-destructive
creature that I am! It's not at all like that. I say, you self-
destructive creature, you . . . But look here, you corrupt man,
see the way it's happening now. Well, where am I to go now?
Well, what, for example, am I going to do with myself now?
Well, what am I good for now? Well, what are you good for
now, for example, you Poor Beggar, you, you unworthy thing,
you! Well, what now? I must get a coach. She says 'Go and get a

coach and have it waiting here for me'; she says, 'We'll get our little feet wet if there isn't a coach' . . . Now, who would have thought it? Now there's a young lady for you; oh, my dear madam! There's a virtuous miss for you! That's our much-praised girl. You've done yourself proud, young lady, I do declare, you've done yourself proud! . . . And all this comes of an immoral upbringing; and now that I have scrutinized it all and gotten to the bottom of it, I finally see that this comes from nothing other than immorality. What they should have done to her when she was young, instead of pampering her, you know . . . they should have used the rod now and then, but they stuffed her with candy and they stuffed her with cakes and that little old fellow gushed over her: 'You're my this', he said, 'and you're my that; you're my good girl', he said, 'and I shall marry you to a count!' . . . And this is why she's turned out the way she has, and shown us her hand now. 'This is the game we have in mind!' she says. They should have kept her home when she was young, but they put her in a boarding school, gave her up to a French madame, to some émigrée named Falbala or some such thing, and a lot of good she's learned from this émigrée named Falbala—and that's why it's all turned out this way. She says, 'Come and be happy!' She says, 'Be in a coach at such-and-such an hour outside my windows and sing a sentimental love song in Spanish; I await you and I know that you love me and we shall run away together and live in a cabin.' Well, really, that cannot be; that, my dear young lady—if it's come to that now—cannot be; it is against the law to carry off an honest and innocent young girl from her family home without the consent of her parents! And, finally, why do it? For what reason? And what need is there? Why, she ought to marry the one she's supposed to, the one intended by fate, and that's that. I am a civil servant; and I can lose my position because of it; I can be taken to court because of it, young lady! That's how it is, if you didn't know! It's that German's doing. She's the source of it all, the witch; all the trouble started with her. They slandered a man and they invented old wives' tales and a cock-and-bull story about him on the advice of Andrei Filippovich; that's where it started. Otherwise, why would Petrushka be involved in it? Why does

he have to be involved? What business is it of that rascal's? No,
young lady, I cannot, I cannot possibly, not at all . . . And you,
young lady, must excuse me somehow this once. You, young
lady, are the source of it all; it's not the German who is the
source of it all, not that witch, but you alone, because the witch
is a good woman, because the witch is not to blame for
anything, while you, my dear young lady, are to blame—so
there! You, young lady, you're the one who's getting me
unjustly accused . . . Here's a man perishing; here's a man losing
sight of himself and unable to restrain himself—how can there
be any talk of a wedding then? And, how will it all end? And how
will it turn out now? I'd give a lot to know all that! . . ."

Thus reasoned our hero in his despair. Coming to his
senses suddenly, he noticed that he was standing somewhere on
Liteynaya Street. The weather was frightful: there was a thaw,
snow was coming down and it was raining—just as it had been at
that unforgettable time when, at the terrible midnight hour, all
of Mr. Golyadkin's misfortunes had begun. "How can there be
any talk of a journey in something like this?" thought Mr.
Golyadkin, looking at the weather. "This is certain death . . .
Dear God! Now where shall I find a coach here, for instance?
Over there on the corner there seems to be something black.
Let's see; let's investigate . . . Dear God!" continued our hero,
directing his feeble and unsteady footsteps to where he had
seen something resembling a coach. "No, here's what I'll do:
I'll go there and throw myself at his feet, if I can, and I'll humbly
entreat him. I'll say, 'This is the way it is. I commend my fate
into your hands, into the hands of my superior.' I'll say, 'Your
Excellency, protect me and give your patronage to me.' 'This is
the way it is,' I'll say; 'such and such and such and such is an
unlawful deed; don't ruin me; you're like a father to me; don't
abandon me . . . save my self-esteem, honor and name . . . save
me, too, from that villain, that corrupt person . . . He is a
different person, Your Excellency, and I am also a different
person; he is separate and I am also separate; really separate,
Your Excellency, really separate'; I'll say, 'That's how it is'. I'll
say, 'I can't resemble him; have him replaced; have the kindness
to do it; give orders for him to be replaced and for the godless,

unwarranted impersonation to be brought to an end . . . so
that it cannot serve as an example to others, Your Excellency.
You're like a father to me; a superior, of course, a beneficent
and protective superior, must encourage such action . . .
There's even something chivalrous about it.' I'll say, 'You,
my beneficent superior, are like a father to me and I entrust
my fate to you and won't cross you; I put myself into your hands
and withdraw my self from my duties . . .' Yes, that's what I'll
say!"

"Well, now, my dear fellow, are you a cabman?"

"Yes, I am . . ."

"I want a coach, brother, for the evening . . ."

"And will you be pleased to journey far, sir?"

"For the evening, for the evening; and to go wherever I
may have to go, my dear fellow, wherever I may have to go."

"Might you be planning then to journey out of town?"

"Yes, my friend, perhaps even out of town. I don't know
yet myself for certain, my friend; I can't tell you for certain,
my dear fellow. You see, my dear fellow, perhaps it will all work
out for the best. You know how it is, my friend. . ."

"Yes, of course, I know how it is, sir; God grant the same
to everyone."

"Yes, my friend, yes; thank you, my dear fellow; well, how
much will it be, my dear fellow? . . ."

"Will you be pleased to go immediately, sir?"

"Yes, immediately; that is, no, you'll have to wait at a
certain spot . . . just a bit; you won't wait long, my dear fellow . . ."

"Well, if you're hiring me for the whole time, I can't ask
less than six rubles in weather like this, sir . . ."

"Well, all right, my friend, all right; and I shall show my
gratitude to you, my dear fellow. Well, so, you'll take me now,
my dear fellow."

"Get in; just let me fix things up a bit; now, be so kind as to
get in. Where do you wish to go?"

"To the Izmaylovsky Bridge, my friend."

The cabman clambered up onto the coachbox, forcibly
tore his pair of emaciated nags away from the hay trough, and
was about to set out for the Izmaylovsky Bridge. But suddenly

Mr. Golyadkin pulled the cord, stopped the coach and in a beseeching voice asked the driver to turn back, to go not to the Izmaylovsky Bridge but to another street. The driver turned into the other street and ten minutes later Mr. Golyadkin's newly acquired carriage stopped before the house in which His Excellency had an apartment. Mr. Golyadkin emerged from the coach, earnestly besought his driver to wait and with a sinking heart ran upstairs to the second floor and pulled the bell-pull. The door opened and our hero found himself in His Excellency's foyer.

"Is His Excellency pleased to be at home?" asked Mr. Golyadkin, addressing himself thus to the servant who had opened the door.

"What do you want?" asked the servant, looking Mr. Golyadkin over from head to foot.

"Well, I, my friend, you know... am Golyadkin, the clerk, Titular Councilor Golyadkin. Tell him this is the way it is; I've come to explain . . ."

"Wait; you can't, sir . . ."

"My friend, I cannot wait; my business is important; an urgent matter . . ."

"But who sent you? Have you come with papers? . . ."

"No, my friend, I have come on my own account . . . Announce me, my friend; say, 'This is the way it is, to explain.' And I will show my gratitude to you, my dear fellow . . ."

"I can't, sir; my orders were not to receive anyone. He has guests, sir. Come back in the morning at ten o'clock, sir . . ."

"Do announce me, my dear fellow; I can't wait; it's impossible for me to wait . . . You will answer for this, my dear fellow . . ."

"Oh, go on, announce him. What's it to you? Afraid to wear out some shoe leather or something?" said another servant sprawled out on a chest and silent until now.

"Who cares about shoe leather? My orders were not to receive anyone. Get it? Their turn is in the morning."

"Announce him. Afraid your tongue will drop off or something?"

"All right, I'll announce him: my tongue won't drop off. My orders were not to receive anyone; I told you those were my orders. Go into that room there."

Mr. Golyadkin entered the first room; there was a clock on the table. He glanced at it: it was half past eight. He began to feel sick at heart. He was just thinking of turning back; but at that very moment the lanky footman standing at the threshold of the next room loudly announced Mr. Golyadkin's name. "What a voice!" thought our hero in indescribable anguish... "Why, you should have said, you know... said, 'This is the way it is, he has humbly and meekly come to explain' . . . you know... 'Will you be so kind as to receive him? ...' But now my case has been ruined; now my entire case is lost; still . . . oh, well—it doesn't matter." There was no time to consider, however. The servant returned, said "If you please," and conducted Mr. Golyadkin into the study.

When our hero entered he felt as though he had been blinded, for he could see absolutely nothing. He had, however, glimpsed two or three figures. "Oh, yes, those are the guests," flashed through Mr. Golyadkin's mind. At last our hero began to distinguish clearly the star on His Excellency's black frock coat; then, by a gradual process he became aware of the black frock coat as well; finally his ability to see was restored completely...

"What is it, sir?" a familiar voice uttered above Mr. Golyadkin.

"Titular Councilor Golyadkin, Your Excellency."

"Well?"

"I've come to explain . . ."

"What? . . . What's that?"

"Why, yes. I say, 'This is the way it is; I've come to explain, Your Excellency, sir . . .' "

"But you . . . But who are you?"

"Mi-Mi-Mister Golyadkin, Your Excellency, a Titular Councilor."

"Well, just what is it you want?"

"I say, 'This is the way it is; he's like a father to me. I withdraw myself from my duties, and protect me from my enemy.' That's what I say!"

"What's that? . . ."

"You know how it is . . ."

"How what is?"

Mr. Golyadkin said nothing; his chin was beginning to twitch slightly . . .

"Well?"

"I thought it was chivalrous, Your Excellency . . . 'that there was something chivalrous in it,' I say, 'and my superior is like a father to me . . .' I say, 'This is the way it is; protect me, I t-tearfully e-entreat you, and that such a-actions m-must b-be en-en-couraged . . .' "

His Excellency turned away. For several moments our hero's eyes could not make anything out. He felt a tightness in his chest. His breathing was labored. He did not know where he was . . . He felt ashamed and sad. God knows what happened next . . . Coming to his senses, our hero noticed that His Excellency was talking with his guests and seemed to be arguing sharply and intensely with them about something. One of the guests Mr. Golyadkin recognized immediately. It was Andrei Filippovich. The other he did not recognize; however, this person also seemed familiar—a tall, thick-set figure, elderly, endowed with very bushy eyebrows and sidewhiskers and a keen, expressive look. Around the stranger's neck was a decoration on a ribbon and in his mouth a small cigar. The stranger was smoking and, without taking the cigar out of his mouth, would nod his head significantly and glance from time to time at Mr. Golyadkin. Mr. Golyadkin began to feel awkward; he averted his eyes and thereupon saw yet another extremely odd guest. In the doorway, which our hero had up until then taken to be a mirror—something which had happened to him once before as well—*he* appeared—we know who—Mr. Golyadkin's very close acquaintance and friend. Mr. Golyadkin Junior had actually been up until then in another, small room, hurriedly writing something; now, apparently, his presence had become necessary—and he appeared with the papers under his arm, went up to His Excellency and very deftly, while waiting to receive His Excellency's undivided attention, succeeded in insinuating himself into the conversation and counsel, taking up his position a little bit behind Andrei Filippovich's back and partly hidden by the stranger smoking the small cigar. Evidently Mr. Golyadkin Junior was intensely interested in the conversation, which he was now listening in on in a noble manner, nodding his head, shifting his feet, smiling, glancing every moment at His Excellency, as though beseeching him with his eyes to permit him as well to put in his few remarks. "Scoundrel!" thought Mr. Golyadkin and involuntarily took a step forward. Just then the general[10] turned around and rather hesitantly approached Mr. Golyadkin.

"Very well, then, very well; go along now. I shall consider your case, and give orders for you to be shown out..." Here the general glanced at the stranger with the bushy sidewhiskers. The latter nodded his head in assent.

Mr. Golyadkin sensed and clearly realized that he was being taken for something other than he was and not at all as he should be. "One way or another I have to explain myself," he thought. 'This is the way it is, Your Excellency,' I'll say." Hereupon, in his bewilderment he looked down at the floor and, to his extreme amazement, saw a sizable white spot on each of His Excellency's shoes. "Can they have split?" thought Mr. Golyadkin. Soon, however, Mr. Golyadkin discovered that His Excellency's shoes had not split at all but were only reflecting the light strongly—a phenomenon completely explainable by the fact that the shoes were of patent leather and had a high gloss. "That's what's called a *highlight*," thought our hero. "The use of this name is reserved particularly for artists' studios, while in other places this sheen is called 'the illuminated edge.'" At this point Mr. Golyadkin raised his eyes and saw that it was time to speak because his case might easily take a turn for the worse ... Our hero took a step forward.

"I say, 'This is the way it is, Your Excellency'," he said, "'but in the age we live in you won't win through imposture.'"

The general did not answer but tugged hard at the bell-pull. Our hero took another step forward.

"He is a vile and corrupt person, Your Excellency," said our hero, beside himself and fainting with fear, but nevertheless boldly and resolutely pointing at his unworthy twin, who was at that moment fidgeting about near His Excellency; "'This is the way it is,' I say, and I am alluding to someone we all know."

A general stir ensued after Mr. Golyadkin's words. Andrei Filippovich and the stranger began nodding their heads; His Excellency in his impatience kept tugging the bell-pull with all his might to summon his servants. At this point Mr. Golyadkin Junior stepped forward in his turn.

"Your Excellency," he said, "I humbly request your permission to speak." There was something decisive in Mr. Golyadkin Junior's voice; everything about him showed that he felt completely within his rights.

"Permit me to ask you," he began again, in his eagerness anticipating His Excellency's answer and turning now to Mr. Golyadkin; "permit me to ask you in whose presence you think you are explaining yourself thus? Before whom do you think you are standing? In whose study do you think you are? . . ." Mr. Golyadkin Junior was in a state of utter and unusual agitation; his face was all red and blazing with indignation and anger; tears had even appeared in his eyes.

"The Bassavryukovs!" roared a servant at the top of his lungs, appearing in the double doors of the study. "A fine noble name, Ukrainians," thought Mr. Golyadkin and thereupon felt someone place a hand on his back in a very friendly way; then another hand was placed on his back; Mr. Golyadkin's vile twin bustled along before them showing the way and our hero saw clearly that they seemed to be directing him towards the big double doors of the study. "Just exactly as it was at Olsufi Ivanovich's," he thought and found himself in the foyer. Looking around, he saw next to him two of His Excellency's servants and one twin.

"The overcoat, the overcoat, the overcoat, the overcoat of my friend! The overcoat of my best friend!" twittered the corrupt person, seizing the overcoat from the hands of one of the servants and tossing it right over Mr. Golyadkin's head, for the sake of a vile and poor jest. Struggling to get out from under his overcoat, Mr. Golyadkin could clearly hear the laughter of the two servants. But shutting his ears to everything and ignoring everything extraneous, he emerged from the foyer and found himself on the lighted stairway. Mr. Golyadkin Junior followed after him.

"Goodbye, Your Excellency!" he shouted after Mr. Golyadkin Senior.

"Scoundrel!" uttered our hero, beside himself.

"So, I'm a scoundrel . . ."

"Corrupt fellow!"

"So, I'm a corrupt fellow . . ." The worthy Mr. Golyadkin's unworthy foe answered him thus and, as was his vile wont, stood looking down from the height of the stairway, without blinking an eye, straight into Mr. Golyadkin's eyes, as though begging him to continue. Our hero spat with indignation and ran out onto the front steps. He was so crushed that he was totally unable to recall who seated him in the coach or how. On coming to his senses, he saw that he was being driven along the Fontanka. "We must be going to the Izmaylovsky Bridge," thought Mr. Golyadkin . . . At this point Mr. Golyadkin tried to think of something else, but could not; it was something so terrible that it could not be explained . . . "Well, it doesn't matter," concluded our hero and drove on to the Izmaylovsky Bridge.

XIII

. . . The weather seemed to be trying to change for the better. The wet snow, which had been coming down in great clouds until then, began to thin out gradually and at last stopped almost completely. The sky became visible and here and there in it tiny stars began to twinkle. But it was wet, muddy, damp and stifling, especially for Mr. Golyadkin, who could hardly breathe as it was. His overcoat, made heavier by being thoroughly soaked, permeated his limbs with an unpleasantly warm dampness, while the weight of it caused his already quite unsteady legs to buckle under him. A feverish shiver sent sharp twinges over his entire body; exhaustion squeezed a cold unhealthy sweat out of him, so that Mr. Golyadkin quite forgot at this convenient opportunity to repeat with his customary firmness and resoluteness his favorite phrase that everything perhaps, maybe, somehow, most likely, certainly would go and turn out for the best. "Still, none of this matters for the time being," added our hero of staunch and unfailing spirit, wiping from his face the drops of cold water running in every direction from the brim of his thoroughly saturated round hat. Having added that all this still didn't matter, our hero attempted to sit down on a rather thick piece of log, which was lying near a woodpile in Olsufi Ivanovich's courtyard. Of course, there was no point any more in thinking about Spanish serenades and silken ladders; but it was indeed necessary to think about a cozy nook, perhaps not altogether warm but at least comfortable and concealed. He was very much enticed, let it be said in passing, by that very nook in the entranceway of Olsufi Ivanovich's apartment where earlier, almost at the beginning of this true story, our hero had stood and waited out his two hours between the cupboard and the old screens, among all sorts of household junk and useless trash and rubbish. The fact of the matter is that now as well Mr. Golyadkin had already been standing and waiting two whole hours in Olsufi Ivanovich's courtyard. But as far as the previous cozy and comfortable nook was concerned, there now existed certain inconveniences which had not existed previously. The first inconvenience was that probably this spot had now been noted and certain precautionary measures taken concerning it since the time of the episode at Olsufi Ivanovich's last ball; while, secondly, it was necessary to wait for the prearranged signal from Klara Olsufyevna, because there certainly had to be some such prearranged signal from Klara Olsufyevna. That is how it was always done, and, as they say, "We aren't the first and we won't be the last." Mr. Golyadkin thereupon appropriately remembered in passing a novel he had read long ago, in which the heroine had given a prearranged signal to Alfred under identical circumstances by tying a pink ribbon to a window. But a pink ribbon now, at night, and in the climate of St. Petersburg, which is notorious for its dampness and unreliability, was out of the question and, in a word, utterly impossible. "No, silken ladders have no place in this," thought our hero, "and I would do better to stay here unobtrusively and cozily . . . I would do better, for instance, to just stay here;" and he chose a spot in the courtyard right opposite the windows and near the woodpile. Of course, many extraneous people, postboys, coachmen, etc., were walking about the courtyard; in addition wheels were clattering and horses were snorting and so forth; but still the spot was convenient: whether they observed him or not, still now at least there was the advantage of being to a certain extent in the shadows and no one could see Mr. Golyadkin; he, however, could see absolutely everything. The windows were brightly illuminated; there was some sort of festive gathering at Olsufi Ivanovich's. The music, however, was not yet audible. "Apparently it's not a ball; they've gathered for some other occasion," thought our hero, his heart sinking somewhat. "Is it today, though?" flashed through his mind. "Can there be a mistake in the date? It could be; anything is possible . . . That's so; anything is possible . . . Perhaps the letter was written yesterday but it didn't reach me, and it didn't

reach me because Petrushka got involved in this matter, rascal
that he is! Or it said tomorrow, that is, that I . . . that it was
necessary to do everything tomorrow, that is, to be waiting
with the coach? . . ." At this point our hero grew absolutely cold
all over and felt in his pocket for the letter in order to check his
information. But to his amazement the letter was not in his
pocket. "How can this be?" whispered Mr. Golyadkin, more
dead than alive. "Where can I have left it? I must have lost it!
That's all I needed!" he concluded finally, with a groan. "And
what if it falls into evil hands now? (Why, perhaps it already
has!) Lord! What will come of this! Something too awful to
contemplate . . . Ah, destestable fate of mine!" At this point Mr.
Golyadkin began to shake like a leaf at the thought that
perhaps his unseemly twin, in tossing his overcoat over his
head, had done it expressly for the purpose of seizing the letter,
the existence of which he had somehow sniffed out from Mr.
Golyadkin's enemies. "What's more, he's seized it," thought
our hero, "as proof . . . but why as proof? . . ." After the initial
stunning horror, the blood rushed to Mr. Golyadkin's head.
Groaning and gnashing his teeth, he clutched his feverish head,
sank down onto his log and began to think about something . . .
But somehow the thoughts were not connecting in his head.
Some faces flashed through his mind; some long-forgotten
events were recalled, now dimly, now sharply; some themes
from stupid songs insinuated themselves into his brain . . . And
oh, the anguish was unnatural! "My God! My God!" thought
our hero, coming to his senses somewhat and suppressing the
dull sobs in his breast, "grant me firmness of spirit in the
bottomless depths of my misfortune! That I am done for, that I
have utterly ceased to exist—of this there is no longer any
doubt, and it is all in the order of things, for it cannot be any
other way. In the first place I've lost my post, lost it for certain;
there is no way I could not have lost it . . . Well, let's even
suppose that it can be put to rights somehow. My money, let's
suppose, will suffice to start off with; I'll get some other small
apartment; I'll need some bits of furniture . . . In the first place
Petrushka won't be with me . . . I can manage without that
rascal . . . manage with the help of the other tenants; well, that's

fine! I can come and go when I feel like it, and Petrushka won't be grumbling that I come home late—that's how it is; that's why it's good to have the other tenants... Well, let's suppose all this is good; only how is it that I keep talking about the wrong thing, completely wrong?" At this point the thought of his real situation again dawned on Mr. Golyadkin. He looked about. "Ah, dear God! Dear God! What have I been talking about now?" he thought, losing his calm completely and clutching his feverish head...

"Will you be pleased to go soon, sir?" a voice uttered above Mr. Golyadkin. Mr. Golyadkin started but before him stood his driver, also soaked to the skin and chilled to the bone. Impatient and having nothing to do, he had taken it into his head to look in on Mr. Golyadkin behind the woodpile.

"I'm fine, my friend, ... I'll come soon, my friend, very soon; you wait..."

The driver went away, muttering under his breath. "Now what's he muttering about?" thought Mr. Golyadkin tearfully. "After all I hired him for the evening; after all, I, you know... am within my rights now ... So there! I hired him for the evening and that's all there is to it. Even if you just stand about, it doesn't matter. Everything has to be as I say. I am free to go and free not to go. And that I am standing here behind the woodpile, why, that doesn't matter at all... and don't you dare say anything; I say, 'The gentleman feels like standing behind the woodpile, and so he's standing behind the woodpile... and he is not sullying anyone's honor—that's what!' That's what, my dear young lady, if you really want to know. As for living in a cabin, I say, 'This is the way it is; nowadays no one does, my dear young lady. So there!' And without good behavior in our industrial age, my dear young lady, you won't get anywhere, something you yourself now serve as a pernicious example of... You say, 'You have to serve as a court clerk and live in a cabin by the sea.' In the first place, my dear young lady, there are no court clerks by the sea, and in the second place, you and I cannot get one, a job as a court clerk, that is. For, let's suppose, for example, I hand in a petition; I appear and say, 'This is the way it is, make me a court clerk;' I say, 'You know... and protect me from my enemy' . . . and they will say to you, 'Young lady,' they'll say, 'you know . . . there are plenty of court clerks and here you are not at the émigrée Falbala's, where you learned good behavior, something you yourself serve as a pernicious example of.' For good behavior, young lady, means sitting at home, respecting your father and not thinking about suitors prematurely. For, suitors, young lady, will be found in good time—so there! Of course, unquestionably, you must have various talents, such as: playing the piano a bit sometimes, speaking French, knowing history, geography, scripture and arithmetic—that's what!—and that's all you need. Oh, and cooking besides; certainly cooking must be part of the area of competence of every well-behaved girl! But what do we have here? In the first place, my beauty, my queen, they won't let you go, but will pursue you and then shut you up in a nunnery. Then what, my dear young lady? What will you have me do then? Will you have me, my dear young lady, in imitation of certain stupid novels, come to a nearby mound and dissolve in tears, looking at the cold walls of your incarceration, and finally die, in imitation of the custom of certain bad German poets and novelists; is that it, young lady? Well, in the first place, permit me to tell you in a friendly manner that things are not done that way, and, in the second place, I would heartily flog both you and your parents for giving you French books to read; for French books do not teach what is good. There is poison in them . . . noxious poison, my dear young lady! Or do you think, permit me to ask you, or do you think that, I say, 'This is the way it is,' we shall run away unpunished, and, well, you know . . . I say, 'a cabin for you by the sea,' and, well, we'll start to bill and coo and discuss our various feelings, and we'll spend our whole life thus, in happiness and contentment; and then we'll have a little one, so we, you know . . . we say, 'This is the way is it, our father and State Councilor, Olsufi Ivanovich; here,' we say, 'a little one has arrived, so will you, on this convenient occasion, remove your malediction and bless this couple?' No, young lady, and once again, let me tell you, things are not done that way, and the first thing is that there'll be no billing and cooing; don't hope for it. Nowadays the husband, my dear young lady, is master and a

good, well-brought-up wife must try to please him in every way.
And they don't like endearments nowadays, young lady, in our
industrial age; 'the time of Jean-Jacques Rousseau is over,' I say.
The husband, for instance, comes home hungry from work
nowadays—he says, 'Darling, how about a little something, a
drop of vodka and a nibble of herring?' And you, young lady,
must immediately have both the vodka and the herring ready.
Your husband will eat and drink with gusto and not even glance
at you, but will say: 'Do go,' he'll say, 'into the kitchen, kitten,
and keep an eye on dinner,' and maybe, just maybe, once a
week he'll kiss you, and even then he'll be indifferent... That's
the way we do it, my dear young lady! 'And even then,' I say,
'he'll be indifferent!' That's how it will be, if we reason thus, if
it's come to that already, that we've begun to look at the matter
in this way... And what do I have to do with it? Why have you
mixed me up in your whims, young lady? You said, 'Beneficent
man, suffering for my sake and dear to my heart in every way,
and so forth.' Well, in the first place, my dear young lady, I'm
not suitable for you; you know yourself I'm no hand at
compliments; I don't like to utter all that scented stuff and
nonsense for the ladies; I don't favor ladies' men; and what's
more, to tell the truth, my figure hasn't done anything for me.
You won't find any false bragging or false shame in me, and I
confess this to you now in all sincerity. I say, 'That's how it is'; a
straightforward and open character and common sense are all I
possess; I don't engage in intrigues. 'I'm not an intriguer,' I say,
'and I'm proud of it—so there!...' I go about without a mask
among good people and, to tell you the whole truth..."

Suddenly Mr. Golyadkin started. The red, thoroughly
soaked beard of his driver again looked in behind the woodpile
at him...

"I'll be there right away, my friend; I'll be there immediately,
my friend, you know; I'll be there at once, my friend," Mr.
Golyadkin answered in a quavering and weary voice.

The driver scratched the back of his head, then smoothed
his beard, then took a step forward... stopped and looked with
mistrust at Mr. Golyadkin.

"I'll be there right away, my friend; I, you see . . . my friend . . . I'm a little, I, you see, my friend, I'm stopping here for just a second . . . you see, my friend . . ."

"Can it be that you won't be going at all?" said the driver at last, accosting Mr. Golyadkin resolutely once and for all . . .

"No, my friend, I'll be there right away. You see, my friend, I'm waiting . . ."

"Yes, sir . . ."

"You see, my friend, I . . . what village are you from, my dear fellow?"

"I'm a serf . . ."

"And is the master a good person? . . ."

"He's all right . . ."

"Yes, my friend; you wait here, my friend. You, you see, my friend, have you been in Petersburg long?"

"I've been driving a year now . . ."

"And are you doing well, my friend?"

"All right."

"Yes, my friend, yes. Thank Providence, my friend. You search for a good person, my friend. Nowadays good people have become rare, my dear fellow; he will take care of you, feed you and give you drink, my dear fellow, a good man will . . . But sometimes you see tears flowing even for the sake of gold, my friend . . . You see a sorry example; that's how it is, my dear fellow . . ."

The driver seemed to feel sorry for Mr. Golyadkin.

"All right, if you please, I'll wait, sir. But are you going to be waiting a long time, sir?"

"No, my friend, no; I'm not going to, you know, um . . . I'm not going to wait any longer, my dear fellow. What do you think, my friend? I'm relying on you. I'm not going to wait here any longer . . ."

"Can it be you won't go at all?"

"No, my friend; no, but I'll show my gratitude to you, my dear fellow . . . that's how it is. How much do I owe you, my dear fellow?"

"Why, what we agreed upon, sir. I've waited a long time, sir. You wouldn't treat a person badly, sir."

"Well, here you are, my dear fellow, here you are." Mr. Golyadkin hereupon gave the full six silver rubles to the driver and seriously resolving to lose no more time, that is, to get away while the getting was good—the moreso since the matter had been decided once and for all and the driver had been let go and, consequently, there was nothing more to wait for—he started out of the courtyard, went through the gates, turned left and without looking back, gasping for breath and rejoicing, set off at a run. "Perhaps it will all turn out for the best," he thought, "and this way I've avoided trouble." And, in fact, Mr. Golyadkin suddenly began to feel unusually lighthearted. "Ah, if only everything would turn out for the best!" thought our hero, but without much believing his own words. "Here's what I'll do. . . ." he thought. "No, I'd better try a different approach . . . Or would it be better for me to do it this way? . . ." While thus doubting and searching for the key to the resolution of his doubts, our hero ran as far as the Semyonovsky Bridge, but having run as far as the Semyonovsky Bridge, decided judiciously and with finality to go back. "This is the better way," he thought. "I'd better use a different approach, that is, do it that way. I'll just be—I'll be an outside observer, and that's all there is to it; I'll say, 'I'm an observer, an outsider—and that's all', and then, no matter what may happen—I'm not to blame. That's how it is! And that's how it will be now."

Having decided to go back, our hero actually did go back, and went readily since, as a result of his happy thought, he had now made himself a complete outsider. "It really is better; you're not responsible for anything, but you'll see what's what . . . that's how it is!" That is, his reckoning was most infallible and that's all there was to it. Having calmed down, he betook himself again to the peaceful safety of his soothing and protective woodpile and began to watch the windows intently. This time he did not have to watch and wait for long. Suddenly a strange commotion was discernible in all of the windows at once; figures appeared here and there; the curtains were opened; whole groups of people thronged to Olsufi Ivanovich's windows; everyone was peering out and searching for something in the courtyard. Protected by his woodpile, our hero, too, in turn, began to follow the general commotion with curiosity and to stick his head out, looking with interest to the right and left, to the extent that the short shadow of the woodpile screening him permitted. Suddenly he became panic-stricken, started and almost collapsed with fear. It seemed to him—in a word, he had guessed fully—that they were searching not for just something and not for just someone; they were searching for him, Mr. Golyadkin. Everyone is looking in his direction; everyone is pointing in his direction. It was impossible to flee: they would see . . . The panic-stricken Mr. Golyadkin pressed himself as closely as he could against the woodpile and only then did he notice that the perfidious shadow was betraying him, that it did not screen all of him. Our hero would have acquiesced now with the utmost pleasure to squeeze into any mousehole between the logs and just sit there quietly, if only that had been possible. But it was absolutely impossible. In his agony he began at last to look resolutely and directly at all of the windows at once; it was better that way . . . And suddenly he burned with utter shame. He had been fully discovered; they had all noticed him at the same time; they were all beckoning to him; they were all nodding to him; they were all calling him; now several ventilation panes clicked and opened; several voices began simultaneously to shout something to him . . . "I'm amazed they don't flog these worthless girls when they're children," our hero muttered, becoming totally flustered. Suddenly *he* (we know who) ran down the front steps, without a coat or hat, breathless, whirling, bouncing along with his mincing gait, and perfidiously expressing how terribly glad he was to see Mr. Golyadkin at last.

"Yakov Petrovich," twittered this person notorious for his worthlessness, "Yakov Petrovich, you here? You'll catch cold. It's cold here, Yakov Petrovich. Do come inside."

"Yakov Petrovich! No, sir, I'm fine, Yakov Petrovich," our hero muttered in a submissive voice.

"No, sir; you mustn't refuse, Yakov Petrovich; they entreat you; they most humbly entreat you; they're waiting for us. They said, 'Do us the pleasure of bringing Yakov Petrovich in.' So there you are, sir."

"No, Yakov Petrovich; you see, I would do better . . . It would be better if I went home, Yakov Petrovich . . ." said our hero, roasting over a slow fire and freezing at the same time, from shame and horror.

"No, no, no, no!" twittered the loathsome person. "No, no, no, I won't take no for an answer! Let's go!" he said resolutely and dragged Mr. Golyadkin Senior towards the front steps. Mr. Golyadkin Senior did not at all want to go, but as everyone was looking and it would have been stupid to resist and dig in his heels, our hero went; however, it cannot be said that he went, for he absolutely did not know what was happening to him. But never mind, still he went!

Before our hero had time to put himself to rights in any way and regain his senses, he found himself in a reception room. He was pale, disheveled and tormented; he took in the whole crowd with lacklustre eyes—horrors! The reception room and all the other rooms were absolutely jam-packed. There were hordes of people and a whole bevy of ladies. All of them were crowding around Mr. Golyadkin; all of them were pressing towards Mr. Golyadkin; all of them were bearing Mr. Golyadkin along; he very clearly noticed that they were pushing him in a certain direction. "But not to the door," flashed through Mr. Golyadkin's mind. And indeed, they were pushing him not to the door but straight towards Olsufi Ivanovich's comfortable armchair. On one side of the armchair stood Klara Olsufyevna, pale, languid, melancholy, but magnificently adorned. What particularly struck Mr. Golyadkin were the tiny white flowers in her black hair, which created a superb effect. On the other side of the armchair Vladimir Semyonovich stood firm in a black morning coat, with his new decoration in his buttonhole. Mr. Golyadkin was being conducted, as has been said above, straight towards Olsufi Ivanovich—on one side by Mr. Golyadkin Junior, who had put on an extraordinarily proper and well-intentioned air, at which our hero was utterly overjoyed; on the other side he was being directed by Andrei Filippovich, whose face bore a most solemn mien. "What can this mean?" thought Mr. Golyadkin. But when he saw that he was being conducted towards Olsufi Ivanovich, it was as if he had suddenly been illumined by a flash of lightning. The thought of the intercepted letter flashed through his mind . . . In immeasurable agony our hero appeared before Olsufi Ivanovich's armchair. "How shall I act now?" he thought to himself. "Fearlessly, of course, that is, with a frankness not devoid of nobility; I'll say, 'This is the way it is and so forth'." But what our hero had apparently been fearing did not happen. Olsufi Ivanovich seemed to receive Mr. Golyadkin extremely well, and although he did not extend his hand to him, at least in looking at him he shook his grey, awe-inspiring head—shook it with a solemn and sad but at the same time benevolent look. So at least it seemed to Mr. Golyadkin. It even seemed to him that a tear glistened in Olsufi Ivanovich's lustreless eyes; he raised his eyes and saw that a little tear seemed also to glisten on the eyelashes of Klara Olsufyevna, who was standing nearby; that in the eyes of Vladimir Semyonovich, too, something similar seemed to be taking place; that, finally, Andrei Filippovich's calm and inviolable dignity was just as eloquent as the general tearful sympathy; that, finally, the youth who had at one time very much looked like an important councilor, taking advantage of the present moment, was now sobbing bitterly . . . Or all of this, perhaps, only seemed so to Mr. Golyadkin because he himself was weeping copiously and distinctly felt the hot tears running down his cold cheeks . . . In a voice shaken by sobs, reconciled to men and fate and at that moment loving greatly not only Olsufi Ivanovich, not only the guests in their entirety, but even his pernicious twin, who now apparently was not at all pernicious and not even Mr. Golyadkin's twin but a complete outsider and an extremely amiable person in his own right, our hero tried to address Olsufi Ivanovich with a touching out-pouring of his soul; but because of the fullness of all that had accumulated within him he could explain nothing at all, and only silently, with a most eloquent gesture, point to his heart . . . At last Andrei Filippovich, probably wishing to spare the sensibilities of the greyhaired old man, drew Mr. Golyadkin slightly aside and left him, it seemed, completely on his own. Smiling, muttering something under his breath, somewhat bewildered, but in any case almost completely reconciled with

187

men and fate, our hero began to make his way somewhere through the dense crowd of guests. Everyone made way for him; everyone looked at him with a strange curiosity and an enigmatic, inexplicable sympathy. Our hero passed into the next room; everywhere he received the same attention; he vaguely heard the entire crowd following close upon his heels, noting his every step, furtively discussing among themselves something extremely interesting, shaking their heads, talking, arguing and whispering. Mr. Golyadkin would have very much liked to find out what they were all discussing and arguing and whispering about so. Looking round, our hero noticed Mr. Golyadkin Junior beside him. Feeling the need to grab his arm and draw him aside, Mr. Golyadkin most earnestly entreated the other Yakov Petrovich to assist him in all his future undertakings and not to abandon him at a critical moment. Mr. Golyadkin Junior nodded gravely and firmly shook Mr. Golyadkin Senior's hand. Our hero's heart began to tremble from an excess of emotion. He was gasping for breath though; he felt that something was squeezing him ever more tightly, that all those eyes turned on him were somehow oppressing and crushing him . . . Mr. Golyadkin caught a glimpse of that councilor who was wearing a wig. The councilor was giving him a stern, searching look, not at all softened by the general sympathy . . . Our hero was about to go straight over to him, give him a smile and have it out with him immediately, but somehow it did not work out. For one instant Mr. Golyadkin almost lost consciousness completely; both his memory and his senses failed him . . . When he regained his senses, he noticed that the guests had gathered around him in a large circle. Suddenly Mr. Golyadkin's name was shouted from the other room. The shout was at once taken up by the entire crowd. Everything began to stir; everything began to hum; everyone rushed for the door of the first reception room; they almost carried our hero along with them, and the hard-hearted councilor with the wig came to find himself side by side with Mr. Golyadkin. Finally, he took Mr. Golyadkin by the arm and sat him down beside him, opposite the seat of Olsufi Ivanovich, but at a rather considerable distance from him. Everyone else from

those rooms sat down in several rows around Mr. Golyadkin
and Olsufi Ivanovich. Everything grew hushed and still; everyone observed a solemn silence; everyone was watching Olsufi
Ivanovich, apparently expecting something rather out of the
ordinary. Mr. Golyadkin noticed that the other Mr. Golyadkin
and Andrei Filippovich had taken their places beside the
armchair of Olsufi Ivanovich and directly opposite the councilor.
The silence continued; they were, in fact, waiting for something.
"Just like in a family, when someone is going on a long journey;
all we have to do now is stand up and say a prayer," thought our
hero. Suddenly an unusual commotion took place, disrupting
all of Mr. Golyadkin's reflections. Something long-awaited had
occurred. "He's coming! He's coming!" ran through the crowd.
"Who is it that's coming?" ran through Mr. Golyadkin's head
and he shuddered from a strange sensation. "It's time!" said the
councilor, looking intently at Andrei Filippovich. Andrei
Filippovich in turn glanced at Olsufi Ivanovich. Olsufi Ivanovich
gravely and solemnly gave a nod of his head. "Let's stand up,"
uttered the councilor, hauling Mr. Golyadkin to his feet.
Everyone rose. Then the councilor took Mr. Golyadkin Senior
by the arm while Andrei Filippovich did the same to Mr.
Golyadkin Junior, and the two of them solemnly brought the
two exactly identical persons together in the midst of the
crowd which had surrounded them and was watching with
intense expectation. Our hero looked about in bewilderment
but they immediately checked him and indicated Mr. Golyadkin
Junior, who had extended his hand to him. "They want to
reconcile us," thought our hero and extended his hand to Mr.
Golyadkin Junior with a feeling of tenderness; then he bent his
head towards him. The other Mr. Golyadkin did the same... At
this point it seemed to Mr. Golyadkin Senior that his perfidious
friend was smiling, that he winked swiftly and roguishly at all
those around them, that there was something malevolent in the
face of the unseemly Mr. Golyadkin Junior, that he even made a
grimace at the moment of his Judas kiss... There was a ringing
in Mr. Golyadkin's head. It went black before his eyes. It
seemed to him that a host, a whole string of exactly identical
Golyadkins was noisily breaking in through all the doors of the

189

room; but it was too late... The resounding, traitorous kiss was heard, and . . .

At this point a completely unexpected event occurred... The door to the reception room opened noisily and on the threshold appeared a man whose very aspect struck terror into Mr. Golyadkin. He stood rooted to the spot. A cry froze in his constricted breast. Still, Mr. Golyadkin had known everything beforehand and had had a premonition of something like this for a long time now. The stranger gravely and solemnly drew near to Mr. Golyadkin... Mr. Golyadkin knew this figure very well. He had seen it before, seen it very frequently, seen it that very day . . . The stranger was a tall, thickset man in a black morning coat with a sizeable cross around his neck and endowed with very black, bushy sidewhiskers; all he needed to complete the resemblance was a small cigar in his mouth . . . Still the stranger's look, as has already been said, struck terror into Mr. Golyadkin. With a grave and solemn mien, the terrifying man approached the pathetic hero of our tale... Our hero stretched his hand out to him; the stranger took his hand and pulled him along after him . . . With a perplexed and crushed look on his face, our hero gazed around . . .

"It's . . . it's Krestyan Ivanovich Rutenshpits, Doctor of Medicine and Surgery, your old acquaintance, Yakov Petrovich!" someone's loathsome voice twittered right in Mr. Golyadkin's ear. He looked round: it was Mr. Golyadkin's twin, made loathsome by the vile qualities of his soul. An unseemly, malevolent glee shone in his face; he was rubbing his hands together with delight; he was turning his head from side to side with delight; he was mincing about near each and every one with delight; he even seemed ready at that point to begin to dance with delight; at last he leapt forward, seized a candle from one of the servants and went ahead lighting the way for Mr. Golyadkin and Krestyan Ivanovich. Mr. Golyadkin clearly heard everyone in the reception room rush after him, heard everyone crowding and crushing each other and all beginning to repeat together, in one voice, after Mr. Golyadkin: "It's all right; don't be afraid, Yakov Petrovich; why, this is your old friend and acquaintance, Krestyan Ivanovich Rutenshpits . . ."

At last they came out onto the brightly illumined main staircase; on the staircase, too, there was a crowd of people; the front door was thrown open noisily and Mr. Golyadkin found himself on the steps together with Krestyan Ivanovich. At the entrance stood a coach, its four horses snorting with impatience. Full of malicious glee, Mr. Golyadkin Junior came down the stairs in three bounds and opened the coach door himself. Krestyan Ivanovich, with an authoritative gesture, requested Mr. Golyadkin to get in. The authoritative gesture was totally unnecessary, however; there were plenty of people to help him get in... Fainting with terror, Mr. Golyadkin looked back: the whole of the brightly illumined staircase was covered with people; inquisitive eyes were looking at him from everywhere; Olsufi Ivanovich presided on the topmost landing in his comfortable armchair, watching with the most intense interest all that was taking place. Everyone was waiting. A murmur of impatience ran through the crowd when Mr. Golyadkin looked back.

"I trust that there is nothing... nothing reprehensible... or capable of provoking severe measures . . . and exciting public attention, as far as my official relations are concerned?" uttered our hero, losing his presence of mind. A hubbub of voices rose all about; everyone began to shake his head to say there wasn't. Tears gushed from Mr. Golyadkin's eyes.

"In that case, I am ready... I have complete confidence... and place my fate in the hands of Krestyan Ivanovich . . ."

No sooner had Mr. Golyadkin uttered the words that he placed his fate completely in the hands of Krestyan Ivanovich than a terrible, deafening shout of joy broke out from all those around him and rolled with a most sinister echo through all of the waiting crowd. At this point Krestyan Ivanovich on one side and Andrei Filippovich on the other took Mr. Golyadkin by the arms and began to help him into the coach; the double, as was his customary vile wont, helped him in from behind. The unfortunate Mr. Golyadkin Senior cast his final glance at everyone and everything and, trembling like a kitten that has been doused with cold water—if we may be permitted the comparison—climbed into the coach; Krestyan Ivanovich climbed in immediately after him. The coach door slammed; the crack of the whip on the horses was heard; the horses started the coach up with a jerk . . . everyone rushed after Mr. Golyadkin. The piercing, furious cries of all his enemies rang out after him like a series of farewell wishes. For some time still a few people could be glimpsed around the coach that was bearing Mr. Golyadkin away; but they gradually began to be left further and further behind and finally disappeared altogether. Mr. Golyadkin's unseemly twin remained longer than any of them. With his hands in the side pockets of his green uniform trousers, he ran along with a satisfied air, leaping up now on one side of the coach, now on the other; and sometimes, grabbing hold of the window frame and hanging from it, he would poke his head in through the window and send Mr. Golyadkin little farewell kisses; but he too began to tire, began to appear less and less frequently and finally disappeared altogether. Mr. Golyadkin's heart began to ache dully in his breast; the blood rushed hotly to his head; it was stifling; he felt like unbuttoning his clothing, baring his breast, sprinkling it with snow and dousing it with cold water. He sank at last into forgetfulness . . . When he regained his senses, he saw that the horses were taking him along an unfamiliar road. To the right and to the left forests loomed darkly; it was godforsaken and lonely. Suddenly he froze in terror: two fiery eyes were looking at him in the darkness, and, those two eyes were shining with sinister, infernal glee. This isn't Krestyan Ivanovich! Who is it? Or is it he? It is! It is Krestyan Ivanovich, only not the previous one; this is another Krestyan Ivanovich! This is a terrifying Krestyan Ivanovich! . . .

"Krestyan Ivanovich, I . . . I believe I'm all right, Krestyan Ivanovich," began our hero, in a timid and trembling manner, wishing by his submissiveness and meekness to propitiate the terrifying Krestyan Ivanovich if only slightly. "You vill recif kvarters at public expenz, mit firevood, licht und serfice, vich you don't deserf," sounded Krestyan Ivanovich's answer, stern and terrible as a judge's sentence.

Our hero uttered a shriek and clutched his head. Alas! He had had a premonition of this for a long time now!

X

1846 Redaction

Mr. Golyadkin's opinion of what constitutes a game with trumps and one without. A corrupt person occupies Mr. Golyadkin's place in practical life. Of how various cabmen and Petrushka, who concurs with them, look upon this entire situation. Mr. Golyadkin wakes up, writes a letter and somewhat wounds the reputation of Grishka Otrepyev. Mr. Golyadkin begins to intrigue. Copyists. Of how Mr. Golyadkin ended his intrigues and what he finally resolved upon.

In general, one might say that the events of the previous day had shaken Mr. Golyadkin to the core; most terrifying of all was his enemies' final word. Of course, this final word had not yet been spoken... All of this was in a mysterious, threatening twilight, but it was this very circumstance—that all of it was in twilight and was mysterious—that was eroding Mr. Golyadkin. "If they would play the game openly," thought Mr. Golyadkin through his sleep, at the moment of waking up, "I would not permit them to trump so; I would show them a game without trumps then." But most of all Vakhrameyev's letter tormented Mr. Golyadkin. What did all those allusions mean? What does that tone, sharp and threatening to the point of bizarreness, mean? Of course, Mr. Golyadkin had had a premonition of all this... that is, he hadn't really, but everything had worked out somehow strangely and it had happened that precisely this had resulted and not something else; consequently, Mr. Golyadkin had had a premonition of this as well. Our hero did not sleep too well, that is, he could in no wise fall completely asleep for even five minutes; it was as if some joker had sprinkled cut-up bristles into his bed. He spent the entire night in a sort of half-sleeping, half-waking state, tossing and turning from side to side, moaning and groaning, falling asleep for one moment and waking up again the next, and all this was accompanied by a kind of strange anguish, dim recollections, hideous apparitions— in a word, by everything unpleasant that one can possibly imagine... Now the figure of Andrei Filippovich would appear before him in a kind of strange, mysterious half-light—a dry figure, an angry figure, with a cold, harsh look and a coldly civil reprimand... And no sooner would Mr. Golyadkin begin to approach Andrei Filippovich to justify himself before him somehow, in this way or that, and to prove to him that he was not at all the way his enemies painted him, that he was like this or like that, and even possessed, above and beyond his usual innate qualities, this one and that one, than thereupon a certain person notorious for his unseemly inclinations would appear and he would forthwith by some means most perturbing to the soul destroy all of Mr. Golyadkin's intended undertakings; he would thereupon, almost before Mr. Golyadkin's very eyes, thoroughly blacken his reputation, trample his self-esteem in the mud and then forthwith take his place at work and in society. Or else Mr. Golyadkin's head would smart from some rap on it, recently acquired and humiliatingly accepted, received either socially or somehow in the line of duty, against which rap it was difficult to protest... And as Mr. Golyadkin was about to start puzzling over just why it was difficult to protest even against such a rap, this very thought about the rap would imperceptibly flow into some other form, into the form of a certain petty or rather considerably base deed seen, heard or recently committed by him, and frequently committed not even on base grounds and not even from some base motive, but just so—sometimes, for example, by chance—out of delicacy, another time because of his own complete helplessness, or, finally, because... because, in a word, well, Mr. Golyadkin knew very well *why*! Hereupon Mr. Golyadkin would blush in his sleep and, suppressing his blushes, would mutter to himself, saying that there, for example, one might have shown firmness of character, one might have shown considerably greater firmness of character in that instance . . . and then he would conclude by saying, "What is firmness of character? . . . Why mention it now? . . ." But what would enrage and irritate Mr. Golyadkin most of all was the fact that hereupon and without fail at such a moment, whether summoned or not, there would appear a person notorious for his disgraceful and slanderous inclinations and he would also—despite the fact that the affair now seemed notorious—he would also, thereupon, mutter with an unseemly smile, "What does firmness of character have to do with it? What firmness of character you and I will have, Yakov Petrovich!" Or else Mr. Golyadkin would dream that he was in a splendid company, famous for the wit and breeding of all the persons comprising it; that he, Mr. Golyadkin, in his turn had distinguished himself by his amiability and wit, that everyone had come to like him, even certain of his enemies who were there had come to like him, which was very pleasant for Mr. Golyadkin; that everyone acknowledged his superiority and that, finally, Mr. Golyadkin himself overheard with pleasure as his host, taking several guests aside, thereupon praised him, Mr. Golyadkin . . . and suddenly, for no reason at all, again there appeared a person notorious for his evil intentions and bestial impulses, in the form of Mr. Golyadkin Junior, and thereupon, forthwith, in an instant, solely by having made his appearance, Golyadkin Junior destroyed all the triumph and all the glory of Mr. Golyadkin Senior, overshadowed Golyadkin Senior, trampled Golyadkin Senior in the mud and, finally, clearly demonstrated that Golyadkin Senior, who was also the real Golyadkin, was not at all the real one but a counterfeit, and that *he* was the real one; that, finally, Golyadkin Senior was not at all what he seemed, the so-and-so, and consequently should not and did not have the right to be in the society of persons who were well-intentioned and well-bred. And all of this happened so quickly that Mr. Golyadkin Senior did not even have time to open his mouth before everyone went over completely to the disgraceful and counterfeit Mr. Golyadkin and with the deepest scorn renounced him, the real and innocent Mr. Golyadkin. There was not one person whose opinion the bestial Mr. Golyadkin would not have altered in an instant to his own way of thinking. There was not one person, even the most insignificant of the entire company, whom the worthless and false Mr. Golyadkin would not fawn over in his own, most saccharine manner, not one person with whom he would not attempt to ingratiate himself in his own way, not one person before whom he would not burn, according to his wont, the most pleasant and sweet-smelling incense, so that the person who was enveloped in its smoke would simply sniff and sneeze till the tears came, in token of his supreme pleasure. And the main thing was that all this would happen in an instant: the swiftness of the suspect and worthless Mr. Golyadkin's progress was astonishing! He would hardly succeed, for example, in currying favor with one person, in getting into his good graces, than before you could blink an eye, he would already be attempting to do so with another. He would quietly work away currying favor with another, gain from him a smile of good will, give a flick of his short little, round little, though rather clumsy little leg, and there he would be with a third; and now he is making advances to the third, fawning over him in a friendly manner; one has not even had time to open one's mouth, one has not even had time to be amazed, when already he is with a fourth and already on those same terms with the fourth; horrors—witchcraft and nothing else! And everyone is glad to see him, and everyone likes him, and everyone exalts him, and everyone proclaims in chorus that the amiability and satiric bent of his mind is by far superior to the amiability and satiric bent of the real Mr. Golyadkin's mind, and they thereby put to shame the real and innocent Mr. Golyadkin, and reject the truth-loving Mr. Golyadkin, and now they are rudely pushing the well-intentioned Mr. Golyadkin and delivering raps to the real Mr. Golyadkin, so well-known for his love of his neighbor! ... In anguish, terror, and rage, the much-suffering Mr. Golyadkin ran out into the street and began trying to hire a cab, so that he could fly straight to His Excellency's or, if not there, then at least to Andrei Filippovich's, but—horrors! The cabman would in no wise agree to take Mr. Golyadkin, saying, "Sir, we cannot take two people who look exactly alike; Your Worship, a good man strives to live honestly, not just any old way, and he never has a double." In an outburst of shame, the completely honest Mr. Golyadkin would look around and really assure himself, with his own eyes, that the cabmen and Petrushka, who was conspiring with them, were all indeed right; for the corrupt Mr. Golyadkin would, in fact, be there close beside him, and in accordance with his base traits of character, would even at this point, even at this critical moment, undeniably be preparing to do something utterly unseemly and not at all indicative of the particular nobility of character that is usually acquired in the course of one's upbringing—a nobility which at every convenient opportunity the repulsive Mr. Golyadkin the Second lauded himself for having. Beside himself with shame and despair, the ruined though completely legitimate Mr. Golyadkin fled blindly, giving himself up to the will of fate, regardless of where it might lead him; but with every step he took, with every thud of his foot against the granite of the pavement there would spring up, out of the ground, an exact likeness of the repulsive Mr. Golyadkin with his corruptness of heart. And all of these exact likenesses, immediately upon making their appearance, began running one after the other and stretched out in a long chain like a string of geese, waddling after Mr. Golyadkin Senior, so that there was nowhere to escape to from these exact likenesses; so that Mr. Golyadkin, who was in every way possible deserving of pity, was breathless with fear; so that finally a terrible host of exact likenesses had sprung into being; so that the entire capital was clogged with exact likenesses and a policeman, seeing such a breach of propriety, was forced to take them, all the exact likenesses, by the scruff of the neck and imprison them in a police booth that happened to be just beside him . . . Frozen and numb with fear, our hero was waking up, and, frozen and numb with fear, he was feeling that his waking hours were hardly more cheerful . . . He felt oppressed and tormented! . . . An anguish that seemed as though someone were consuming his heart out of his breast began to come over him . . .

Finally Mr. Golyadkin could bear it no longer. "It shall not be!" he shouted, raising himself up in bed with determination and waking up altogether after this exclamation.

The day was evidently well under way. It was unusually bright in the room; the sun's rays filtered densely through the frost-covered panes and spilled profusely about the room, which astonished Mr. Golyadkin more than a little; for after all it was only at noon that the sun peeped into his room in its normal round; there had almost never been such exceptions in the course of the heavenly body before, at least not insofar as Mr. Golyadkin himself could recall. Our hero had no sooner marvelled at this than the wall clock behind the partition began to whir as if it were going to strike. "Ah, there it goes!" thought Mr. Golyadkin and anxiously and apprehensively prepared to listen... But to Mr. Golyadkin's utter and final frustration, his clock strained itself and struck only once. "What's going on here?" our hero cried, jumping out of bed altogether. Without dressing, just as he was, he rushed behind the partition, not believing his ears. The clock really did say one. Mr. Golyadkin glanced at Petrushka's bed, but there wasn't even the least hint of Petrushka anywhere in the room: his bed had evidently been made up for some time now and left; his shoes were also nowhere to be seen—an unmistakeable sign that Petrushka really was not home. Mr. Golyadkin rushed to the door; it was locked. Mr. Golyadkin straightaway ran back into his room, threw himself on the bed, wrapped himself up in the counterpane and closed his eyes tightly...

For a minute our hero lay motionless, then carefully, timidly, slowly opened both eyes. No! No change of any kind! Everything was the same as before. "It can't be a dream at all!" cried Mr. Golyadkin. "It must be that I actually, in fact, and in reality did sleep past noon! But where can Petrushka be?" he continued in a whisper, overcome with intense excitement and feeling a rather considerable trembling in all his limbs... Suddenly a thought flashed through his mind... Mr. Golyadkin rushed to his desk, surveyed it, and rummaged about—just as he thought: his letter of the day before to Vakhrameyev was not there... Petrushka was also nowhere behind the partition now; it had struck one on the wall clock, while in Vakhrameyev's letter of the day before some new points had been introduced which, though they had at first glance been extremely obscure, had now become perfectly clear points that concerned Mr. Golyadkin personally and familially . . . Finally, Petrushka, too—although drunk (and consequently, he was within his rights and therefore there was no reason to hold him responsible), had announced yesterday that others do not live having doubles, but live honestly . . . It must be that all of this was so! The allusion was clear, the enemies' machinations had been revealed, and the game was on the verge of coming out into the open; yes, the game must now be moving toward open warfare . . . It was clear that now they were eroding the very core of his well-being; it was clear that they were bribing, nosing about, concocting, conjecturing, spying, that, finally, they wanted Mr. Golyadkin's destruction once and for all; perhaps they had already set the day . . . perhaps they had already set the hour . . . It must be that Petrushka had been bribed and had now also deserted to their side. It must be that way! It must be that this was the kind of turn that matters had now begun to take! . . . Otherwise, how exactly could one explain Petrushka's disappearance, Petrushka's behavior of the day before, Vakhrameyev's letter with its accusatory points, the coldness and harshness of his relations with his superiors, and finally, the disappearance of the letter and the fact that Mr. Golyadkin had slept past noon—how exactly could one explain all this if not by the presence, if not by the evil-intentioned participation of a new, unseemly person in all of his misfortunes, if not by the secret and underground machinations of that person to cause every kind of unconscionable damage to Mr. Golyadkin . . . And Mr. Golyadkin knew what sort of person this was, knew what sort of new person had gotten mixed up in this—and knew why he had gotten mixed up in it. "And that is sufficient for subsequent comprehension," thought Mr. Golyadkin. "And, of course, the thing was clear! But still, how did such a simple thought escape me as recently as yesterday? How is it that I didn't realize it all immediately long ago? That was the beginning of it all; and though it's only gossip, though it's all nothing but the invention of old wives and old biddies, the invention of certain old ladies secretly conspiring with certain persons in order to confound people, in order to finish a person off in the moral sense once and for all—still, this is how it all was! So that's where the main plot was being hatched!" cried Mr. Golyadkin, striking his forehead and opening his eyes wider and wider. "So, it's in the den of that stingy German that all the main forces of darkness are hiding now! So, it must be that she was only creating a strategic diversion when she directed me to the Izmailovsky Bridge; she was distracting my attention; she was destroying my peace; she was confusing me (the good-for-nothing witch!) and that's how she was undermining me!!! Yes, that's it! That's it! If only one looks at the matter from this aspect, then that's exactly how it all is! It absolutely must be that way! And the appearance of that utter heel can also be explained now, explained completely; so it's all connected. They've been keeping him in reserve for a long time now, getting him ready and saving him for a rainy day. He's their leaven for this whole unseemly intrigue and he's been made by them to aid them in achieving their main and their most evil-intentioned goals. Why, that's how it is now, how it has all resulted! That's how it has all been resolved! So that's what has affected my case now! The mask must be falling off now; everything must be coming out into the open! It must be that brazenness, corruptness and dissoluteness are not ashamed now of their nakedness and are resolved to walk in broad daylight openly and with head held high . . . But this is just where they will be taken by surprise; now this is just where they will stub their toes!" cried our hero, reminding himself in this difficult situation that innocence is strong simply by virtue of its innocence . . .—"And how amazing it is that yesterday I was negligent and noticed nothing! Ah, well, it doesn't matter! No time has been lost so far; thank God that so far only a little of it has passed and that hardly any time has been lost so far! At this point Mr. Golyadkin recalled with horror that it was already one in the afternoon. "What if they have succeeded by now! . . ." A groan escaped from his breast. . . "But, of course not; they're lying; they haven't succeeded—we'll see . . . 'we'll just go and see now,' I say, 'you know, expose it and damn the expense . . . we'll just see . . .'" muttered Mr. Golyadkin, not understanding too well himself what he was saying, losing his calm, growing pale

and trembling with anguish and excitement. At last our hero,
seizing his clothing, began to dress as quickly as possible . . .

Somehow he got dressed; losing no time, he unlocked the
apartment with another key, ran down the stairway and, not
stopping now to interrogate the janitor about his servant,
knowing that it was all superfluous, that all of them were united
in a conspiracy and making use of one another, ran out the gate
and to the office. However, on the corner of Italyanskaya and
Shestilavochnaya streets our hero wisely managed to think
better of it while there was still time and to revoke his decision,
and decided to return home for a while. "Well, never mind," he
thought, "that I shall be a bit late. For after all I must not leave
what I have to say unsaid. In the first place, as far as work is
concerned, I'll get there; whether sooner or later—the outcome
will still be the same. It all centers around this . . . Of course, I
can also . . . that's what I'll do . . . I can go see His Excellency in
the evening. I'll say, 'You know, this is the way it is'; I'll say
'. . . extra special . . . I entrust myself'—and at the same time, I
imagine, you know . . . That's just how it all will be! As far as the
main issue is concerned, it doesn't seem as if it could be made
any worse now. Even as it is, everything is in good shape,
everything is very fine. But in any case I still must write to *that*
one and make haste to write, to forewarn and intimidate the
fool—expressly to intimidate him, intimidate him without fail;
I'll say, 'This is the way it is, sir; and to, you know . . . intimidate
you! I'm opening your eyes for you, my dear sir, but still I desire
with all my heart to remain on friendly terms with you and so
forth'—that's absolutely necessary. And to that other person I
must announce firmly and in a straightforward manner that his
game is very intricate; I'll say, 'Very intricate, I assure you. That
regardless of how one looks at the matter, my dear sir and utter
heel, we shall leave the untangling of your game to someone
higher up, to someone better than you and me,' I'll say; 'We'll
take it to another instance; we'll go,' I'll say, 'somewhere higher
up'; I'll say, 'We know what's good for us, sir'; I'll say, 'Every
person protects his own nose, sir, cherishes and guards it, and
we, sir, don't blow ours just any old way', and so forth. That's
how I'll do it, that's how, that is, boldly; I shall speak using

direct and noble language, with steely resoluteness, as they say in good style, and with iron firmness, which, as everyone knows, all villains fear, and so forth. Or perhaps it can be done this way . . . that is, you know . . . that is, give the matter a different turn, that is, thus, this way, and cunningly ingratiate myself . . . that is, no, why cunningly ingratiate myself? . . . that's base—to cunningly ingratiate oneself! Or one can do it this way as well—in direct and noble language and utterly boldly, that is, you know . . . 'That's how it is,' I'll say; I'll say, 'If I am to blame for something, then I'm prepared to come to an agreement, very likely, prepared, it's my fault,' I'll say . . . but still, you know . . . well, in a noble manner, of course . . ."

Here Mr. Golyadkin stopped and noticed that he was throwing his well-known, terrible, defiant glance at the engraved portrait of the jester Balakirev which hung in his room over his bed. But Balakirev only grinned as he looked at Mr. Golyadkin. Our hero looked about in confusion and only then saw that he had returned to his room a long time ago, something he had at first not noticed at all because he was so deeply absorbed in what he was saying . . . Spitting in annoyance, Mr. Golyadkin threw off his overcoat and everything else that one did not need to wear indoors, sat down at the desk, seized a pen and without hesitating for very long scribbled the following two epistles—one to Vakhrameyev and the other to the ignoble Mr. Golyadkin Junior. The content of the letter to Vakhremeyev was as follows:

My Dear Nestor Ignatyevich,
    Sir!
Having kept inviolable and intact my nobility of soul, my uncorrupted heart and my untroubled conscience (the true riches and happiness of every mortal!), I am compelled, my dear sir, for the second time and without waiting for your reply to my letter of yesterday, to have it out with you and to pronounce my last word once and for all now. I am ashamed of my letter of yesterday, for in my innocence and in my artlessness—qualities which bear the earmarks of a

truly noble grounding received primarily through one's upbringing (which certain insincere and in any case useless people are so falsely and insolently proud of)—in my innocence and in my artlessness, I repeat, I spoke with you, my dear sir, in my last letter in the language not of stratagems and not of underground and secret machinations, but in an open and noble language inculcated in me by a true belief in the purity of my conscience and in the contempt which I harbor for hypocrisy, which is loathsome and in every respect worthy of pity. I am changing my language and at the same time most earnestly request you, my dear sir, to look upon my letter of yesterday to you, obtained by Petrushka through stealth, as though you had not received it, as though it did not exist at all, or , if all of this is impossible, then, I beg you, at least, my dear sir, to read it absolutely the other way round, in the reverse sense, that is, deliberately understanding the meaning of my words in exactly the opposite sense. For not only do I now not desire a meeting with a certain person of the female sex whom you know, but I utterly reject, for the sake of my own personal safety and that of my interests, even the most remote and most innocent dealings with her. Indeed, I rejected this person and avoided her even when, without any cause on my part to breach the rules of propriety, I lived together with you and others, people forever dear to my heart, in the apartment of that person, with benefit of board and maid service from her. In precisely the same manner do I intend to avoid her now, too, having been informed in the letter written by you on the ** of this month, of the illegal, and in any case, for a person of trustworthy upbringing, the dishonorable acquisition of a pound of sugar in pieces via the thief, Petrushka, of which I am even glad; for I now have in my hands a written and original document about her false virtues. Finally, I also hope that you, in the uprightness of your truly frank character, will fully agree that the bribing of Petrushka, the enticing of him into your service, and the palming off on your part, my dear sir, of Yevstafi as suitable, according to your cunning words, for service to a young bachelor of good conduct—whereas Yevstafi is a scoundrel the likes of whom the world has not produced even to this day—speaks in my behalf even more than it should. Believe me, my dear sir (if you have not managed by now to be convinced of it), that there is reprisal for everything in the world and that above us there are also our superiors. As for untruthful letters of mine to that person, as you unjustly avow, sir, in your letter, they have never existed, and, consequently, there are no documents of any kind against me. As for the unfortunate person who is known for the disreputableness of his inclinations and who is now playing the pitiful and, moreover, dangerous role of a figurehead and impostor, tell him that in the first place, 1)[111] imposture and most of all shamelessness and brazenness have never led anyone to anything good and moral; 2) that Otrepyevs are impossible in the age in which we live; 3) that the quatrain supposedly composed by him and written by him while at my place, with crocodile and, therefore, with deceptive tears of tender emotion, I am holding onto as evidence before the entire world against a corruptness and shamelessness that make the heart indignant—qualities that lead to perdition, and that, finally, 4) I have never called myself and never been anyone's twin, that this claim will sooner earn him the derision and odium of everyone than any fulfillment of his infamous desires, and that, finally, I will not permit him to trifle with me. Tell them all, my dear sir, that I am not one of those people who are afraid of judgment or of a confrontation because they sense that they have some sins on their soul, and who therefore ingratiate themselves through flattery;

that I am not one of those people who are in every possible way ready to stick their nose out to be rapped and then express their gratitude for it besides; that, finally, I am not one of those people who, if, for example, they have a tailor sew them a pair of fashionable trousers with fine footstraps, feel, in their stupidity, utterly happy the whole day long, like fools. In conclusion, I shall say that the money owed to you, my dear sir, for the sale of razors to me I deem it my most sacred duty to return in its entirety and with deepest gratitude withal.

Moreover, I remain respectfully yours and, my dear sir,

Your most humble servant,
Ya. Golyadkin.

The letter to Mr. Golyadkin Junior bore the following content:

Dear Yakov Petrovich,
Sir!
Either you or I, but not the two of us! And therefore I am declaring to you that your strange, ludicrous and at the same time utterly impossible desire to seem to be my twin and to pass yourself off as such will only lead to your utter dishonor and defeat. I do not know, or, to put it better, do not well remember from what parts you hail, but I am warning you in a Christian manner that here among us and in the age in which we live you will not win us over by imposture and that we know what's what. And therefore I beg you, for the sake of your own good, to throw off your mask, withdraw and make way for people who are truly honorable and well-intentioned. If not, I will be prepared to decide on the most extreme measures; then the mask will fall off itself and certain things will be revealed of themselves; out of pity for you I am informing you of

this. But in any case I am warning you now for the last time. Afterwards it will be too late. I lay down my pen and wait . . . However, I am, in any case, at your service.

> Ya. Golyadkin.

Our hero rubbed his hands together energetically when he had finished both his letters. One could see that Mr. Golyadkin was in a state of powerful agitation, as if he had already utterly routed all his enemies and once and for all frustrated all their loathsome and base machinations. He had grown particularly excited as he was finishing his last lines. The fact of the matter is that he himself felt strongly at last that he was within his rights. With love and with hope he looked once more at the hot, but already cooling, lines, then folded both letters and sealed them in two separate envelopes. "And now to work," said Mr. Golyadkin without delay, getting up from his ottoman. "Now I shall work at odds against them and as quickly as possible. For they can very possibly be forestalled. If only it's not too late. Dear, dear, why, it's already after two!"

In actuality Mr. Golyadkin's clock was already showing a quarter past two when he came to finish his correspondence. Depsite the fact that both letters were extremely brief, their style had not come very easily to our hero. It had been particularly necessary to work hard at the start, on the first pages. Mr. Golyadkin took his hat without a word and rather slowly began to pull on his overcoat. It really was a strange business. Moreover, an extremely bad joke was resulting again! Of course, though, if one judged that way and looked at the matter from one side, then it was probably nothing—well, yes; but if one went and looked at it from the other side, it did not come out right; it looked completely different. The fact of the matter was that even now, after writing both his letters, admiring them, and at last sealing them up, our hero still continued to hesitate. "Why did I write them, though, those letters?" he said to himself, taking his hat and going out of the apartment a second time. "Why really did I write them? It may be risky, of course . . . and isn't it too soon? Wouldn't it be better to bide my time? So . . . to prudently keep silent until the right time; to pretend that I don't wish to challenge, that I myself do not wish to encounter unpleasantness, and for the time being take no heed of it—that's the way! Or else, after all, this will be a decisive step, a bold step, even too decisive a step, if I begin by saying everything, a step which can entail—can entail something extremely unpleasant . . . Hm . . . dear, it's bad, bad! Dear, my case is pretty bad now . . . hm! And the fact that I am so unpardonably late is extremely bad, too. What shall I do now? It's sort of frightening to go there. Besides, it's almost dusk . . . Dear, it's bad, bad! . . . Still, I'd be curious to know how he's doing there, you know, and on what footing he is now . . . I'll say, 'What sort of footing are you on there now, my dear sir?' " muttered Mr. Golyadkin, who had arrived and was getting down from the hired carriage. "I'll say, 'What have you resolved on and just what are you doing now, I'd like to know? . . .' " he continued to mutter, settling with the cabman and somewhat beside himself with agitation. "Oh, well, it's nothing, though," he said at last in conclusion, "but there, I keep going on about it, though . . . It's bad, really bad that I wrote those two letters and wrote them in such a style, finally. It would have been much better if I had written them in a more friendly and amicable tone . . . to Vakhrameyev, for example, by the way . . . I'd say, 'This is the way it is, dear friend; I remember the pleasant moments spent with you and particularly that unforgettable evening, etc.,' and at this point only, by the way, reproach him . . . I'd say, 'I am sending you, dear friend, two rubles for the razors; thank you for reminding me and, by the way, permit me to tell you in a friendly way, dear friend, that I, this is the way it is, read your letter,' (here I can even joke somewhat), 'and see that you, you ladykiller and perfidious traitor (you so-and-so), are playing knight to the German beauty with a walleye, that is, to a person of the female sex whom we both know . . .' It might not be a bad idea, though, to keep quiet about the walleye. The fool really does have designs in that direction . . . oh, well, it's nothing; it's superfluous, but how about this: 'And so, dear friend, having explained this and that to you, I conclude my letter and remain your most faithful Golyadkin, etc.'—that's the way! However, one way or the other, it's still risky . . . Dear, it's bad, bad! I should have been wary; I should have waited until the time was right, and then the whole business would have been revealed even more... Um... Oh, well, it's nothing! Live—and get used to it; but there, now we'll, you know, investigate the matter. It's really up to me to investigate the matter. It was always, finally, up to me to investigate any matter . . . To just up and go right in . . ." said Mr. Golyadkin, stopping hesitantly at the office stairway.—"The fact of the matter is shall I actually go in or not? Of course, on the one hand, perhaps it's risky, but, on the other hand, perhaps it will just be the same thing all over again. Dear, it's bad, bad! Dear, my case is pretty bad now!..." At last Mr. Golyadkin did somewhat make up his mind. However, having made up his mind somewhat, Mr. Golyadkin hereupon discovered that mightn't it be better to do it later, mightn't it be better like that, to do it another way, I say, later; but right now do it boldly and do it by some other means; or else, why, it meant revealing the game too much and putting one's own head in the noose. And it's never really good to reveal a lot; to be perfectly frank, if it's come to that, to being perfectly frank, then it's not always good to stick one's nose out far and to permit one's cards to be peeked at. The fact of the matter was that Mr. Golyadkin actually and quite accurately had had a premonition that the decisive moment was approaching, that matters were coming to a head, that intrigue, perfidy and treachery were at work, and that, finally, his enemies had forestalled him altogether and gotten the upper hand, and that now, at last, the final solution was at hand. "Of course," thought our hero, "of course, I can make inquiries about everything beforehand on the quiet; I can find out about all of this beforehand; I can find out, for example, even in the vestibule what he's really like and what footing he's on, without sticking my nose out far; I say, 'It's necessary to take care of one's nose now, because it's harmful for a person to stick his nose out far;' I say, 'That's how it is, etc.'"

This is the manner in which our hero flagged and became flustered, at a loss to know what to do and how to proceed in his difficult situation. Suddenly an apparently extremely trivial occurrence dispelled certain of Mr. Golyadkin's doubts, and although it only partially helped him out, at least it put him on the beaten path and the true way. From behind the corner of the office building a figure suddenly appeared, breathless and redfaced, probably from walking fast, and with a stealthy, ratlike gait darted up the entrance steps and then immediately into the vestibule. It was the copyist, Ostafyev, a person very well known to Mr. Golyadkin, a person who was quite useful and ready to do anything for ten kopeks. Knowing Ostafyev's weak spot and realizing that after an absence due to most urgent business he had probably become even more avid than before for ten-kopek coins, our hero determined not to begrudge them and immediately darted up the entrance steps and then also into the vestibule after Ostafyev, called to him, and with a mysterious air invited him to step over into a secluded corner behind an enormous iron stove. Once there our hero began to interrogate him.

"Well, now, my friend, how are things, you know . . . do you understand what I mean? . . ."

"At your service, Your Worship; I wish Your Worship good health."

"All right, my friend, all right; but I shall show my gratitude to you later, dear friend. Well, look now, how is it, my friend?"

"What is it that you would like to ask about, sir?" Here Ostafyev put his hand up to his mouth, which had inadvertently fallen open, and tried to close it somewhat.

"Well, I, look, my friend, I, you know . . . now don't you go thinking anything . . . Well, now, is Andrei Filippovich here? . . ."

"He's here, sir."

"And are the clerks here?"

"Yes, the clerks too, sir, as they should be, sir."

"And His Excellency, too?"

"Yes, His Excellency too, sir." Here the copyist once more put his hand up to close his mouth, which had again fallen open, and looked at Mr. Golyadkin somewhat curiously and strangely. At least so it seemed to our hero.

"And there's nothing special, my friend?"

"No, sir; not at all, sir."

"Have you heard anything about me, my friend? Any little thing, eh? Just maybe, my friend; do you understand what I mean?"

"No, sir, nothing yet." Here the copyist again put his hand up to close his mouth and again looked somewhat strangely at Mr. Golyadkin. The fact of the matter is that now our hero was trying to penetrate Ostafyev's countenance, to read something in it, to see whether he wasn't hiding something. And actually, it seemed as if he was hiding something; the fact of the matter is that somehow Ostafyev was becoming more and more rude and cold and was now less sympathetic to Mr. Golyadkin's interests than he had been at the start of their conversation. "He is partly within his rights," thought Mr. Golyadkin. "After all, what am I to him? Perhaps he has already received something from the other side, and that's why he has been absent due to most urgent business. And so I'll take a chance and give him something . . ." Mr. Golyadkin realized that the time for handing out ten-kopek pieces had come.

"Here, this is for you, dear friend . . ."

"I'm most deeply grateful to Your Worship."

"I'll give you even more."

"Yes, sir, Your Worship."

"I'll give you even more in just a moment and when this business is over I'll give you as much again. Understand?"

The copyist said nothing, stood at attention, and looked fixedly at Mr. Golyadkin.

"Well, tell me now: have you heard anything about me? . . ."

"So far it seems . . . you know, sir . . . so far there's nothing, sir." Ostafyev responded slowly and deliberately, also putting on, like Mr. Golyadkin, a somewhat mysterious air, wiggling his eyebrows slightly, looking at the ground, trying to find the right tone and, in a word, attempting with all his might to earn what had been promised him because he considered that what he had been given was already his and his in no uncertain terms.

"And hasn't anything been made known?"

"No, not yet, sir."

"But, listen . . . you know . . . perhaps it will be made known?"

"Later, of course, perhaps it will be made known, sir."

"It's bad!" thought our hero.

"Listen, here's some more, old chap."

"I'm most deeply grateful to Your Worship."

"Was Vakhrameyev here yesterday? . . ."

"He was, sir."

"And wasn't there someone else? . . . Try to remember, old chap."

The copyist searched his memory for a moment but could recall nothing appropriate.

"No, sir; there wasn't anyone else, sir."

"Hm!" Silence ensued.

"Listen, old chap, here's some more for you. Tell me everything down to the last detail."

"Yes, sir." Now Ostafyev stood there as meek as a lamb: this was just what Mr. Golyadkin wanted.

"Explain to me now, old chap; what sort of a footing is he on?"

"All right, sir; a good one, sir," responded the copyist, staring wide-eyed at Mr. Golyadkin.

"What do you mean 'a good one'?"

"Just that, sir." Here Ostafyev wiggled his eyebrows significantly. However, he was decidedly coming to a dead end and did not know what else to say. "It's bad!" thought Mr. Golyadkin.

"Hasn't there been anything more concerning Vakhrameyev?"

"Why, no, everything is the same as it was, sir."

"Try and think."

"There is, they say, sir."

"Well, and what is it?"

Ostafyev put his hand up to his mouth.

"Isn't there a letter from there to me?"

"Today the guard, Mikheyev, went to Vakhrameyev's apartment, to his German landlady there, sir. So I'll go and ask, if you want."

"Be so kind, old chap, for God's sake!... I'm just... Don't you go thinking anything, old chap; I'm just asking. Go and make inquiries, old chap; find out whether they're cooking something up on my account. What is *he* doing? That's what I need to know. Now you find *that* out, dear friend, and I shall show my gratitude to you later, dear friend..."

"Yes, sir, Your Worship, and Ivan Semyonych sat in your place today, sir."

"Ivan Semyonych? Ah, yes! Really?"

"Andrei Filippovich told him to sit there, sir..."

"Really? For what reason? Find that out, old chap; for God's sake, find that out, old chap. Find it all out—and I shall show my gratitude to you, my dear fellow; that's what I need... But don't you go thinking anything, old chap..."

"Yes, sir, yes, sir. I'll come right back down here, sir. But, Your Worship, aren't you coming in today?"

"No, my friend. I just happened to come by; why, I just happened to; I only came to have a look, dear friend, but I shall show my gratitude to you later, my dear fellow."

"Yes, sir." The copyist ran quickly and eagerly up the stairs and Mr. Golyadkin was left alone.

"It's bad," he thought. "Dear, it's bad, bad! Oh, my case... is really pretty bad now! What was the meaning of it all? What else have they gotten hold of? Just what did certain of that drunkard's allusions mean, for example, and who's doing is this? Ah! Now I know who's doing this is. Here's what's going on. They most likely found out and then they put him... But, why am I saying—*they* put? It was Andrei Filippovich who put him, put Ivan Semyonovich in my place. But why did he put him in my place and just what was his purpose in doing it? They probably found out... This is Vakhrameyev's work, I mean, not Vakhrameyev's—he's as stupid as a post, that Vakhrameyev. It's all of them who are working on his behalf and who have also put that scoundrel up to coming here for the same purpose. And the German complained, that one-eyed witch! I always suspected that all this intriguing had more to it than meets the eye and that there surely had to be something in all those old-wives' tales and that old-biddy gossip. I even told Krestyan

Ivanovich as much; 'They've sworn to murder a person, speaking in the moral sense,' I said, 'and they've seized upon Karolina Ivanovna.' No, experts are at work here, it's obvious! The hand of a master is at work here, sir, and not some Vakhrameyev. I've already said Vakhrameyev is stupid, but this . . . Now I know who's working here on their behalf: that scoundrel, that impostor is! On the basis of this alone he makes his way, which also partly explains his success in high society. But actually it might be well to know what sort of footing he's on now . . . where does he stand with them? But why ever did they take on Ivan Semyonovich? What the devil did they need Ivan Semyonovich for? As if they couldn't find anyone else. Still, no matter who they put in my place, it would all have been just the same. All I know is that I have suspected that Ivan Semyonovich for a long time; I noticed a long time ago what he was like: such a nasty little old fellow, so vile—they say he lends money and charges interest rates as high as any Jew. But the bear is responsible for putting all this together. The bear is involved in the whole affair. That's how it started. It started at the Izmaylovsky Bridge; that's how it started . . ." Here Mr. Golyadkin puckered up his face as though he had bitten into a lemon, probably because he had recalled something highly unpleasant. "Well, it doesn't matter anyway!" he thought. "But here I am going on about my own affairs. Why doesn't Ostafyev come? He probably settled down to some work or got held up somehow. Why, to some extent it's even a good thing that I am carrying on an intrigue in this way and engaging in some undermining of my own. All I have to do is give Ostafyev ten kopeks and he's, you know . . . he's on my side. Only here's the point: is he really on my side? Perhaps the other side has been getting at him too . . . and they have an agreement with him and are carrying on an intrigue. Why, he has the look of a villain, the fraud, a veritable villain! He's hiding something, the rogue! 'No, nothing', he says, and 'I am most deeply', he says, 'grateful to you', he says, 'Your Worship.' What a villain you are! That's just the way it all is. And, as I just said, for sure one is making use of the other; but perhaps it's not like that . . . indeed, perhaps it's not like that at all but is simply being done in some other secret way. Dear, it's bad, bad! Oh, well, it's nothing at all! Perhaps it's nothing at all; but if only *he* would come; if only he would come to *me*! What is it he's doing? Or else if a fine intrigue would result and come about to spite them. I'd say, 'This is my affair; go ahead and do things this way and that way and your own way, but here,' I'd say, 'among us, there is such a thing as our way. That's how it is, sir; we are carrying on an intrigue,' I'd say, 'to spite you; we are carrying on an intrigue in an honorable and open manner . . .' "

There was a noise . . . Mr. Golyadkin hunched himself up and leapt behind the stove. Someone came down the stairway and went out into the street. "Who would be leaving now?" our hero thought to himself. A moment later other footsteps could be heard . . . At this point Mr. Golyadkin could not restrain himself and poked just the tip of his nose ever so slightly out from behind his bulwark—poked it out and immediately pulled back as though someone had pricked it with a pin. This time you-know-who was going by, that is, the rogue, intriguer, and profligate was going by, with his usual vile small step, mincing along and throwing his feet out as though getting ready to kick someone. "Scoundrel!" uttered our hero to himself. However, Mr. Golyadkin could not help noticing that the scoundrel had under his arm an enormous green portfolio belonging to His Excellency. "There he goes again on a special assignment," thought Mr. Golyadkin, flushing, and hunching himself up even more than before in vexation. Hardly had Mr. Golyadkin Junior flashed by Mr. Golyadkin Senior without noticing him in the least than someone's footsteps were heard for the third time and this time Mr. Golyadkin guessed that these footsteps were the copyist's. Indeed, the sleeked-down figure of a copyist peeped in at him, behind the stove; it was not, however, Ostafyev's figure, but that of another copyist, Pisarenko by name. This astounded Mr. Golyadkin. "Why is it that he has let others in on the secret?" thought our hero. "What barbarians! They hold nothing sacred!"

"Well, what is it, my friend?" he uttered, turning to Pisarenko. "Who sent you, my friend? . . ."

"I've come, sir, on the matter of your business, sir. For the time being there isn't any news from anyone, sir. But if there is, we'll inform you, sir."

"What about Ostafyev? . . ."

"Oh, he can't come at all, Your Worship, sir. His Excellency has walked through the division twice already and I, too, have no time now."

"Thank you, my dear fellow, thank you . . . But just tell me . . ."

"Really and truly, I have no time, sir . . . He's constantly asking for us, sir . . . But if you would please to stand here a while longer, sir, then if there should be anything concerning your case, sir, then we'll inform you, sir . . ."

"No, my friend, you just tell me . . ."

"Excuse me, sir; I have no time, sir," said Pisarenko, pulling away from Mr. Golyadkin, who had grabbed hold of the front of his jacket. "I really can't. You be so kind as to stand here a while longer, sir, and we'll inform you."

"Just a moment, just a moment, my friend! Just a moment, dear friend! Now this is what I ask: here are two letters, my friend, and I'll show my gratitude to you, my dear fellow."

"Yes, sir."

"You will take this letter here, my dear fellow. Then you will get a guard or errand-boy, someone, and will entrust him to deliver it to the address of Provincial Secretary Vakhrameyev. And I shall show my gratitude to you, my dear fellow . . ."

"I understand, sir. Just as soon as I can get away, I'll deliver it."

"Now this other letter here, my dear fellow, you try and give it to Mr. Golyadkin, my dear fellow."

"To Golyadkin?"

"Yes, my friend, to Mr. Golyadkin. You see, my friend, there are two Mr. Golyadkins here. It just happened that way . . . a strange story, my dear old fellow," added our hero, forcing himself to smile for the sake of propriety, so that Pisarenko would not go thinking anything, and in order to clearly give him to understand that this was nothing at all and that Mr. Golyadkin himself was not at all embarrassed.

"All right, sir. As soon as I can get away, I'll deliver it, sir. And in the meantime you stand here. No one will see you here..."

"No, I... my friend, don't you go thinking... why, I'm not standing here so that no one will see me. But I'm not going to be here now, my friend..."

"Yes, sir; yes, sir..."

"Rather, I shall be right there in the sidestreet, my friend. There's a coffee house there; and I shall be waiting there, and, if anything happens, you inform me about everything. Understand?"

"Fine, sir. Just let me go. I understand..."

"And I shall show my gratitude to you, my dear fellow!" Mr. Golyadkin shouted after Pisarenko, who had finally freed himself... "The scoundrel seemed to get ruder after a while," thought our hero, furtively coming out from behind the stove. "There's a further twist here. That's clear... At first it was one thing and another... Still, he really was in a hurry. Perhaps there *is* a great deal of work. And His Excellency has been through the division twice... What could be the occasion for that?... Ugh! Well, never mind! Still, perhaps it's nothing, but now we shall see..."

At this point Mr. Golyadkin was going to open the door and wanted to go out into the street, when suddenly at that very instant His Excellency's coach thundered up to the entrance. Mr. Golyadkin barely had time to recover from the shock when the coach door was opened from within, and the gentleman sitting inside jumped out onto the front steps. The passenger was none other than that same Mr. Golyadkin Junior who had left some ten minutes before. Mr. Golyadkin Senior recalled that the director's apartment was only a few steps away. "He's on a special assignment," our hero thought to himself. In the meantime Mr. Golyadkin Junior, after taking a bulging green portfolio and some other papers out of the coach and finally giving some instructions to the coachman, opened the door, almost hitting Mr. Golyadkin Senior with it and, deliberately taking no notice of him just to spite him, set off at a run up the office stairway. "It's bad!" thought Mr. Golyadkin; "oh, dear, so that's the turn my case has taken now! Oh, dear God, look at him, will you!" Our hero stood motionless for half a minute longer; finally, he made up his mind. Not giving it much thought, but feeling a powerful trepidation in his heart and a trembling in all his limbs, he ran up the stairs after his friend.

"Ah! Here goes! What do I care? I'm not a party to this matter," he thought, taking off his hat, overcoat and galoshes in the anteroom. "Things are still to come, though. Well, just let them! But now I shall act in a bold manner, just so, resolutely and boldly, in an honorable way, taking off the mask—and besides I'm a person within his rights . . . you know, etc.; oh, well, it doesn't matter!"

XI

Mr. Golyadkin's enemies move towards open warfare, during which the mask falls once and for all from several persons, and much—that is absolutely unnecessary, however—is revealed. Mr. Golyadkin argues on this convenient occasion that there are motions of the soul such that all superiors should feel utter sympathy for them; but Anton Antonovich Setochkin, who has gone over to the side of Mr. Golyadkin's enemies, argues the exact opposite. Of the extent to which Mr. Golyadkin's course is well-intentioned. Despite this, no one sympathizes with Mr. Golyadkin and he absolutely cannot come to an understanding with anyone.

When Mr. Golyadkin entered his division, dusk had already fallen completely. Neither Andrei Filippovich nor Anton Antonovich was in the room. They were both in the Director's office, handing in his reports; the Director, as rumor had it, was in turn in a hurry to report to his superior. As a result of these circumstances and also because the dusk contributed to it and office hours were ending, some of the clerks, chiefly the younger ones, were, at the very moment that our hero entered, engaged in some form of idleness; they were gathering together, conversing, discussing and laughing, and some of the youngest ones, that is, some of those with the lowest rank, were even secretly and under cover of the general hubbub playing pitch-and-toss in a corner by a window. Cognizant of what constitutes proper behavior and feeling at the present moment a particular need to purchase and find favor, Mr. Golyadkin immediately went up to those with whom he was on better terms to wish them good day and so forth. But his colleagues responded somewhat strangely to Mr. Golyadkin's greeting.

He was unpleasantly struck by a general coldness, dryness, one might even say, severity in their reception of him. No one shook hands with him. Some simply said, "Hello" and walked away; others merely nodded; a few simply turned away and pretended that they hadn't noticed anything; finally, some—and what was most offensive of all to Mr. Golyadkin, some of the young ones with the lowest ranks, boys who, as Mr. Golyadkin had rightly expressed himself concerning them, knew only how to play pitch-and-toss when the occasion arose and gad about—gradually surrounded Mr. Golyadkin, forming a group about him and almost cutting off his escape. All of them looked at him with a kind of insulting curiosity.

It was a bad sign. Mr. Golyadkin sensed this and was for his part prudently prepared to ignore it. "It's nothing, though; perhaps it will all be for the best," he thought, becoming, in his indescribable embarrassment, completely flustered. Suddenly a quite unexpected occurrence completely finished Mr. Golyadkin, as they say, and made him utterly desolate.

In the small group of young colleagues surrounding him, suddenly and as if deliberately, at what was Mr. Golyadkin's most anguished moment, there appeared Mr. Golyadkin Junior, jovial as always, with a little smile as always, overvivacious, too, as always; in a word, playing pranks, cavorting about, fawning, guffawing, quick with his tongue and quick on his feet, as always, as before, just as he had been yesterday, for example, at a moment that had been most unpleasant for Mr. Golyadkin Senior. Grinning, whirling about, mincing along, with his little smile that so clearly said, "Good evening" to everyone, he pushed his way into the little group of clerks, shook this one's hand, clapped that one on the shoulder, lightly embraced another, explained to a fourth exactly on what business His Excellency had sent him, where he had gone, what he had done, what he had brought back with him; to a fifth and most likely his best friend he gave a smacking kiss right on the lips—in a word, everything was happening exactly as it had in Mr. Golyadkin Senior's dream. After cavorting his fill, dealing with each one in his own inimitable way, disposing them all favorably towards himself, whether he needed to or not, and sucking up

to all of them to his heart's content, Mr. Golyadkin Junior
suddenly, and probably by mistake, because he had failed up to
that point to notice his oldest friend, held his hand out to Mr.
Golyadkin Senior as well. Probably also by mistake, although,
however, he had by no means failed to take full notice of the
ignoble Mr. Golyadkin Junior, our hero thereupon eagerly
seized the hand which had been extended to him so unexpectedly and shook it in the firmest and friendliest manner,
shook it with a strange, totally unexpected inner stirring and a
weepy feeling. Whether our hero was deceived by his unseemly
enemy's first move, whether he was simply at a loss to know
what to do, or whether he sensed and acknowledged in the
depths of his soul the full extent of his helplessness is difficult
to say. The fact remains that Mr. Golyadkin Senior, being of
sound mind and body, did of his own free will and in the
presence of witnesses, solemnly shake the hand of one whom
he called his mortal enemy. But what was the amazement,
frenzy and rage, what was the horror and shame of Mr.
Golyadkin Senior, when his foe and mortal enemy, the ignoble
Mr. Golyadkin Junior, on noticing his mistake, thereupon,
before the very eyes of the persecuted, innocent person whom
he had so perfidiously deceived, without shame, without
feeling, without compassion or conscience, and with intolerable
effrontery and crudity, suddenly tore his hand out of Mr.
Golyadkin Senior's hand; as if that were not enough, he flicked
his hand as though he had soiled it with something quite awful;
as if that were not enough, he spat to one side, accompanying
all this with the most insulting gesture; and as if that were not
enough, he took out his handkerchief and thereupon, in the
most excessive manner, wiped all of the fingers that had for a
moment lain in Mr. Golyadkin Senior's hand. While doing this,
Mr. Golyadkin Junior, as was his vile wont, deliberately looked
about, making sure that everyone should see what he was
doing, looked everyone in the eye, and obviously tried to
convey to everyone all that was most unfavorable about Mr.
Golyadkin. The behavior of the revolting Mr. Golyadkin
Junior seemed to arouse the general indignation of the clerks
surrounding them; even the flighty young people showed their

displeasure. A grumbling and murmuring arose on all sides. The general stir could not fail to reach the ears of Mr. Golyadkin Senior; but suddenly an apropos little joke occurred to Mr. Golyadkin Junior and erupted from his lips, smashing and destroying our hero's last hopes and tipping the balance again in favor of his mortal and worthless enemy.

"This is our Russian Faublas, gentlemen; permit me to introduce the young Faublas," piped Mr. Golyadkin Junior, mincing and whirling about among the clerks with his customary brazenness, and pointing out to them the benumbed but infuriated real Mr. Golyadkin. "Let's give each other a kiss, duckie!" he continued with intolerable familiarity, moving toward the person he had so perfidiously insulted. The worthless Mr. Golyadkin Junior's little joke, it seems, found a ready response, the moreso since it contained an insidious allusion to an incident which evidently had already been made public and was known to everyone. Our hero felt the hand of his enemies heavy upon him. However, he had already made a resolve. With a burning look, pale face, and a fixed smile he somehow made his way out of the crowd and with uneven, quickened steps set his course straight for His Excellency's office. In the room just before it he was met by Andrei Filippovich, who had just emerged from seeing His Excellency, and although there was a sizeable number of all sorts of other persons in the room at that moment who were complete strangers to Mr. Golyadkin, still our hero did not wish to pay any attention to this fact. Directly, resolutely, boldly, almost surprised at himself and yet lauding himself inwardly for his boldness, losing no time, he assailed Andrei Filippovich, who was quite amazed at such an unexpected assault.

"Ah! What do you . . . What do you want?" asked the division chief, not listening to the stammering Mr. Golyadkin.

"Andrei Filippovich, I . . . may I have a conversation with His Excellency, Andrei Filippovich, now, right now and in private?" uttered our hero, volubly and distinctly, while casting a most determined look at Andrei Filippovich.

"What, sir? Of course not, sir." Andrei Filippovich measured Mr. Golyadkin from head to foot with his glance.

"Andrei Filippovich, I'm saying all this because I am amazed that no one here unmasks the imposter and scoundrel."

"Wha-a-at, sir?"

"Scoundrel, Andrei Filippovich."

"And just whom are you pleased to speak of thus?"

"Of a certain person, Andrei Filippovich. I am alluding to a certain person, Andrei Filippovich; I am within my rights . . . I think, Andrei Filippovich, that our superiors should encourage such action," added Mr. Golyadkin, obviously beside himself; "Andrei Filippovich . . . you probably see yourself, Andrei Filippovich, that this noble action signifies that I have every good intention of accepting our superior as a father, Andrei Filippovich. 'I accept our beneficent superior as a father,' I say, 'and blindly entrust my fate to him. This is the way it is,' I say . . . 'that's how it is . . .' " Here Mr. Golyadkin's voice began to quaver, his face turned red, and two tears gathered on his eyelashes.

Andrei Filippovich was so astonished at what Mr. Golyadkin had said that he involuntarily took a couple steps back. Then he looked about uneasily . . . It is difficult to say how the matter would have ended . . . But suddenly the door of His Excellency's office opened and he himself emerged, accompanied by several other officials. Everyone in the room trailed after him. His Excellency called Andrei Filippovich and began to walk along with him, conversing about some matters of business. When everyone had moved off and left the room, Mr. Golyadkin came to his senses. Calming down, he took refuge under the wing of Anton Antonovich Setochkin, who in turn was hobbling along behind everyone else and, so it seemed to Mr. Golyadkin, had a most severe and preoccupied look on his face. "I've just talked a lot of nonsense and made a mess again," he thought to himself; "well, it doesn't matter."

"I hope that at least you, Anton Antonovich, will agree to hear me out and understand my situation," he uttered quietly in a voice still trembling slightly from agitation. "Cast aside by everyone, I turn to you. I am still at a loss to understand what Andrei Filippovich's words meant, Anton Antonovich. Explain them to me, if you can . . ."

223

"Everything will be explained in good time, sir," answered Anton Antonovich severely and without haste, and, so it seemed to Mr. Golyadkin, with a look which clearly gave to understand that Anton Antonovich did not at all wish to continue the conversation. "You will shortly know everything, sir. This very day you will be officially informed of everything."

"What do you mean by officially, Anton Antonovich? Just why will it be officially, sir?" asked our hero timidly.

"It's not for you and me to reason why our superiors decide as they do, Yakov Petrovich."

"But why our superiors, Anton Antonovich," uttered Mr. Golyadkin, feeling even more timid, "why our superiors? I don't see why it's necessary to bother our superiors, Anton Antonovich . . . Perhaps you mean something to do with what happened yesterday, Anton Antonovich?"

"Oh, no, sir; not yesterday, sir, but the fact that you decided upon something bad, Yakov Petrovich; there's something else that leaves much to be desired where you're concerned, sir."

"What leaves much to be desired, Anton Antonovich? It seems to me, Anton Antonovich, there's nothing that leaves much to be desired where I'm concerned."

"And whom were you planning to be crafty with?" Anton Antonovich sharply cut short the absolutely dumbfounded Mr. Golyadkin. Mr. Golyadkin shuddered and turned white as a sheet.

"Of course, Anton Antonovich," he uttered in a barely audible voice, "if one heeds the voice of slander and listens to a person's enemies without hearing the justification offered by the other side, then, of course . . . of course, Anton Antonovich, then a person can suffer for it, Anton Antonovich, suffer innocently and for nothing."

"Just so, sir; but what about that unseemly performance of yours that hurt the reputation of an honorable young lady from that beneficent, esteemed and well-known family that was so good to you?"

"What performance is that, Anton Antonovich?"

"Just so, sir; and as far as another young lady is concerned, who although poor is nevertheless of honest foreign extraction, you don't know what admirable deed you performed there either, sir?"

"Permit me, Anton Antonovich . . . do me the kindness, Anton Antonovich, of hearing me out . . ."

"And your perfidious behavior and slander of another person—your accusing another of what you are guilty of yourself? Eh? What do you call that?"

"I did not chase him out, Anton Antonovich," uttered our hero, all aflutter, "nor did I instruct Petrushka, that is, my servant, to do anything of the sort, sir . . . He ate my bread, Anton Antonovich; he enjoyed my hospitality," our hero added so expressively and with such deep feeling that his chin began to tremble slightly and the tears were ready to come again.

"You're just saying that, Yakov Petrovich, that he ate your bread," answered Anton Antonovich, grinning, and a slyness could be heard in his voice that made Mr. Golyadkin's heart ache. "You're just saying that, Yakov Petrovich, just to say something."

"Of course, Anton Antonovich . . . You're right, Anton Antonovich," said our hero, insulted. "Nowadays virtues are on the decline, and hospitality is no longer taken into account."

"But that's just where you are wrong, Yakov Petrovich. Now this, sir, is called freethinking."

"It's not freethinking at all, Anton Antonovich. I shun freethinking, Anton Antonovich. It's Petrushka, Anton Antonovich. He's always getting drunk and you can't rely on him for anything, sir."

"But Petrushka is not the point here, sir. Petrushka has nothing to do with the matter at all."

"Of course, Petrushka doesn't have anything to do with the matter, Anton Antonovich. What you are pleased to say is true. Permit me most humbly to ask you something else, Anton Antonovich: does His Excellency know all about this matter?"

"Of course, sir! But do let me go now, sir. I have no time for you now . . . This very day you'll find out about everything you need to know, sir."

"Stay just a minute longer, Anton Antonovich, for God's sake . . ."

"No, sir; I don't have time for you, sir . . . Later sir, perhaps . . ."

"One minute, just one word, Anton Antonovich . . ."

"You can tell me later, sir . . ."

"No, Anton Antonovich, sir; I, sir . . . you see, sir . . . just listen, Anton Antonovich . . . This isn't at all freethinking on my part, Anton Antonovich; I shun freethinking; I'm quite prepared for my part and have even expressed the idea that . . ."

"All right, sir, all right. I've already heard it, sir . . ."

"No, sir, you haven't heard it, Anton Antonovich. This is something else, Anton Antonovich. This is good, really good, and pleasant to hear . . . I have expressed, as I explained before, Anton Antonovich, the idea that Divine Providence created two absolutely identical beings, and that our beneficent superiors, seeing that it was Divine Providence, took the two twins to their bosom, sir. This is good, Anton Antonovich. You can see that this is very good, Anton Antonovich, and that I am far from being a freethinker. Our beneficent superior is like a father to me. 'This is the way it is,' I say, 'our beneficent superior, and you, you know' . . . I say . . . 'a young man must have work' . . . Back me up, Anton Antonovich; intercede for me, Anton Antonovich . . . I don't mean anything, sir . . . Anton Antonovich, for God's sake, just one little word more . . . Anton Antonovich . . ."

But Anton Antonovich was already far away from Mr. Golyadkin . . . Our hero did not know where he was standing, what he was hearing, what he was doing, what had happened to him, and what more was going to happen to him—because everything he had heard and everything that had happened to him had so confused and shaken him.

With a beseeching look he sought out Anton Antonovich in the crowd of clerks in order to justify himself still further in his eyes and tell him something extremely well-intentioned and quite honorable and pleasant about himself . . . However, little by little, a new light was beginning to break through the confusion of Mr. Golyadkin's mind, a new and terrible light that revealed suddenly and at once an entire perspective of circumstances hitherto completely unknown and totally unsuspected . . . At that moment someone gave our utterly disconcerted hero a poke in the ribs. He looked around. Before him stood Pisarenko.

"A letter, Your Honor, sir."

"Ah! . . . You've already been there, my dear fellow?"

"No, it was brought here this morning at ten o'clock, sir. Sergey Mikheyev, the guard, brought it from Provincial Secretary Vakhrameyev's apartment, sir."

"All right, my friend, all right. I shall show my gratitude to you, my dear fellow."

Saying this, Mr. Golyadkin put the letter away in the side pocket of his jacket and buttoned it all the way up; then he looked around and, to his amazement, noticed that he was already in the vestibule among a little group of clerks that had clustered at the exit, for office hours had ended. Up until then Mr. Golyadkin had not only failed to notice this last circumstance, but had also failed to notice and could not remember how he had suddenly come to be wearing his overcoat and galoshes and to be holding his hat in his hands. All the clerks were standing motionless in respectful expectation. The fact of the matter is that His Excellency had stopped at the bottom of the stairs and while waiting for his carriage, which for some reason had been delayed, was carrying on a highly interesting conversation with two councilors and Andrei Filippovich. A short distance from the two councilors and Andrei Filippovich stood Anton Antonovich Setochkin and some other clerks, who, seeing that His Excellency was pleased to joke and laugh, were smiling broadly. The clerks clustered at the top of the stairs were also smiling and waiting for His Excellency to laugh again. The only one who was not smiling was Fedoseyich, the potbellied doorman, who stood stiffly at attention holding the door handle and awaiting with impatience that portion of his daily pleasure which consisted in suddenly flinging one half of the double doors wide open with a single sweep of his arm, and then bowing low and respectfully letting His Excellency pass. But the one who obviously was gladdest of all and felt the most pleasure was Mr. Golyadkin's unworthy and ignoble enemy. At that moment he even forgot all the clerks and even left off flitting and mincing about among them, as was his vile wont; he even forgot to take advantage of the opportunity to fawn over anyone at that moment. He was all eyes and ears, and scrunching himself up somewhat oddly— probably in order to hear better— never took his eyes off His Excellency; and only occasionally did his arms, legs and head give a barely noticeable twitch, betraying all the innermost, hidden stirrings of his soul.

"See how excited he is by it!" thought our hero; "he looks the favorite, the rogue! I'd like to know— what is it that makes him get on in well-bred society? No brains, no character, no education, no feeling . . . the rascal is lucky! Dear God! Why, how fast a person can get on, when you think of it, and ingratiate himself with everyone! And the man will go far; I give my oath that he'll go far, the rascal; he'll make it— the rascal is lucky! I'd also like to know— just what is it that he keeps whispering to them all? What sort of mysterious things is he concocting with all these people and what sort of secrets are they talking about? Dear God! If only I could . . . you know . . . and if only I could talk with them a bit, too . . . I'd say, 'This is the way it is' . . . perhaps I should ask him . . . I'd say, 'This is the way it is, but I won't do it any more'; I'd say, 'I'm to blame, but a young man, Your Excellency, has to work these days; I'm not at all embarrassed by my obscure situation.' That's how it is! I won't protest in any way either, but will bear everything with patience and humility— that's what I'll do! Is this really the way to proceed? . . . You'll never get through to him, the rascal; no words penetrate; you can't pound any sense into his unruly head . . . Still, we'll try. I may happen to find an opportune moment and then I'll try . . ."

Feeling in his agitation, anguish and confusion that he could not go on this way, that the decisive moment was approaching and that he simply had to come to an understanding with someone, our hero was about to begin moving gradually toward the spot where his unworthy and mysterious friend was standing; but just then His Excellency's long-awaited carriage came rumbling up to the entrance. Fedoseyich jerked open the door and, bowing as low as could be, let His Excellency pass. All those who had been waiting at once surged to the exit and for a moment separated Mr. Golyadkin Senior from Mr. Golyadkin Junior. "You won't get away!" said our hero, forcing his way through the crowd and keeping his eyes pinned on his man. At last the crowd gave way. Our hero felt he was free and dashed off in pursuit of his foe.

XII

The coffee house. Of how Mr. Golyadkin Junior's utter immorality expressed itself and how Mr. Golyadkin Senior defended himself. Deceit and perfidy. A whirlwind, a blizzard, a snowstorm and—the downfall of Mr. Golyadkin Senior. A comparison between Mr. Golyadkin Senior and a sack of flour. Mr. Golyadkin Senior decides, however, that this is still nothing at all and that everything may still turn out for the best. Of how, through two peasant women, one waiter and one gentleman reading "The Police Gazette", Mr. Golyadkin discovered that they wanted to poison him. The final blow to Mr. Golyadkin.

Mr. Golyadkin's breathing became labored. He sped as if on wings after his rapidly retreating foe. He felt within him the presence of an enormous energy. However, despite the presence of this enormous energy, Mr. Golyadkin could be perfectly confident that at that moment even a mere mosquito, if only it had been able to live in Petersburg in such a season, could very easily have knocked him over with one wing. He felt further-more that his strength had flagged and that he had become utterly weak, that he was being borne along by a completely separate and external force, that he was moving not of his own volition, but that, on the contrary, his legs were giving way beneath him and refusing to function. Still, it was all, as yet, absolutely nothing, and, in spite of everything, certainly might turn out for the best. "For the best—not for the best," thought Mr. Golyadkin, almost breathless from running so fast, "but that the case has been lost, of that there is not the slightest doubt now; that I am completely done for is certain and has been signed, sealed and delivered." Despite all this, it was as if our hero had been resurrected from the dead, had weathered the battle and seized the victory, when he succeeded in laying hold of the overcoat of his foe, who was already placing one foot on the step of a droshky, with the driver of which he had just contracted to be taken somewhere. "Sir! Sir!" he shouted to the ignoble Mr. Golyadkin Junior, whom he had finally overtaken. "Sir, I hope that you . . ."

"No, don't you go hoping for anything, please," Mr. Golyadkin's unfeeling foe answered evasively, standing with one foot on one step of the droshky and trying with all his might to land the other inside the carriage, but instead waving it vainly in the air; trying to maintain his equilibrium and at the same time trying with all his might to disengage his overcoat from the grasp of Mr. Golyadkin Senior who, for his part, had laid hold of it with all the means that nature had bestowed on him.

"Yakov Petrovich! Just ten minutes . . ."

"Excuse me, I haven't time, sir."

"You must agree, Yakov Petrovich . . . Please, Yakov Petrovich . . . For God's sake, Yakov Petrovich . . . This is the way it is—let's have it out . . . man to man . . . One little second, Yakov Petrovich! . . ."

"My dear boy, I don't have time," answered Mr. Golyadkin's falsely noble foe with uncivil familiarity disguised as goodheartedness. "Another time, believe me, I'll do it out of the goodness of my heart and with utmost sincerity, but now, I really just can't."

"Scoundrel!" thought our hero. "And with utmost sincerity yet, you villain, you! . . ."

"Yakov Petrovich!" he cried in anguish, "I have never been your enemy. Malicious people have painted an unfair picture of me . . . For my part I am prepared . . . Yakov Petrovich, if you like, let's you and I go somewhere right now, shall we, Yakov Petrovich? . . . And there with utmost sincerity, as you so rightly said just now, and in direct and noble language . . . Let's go into that coffee house there; then everything will explain itself—yes, indeed, Yakov Petrovich! Then everything will surely explain itself . . ."

"Into the coffee house? Very well, sir. I have no objection. Let's go into the coffee house, but on one condition, my dear, and on one condition only, that there everything *will* explain itself. I say, 'This is the way it is, duckie'," uttered Mr. Golyadkin Junior, climbing down from the droshky and shamelessly clapping our hero on the shoulder. "What a dear old chap you are. For you, Yakov Petrovich, I am prepared to go by way of a sidestreet (as you were once pleased to note so rightly, Yakov Petrovich.). Why, you really are a rascal; you do what you will with a person!" continued Mr. Golyadkin's false friend with an easy smile, hovering about him and fawning over him, peeping under his hat at him and, in a word, attempting by every means to falsely depict himself as a wit and an amiable person, but meanwhile behaving with all the brazenness of immorality just to spite Mr. Golyadkin Senior, and having as his sole purpose to deceive him in some new shameless manner and later in a friendly company somewhere over a goblet of wine, for the sake of a witticism, to make a laughing stock of him.

The coffee house which both Mr. Golyadkins entered was located far from the main streets and was at that moment completely deserted. A rather fat German woman appeared at the counter the moment the bell sounded. Mr. Golyadkin and his unworthy foe went on into a second room, where a puffy-looking boy with cropped hair was fussing about near the stove with a bundle of kindling, trying to remake the fire that had gone out in it. At the request of Mr. Golyadkin Junior chocolate was served.

"She's a tasty morsel, all right," uttered Mr. Golyadkin Junior, winking roguishly at Mr. Golyadkin Senior.

Our hero blushed and said nothing.

"Oh, yes, I forgot; excuse me. I know your taste. We, sir, are partial to slender little German ladies. We, I say, you upright soul, Yakov Petrovich, are both partial to slender little German ladies who, however, have not yet lost all their charms. We rent apartments from them; we corrupt their morals; we give our hearts to them for beer soup and milk soup and give various written promises. That's what we do, isn't it? Oh, you Faublas, you, you traitor, you!"

In saying all this Mr. Golyadkin Junior was making a completely worthless but maliciously cunning allusion to a certain person of the female sex, and he was fawning over Mr. Golyadkin, smiling at him under the pretext of amiability, and thus falsely exhibiting cordiality toward him and joy at having met him. Noting, however, that Mr. Golyadkin Senior was by no means so stupid and so lacking in education and good manners as to believe him at once, the ignoble person resolved to change his tactics and conducts matters openly. Hereupon, having uttered his vile remarks, the false Mr. Golyadkin concluded by clapping the solid Mr. Golyadkin on the shoulder with a perturbing shamelessness and familiarity, and, not satisfied with this, set about making fun of him in a manner that was utterly unseemly in good society, namely, he intended to repeat his earlier vile gesture, that is, despite the resistance and faint cries of the perturbed Mr. Golyadkin Senior, to pinch his cheek. At the sight of such corruptness our hero's blood boiled but he held his tongue . . . that is, until an opportune moment should present itself.

"That is the talk of my enemies," he answered at last, in a quavering voice, prudently restraining himself. "That is the talk of my enemies," our hero added with dignity, feeling, incidentally, that he was completely within his rights, and stung to the quick by the familiarity and shamelessness of his unworthy enemy . . . At the same time our hero looked back uneasily at the door. The fact of the matter is that Mr. Golyadkin Junior was evidently in fine fettle and ready to engage in various pranks which were inadmissible in a public place and, generally speaking, not permitted by the laws of society, chiefly of well-bred society.

"Come, come, now; I won't, I won't!" uttered Mr. Golyadkin Junior, moving away from Mr. Golyadkin Senior in a conciliatory manner, thus dissembling before him cunningly, donning his mask and, with subtle deception and under the guise of humility, luring him into new snares. However, our hero understood and understood clearly that his immoral twin, who was having a confrontation with him here in an open and bold manner and with a frankness not devoid of nobility, would gain little. I say, "This is the way it is and you will do yourself in." I say, "This is the way it is and you, my dear sir and utter heel, will gain little." I say, "You know, etc."

"Ah, well, in that case, have it your own way," Mr. Golyadkin Junior retorted seriously to Mr. Golyadkin Senior's thought, placing his empty cup, which he had drunk down with unseemly greediness, on the table. "Well, sir, there's no point in my spending much time with you . . . Well, sir, how are you getting on now, Yakov Petrovich?"

"There's only one thing I can say to you, Yakov Petrovich," answered our hero with composure and dignity; "I have never been your enemy."

"Hm . . . Well, and how is Petrushka getting on? What's his name? It *is* Petrushka, I believe?—Why, yes! Well, how is he? Fine? Same as ever?"

"He is also the same as ever, Yakov Petrovich," answered the somewhat astonished Mr. Golyadkin Senior. "I don't know, Yakov Petrovich . . . for my part . . . that is, looking at things nobly and frankly, Yakov Petrovich, you must admit yourself, Yakov Petrovich . . ."

"Yes, sir. But you know yourself, Yakov Petrovich," answered Mr. Golyadkin Junior in a quiet and expressive voice, thus falsely portraying himself as sad, full of remorse and deserving of pity; "you know yourself, these are hard times we live in . . . I appeal to you, Yakov Petrovich; you're an intelligent man and will judge rightly," threw in Mr. Golyadkin Junior, basely flattering Mr. Golyadkin Senior. "You will judge rightly that I could not have acted otherwise. Life is no picnic, you know yourself, Yakov Petrovich," concluded Mr. Golyadkin Junior significantly, pretending thus to be an intelligent and learned man capable of discussing lofty subjects.

"For my part, Yakov Petrovich," answered our hero animatedly, "for my part, scorning roundabout means and speaking boldly and frankly, using direct and noble language and placing the entire matter on an honorable level, I shall tell you, I can frankly and nobly affirm, Yakov Petrovich, that I am absolutely innocent and that, you know yourself, Yakov Petrovich, a mutual error—anything can happen—the world's judgment, the opinion of the servile mob . . . I am speaking frankly, Yakov Petrovich; anything can happen. I shall say further, Yakov Petrovich, if we judge thus, if we look at the matter from a noble and lofty point of view, then I shall say boldly, I shall say without false shame, Yakov Petrovich, that I shall even find it pleasant to disclose that I have been in error, I shall even find it pleasant to admit the fact that I have been in error, Yakov Petrovich. You know it yourself; you are an intelligent man and, what is more, an honorable one, I am ready to admit it; without shame, without false shame, I am ready to admit it . . ." concluded our hero with dignity and nobility.

"Destiny, fate! Yakov Petrovich . . . But let's put all this aside," uttered Mr. Golyadkin Junior with a sigh. "Let us rather use the brief moments of our encounter for a more profitable and pleasant conversation, as two colleagues should with one another . . . I really have not been able to say two words to you in all this time . . . It's not I who am to blame for this, Yakov Petrovich . . ."

"Nor I either," interrupted our hero heatedly, "not me! My heart tells me, Yakov Petrovich, that it's not I who am to blame for all this. Let us blame fate for all this, Yakov Petrovich," added Mr. Golyadkin Senior in a utterly conciliatory tone. His voice was gradually beginning to weaken and tremble.

"Well, now! How is your health in general?" said the errant one in a sweet voice.

"I have a bit of a cough," answered our hero even more sweetly.

"Take care of yourself. There are many infections going about now; you can easily catch tonsilitis and I, I confess to you, am already starting to bundle myself up in flannel."

"Yes, Yakov Petrovich, you can easily catch tonsilitis, sir . . . Yakov Petrovich!" uttered our hero after a modest silence. "Yakov Petrovich! I see that I was in error . . . I am touched by the recollection of those happy moments which we were able to spend together under my humble, but, I make so bold as to say, cordial roof . . ."

"In your letter, however, you wrote something else," uttered Mr. Golyadkin Junior somewhat reproachfully, and he was absolutely right (though only in this one respect was he absolutely right).

"Yakov Petrovich! I was in error... I see clearly now that I was in error in that unfortunate letter of mine, too. Yakov Petrovich, it pains me to look at you; Yakov Petrovich, you won't believe . . . Give me that letter so that I can tear it up before your very eyes, Yakov Petrovich, or if this is utterly impossible, then I beseech you to read it the other way round—quite the other way round, that is, with a deliberately friendly intent, giving the opposite sense to every word in my letter. I was in error. Forgive me, Yakov Petrovich, I was completely... I was sadly in error, Yakov Petrovich."

"You were saying?" asked Mr. Golyadkin Senior's perfidious friend rather absentmindedly and indifferently.

"I was saying that I have been completely in error, Yakov Petrovich, and that for my part, utterly without false shame, I . . ."

"Ah, well, all right! It's quite all right that you were in error," Mr. Golyadkin Junior answered rudely.

"I even had the idea," added our frank hero in a noble manner, completely oblivious to the terrible perfidy of his false friend, "I even had the idea of saying, 'Look, two absolutely identical persons were created . . .'"

"Ah! That's your idea! A good one, a good one, indeed, extremely good. Still, even though it's good, we shall leave . . . you know, this idea of yours," uttered Mr. Golyadkin Junior, insolently and shamelessly, screwing up his eyes, smiling and nodding his head at Mr. Golyadkin Senior. "We shall leave this idea of yours until another time, but now . . ."

Hereupon Mr. Golyadkin Junior, notorious for his worthlessness, got up and grabbed his hat. Still failing to notice the ruse, Mr. Golyadkin Senior also got up, smiling ingenuously and nobly at his false friend and trying in his innocence to be nice to him, to reassure him and in this way to start up a new friendship . . .

237

"We shall leave it until tomorrow, this idea of yours, but now, to use your accurate expression, Yakov Petrovich, we all must labor," added Mr. Golyadkin Junior, obviously speaking all sorts of nonsense in order to mock Mr. Golyadkin Senior. "We all must labor, you understand, Petrushka?! ... Oh, well, it's nothing, it's nothing; don't be embarrassed ... Well, now, goodbye, Yakov Petrovich; I've had enough of you for the time being ... If we should somehow get together, we'll drink a bottle or two of wine, of sweet light beer, as the hicks say (which is neither here nor there), we'll talk, we'll chat, we'll have a discussion," continued that immoral person, astonishing Mr. Golyadkin with the immorality and corruptness of his heart. "We'll be nice, perhaps, to Petrushka and tell him that we all must labor," that deluded person added, immorally, winking at Mr. Golyadkin Senior and continuing to spin and mince about near him and partly tease him. "We'll rehabilitate, though, the reputation of our mutual friend Mohammed, the Turkish prophet, which has been somewhat sullied by various German scholars," that utterly corrupt person decided to add with even greater brazen insolence than before, smiling in a depraved manner at the worthy Mr. Golyadkin Senior and thus mocking him shamefully. "And, finally, finally, give me your hand, hero, give me your hand! 'Give me your hand in parting, etc.' "

Hereupon the godless Mr. Golyadkin Junior, who believed in nothing, probably fancying that he would wound the proud hero of our tale, performed an unseemly entrechat before his eyes, gave a flick of his little leg, and, to crown his disgrace, made a popping sound with his mouth using his finger and tongue, wishing to show in this manner that he was pretending to uncork a bottle of champagne, and all the while obviously amusing himself in a most worthless manner, like a five-year-old child, but without its innocence. Finally, to put the finishing touch on the whole loathsome picture of his utterly scandalous behavior, with a most insolent, caustic and bacchanalian smile he extended his hand to the chaste Mr. Golyadkin Senior (this is intended as a compliment to him) and shouted in a frenzied and at the same time mocking voice: "Goodbye, Your Excellency!"

At the sight of such fanatic corruption personified, our hero involuntarily reeled back . . . But the corrupted child of nature, the worthless Mr. Golyadkin Junior, seemed to have given his word to himself to go all the way in outraging the real Mr. Golyadkin. Solely for the purpose of getting rid of him, our hero shoved two of his fingers into the extended hand of the fanatic; but at this point . . . at this point Mr. Golyadkin Junior's brazenness exceeded all human limits. Seizing Mr. Golyadkin Senior's two fingers and at first pressing them, that unworthy person thereupon, before Mr. Golyadkin's very eyes, resolved to repeat his shameless joke of that morning. The limits of human patience were exhausted . . .

He was already putting into his pocket the handkerchief with which he had wiped his fingers, when Mr. Golyadkin Senior came to his senses. "Base and corrupt person!" our hero cried out in a low voice, timidly looking round at the door into the next room, shaking all over in painfully anguished agitation, and obviously utterly distraught over the inexhaustible brazenness of his enemy.

Then a rather strange scene occurred. Mr. Golyadkin Junior, having committed an indecency, and hastening now, according to his nasty habit, to slip away into the next room, quickly turned toward Mr. Golyadkin Senior with a most malevolent expression on his face. Our hero involuntarily took two steps back. That immoral person took two steps forward. Our hero took two more steps back, prudently trying to select as the target for his retreat a corner which would neither be visible from the next room, where there were strangers, nor in a mirror, where the people in the next room could see everything reflected; it was necessary to avoid any new unseemly and loathsome trick as a result of which self-esteem could suffer in the presence of strangers. At last Mr. Golyadkin Senior made his way to his corner. The enemies were now standing absolutely nose to nose and our hero was trying with all his might to look directly, resolutely and unblinkingly into the eyes of his unworthy enemy in order to show him, in this way, that he was not at all afraid of him but even quite the contrary. There was prolonged silence and expectation. "Why did I bring him here!" flashed through Mr. Golyadkin's mind. "For here we stand now, nose to nose," thought our hero apropos of the situation. "What if our noses were to grow together inseparably . . ." He thereupon recalled the fairy tale which told of a sausage that stuck to the nose of an old man's wife who was imprudent in her desires.

"Greed for possessions and imprudence in our desires is our undoing," thought Mr. Golyadkin, continuing to look into the eyes of his enemy resolutely, fearlessly and without blinking an eye.

"Faublas?" uttered that immoral person at last in a semi-mysterious whisper and interrogatory tone.

Our hero looked with anguish at the door into the next room.

"You are Faublas, aren't you?" continued Mr. Golyadkin Junior even more insistently, utterly on the offensive against Mr. Golyadkin Senior.

"Come to your senses—we are not alone. Let's go out into the street, Yakov Petrovich. It will be better for us on the street, Yakov Petrovich . . ."

Our hero did not finish and stopped short. The limits of outrageous behavior had exceeded all his anguished expectations. . . . .
. . . .

Meanwhile, deprived of his senses by his amazement, our hero stood immobile . . . At last he recovered his senses. The fact of the matter is that Mr. Golyadkin Junior, having carried out his latest act of infamy, which he perfidiously called a joke, had made a run for the next room as fast as his legs could carry him. But perfidy could not be left unpunished! However, when our hero in his frenzy arrived in the next room, his immoral foe was just standing at the counter as if nothing was wrong, eating pasties and with great composure, like a virtuous man, exchanging pleasantries with the German woman. "I mustn't— not in front of ladies," thought our hero and also went up to the counter, beside himself with agitation.

"No, she's really not bad looking! What do you think?" Mr. Golyadkin Junior began his unseemly pranks again, probably counting on Mr. Golyadkin's endless patience. The fat German woman, for her part, looked at both her customers with inexpressive, vacant eyes, evidently not understanding any Russian, and smiled affably. Our hero blushed a fiery red at the words of the shameless Mr. Golyadkin Junior and, unable to restrain himself, flung himself at last upon him with the intention of tearing him to pieces and thus finishing him off once and for all; but Mr. Golyadkin Junior, as was his vile wont, was already far away: he had taken to his heels and was now at the entrance. It goes without saying that after the initial moment of stupor which naturally seized Mr. Golyadkin Senior, he came to his senses and dashed full speed after his insulter, who was already getting into the carriage, the driver of which had obviously agreed to wait for him. But at that very moment the fat German woman, witnessing the flight of the two customers, let out a scream and rang her little bell furiously. Our hero, turned, almost on the wing, threw her the money for himself and for that shameless person who had not paid, without demanding any change, and, despite the fact that he had lost time, nevertheless succeeded, although once again only on the wing, in catching up with his foe. Hanging onto the splashboard of the droshky with every means bestowed on him by nature, our hero was borne along the street for some time, trying to clamber into the carriage, while Mr. Golyadkin Junior repulsed him with all his might. Meanwhile the driver, using whip and reins and foot and words, urged on his exhausted jade, which quite unexpectedly broke into a gallop like a whirlwind, taking hold of the bit with its teeth and kicking out, as was its nasty habit, with its back legs at every third step. Finally our hero did succeed after all in clambering into the droshky, and sat back to back with the driver, and face to face with his foe, knee to knee with that shameless person, and with his right hand used every means to hang onto the extremely shabby fur collar on the overcoat of his corrupt and most bitter foe . . .

The enemies were borne along and for some time said nothing. Our hero could scarcely catch his breath; the road was utterly dreadful and he continually bounced up and down, in danger of breaking his neck. Moreover, his most bitter foe continued to refuse to acknowledge himself vanquished and was trying to topple his opponent into the mud. To crown all this unpleasantness, the weather was really terrible. The snow was coming down in large flakes and trying as hard as it could in every way to get inside the real Mr. Golyadkin's open overcoat. All around it was foggy and pitch dark. It was difficult to distinguish in what direction and along what streets they were rushing... It seemed to Mr. Golyadkin that something familiar was happening to him. For one instant he tried to recall whether he had had a presentiment of anything yesterday... in a dream, for example ... Finally his anguish became utterly excruciating. He pressed against his merciless opponent and was going to shout ... But his shout was already dying on his lips ... There was a moment when Mr. Golyadkin forgot everything and decided that all of this was absolutely nothing and that it was happening just like that, somehow, in an inexplicable manner, and to protest it would be a superfluous and utterly wasted effort ... But suddenly and almost at the same instant as our hero was coming to all these conclusions, a careless jolt put an entirely different complexion on the matter. Like a sack of flour Mr. Golyadkin fell off the droshky and rolled away somewhere, acknowledging quite rightly at the moment of his fall that he really had gotten somewhat angry most inopportunely and that everything had come about as a result of his having gotten somewhat angry. Jumping to his feet at last, he saw that they had arrived somewhere; the droshky was standing in the middle of someone's courtyard, and our hero noticed from the first glance that it was the courtyard of the very house in which Olsufi Ivanovich had an apartment. At that very same instant he noticed that his friend was already making his way up the front steps and was probably going to Olsufi Ivanovich's. In his indescribable anguish he was going to rush to catch up with his foe, but luckily for him he wisely thought better of it in time. Not forgetting to settle with the cabman, Mr. Golyadkin rushed out into the street and began to run as fast as he could, somewhere, anywhere. The snow was coming down as before in large flakes; as before it was foggy, wet and dark. Our hero did not walk but flew, knocking over everyone in his path—peasant men and women and children—and himself in turn rebounding off peasant women and men and children. Around him and in his wake could be heard the sound of frightened voices, squealing and shouting . . . But Mr. Golyadkin seemed to have lost consciousness and refused to pay attention to anything . . . He came to his senses, however, at the Semyonovsky Bridge and then only because he had awkwardly managed somehow to bump into and knock down two peasant women with their street wares and at the same time to fall down himself. "It's nothing," thought Mr. Golyadkin; "all of this still has a very good chance of turning out for the best." And hereupon he put his hand into his pocket, wishing to make amends with a silver ruble for spilling the cakes, apples, peas and various other items. Suddenly a new light dawned on Mr. Golyadkin; in his pocket he felt Vakhrameyev's letter. Throwing them the silver ruble, he set out running again, without stopping or looking back at anything. Recalling, however, along the way, that there was an eating establishment he knew nearby, he rushed into the eating establishment, lost no time in settling down at a table lit by a tallow candle and, paying no attention to anything nor listening to the waiter who had appeared to take his order, he broke the seal and began to read the following, which utterly staggered him:

> My dear Yakov Petrovich,
>   Sir
>
> In my previous letter, my dear sir, I clearly gave you to understand that further relations between us would not only be extremely unpleasant for me but would even be detrimental to my personal interests. For everyone knows that association with persons who do not value the opinion of well-intentioned people, with persons rejected out of hand by well-bred society, can not only be ruinous for people uncorrupted and uncontaminated in their innocence by the pernicious breath of vice, but can even lead

them to ultimate perdition. Despite all this, you did not desist and continue to seek my friendship! A clear proof of my opinion about the pernicious poison conveyed by you is, in the first place, your sullied reputation at the Izmaylovsky Bridge and in that vicinity. In the second place, the public knowledge and general official announcement of your disorderly life; in the third place, your incessant fraudulent substitution of complete outsiders for yourself, and, in the fourth place, the wrongs and contrivances undertaken by you against persons known for the well-intentioned and frank quality of their character and for their uprightness of soul. For certain people falsely avow their friendship to one's face while behind one's back they have the pernicious habit of reviling those acknowledged as their friends and doing this not only in the most disgraceful manner but even through the use of abusive and insulting words, as, for example, by calling someone "hollow nut", probably to explain through the use of this word that their friends are stupid and have nothing in their heads and consequently their heads are likened to a hollow nut, an expression used by hicks. You did all this, my dear sir, exactly five months ago when you were present at the home of our mutual acquaintance, Nikolay Sergeyevich Skoroplyokhin, and, to boot, in the presence of strangers. I am far from justifying myself to you, but nevertheless everybody knows that superfluous wit is not only not a chief human requirement but even does harm in practical life, of which you yourself serve as an example worthy of pity, for you are perishing from nothing other than your superfluous wit. I, however, am still inexperienced; I have recently come from Vyatka Province; I do not know the local customs and therefore prudently avoid superfluous wit, striving on the contrary to become famous through my goodnaturedness and the uprightness of

my character—qualities which I am justly proud of.
You write, finally, my dear sir, as if in self-justification,
that one won't win through imposture in our age of
business and industry (based chiefly on steamships
and railways) and, as you are pleased to assert rightly,
that Grishka Otrepyev cannot appear again. This is
true, and I am prepared to agree; but again, by means
of this point in your letter as well, you, sir, not only
have offered nothing in justification of yourself, but
have even turned your accusation upon yourself, for
by it you have demonstrated, in the first place, that
you are an educated person and know the history of
our precious fatherland, and consequently, in the
second place, that even though you are an educated
and witty person you have not safeguarded yourself
and have succumbed to those same faults which you
now censure in others. I say this, my dear sir, because
you yourself operate with deceit and imposture,
alluding to certain persons, laying upon them all
your own transgressions, and thus attempting to
save yourself from the implacable severity of the law.
Your coarse and harsh actions against a person of the
female sex, whose name I do not mention out of
respect for her, deserve nothing but contempt and
recoil upon you to your own, my dear sir, shame and
disgrace. But if you, my dear sir, having forgotten
honor and duty and having made this person forever
unhappy, have now also repudiated all further connections with her, there still are and exist people of
upright and truthful character, who would consider
it an honor to take upon themselves, my dear sir, all
the damage caused by you in order to make amends
for it once and for all and in a noble manner. For here
everyone says that to seek the hand of this person is
both honorable and advantageous; for this person is
of an origin that is neither disreputable nor servile and
would do you an honor in offering you her hand. For
you already know that her father served as a junker in

the German horse artillery. Moreover, on Obukhovsky Prospect she has her close acquaintance and friend engaged in the art of metalworking, who, in the words of this person very well known to you and in every way possible insulted by you, absolutely does not look like some hick metalworker, and consequently is an educated man. Next, she has her second cousin, a person sincere and pious and known to me in the most positive sense—a baker from Bolshaya Podyacheskaya Street. Then, she further has a former pastrycook, a person who though poor has an extremely solid and firm character and, finally, her blood uncle, a learned gentleman and what's more a chemist, who has his own apothecary shop on Sergiyevskaya Street. Finally, even Doctor of Medicine and Surgery, Krestyan Ivanovich Rutenshpits, whom you know, will not refuse to lend all of his powerful influence to further the well-being and protection of his outraged fellow countrywoman. In conclusion I shall tell you that Karolina Ivanovna's petition with respect to your case was submitted long ago; that our mutual acquaintance, Nikolay Sergeyevich Skoroplyokhin, is acting in this case on behalf of Karolina Ivanovna; that her case has already become public knowledge and been announced; that no one anywhere with an apartment will take you in as a lodger; that you have lost all credit and credibility; that you will lose out at work, for this very morning all your machinations were forestalled and wrecked by Karolina Ivanovna's petitions and supplications to your superiors; that, finally, all your hopes and foolish ravings about the Izmaylovsky Bridge and that vicinity must, when public knowledge and announcement are made of your corrupt life, of themselves be dashed and you, rejected by all and wracked by pangs of conscience, will not know where to bow your head, and will wander the entire world and vainly nurture within your heart the serpent of your corruptness and vengeance. And so, I remain,

Sir,

Your Humble Servant
N. Vakhrameyev.

After reading Vakhrameyev's letter, our hero remained for several minutes as though thunderstruck. And so, everything had been explained, everything, everything! Everything had been revealed and the infamy of the infernal intrigue had prevailed over innocence. Still, Mr. Golyadkin did not yet understand everything completely. He still could not recover from the stupor which had come over him. Feeling terrible anguish and terrible agitation, white as a sheet, with the letter in his hands, he walked up and down the room several times; to crown his unfortunate situation, our hero was unaware that he was at that moment the object of special attention for everyone in the room. Probably the disorder of his dress, his uncontrolled agitation, his walking, or rather, running, his gesticulations with both hands, and perhaps his few enigmatic words absent-mindedly addressed to the air—all this probably spoke very badly for Mr. Golyadkin in the opinion of all the customers; and even the waiter was beginning to cast suspicious glances at him. Coming to his senses, our hero noticed that he was standing in the middle of the room and staring in an almost unseemly and impolite manner at an old man of very respectable appearance who, having dined and said some prayers before an icon, had settled himself in his seat again and had in turn riveted his eyes on Mr. Golyadkin. Our hero looked vaguely about him and noticed that everyone, absolutely everyone, was giving him the most ominous and suspicious looks. Suddenly a retired military man with a red collar on his uniform loudly requested "The Police Gazette." Mr. Golyadkin shuddered and blushed. Vakhrameyev's letter and the official announcement flashed through his mind. At that very same instant our hero inadvertently lowered his eyes and saw that he was in clothing so disreputable that he would not wear it even at home let alone in a public place. His shoes, his trousers and his entire left side were completely covered with mud, his right footstrap was torn loose and his coat was even ripped in many places. In his unending anguish our hero went over to the table at which he had been reading and saw that the waiter was approaching him with a strange and brazenly insistent expression on his face. Utterly flustered and downcast, our hero began to examine the table at which he was now standing. On the table lay the dirty plates from someone's dinner, a soiled napkin, and a knife, fork and spoon which had just recently been used. "Why, who's been having dinner?" thought our hero. "Can it have been me? Well, anything is possible! I had dinner and didn't even notice it. What shall I do?" Raising his eyes, Mr. Golyadkin once again saw the waiter standing beside him and getting ready to say something to him.

"How much do I owe you, old chap?" asked our hero in a quavering voice.

Loud laughter resounded around Mr. Golyadkin; even the waiter gave a funny smile. Mr. Golyadkin realized that in this as well he had come off badly and had committed a terrible blunder. When he realized all this, he became so embarrassed that he was forced to reach into his pocket for his handkerchief, probably for the sake of having something to do instead of just standing there; but to his indescribable amazement and that of all those around him, instead of the handkerchief he pulled out a vial containing some kind of medicine which had been prescribed four days earlier by Krestyan Ivanovich. "The medicines are obtained at the same apothecary shop," flashed through Mr. Golyadkin's mind . . . Suddenly he shuddered and almost cried out in horror. New light was dawning . . . On the label it said: "Apothecary *** on Sergiyevskaya Street". Ignoring everything else, Mr. Golyadkin seized Vakhrameyev's letter and—oh, horrors!—among those making efforts on behalf of Karolina Ivanovna were Krestyan Ivanovich and the apothecary on Sergiyevskaya Street. In the letter it also said that this morning his affairs had taken a different turn and that he had been given a warning in the presence of his highest-ranking superiors. This morning, too, Petrushka had disappeared and, finally, Mr. Golyadkin had slept past noon. "Perhaps it's poison! And through the action of the poison I slept past noon," rushed through Mr. Golyadkin's mind. He absentmindedly shook the medicine and held the vial up to the light... The dark, revolting, reddish liquid gleamed ominously before Mr. Golyadkin's eyes . . . The vial fell out of his hands and instantly shattered to pieces. Our hero cried out and leapt back a few steps from the spilled liquid . . . Our hero was shaking in every limb and sweat was breaking out on his temples and brow. "My life must be in danger!" Meanwhile a stir and commotion arose in the room; everyone was surrounding Mr. Golyadkin; everyone was talking to Mr. Golyadkin. But our hero was mute and motionless, seeing nothing, hearing nothing, feeling nothing . . . At last, as though tearing himself from the spot, he dashed out of the eating establishment, shoved aside each and every one attempting to restrain him, fell almost senseless into the first droshky for hire that came along and flew off to his apartment.

In the entranceway of his apartment he met Mikheyev, the office guard, with an official envelope in his hands. "I know, my friend, I know everything," our exhausted hero answered in a weak, anguished voice; "it's the official. . ." The envelope did in fact contain an order to Mr. Golyadkin, signed by Andrei Filippovich, to turn over his duties to Ivan Semyonovich. Taking the envelope and giving the guard ten kopeks, Mr. Golyadkin entered his apartment and saw that Petrushka was getting all his odds and ends and all his things ready and gathering them in a pile, obviously with the intention of leaving Mr. Golyadkin and moving from his place to that of Karolina Ivanovna, who had enticed him into replacing Yevstafi. Without a word Petrushka helped his master off with his overcoat; he was going to take the galoshes but there were no galoshes because Mr. Golyadkin had lost them; he saw his master to his room, gave him a candle, and without a word pointed out to him an envelope lying on a little table. The envelope had arrived by regular post. Absentmindedly and almost beside himself, our hero opened it and read, to his great amazement and to his utter devastation, the following:

249

Noble man, suffering for me and forever dear
to my heart!

I suffer, I perish—save me! A slanderer, an
intriguer, a man notorious for his worthless tendencies has ensnared me in his nets and I am undone!
(But he is repulsive to me, while you! . . .) We have
been kept apart, my letters to you have been intercepted—and all this has been done by an immoral
person, taking advantage of his one good quality—
his resemblance to you. In any case one can be ugly
but still captivate with one's intellect, strong feelings
and pleasing manners... I perish! I am being married
off against my will, forcibly, and the one who
intrigues in this most of all is my father, my benefactor
and State Councilor Olsufi Ivanovich, who probably
desires to take over my place and my relationships in
well-bred society ... But I have made up my mind
and am protesting with every means bestowed on me
by nature. I say 'This is the way it is, but I protest;' I
say, 'This is the way it is... but you, my dear sir and
utter heel, you know... and Otrepyevs are impossible
in the times in which we live...'; I say, 'Save me, man
dear to my heart!' Do not let me perish and await me
in your coach today at exactly nine o'clock by the
windows of Mr. Berendeyev's apartment. We are
giving a ball. I shall come out and we shall fly; we
shall fly ... and shall live in a cabin on the shore of
Khvalynskoye Sea.[12] Besides, there are other posts,
such as: a clerk in chambers in the provinces. As far
as our aged aunt, Pelageya Semyonovna, is concerned,
we won't take her with us: she refuses to go. But in
any case, remember, my friend, that innocence is
strong by virtue of its innocence. One further moral
idea—that concerning our places—is a good one and
so is the historical idea that Otrepyevs are impossible
in the times in which we live. Farewell; think of me,

and for heaven's sake, await me at the entrance with your coach. For my part, I shall throw myself into the protection of your embracing arms at exactly 2 a.m.

Yours till the grave,
Klara Olsufyevna

XIII

*Of how Mr. Golyadkin resolves to kidnap Klara Olsufyevna,
noting, however, that immorality in their upbringing ruins
inexperienced young ladies. Something about Spanish serenades
and about a great variety of things which are inconvenient in
our severe climate. Of how Mr. Golyadkin explained himself
the way it is. Something about artists' studios and noble
families having their origins in the Ukraine. Mr. Golyadkin
drives to the Izmaylovsky Bridge.*

Mr. Golyadkin's face was, as they say, blank with fear
when he came to finish the unexpected letter, which was
terrible and frightening solely by virtue of its being totally
unexpected. So many contradictory circumstances, so many
blows, so many horrors inconsistent with one another! Pale,
shaken, alarmed, Mr. Golyadkin got up from the chair. He felt
dizzy; he felt faint. In a minute, however, he collected himself
and called Petrushka. Petrushka entered with a swagger, his
manner strangely casual and his mien boorishly triumphant. It
was evident that Petrushka had gotten some idea into his head,
that he felt himself to be completely within his rights, and that
he looked like a complete outsider, that is, like someone else's
servant, but certainly in no way like Mr. Golyadkin's former
servant.

"Well, so you see, my dear fellow," began our hero,
gasping for breath, "what time is it now, my dear fellow?"

Without a word Petrushka headed behind the partition,
then returned and in a rather independent tone announced that
it was nearly half past seven.

"That's fine, my dear fellow, that's fine. Well, you see, my
dear fellow . . . permit me to tell you, my dear fellow, that
everything seems to be over between us now."

Petrushka said nothing.

"Well, now that everything is over between us, tell me frankly now, tell me as you would a friend, where have you been, old chap?"

"Where have I been? With good people, sir."

"I know, my friend, I know. I've always been satisfied with you, my dear fellow, and I shall give you a reference... Well, what are you doing with them now?"

"What indeed, sir! You know yourself, sir. It's clear, sir, a good person doesn't teach you to do bad."

"I know, my dear fellow, I know. Nowadays good people are rare, my friend; treasure them, my friend. Well, and how are they?"

"You know how, sir... Only I can't serve you any longer now, sir; you must know that, sir."

"I know, my dear fellow, I know; I know your zeal and diligence; I've seen it all, my friend; I've noticed it. I respect you, my friend. I respect a good and honest person, even if he's a servant."

"Of course, I know, sir! I know, sir, that it's good to be with a good person. For various things happen, sir; it depends on who you come across... Our kind, of course, as you yourself must know, sir, earn their bread where it's best. That's just the way it is, sir. I'm the same way! I know, sir, that one just can't get along without a good person, sir. They say: 'What are you going to do there, good person? There's nothing for you to do there, good person, at his place,' they say. I know that that's just the way it is, you know, sir... We aren't the first and we won't be the last. But our kind have their place everywhere... I know, sir."

"Well, that's fine, old chap, that's fine; I sense it, my friend, I sense it . . . Well, here's your money and your reference. Now let's kiss one another, old chap, and say goodbye... Well now, my dear fellow, I shall ask a favor of you, one last favor," said Mr. Golyadkin in a solemn tone. "You see, my dear fellow, that's how it is. All sorts of things can happen. Sorrow, my friend, lies in wait even in gilded palaces, and there is no escape from it. You know, my friend, it seems to me I've always been kind to you . . ."

Petrushka said nothing.

"It seems to me I've always been kind to you, my dear fellow . . . Well, how much linen do we have now, my dear fellow?"

"Why, everything's there, sir. Linen shirts six, sir; socks three pairs; four dickeys, sir; one jersey flannel; underwear two sets, sir. You know yourself that's all, sir. I haven't taken anything of yours, sir . . . I take care of my master's property, sir. I may have my moments, sir, you know . . . I know, sir . . . but that I should be guilty of that—never, sir; you know that yourself, sir . . ."

"I believe it, my friend, I believe it. That's not what I'm talking about, my friend, that's not what I'm talking about; you see, here's what, my friend . . ."

"I know, sir. I know it already, sir. Now when I was working for General Stolbnyakov, sir, he let me go because he was going away to Saratov . . . he had an estate there . . ."

"No, my friend, that's not what I'm talking about. I don't mean anything . . . don't you go thinking anything, my dear friend . . ."

"I know, sir. It's easy to slander people of our sort, sir. But I've given satisfaction everywhere, sir. Ministers, generals, senators, counts, sir. I've been with all of them, sir; at Prince Svinchatkin's, sir; at Pereborkin's, the colonel's, sir; at Nedobarov's, the general's. They visited us, too, sir; they came out to the estate, sir, to see our folks. You know, sir . . ."

"Yes, my friend, yes; fine, my friend, fine. And now I, too, am going away, my friend . . . A different way lies before everyone, my dear fellow, and no one knows what road he may find himself on. Well, my friend, help me get dressed now; and also lay out my uniform jacket . . . another pair of trousers, sheets, blankets, pillows . . ."

"Do you wish everything to be tied up into a bundle, sir?"

"Yes, my friend, yes; why not into a bundle? Who knows what may happen to us? Well, and now, my dear fellow, you go find me a coach . . ."

"A coach, sir? . . ."

"Yes, my friend, a coach, a really roomy one and for a specific time. And don't you go thinking anything, my friend..."

"And do you mean to go far away, sir?"

"I don't know, my friend; that I also don't know. I think you'd better put a down quilt in there as well. What do you think, my friend? I am relying on you, my dear fellow . . ."

"You mean you're going away right now, sir?"

"Yes, my friend, yes! Something has come up—something rather odd... that's how it is, my dear fellow, that's how it is..."

"I know, sir; the same thing happened to a lieutenant in our regiment, sir; at a landowner's, sir . . . he carried her off, sir . . ."

"Carried her off? . . . What do you mean? My dear fellow, you . . ."

"Yes, sir; he carried her off, sir, and they were married at another estate. Everything had been arranged in advance, sir. There was a pursuit, sir. But the prince took their part at that point, sir, the late prince, sir,—well, and things were smoothed over, sir . . ."

"They were married, but... how is it that you know, my dear fellow? By what manner of means did you get to know, my dear fellow?"

"Why, I just know, sir; what do you think, sir! News flies quickly, sir. We know everything, sir . . ."

"So then you know what's going on here as well, my dear fellow? How is it that you know? . . . Well, that's all right, that's all right... I'm relying on you. You see, my friend, something has come up . . . I don't think I need to explain anything to you . . ."

"I know, sir; I know that it could happen to anyone, of course. Only I shall tell you now, sir, permit me to say it in my plain servant's way, sir, since it's come to that now, I'll tell you, sir: you have an enemy; you have a rival, sir, a powerful rival; so there you are, sir . . ."

"I know, my friend, I know; you know yourself, my dear fellow... Well, then, I'm relying on you. What shall we do now, my friend? How can we do this thing the way those other people did?"

"Here's how, sir. If you've chosen that way of doing things, roughly speaking, sir, then you are going to have to buy some things, sir—well, like sheets, pillows, another down quilt, sir, a good blanket, sir—why, right here at our neighbor's downstairs, sir—she's a tradeswoman, sir—there's a fine lady's fox cloak; you can have a look at it right now, sir. It's just what you'll need now, sir; a fine cloak, sir, satin, lined with fox, sir..."

"Very well, my friend, very well. I agree, my friend. I'm relying on you, I'm relying on you completely. Why not have a cloak, too, my dear fellow . . . Only hurry, hurry! For God's sake, hurry! I'll buy the cloak, too, only please hurry! It will soon be eight! Hurry, for God's sake, my friend! Hasten, be quick, my friend! . . ."

Petrushka dropped the bundle of linen, pillows, blankets, sheets and odds and ends that he had been about to gather together and tie up and rushed headlong out of the room. Mr. Golyadkin meanwhile seized the letter once more . . . but he was unable to read it. Clutching his wretched head with both hands, he leaned against the wall in amazement. He was unable to think about anything; he was unable to do anything either; he didn't know himself what was happening to him. At last, seeing that time was passing and that neither Petrushka nor the clerk were making their appearance, Mr. Golyadkin decided to go himself. Opening the door into the entranceway, he heard a hubbub of conversation, arguing and gossiping below . . . Several female neighbors were babbling, shouting, discussing and dickering over something—Mr. Golyadkin already knew exactly what it was about. Petrushka's voice was audible; then there was the sound of footsteps. "Oh, my God! They'll drag everybody and his brother into it!" groaned Mr. Golyadkin, wringing his hands in despair and dashing back into his room. Back in his room he fell almost senseless onto the ottoman, face down on a cushion. For a minute he lay like this, then leapt up and, not waiting for Petrushka, put on his galoshes, hat and overcoat, grabbed his wallet and ran headlong down the stairs. "I don't need anything, anything, my dear fellow! I'll do it myself; I'll do it all myself. For the time being I have no need of you and meanwhile perhaps this matter will turn out for the best," Mr. Golyadkin muttered to Petrushka, meeting him on the stairway. Then he ran out into the courtyard and was off; his heart was fainting; he had not yet made up his mind... how to proceed, what to do, how to act at this critical moment...

"That's the question—dear God, how ought I to act! Why did all this have to happen?" he cried out at last in despair, hobbling along the street aimlessly and haphazardly; "why did all this have to happen? Why, if it were not for this, for this very thing, then everything would have been settled; at one go, with a single stroke, a single, deft, energetic, firm stroke, it would have been settled! And I even know just how it would have been settled. Here's how it would all have happened: I would have gone and said, 'This is the way things are, but I, sir, with your permission, could not care less'; I would have said, 'Things aren't done that way'; I would have said, 'Sir, dear sir, things are not done that way and you won't win us over by imposture; an impostor, sir, is a person, you know... who is worthless and of no use to his native land. Do you understand that?' I would have said, 'Do you understand that, my dear sir?!' That's how it would have happened... But no, on the other hand, what am I saying? It's not at all like that, absolutely not... What nonsense I'm talking, fool that I am, self-destructive creature that I am! It's not at all like that. I say, you self-destructive creature, you ... But look here, you corrupt man, see the way it's happening now. Well, where am I to go now? Well, what, for example, am I going to do with myself now? Well, what am I good for now? Well, what are you good for now, for example, you Poor Beggar, you, you unworthy thing, you! Well, what now? I must get a coach. She says 'Go and get a coach and have it waiting here for me'; she says, 'We'll get out little feet wet if there isn't a coach' ... Now, who would have thought it? Now there's a fine miss for you! Oh, my dear young lady! There's a virtuous maiden for you! There's the much-praised ninny.[113] You've done yourself proud, young lady, I do declare, you've done yourself proud! ... And all this comes of an immoral upbringing; and now that I have scrutinized it all and gotten to the bottom of it, I finally see that this comes from nothing other than immorality. What they should have done to her when she

was young, instead of pampering her, you know . . . they should
have used the rod now and then, but they stuffed her with candy
and they stuffed her with cakes and that little old fellow gushed
over her: 'You're my this', he said, 'and you're my that; you're
my good girl', he said, 'and I shall marry you to a count, my little
aristocrat!' . . . And this is the kind of little aristocrat she's
turned out to be! You're our this and our that—and now she's
gone and shown us her hand. 'This is the game we have in mind!'
she says. They should have kept her home when she was young,
but they put her in a boarding school, gave her up to a French
madame, to some émigrée named Falbala or some such thing,
and a lot of good she's learned from this émigrée named
Falbala—and that's why it's all turned out this way. She says,
'Come and be happy!' She says, 'Be in a coach at such-and-such
an hour outside my windows and sing a sentimental love song in
Spanish; I await you and I know that you love me and we shall
run away together and live in a cabin; and as for you, sir, you
shall be a court clerk! . . . Well, really, that cannot be; that, my
dear young lady—if it's come to that now—cannot be; it is
against the law to carry off an honest and innocent young girl
from her family home without the consent of her parents! And,
finally, why do it? For what reason? And what need is there?
Why, she ought to marry the one she's supposed to, the one
intended by fate, and that's that. I am a civil servant; and I can
lose my position because of it; I can be taken to court because
of it, young lady! That's how it is, if you didn't know! And I
know all this; I've found it all out; I know where the source of it
all is and who's working away at it! It's that German's doing.
She's the source of it all, the witch; all the trouble started with
her. They slandered a man and they invented old wives' tales
and a cock-and-bull story about him on the advice of Andrei
Filippovich; that's where it started. Otherwise, why would
Petrushka be involved in it? Why does he have to be involved?
What business is it of that rascal's? No, young lady, I cannot, I
cannot possibly, not at all . . . And you, young lady, must excuse
me somehow this once. You, young lady, are the source of it all;
it's not the German who is the source of it all, not that witch,
but you alone, because the witch is a good woman, because the

witch is not to blame for anything, while you, my dear young lady, are to blame—so there! You, young lady, you're the one who's getting me unjustly accused . . . Here's a man perishing; here's a man losing sight of himself and unable to restrain himself—how can there be any talk of a wedding then? And how will it all end? And how will it all turn out and end now? I'd give a lot to know all that! . . ."

Thus reasoned our hero in his despair. Coming to his senses suddenly, he noticed that he was standing somewhere on Liteynaya Street. The weather was frightful: there was a thaw, snow was coming down and it was raining—just as it had been at that unforgettable time when, at the terrible midnight hour, all of Mr. Golyadkin's misfortunes had begun. "How can there be any talk of a journey in something like this?" thought Mr. Golyadkin, looking at the weather. "This is death; this is certain death . . . Dear God! Now where shall I find a coach here, for instance? Over there on the corner there seems to be something black. Let's see; let's investigate . . . Dear God!" continued our hero, directing his feeble and unsteady footsteps to where he had seen something resembling a coach. "No, here's what I'll do: I'll go there and throw myself at his feet, if I can, and I'll humbly entreat him. I'll say, 'This is the way it is. I commend my fate into your hands, into the hands of my superior.' I'll say, 'Your Excellency, protect me and give your patronage to me.' 'This is the way it is,' I'll say; 'such and such and such and such is an unlawful deed; don't ruin me; you're like a father to me; don't abandon me . . . save my self-esteem, honor and name . . . save me, too, from that villain, that corrupt person . . . He is a different person, Your Excellency, and I am also a different person; he is separate and I am also separate; really separate, Your Excellency, really separate'; I'll say, 'That's how it is'. I'll say, 'I can't resemble him; have him replaced; have the kindness to do it; give orders for him to be replaced and for the godless, unwarranted impersonation to be brought to an end . . . so that it cannot serve as an example to others, Your Excellency. You're like a father to me; a superior, of course, a beneficent and protective superior, must encourage such action . . . There's even something chivalrous

about it.' I'll say, 'You, my beneficent superior, are like a father
to me and I entrust my fate to you and won't cross you; I put
myself into your hands and withdraw myself from my duties...'
Yes, that's what I'll say!"

"Well, now, my dear fellow, are you a cabman?"

"Yes, I am..."

"I want a coach, brother, for the evening..."

"And will you be pleased to journey far, sir?"

"For the evening, for the evening; and to go wherever I
may have to go, my dear fellow, wherever I may have to go."

"Might you be planning then to journey out of town?"

"Yes, my friend, perhaps even out of town. I don't know
yet myself for certain, my friend; I can't tell you for certain, my
dear fellow. You see, my dear fellow, perhaps it will all work out
for the best and change for the better, when the mask falls from
certain persons and a few things are revealed. You know how it
is, my friend..."

"Yes, of course, I know how it is, sir; God grant everyone
joy and happiness..."

"Yes, my friend, yes; thank you, my dear fellow; well, how
much will it be, my dear fellow?..."

"Will you be pleased to go immediately, sir?"

"Yes, immediately; that is, no, you'll have to wait at a
certain spot . . . just a bit; you won't wait long, my dear
fellow..."

"Well, if you're hiring me for the whole time, I can't ask
less than six rubles in weather like this, sir..."

"Well, all right, my friend, all right; and I shall show my
gratitude to you, my dear fellow. Well, so, you'll take me now,
my dear fellow."

"Get in; just let me fix things up a bit; now, be so kind as to
get in. Where do you wish to go?"

"To the Izmaylovsky Bridge, my friend."

The cabman clambered up onto the coachbox, forcibly
tore his pair of emaciated nags away from the hay trough, and
was about to set out for the Izmaylovsky Bridge. But suddenly
Mr. Golyadkin pulled the cord, stopped the coach and in a
beseeching voice asked the driver to turn back, to go not to the

Izmaylovsky Bridge but to another street. The driver turned
into the other street and ten minutes later Mr. Golyadkin's
newly acquired carriage stopped before the house in which His
Excellency had an apartment. Mr. Golyadkin emerged from
the coach, earnestly besought his driver to wait and with a
sinking heart ran upstairs to the second floor and pulled the
bell-pull. The door opened and our hero found himself in His
Excellency's foyer.

"Is His Excellency pleased to be at home?" asked Mr.
Golyadkin, addressing himself thus to the servant who had
opened the door.

"What do you want?" asked the servant, looking Mr.
Golyadkin over from head to foot.

"Well, I, my friend, you know... am Golyadkin, the clerk,
Titular Councilor Golyadkin. Tell him this is the way it is; I've
come to explain..."

"Wait; you can't, sir..."

"My friend, I cannot wait; my business is important; an
urgent matter..."

"But who sent you? Have you come with papers?..."

"No, my friend, I have come on my own account...
Announce me, my friend; say, 'This is the way it is, to explain.'
And I will show my gratitude to you, my dear fellow..."

"I can't, sir; my orders were not to receive anyone. He has
guests, sir. Come back in the morning at ten o'clock, sir..."

"Do announce me, my dear fellow; I can't wait; it's
impossible for me to wait... You will answer for this, my dear
fellow..."

"Oh, go on, announce him. What's it to you? Afraid to
wear out some shoe leather for nothing?" said another servant
sprawled out on a chest and silent until now.

"Who cares about shoe leather? My orders were not to
receive anyone. Get it? Their turn is in the morning."

"Announce him. Afraid your tongue will drop off or
something?"

"All right, I'll announce him: my tongue won't drop off.
My orders were not to receive anyone, I told you; those were my
orders. Go into that room there."

Mr. Golyadkin entered the first room; there was a clock on the table. He glanced at it: it was half past eight. He began to feel sick at heart. He was just thinking of turning back; but at that very moment the lanky footman standing at the threshold of the next room loudly announced Mr. Golyadkin's name. "What a voice!" thought our hero in indescribable anguish... "Why, you should have said, you know... said, 'This is the way it is, he has humbly and meekly come to explain' . . . you know... 'Will you be so kind as to receive him? ...' But now my case has been ruined; now my entire case is lost; still . . . oh, well—it doesn't matter." There was no time to consider, however. The servant returned, said, "If you please," and conducted Mr. Golyadkin into the study.

When our hero entered he felt as though he had been blinded, for he could see absolutely nothing. He had, however, glimpsed two or three figures. "Oh, yes, those are the guests," flashed through Mr. Golyadkin's mind. At last our hero began to distinguish clearly the star on His Excellency's black frock coat; then, by a gradual process he became aware of the black frock coat as well; finally his ability to see was restored completely.

"What is it, sir?" a familiar voice uttered above Mr. Golyadkin.

"Titular Councilor Golyadkin, Your Excellency."

"Well?"

"I've come to explain . . ."

"What? . . . What's that?"

"Why, yes. I say, 'This is the way it is; I've come to explain, Your Excellency, sir . . .' "

"But you . . . But who are you?"

"Mi-Mi-Mister Golyadkin, Your Excellency, a Titular Councilor."

"Well, just what is it you want?"

"I say, 'This is the way it is; he's like a father to me. I withdraw myself from my duties, and protect me from my enemy.' That's what I say!"

"What's that? . . ."

"You know how it is . . ."

"How what is?"

Mr. Golyadkin said nothing; his chin was beginning to twitch slightly . . .

"Well?"

"I thought it was chivalrous, Your Excellency . . . 'that there was something chivalrous in it,' I say, 'and my superior is like a father to me . . .' I say, 'This is the way it is; protect me, I t-tearfully e-entreat you, and that such a-actions m-must b-be en-en-encouraged . . .' "

His Excellency turned away. For several moments our hero's eyes could not make anything out. He felt a tightness in his chest. His breathing was labored. He did not know where he was . . . He felt ashamed and sad. God knows what happened next . . . Coming to his senses, our hero noticed that His Excellency was talking with his guests and seemed to be arguing sharply and intensely with them about something. One of the guests Mr. Golyadkin recognized immediately. It was Andrei Filippovich. The other he did not recognize; however, this person also seemed familiar—a tall, thick-set figure, elderly, endowed with very bushy eyebrows and sidewhiskers and a keen, expressive look. Around the stranger's neck was a decoration on a ribbon and in his mouth a small cigar. The stranger was smoking and, without taking the cigar out of his mouth, would nod his head significantly and glance from time to time at Mr. Golyadkin. Mr. Golyadkin began to feel awkward; he averted his eyes and thereupon saw yet another extremely odd guest. In the doorway, which our hero had up until then taken to be a mirror—something which had happened to him once before as well—*he* appeared—we know who—Mr. Golyadkin's very close acquaintance and friend. Mr. Golyadkin Junior had actually been up until then in another, small room, hurriedly writing something; now, apparently, his presence had become necessary—and he appeared with the papers under his arm, went up to His Excellency and very deftly, while waiting to receive His Excellency's undivided attention, succeeded in insinuating himself into the conversation and counsel, taking up his position a little bit behind Andrei Filippovich's back and partly hidden by the stranger smoking the small cigar. Evidently

Mr. Golyadkin Junior was intensely interested in the conversation, which he was now listening in on in a noble manner, nodding his head, shifting his feet, smiling, glancing every moment at His Excellency, as though beseeching him with his eyes to permit him as well to put in his few remarks. "Scoundrel!" thought Mr. Golyadkin and involuntarily took a step forward. Just then the general turned around and rather hesitantly approached Mr. Golyadkin.

"Very well, then, very well; go along now. I shall consider your case, and give orders for you to be shown out..." Here the general glanced at the stranger with the bushy sidewhiskers. The latter nodded his head in assent.

Mr. Golyadkin sensed and clearly realized that he was being taken for something other than he was and not at all as he should be. "One way or another I have to explain myself," he thought. 'This is the way it is, Your Excellency,' I'll say." Hereupon, in his bewilderment he looked down at the floor and, to his extreme amazement, saw a sizable white spot on each of His Excellency's shoes. "Can they have split?" thought Mr. Golyadkin. Soon, however, Mr. Golyadkin discovered that His Excellency's shoes had not split at all but were only reflecting the light strongly—a phenomenon completely explainable by the fact that the shoes were of patent leather and had a high gloss. "That's what's called a *highlight*," thought our hero. "The use of this name is reserved particularly for artists' studios, while in other places this sheen is called 'the illuminated edge.'" At this point Mr. Golyadkin raised his eyes and saw that it was time to speak because his case might easily take a turn for the worse . . . Our hero took a step forward.

"I say, 'This is the way it is, Your Excellency'," he said, " 'but in the age we live in you won't win through imposture.' "

The general did not answer but tugged hard at the bell-pull. Our hero took another step forward.

"He is a vile and corrupt person, Your Excellency," said our hero, beside himself and fainting with fear, but nevertheless boldly and resolutely pointing at his unworthy twin, who was at that moment fidgeting about near His Excellency; " 'This is the way it is,' I say, and I am alluding to someone we all know."

A general stir ensued after Mr. Golyadkin's words. Andrei Filippovich and the stranger began nodding their heads; His Excellency in his impatience kept tugging the bell-pull with all his might to summon his servants. At this point Mr. Golyadkin Junior stepped forward in his turn.

"Your Excellency," he said, "I humbly request your permission to speak." There was something decisive in Mr. Golyadkin Junior's voice; everything about him showed that he felt completely within his rights.

"Permit me to ask you," he began again, in his eagerness anticipating His Excellency's answer and turning now to Mr. Golyadkin; "permit me to ask you in whose presence you think you are explaining yourself thus? Before whom do you think you are standing? In whose study do you think you are? . . ." Mr. Golyadkin Junior was in a state of utter and unusual agitation; his face was all red and blazing with indignation and anger; tears had even appeared in his eyes.

"The Bassavryukovs!" roared a servant at the top of his lungs, appearing in the double doors of the study. "A fine noble name, Ukrainians," thought Mr. Golyadkin and thereupon felt someone place a hand on his back in a very friendly way; then another hand was placed on his back; Mr. Golyadkin's vile twin bustled along before them showing the way and our hero saw clearly that they seemed to be directing him towards the big double doors of the study. "Just exactly as it was at Olsufi Ivanovich's," he thought and found himself in the foyer. Looking around, he saw next to him two of His Excellency's servants and one twin.

"The overcoat, the overcoat, the overcoat, the overcoat of my friend! The overcoat of my best friend!" twittered the corrupt person, seizing the overcoat from the hands of one of the servants and tossing it right over Mr. Golyadkin's head, for the sake of a vile and poor jest. Struggling to get out from under his overcoat, Mr. Golyadkin could clearly hear the laughter of the two servants. But shutting his ears to everything and ignoring everything extraneous, he emerged from the foyer and found himself on the lighted stairway. Mr. Golyadkin Junior followed after him.

"Goodbye, Your Excellency!" he shouted after Mr. Golyadkin Senior.

"Scoundrel!" uttered our hero, beside himself.

"So, I'm a scoundrel . . ."

"Corrupt fellow!"

"So, I'm a corrupt fellow. . ." The worthy Mr. Golyadkin's
unworthy foe answered him thus and, as was his vile wont,
stood looking down from the height of the stairway, without
blinking an eye, straight into Mr. Golyadkin's eyes, as though
begging him to continue. Our hero spat with indignation and
ran out onto the front steps. After running out onto the front
steps, he was so crushed that he was totally unable to recall who
seated him in the coach or how. On coming to his senses, he saw
that he was being driven along the Fontanka. "We must be
going to the Izmaylovsky Bridge," thought Mr. Golyadkin...
At this point Mr. Golyadkin tried to think of something else,
but could not; it was something so terrible that it could not be
explained . . . "Well, it doesn't matter," concluded our hero
and drove on to the Izmaylovsky Bridge.

XIV

Of how Mr. Golyadkin kidnaps Klara Olsufyevna. Of how everything that Mr. Golyadkin had had a premonition of came to pass. The end of all of this completely improbable story.

. . . The weather seemed to be trying to change for the better. The wet snow, which had been coming down in great clouds until then, began to thin out gradually and at last stopped almost completely. The sky became visible and here and there in it tiny stars began to twinkle. But it was wet, muddy, damp and stifling, especially for Mr. Golyadkin, who could hardly breathe as it was. His overcoat, made heavier by being thoroughly soaked, permeated his limbs with an unpleasantly warm dampness, while the weight of it caused his already quite unsteady legs to buckle under him. A feverish shiver sent sharp twinges over his entire body; exhaustion squeezed a cold unhealthy sweat out of him, so that Mr. Golyadkin quite forgot at this convenient opportunity to repeat with his customary firmness and resoluteness his favorite phrase that everything perhaps, maybe, somehow, most likely, certainly would go and turn out for the best. "Still, none of this matters for the time being," added our hero of staunch and unfailing spirit, wiping from his face the drops of cold water running in every direction from the brim of his thoroughly saturated round hat. Having added that all this still didn't matter, our hero attempted to sit down on a rather thick piece of log, which was lying near a woodpile in Olsufi Ivanovich's courtyard. Of course, there was no point any more in thinking about Spanish serenades and silken ladders; but it was indeed necessary to think about a cozy nook, perhaps not altogether warm but at least comfortable and concealed. He was very much enticed, let it be said in passing, by that very nook in the entranceway of Olsufi Ivanovich's apartment where earlier, almost at the beginning of this true story, our hero had been standing and waiting out his two hours among the cupboard and the old screens and all sorts of household junk and useless trash and rubbish. The fact of the matter is that now as well Mr. Golyadkin had already been standing and waiting two whole hours in Olsufi Ivanovich's courtyard. But as far as the previous cozy and comfortable nook was concerned, there now existed certain inconveniences which had not existed previously. The first inconvenience was that probably this spot had now been noted and certain precautionary measures taken concerning it since the time of the episode at Olsufi Ivanovich's last ball; while, secondly, it was necessary to wait for the prearranged signal from Klara Olsufyevna, because there certainly had to be some such prearranged signal from Klara Olsufyevna. That is how it was always done, and, as they say, "We aren't the first and we won't be the last." Mr. Golyadkin thereupon appropriately remembered in passing a novel he had read long ago, in which the heroine had given a prearranged signal to Alfred under identical circumstances by tying a pink ribbon to a window. But a pink ribbon now, at night, and in the climate of St. Petersburg, which is notorious for its dampness and unreliability, was out of the question and, in a word, utterly impossible. "No, silken ladders have no place in this," thought our hero, "and I would do better to stay here unobtrusively and cozily ... I would do better, for instance, to just stay here;" and he chose a spot in the courtyard right opposite the windows and near the woodpile. Of course, many extraneous people, postboys, coachmen, etc., were walking about the courtyard; in addition wheels were clattering and horses were snorting and so forth; but still the spot was convenient: first of all, he could operate here on the quiet, while secondly, whether they observed him or not, still now at least there was the advantage of being to a certain extent in the shadows and no one could see Mr. Golyadkin; he, however, could see absolutely everything. The windows were brightly illuminated; there was some sort of festive gathering at Olsufi Ivanovich's. The music, however, was not yet audible. "Apparently it's not a ball; they've gathered for some other occasion," thought our hero, his heart sinking somewhat. "Is it today, though?" flashed through his mind. "Can there be a mistake in the date? It could be; anything is possible . . . That's so; anything is possible . . . Perhaps the letter was written yesterday but it didn't reach me, and it didn't reach me because Petrushka got involved in this matter, rascal that he is! Or it said tomorrow, that is, that I . . . that it was necessary to do everything tomorrow, that is, to be waiting with the coach? . . ." At this point our hero grew absolutely cold all over and felt in his pocket for the letter in order to check his information. But to his amazement the letter was not in his pocket. "How can this be?" whispered Mr. Golyadkin, more dead than alive. "Where can I have left it? I must have lost it! That's all I needed!" he concluded finally, with a groan. "And what if it falls into evil hands now? (Why, perhaps it already has!) Lord! What will come of all this! Oh, what will come of it? Something too awful to contemplate . . . Ah, destestable fate of mine!" At this point Mr. Golyadkin began to shake like a leaf at the thought that perhaps his unseemly twin, in tossing his overcoat over his head, had done it expressly for the purpose of seizing the letter, the existence of which he had somehow sniffed out from Mr. Golyadkin's enemies. "What's more, he's seized it," thought our hero, "as proof . . . but why as proof? . . ." After the initial stunning horror, the blood rushed to Mr. Golyadkin's head. Groaning and gnashing his teeth, he clutched his feverish head, sank down onto his log and began to think about something . . . But somehow the thoughts were not connecting in his head. Some faces flashed through his mind; some long-forgotten events were recalled, now dimly, now sharply; some themes from stupid songs insinuated themselves into his brain . . . And oh, the anguish was unnatural! "My God! My God!" thought our hero, coming to his senses somewhat and suppressing the dull sobs in his breast, "grant me firmness of spirit in the bottomless depths of my misfortune! That I am done for, that I have utterly ceased to exist—of this there is no longer any doubt, and it is all in the order of things, for it cannot be any other way. In the first place I've lost my post, lost it for certain; there is no way I could not have lost it . . . Well, let's even suppose that it can be put to rights somehow. My money, let's suppose, will suffice to start off with; I'll get some other small apartment; I'll need some bits of furniture . . . In the first place Petrushka won't be with me . . . I can manage without that rascal . . . manage with the help of the other tenants; well, that's fine! I can come and go when I feel like it, and Petrushka won't be grumbling that I come home late—that's how it is; that's why it's good to have the other tenants . . . Well, let's suppose all this is good; only how is it that I keep talking about the wrong thing, completely wrong?" This is how it will be . . . It will be like this . . ." At this point the thought of his real situation again dawned on Mr. Golyadkin. He looked about. "Ah, dear God! Dear God! What have I been talking about now?" he thought, losing his calm completely and clutching his feverish head . . .

"Will you be pleased to go soon, sir?" a voice uttered above Mr. Golyadkin. Mr. Golyadkin started but before him stood his driver, also soaked to the skin and chilled to the bone. Impatient and having nothing to do, he had taken it into his head to look in on Mr. Golyadkin behind the woodpile.

"I'm fine, my friend, . . . I'll come soon, my friend, very soon; you wait . . ."

The driver went away, muttering under his breath. "Now what's he muttering about?" thought Mr. Golyadkin tearfully. "After all I hired him for the evening; after all, I, you know . . . am within my rights now . . . So there! I hired him for the evening and that's all there is to it. I say, 'And that, my dear old fellow, is all there is to it. Even if you just stand about, it doesn't matter. Everything has to be as I say. I am free to go and free not to go. And that I am standing here behind the woodpile, why, that doesn't matter at all . . . and don't you dare say anything'; I say, 'The gentleman feels like standing behind the woodpile, and so he's standing behind the woodpile . . . and he is not sullying anyone's honor—that's what!' That's what, my dear young lady, if you really want to know. As for living in a cabin, I say, 'This is the way it is; nowadays no one does, my dear young lady. So there!' And without good behavior in our industrial age, my dear young lady, you won't get anywhere, something you yourself now serve as a pernicious example of... You say, 'You have to serve as a court clerk and live in a cabin by the sea.' In the first place, my dear young lady, there are no court clerks by the sea, and in the second place, you and I cannot get one, a job as a court clerk, that is. For, let's suppose, for example, I hand in a petition; I appear and say, 'This is the way it is, make me a court clerk;' I say, 'You know . . . and protect me from my enemy' . . . and they will say to you, 'Young lady,' they'll say, 'you know . . . there are plenty of court clerks and here you are not at the émigrée Falbala's, where you learned good behavior, something you yourself serve as a pernicious example of.' For good behavior, young lady, means sitting at home, respecting your father and not thinking about suitors prematurely. For, suitors, young lady, will be found in good time—so there! Of course, unquestionably, you must have various talents, such as: playing the piano a bit sometimes, speaking French, knowing history, geography, scripture and arithmetic—that's what!—and that's all you need. Oh, and cooking besides; certainly cooking must be part of the area of competence of every well-behaved girl! But what do we have here? In the first place, my beauty, my queen, they won't let you go, but will pursue you and then shut you up in a nunnery. Then what, my dear young lady? What will you have me do then? Will you have me, my dear young lady, in imitation of certain stupid novels, come to a nearby mound and dissolve in tears, looking at the cold walls of your incarceration, and finally die, in imitation of the custom of certain bad German poets and novelists; is that it, young lady? Well, in the first place, permit me to tell you in a friendly manner that things are not done that way, and, in the second place, I would heartily flog both you and your parents for giving you French books to read; for French books do not teach what is good. There is poison in them . . . noxious poison, my dear young lady! Or do you think, permit me to ask you, or do you think that, I say, 'This is the way it is,' we shall run away unpunished, and, well, you know . . . I say, 'a cabin for you on the shore of the Khvalynskoye Sea, while I, for my part, shall be a court clerk;' and, well, we'll start to bill and coo and discuss our various feelings, and we'll spend our whole life thus, in happiness and contentment; and then we'll have a little one, so we, you know . . . we say, 'This is the way is it, our father and State Councilor, Olsufi Ivanovich; here,' we say, 'a little one has arrived, so will you, on this convenient occasion, remove your malediction and bless this couple?' No, young lady, and once again, let me tell you, things are not done that way, and the first thing is that there'll be no billing and cooing; don't hope for it. Nowadays the husband, my dear young lady, is master and a good, well-brought-up wife must try to please him in every way. And they don't like endearments nowadays, young lady, in our industrial age; 'the time of Jean-Jacques Rousseau is over,' I say. The husband, for instance, comes home hungry from work nowadays—he says, 'Darling, how about a little something, a drop of vodka and a nibble of herring?' And you, young lady, must immediately have both the vodka and the herring ready. Your husband will eat and drink with gusto and not even glance at you, but will say: 'Do go,' he'll say, 'into the kitchen, kitten, and keep an eye on dinner,' and maybe, just maybe, once a week he'll kiss you, and even then he'll be indifferent . . . That's the way we do it, my dear young lady! That's how it will be, if we reason thus, if it's come to that already, that we've begun to look at the matter in this way . . . And what do I have to do with it? Why have you mixed me up in your whims, young lady? You said, 'Beneficent man, suffering for my sake and dear to my heart in every way, etc.' Well, in the first place, my dear young lady, I'm not suitable for you; you know yourself I'm no hand at compliments; I don't like to utter all that scented stuff and nonsense for the ladies; I don't favor ladies' men; and what's more, to tell the truth, my figure hasn't done anything for me. You won't find any false bragging or false shame in me, and I confess this to you now in all sincerity. I say, 'That's how it is'; a straightforward and open character and common sense are all I possess; I don't engage in intrigues. 'I'm not an intriguer,' I say, 'and I'm proud of it—so there! . . .' I go about without a mask among good people and, to tell you the whole truth . . ."

Suddenly Mr. Golyadkin started. The red, thoroughly soaked beard of his driver again looked in behind the woodpile at him . . .

"I'll be there right away, my friend; I'll be there immediately, my friend, you know; I'll be there at once, my friend," Mr. Golyadkin answered in a quavering and weary voice.

The driver scratched the back of his head, then smoothed his beard, then took a step forward . . . stopped and looked with mistrust at Mr. Golyadkin.

"I'll be there right away, my friend; I, you see . . . my friend . . . I'm a little, I, you see, my friend, I'm stopping here for just a second . . . you see, my friend . . ."

"Can it be that you won't be going at all?" said the driver at last, accosting Mr. Golyadkin resolutely once and for all . . .

"No, my friend, I'll be there right away. You see, my friend, I'm waiting . . ."

"Yes, sir . . ."

"You see, my friend, I . . . what village are you from, my dear fellow?"

"I'm a serf . . ."

"And is the master a good person? . . ."

"He's all right . . ."

"Yes, my friend; you wait here, my friend. You, you see, my friend, have you been in Petersburg long?"

"I've been driving a year now . . ."

"And are you doing well, my friend?"

"All right."

"Yes, my friend, yes. Thank Providence, my friend. You search for a good person, my friend. Nowadays good people have become rare, my dear fellow; he will take care of you, feed you and give you drink, my dear fellow, a good man will . . . But sometimes you see tears flowing even for the sake of gold, my friend . . . You see a sorry example; that's how it is, my dear fellow . . ."

The driver seemed to feel sorry for Mr. Golyadkin.

"All right, if you please, I'll wait, sir. But are you going to be waiting a long time, sir?"

"No, my friend, no; I'm not going to, you know, um . . .
I'm not going to wait any longer, my dear fellow. What do you
think, my friend? I'm relying on you. I'm not going to wait here
any longer . . ."

"Can it be you won't go at all?"

"No, my friend; no, but I'll show my gratitude to you, my
dear fellow . . . that's how it is. How much do I owe you, my dear
fellow?"

"Why, what we agreed upon, sir. I've waited a long time,
sir. You wouldn't treat a person badly, sir."

"Well, here you are, my dear fellow, here you are." Mr.
Golyadkin hereupon gave the full six silver rubles to the driver
and seriously resolving to lose no more time, and concluding
that it all had most likely been that way and that the best thing
to do was to leave it that way, that is, to get away while the
getting was good—the moreso since the matter had been
decided once and for all and the driver had been let go and,
consequently, there was nothing more to wait for—he started
out of the courtyard himself, went through the gates, turned
left and without looking back, gasping for breath and rejoicing,
set off at a run. "Perhaps it will all turn out for the best," he
thought, "and this way I've avoided trouble." And, in fact, Mr.
Golyadkin suddenly began to feel unusually lighthearted. "Ah,
if only everything would turn out for the best!" thought our
hero, but without much believing his own words. "Here's what
I'll do . . ." he thought. "No, I'd better try a different approach.
. . Or would it be better for me to do it this way? . . ." While thus
doubting and searching for the key to the resolution of his
doubts, our hero ran as far as the Semyonovsky Bridge, but
having run as far as the Semyonovsky Bridge, decided judiciously and with finality to go back. "This is the better way," he
thought. "I'd better use a different approach, that is, do it that
way. I'll just be—I'll be an outside observer, and that's all there
is to it; I'll say, 'I'm an observer, an outsider—and that's all', and
then, no matter what may happen—I'm not to blame. That's
how it is! And that's how it will be now."

Having decided to go back, our hero actually did go back,
and went readily since, as a result of his happy thought, he had

now made himself a complete outsider. "It really is better; you're not responsible for anything, but you'll see what's what ... that's how it is!" That is, his reckoning was most infallible and that's all there was to it. And since that was absolutely all there was to it and there was no one else to feel rancor toward, and since everyone was supposed to be utterly happy and content, our hero in turn also calmed down completely. Having calmed down, he betook himself again to the peaceful safety of his soothing and protective woodpile and and began to watch the windows intently. This time he did not have to watch and wait for long. Suddenly a strange commotion was discernible in all of the windows at once; figures appeared here and there; the curtains were opened; whole groups of people thronged to the windows of Olsufi Ivanovich's apartment; everyone was peering out and searching for something in the courtyard. Protected by the safety of his woodpile, our hero, too, in turn, began to follow the general commotion with curiosity and to stick his head out, looking with interest to the right and left, to the extent that the short shadow of the woodpile screening him permitted. Suddenly he became panic-stricken, started and almost collapsed with fear. So that's how it was ... So that's the way the whole business was going now ... They were searching not for just something and not for just someone; they were searching for him, Mr. Golyadkin. Why, it really is so and there is no longer any doubt about it. I say, 'That's how it is.' I say, 'This is the way it is, but it's Mr. Golyadin they're searching for.' Everyone is looking in his direction; everyone is pointing in his direction. It was impossible to flee: they would see ... The panic-stricken Mr. Golyadkin pressed himself as closely as he could against the woodpile and only then did he notice that the perfidious shadow was betraying him, that it did not screen all of him. Our hero would have acquiesced now with the utmost pleasure to squeeze into any mousehole between the logs and just sit there quietly, if only that had been possible. But it was absolutely impossible. In his agony our hero began at last to look resolutely and directly at all of the windows at once; it was better that way ... And suddenly he burned with utter shame. He had been fully discovered; they had all noticed him at the same time; they were all beckoning to him; they were all nodding to him; they were all calling him; now several ventilation panes clicked and opened; several voices began simultaneously to shout something to him . . . "I'm amazed they don't flog these worthless girls when they're children," our hero muttered, becoming totally flustered. Suddenly he (we know who) ran down the front steps, without a coat or hat, breathless, worn out, whirling, bouncing along with his mincing gait, and perfidiously expressing how terribly glad he was to see Mr. Golyadkin at last.

"Yakov Petrovich," twittered this person notorious for his worthlessness, "Yakov Petrovich, you here? You'll catch cold. It's cold here, Yakov Petrovich. Do come inside."

"Yakov Petrovich! No, sir, I'm fine, Yakov Petrovich," our hero muttered in a submissive voice.

"No, sir; you mustn't refuse, Yakov Petrovich; they entreat you; they most humbly entreat you; they're waiting for us. They said, 'Do us the pleasure of bringing Yakov Petrovich in.' So there you are, sir."

"No, Yakov Petrovich; you see, I would do better . . . It would be better if I went home, Yakov Petrovich . . ." said our hero, roasting over a slow fire and freezing at the same time, from shame and horror.

"No, no, no, no!" twittered the loathsome person. "No, no, no, I won't take no for an answer! Let's go!" he said resolutely and dragged Mr. Golyadkin Senior towards the front steps. Mr. Golyadkin Senior did not at all want to go, but as everyone was looking and it would have been stupid to resist and dig in his heels, our hero went; however, it cannot be said that he went, for he absolutely did not know what was happening to him. But never mind, still he went!

Before our hero had time to put himself to rights in any way and regain his senses, he found himself in a reception room. He was pale, disheveled and tormented; he took in the whole crowd with lacklustre eyes—horrors! The reception room and all the other rooms were absolutely jam-packed. There were hordes of people and a whole bevy of ladies. All of them were crowding around Mr. Golyadkin; all of them were pressing towards Mr. Golyadkin; all of them were bearing Mr. Golyadkin along; he very clearly noticed that they were pushing him in a certain direction. "But not to the door," flashed through Mr. Golyadkin's mind. And indeed, they were pushing him not to the door but straight towards Olsufi Ivanovich's comfortable armchair. On one side of the armchair stood Klara Olsufyevna, pale, languid, melancholy, but magnificently adorned. What particularly struck Mr. Golyadkin were the tiny white flowers in her black hair, which created a superb effect. On the other side of the armchair Vladimir Semyonovich stood firm in a black morning coat, with his new decoration in his buttonhole. Mr. Golyadkin was being conducted, as has been said above, straight towards Olsufi Ivanovich—on one side by Mr. Golyadkin Junior, who had put on an extraordinarily proper and well-intentioned air, at which our hero was utterly overjoyed; on the other side he was being directed by Andrei Filippovich, whose face bore a most solemn mien. "What can this mean?" thought Mr. Golyadkin. But when he saw that he was being conducted towards Olsufi Ivanovich, it was as if he had suddenly been illuminated by a flash of lightning. The thought of the intercepted letter flashed through his mind . . . In immeasurable agony our hero appeared before Olsufi Ivanovich's armchair. "How shall I act now?" he thought to himself. "Fearlessly, of course, that is, with a frankness not devoid of nobility; I'll say, 'This is the way it is, etc.'" But what our hero had apparently been fearing did not happen. Olsufi Ivanovich seemed to receive Mr. Golyadkin extremely well, and although he did not extend his hand to him, at least in looking at him he shook his grey, awe-inspiring head—shook it with a solemn and sad but at the same time benevolent look. So at least it seemed to Mr. Golyadkin. It even seemed to him that a tear glistened in Olsufi Ivanovich's lustreless eyes; he raised his eyes and saw that a little tear seemed also to glisten on the eyelashes of Klara Olsufyevna, who was standing nearby; that in the eyes of Vladimir Semyonovich, too, something similar seemed to be taking place; that, finally, Andrei Filippovich's calm and inviolable dignity was just as eloquent as the general tearful sympathy; that, finally, the youth who had at one time

279

very much looked like an important councilor, taking advantage of the present moment, was now sobbing bitterly . . . Or all of this, perhaps, only seemed so to Mr. Golyadkin because he himself was weeping copiously and distinctly felt the hot tears running down his cold cheeks . . . In a voice shaken by sobs, reconciled to men and fate and at that moment loving greatly not only Olsufi Ivanovich, not only the guests in their entirety, but even his pernicious twin, who now apparently was not at all pernicious and not even Mr. Golyadkin's twin but a complete outsider and an extremely amiable person in his own right, our hero tried to address Olsufi Ivanovich with a touching outpouring of his soul; but because of the fullness of all that had accumulated within him he could explain nothing at all, and only silently, with a most eloquent gesture, point to his heart . . . At last Andrei Filippovich, probably wishing to spare the sensibilities of the greyhaired old man, drew Mr. Golyadkin slightly aside and left him, it seemed, completely on his own. Smiling, muttering something under his breath, somewhat bewildered, but in any case almost completely reconciled with men and fate, our hero began to make his way somewhere through the dense crowd of Olsufi Ivanovich's guests. Everyone made way for him; everyone looked at him with a strange curiosity and an enigmatic, inexplicable sympathy. Our hero passed into the next room; everywhere he received the same attention; he vaguely heard the entire crowd following close upon his heels, noting his every step, furtively discussing among themselves something extremely interesting, shaking their heads, talking, arguing and whispering. Mr. Golyadkin would have very much liked to find out what they were all discussing and arguing and whispering about so. He knew very well, though, what it was about. Looking round, our hero noticed Mr. Golyadkin Junior beside him. Feeling the need to grab his arm and draw him aside, Mr. Golyadkin most earnestly entreated the other Yakov Petrovich to assist him in all his future undertakings and not to abandon him at a critical moment. Mr. Golyadkin Junior nodded gravely and firmly shook Mr. Golyadkin Senior's hand. Our hero's heart began to tremble from an excess of emotion. He was gasping for breath though; he felt that something was squeezing him ever more tightly, that all those eyes turned on him were somehow oppressing and crushing him . . . Mr. Golyadkin caught a glimpse of that councilor who was wearing a wig. The councilor was giving him a stern, searching look, not at all softened by the general sympathy . . . Our hero was about to go straight over to him, give him a smile and have it out with him immediately, but somehow it did not work out. For one instant Mr. Golyadkin almost lost consciousness completely; both his memory and his senses failed him. When he regained his senses, he noticed that the guests had gathered around him in a large circle. Somehow our hero managed to extricate himself from the large circle and was about to make his way to the door. Suddenly Mr. Golyadkin's name was shouted from the other room. The shout was at once taken up by the entire crowd. Everything began to stir; everything began to hum; everyone rushed for the door of the first reception room; they almost carried our hero along with them, and the hard-hearted councilor with the wig came to find himself side by side with Mr. Golyadkin. Finally, he took Mr. Golyadkin by the arm and sat him down beside him, opposite the seat of Olsufi Ivanovich, but at a rather considerable distance from him. Everyone else from those rooms sat down in several rows around Mr. Golyadkin and Olsufi Ivanovich. Everything grew hushed and still; everyone observed a solemn silence; everyone was watching Olsufi Ivanovich, apparently expecting something rather out of the ordinary. Mr. Golyadkin noticed that the other Mr. Golyadkin and Andrei Filippovich had taken their places beside the armchair of Olsufi Ivanovich and directly opposite the councilor. The silence continued; they were, in fact, waiting for something. "Just like in a family, when some member of that family is going on a long journey; all we have to do now is stand up and say a prayer," thought our hero. Suddenly an unusual commotion took place, disrupting all of Mr. Golyadkin's reflections. Something long-awaited had occurred. "He's coming! He's coming!" ran through the crowd. "Who is it that's coming?" ran through Mr. Golyadkin's head and he shuddered from a strange sensation. "It's time!" said the councilor, looking intently at Andrei Filippovich. Andrei Filippovich in turn glanced at Olsufi Ivanovich. Olsufi Ivanovich gravely and solemnly gave a nod of his head. "Let's stand up," uttered the councilor, hauling Mr. Golyadkin to his feet. Everyone rose. Then the councilor took Mr. Golyadkin Senior by the arm while Andrei Filippovich did the same to Mr. Golyadkin Junior, and the two of them solemnly brought the two exactly identical persons together in the midst of the crowd which had surrounded them and was watching with intense expectation. Our hero looked about in bewilderment but they immediately checked him and indicated Mr. Golyadkin Junior, who had extended his hand to him. "They want to reconcile us," thought our hero and extended his hand to Mr. Golyadkin Junior with a feeling of tenderness; then he bent his head towards him. The other Mr. Golyadkin did the same . . . At this point it seemed to Mr. Golyadkin Senior that his perfidious friend was smiling, that he winked swiftly and roguishly at all those around them, that there was something malevolent in the face of the unseemly Mr. Golyadkin Junior, that he even made a grimace at the moment of his Judas kiss . . . There was a ringing in Mr. Golyadkin's head. It went black before his eyes. It seemed to him that a host, a whole string of exactly identical Golyadkins was noisily breaking in through all the doors of the room; but it was too late . . . The resounding, traitorous kiss was heard, and . . .

At this point a completely unexpected event occurred . . . The door to the reception room opened noisily and on the threshold appeared a man whose very aspect struck terror into Mr. Golyadkin. He stood rooted to the spot. A cry froze in his constricted breast. Still, Mr. Golyadkin had known everything beforehand and had had a premonition of something like this for a long time now. The stranger gravely and solemnly drew near to Mr. Golyadkin . . . Mr. Golyadkin knew this figure very well. He had seen it before, seen it very frequently, seen it that very day . . . The stranger was a tall, thickset man in a black morning coat with a sizeable cross around his neck and endowed with very black, bushy sidewhiskers; all he needed to complete the resemblance was a small cigar in his mouth . . . Still the stranger's look, as has already been said, struck terror into Mr. Golyadkin. With a grave and solemn mien, the terrifying man approached the pathetic hero of our tale... Our hero stretched his hand out to him; the stranger took his hand and pulled him along after him . . . With a perplexed and crushed look on his face, our hero gazed around . . .

"It's . . . it's Krestyan Ivanovich Rutenshpits, Doctor of Medicine and Surgery, your old acquaintance, Yakov Petrovich!" someone's loathsome voice twittered right in Mr. Golyadkin's ear. He looked round: it was Mr. Golyadkin's twin, made loathsome by the vile qualities of his soul. An unseemly, malevolent glee shone in his face; he was rubbing his hands together with delight; he was turning his head from side to side with delight; he was mincing about near each and every one with delight; he even seemed ready at that point to begin to dance with delight; at last he leapt forward, seized a candle from one of the servants and went ahead lighting the way for Mr. Golyadkin and Krestyan Ivanovich. Mr. Golyadkin clearly heard everyone in the reception room rush after him, heard everyone running ahead, crowding and crushing each other and all beginning to repeat together, in one voice, after Mr. Golyadkin: "It's all right; don't be afraid, Yakov Petrovich; why, this is your old friend and acquaintance, Krestyan Ivanovich Rutenshpits . . ." At last they came out onto the brightly illumined main staircase; on the staircase, too, there was a crowd of people; the front door was thrown open noisily and Mr. Golyadkin found himself on the steps together with Krestyan Ivanovich. At the entrance stood a coach, its four horses snorting with impatience. Full of malicious glee, Mr. Golyadkin Junior came down the stairs in three bounds and opened the coach door himself. Krestyan Ivanovich, with an authoritative gesture, requested Mr. Golyadkin to get in. The authoritative gesture was totally unnecessary, however; there were plenty of people to help him get in . . . Fainting with terror, Mr. Golyadkin looked back: the whole of the brightly illumined staircase was covered with people; inquisitive eyes were looking at him from everywhere; Olsufi Ivanovich presided on the topmost landing in his comfortable armchair, watching with the most intense interest all that was taking place.

Everyone was waiting. A murmur of impatience ran through the crowd when Mr. Golyadkin looked back.

"I trust that there is nothing... nothing reprehensible... or capable of provoking severe measures . . . and exciting public attention, as far as my official relations are concerned?" uttered our hero, losing his presence of mind. A hubbub of voices rose all about; everyone began to shake his head to say there wasn't. Tears gushed from Mr. Golyadkin's eyes.

"In that case, I am ready; I have complete confidence... 'This is the way it is,' I say; I withdraw myself from my duties and place my fate in the hands of Krestyan Ivanovich . . . ."

No sooner had Mr. Golyadkin uttered the words that he placed his fate completely in the hands of Krestyan Ivanovich than a terrible, deafening shout of joy broke out from all those around him and rolled with a most sinister echo through all of the waiting crowd. At this point Krestyan Ivanovich on one side and Andrei Filippovich on the other took Mr. Golyadkin by the arms and began to help him into the coach; the double, as was his customary vile wont, helped him in from behind. The unfortunate Mr. Golyadkin Senior cast his final glance at everyone and everything and, trembling like a kitten that has been doused with cold water—if we may be permitted the comparison—climbed into the coach; Krestyan Ivanovich climbed in immediately after him. The coach door slammed; the crack of the whip on the horses was heard; the horses started the coach up with a jerk... everyone rushed after Mr. Golyadkin. The piercing, furious cries of all his enemies rang out after him like a series of farewell wishes. For some time still a few people could be glimpsed around the coach that was bearing Mr. Golyadkin away; but at last they too began to be left further and further behind and finally disappeared altogether. Mr. Golyadkin's unseemly twin remained longer than any of them; with his hands in the side pockets of his green uniform trousers, he ran along with a satisfied air, leaping up now on one side of the coach, now on the other; sometimes he even ran ahead of the horses; and sometimes, grabbing hold of the window frame and hanging from it with the full weight of his body, he would poke his head in through the window and cast tender glances at Mr. Golyadkin Senior, smiling at him and saying goodbye to him, and would nod his head and throw him endless little kisses . . . At last he too seemed to tire, began to appear less and less frequently at the sides of the coach and finally disappeared altogether. Mr. Golyadkin's heart began to ache dully in his breast; the blood rushed hotly to his head; it was stifling; he felt like unbuttoning his clothing, baring his breast, sprinkling it with snow and dousing it with cold water . . . He sank at last into forgetfulness . . . When he regained his senses, he saw that the horses were taking him along an almost unfamiliar road; to the right and to the left forests of some kind loomed darkly; it was godforsaken and lonely. There was not a living soul about. It began to snow. Anguish weighed heavy on Mr. Golyadkin Senior's breast like an incubus. He became terrified . . . Totally overcome by exhaustion, by anguish, and by agony, totally cowed and crushed, he pressed his shoulder against that of the taciturn Krestyan Ivanovich . . . But suddenly he recoiled from him in horror and huddled into the other corner of the coach. His hair stood on end. A cold sweat rolled down his temples. He glanced—and froze in terror . . . Two fiery eyes were looking at him in the darkness, and those two eyes were shining with sinister, infernal glee. Those eyes came closer and closer to Mr. Golyadkin . . . He already felt someone's touch, someone's burning breath on his face, someone's hands stretched out above him and ready to seize him. This isn't Krestyan Ivanovich! Who is it? . . . Or is it he? . . . It is! It is Krestyan Ivanovich, only not the former one; this is another Krestyan Ivanovich.

"You must not be an enemy of the bottle," flashed through Mr. Golyadkin's mind . . . However, he was no longer thinking anything. Slowly, with trepidation, he closed his eyes. Numbly he awaited something horrible; he awaited it . . . he already heard it, felt it and—at last . . .

But here, ladies and gentlemen, ends the story of Mr. Golyadkin's adventures.

Notes

1. According to Peter the Great's Table of Ranks, a Titular Councilor was ninth on a scale of one to fourteen in the civil service, with fourteen the lowest rank. Most of the civil service ranks had corresponding military and court ranks. For a useful chart showing all the ranks, see *The Collected Tales and Plays of Nikolai Gogol*, trans. Constance Garnett, rev. Leonard J. Kent (New York: The Modern Library, 1969), p. xli.
2. From July 1, 1839 to June 1, 1843 one silver ruble was equal to 3½ ruble notes (assignatsiya) (Franz Pick and Renè Sèdillot, *All the Monies of the World* (New York: Pick Publishing Corporation, 1971), p. 488). The colors of the ruble notes signified their denomination: green = 3 rubles, grey = 50, blue = 5, red = 10, multicolored = 100.
3. Collegiate Assessor: Grade 8, i.e., one rank above Titular Councilor, in the civil service.
4. Collegiate Registrar: Grade 14 in the civil service.
5. State Councilor: Grade 5 in the civil service.
6. Collegiate Councilor: Grade 6 in the civil service.
7. The name Golyadkin means poor beggar, poor devil.
8. The concluding line of I. A. Krylov's fable "The Coffer," in which an expert attempts to open a coffer in every way except by lifting the lid and withdraws in defeat. The solution to a problem may be quite simple, but some people fail to find it because they anticipate a complexity that does not exist. Krylov was also alluding to the dangers of being an expert.
9. Provincial Secretary: Grade 13.
10. The rank of general was the army rank corresponding to Actual Privy Councilor in the civil service (Grade 2).
11. The editors of the edition of Dostoevsky's works from which this translation was made supplied this footnote, which reads: [1] This is in the text of the journal publication.
12. The Old Russian name for the Caspian Sea (*PSS*, p. 496).
13. A footnote has been supplied here by the editors of the *PSS* edition of "The Double". It reads: "[1] In the 1866 text - 'our much-praised girl.' The given variant may be a misprint. It is also possible to see in it an allusion to a saying, an allusion later removed because of the inexactness of its meaning: the porridge praises itself."

    There is an expression in Russian: Vsyakaya falya sama sebya khvalit. "Falya" means a "simpleton" or "ninny". "Kasha" also has these meanings. (See *Slovar' russkikh narodnykh govorov*, vypusk 13, [Leningrad: Izd-stvo "Nauka", 1977], p. 148). "Khvalenaya kasha" could therefore mean "much-praised ninny" and be appropriate here.

Rough Drafts for a Proposed Reworking of *The Double*[1]

Notebook No. 1   1860-62

Into *Golyadkin*

Mr. Golyadkin is being destroyed by a cup of sorrows and writes a letter to Golyadk/in/ Junior, his mortal enemy, about *a helping hand* (a chivalrous letter). (I am at the Beketovs.[2] I am going to Turg/enev's/.)[3]

Mr. Golyadkin Junior meets with Senior. Junior romanticizes and draws Senior into romanticism. He goes as far almost as Manilov's generals.[4] Sometimes he shows his true self at the same time, i.e., displays some *vile calculation.* This jars on Senior, but he keeps silent *out of comradeliness* and reproaches himself: why does he keep silent.

Junior's dreams, aloud, about a duel with the lieutenant, with the general (Junior's practical advice—to challenge /Senior/ the general to a duel). Mr. Golyadkin's astonishment, but he agrees, out of romanticism and out of the raptures of the herd instinct. Mr. Golyadkin Junior explains to Senior: what I accept my beneficent superiors as a father means and what is chivalrous about this. The juridical and patriarchal relationship to authority and that the government itself seeks /to be accepted, looked upon EJH/ *as a father.*

NB Herein is the anatomy of all Russian attitudes to authority. The mutual dreams of both Golyadkins under the command of Junior, how the general will understand chivalrousness and come forth to duel, how he will not shoot; *one can stand at the barrier and do nothing* further, say, "I am satisfied, Your Excellency." How then Golyadkin marries the general's daughter. Manilov. That would be *paradise.*

The next day at the office Mr. Golyadkin Junior whispers to senior, pointing to the general: *"Go on and challenge him."*

Golyadkin Junior tells about the lieutenant, about Senior, and basely fawning, amuses the company. Mr. Golyadkin Senior hears. The duel. Pargolovo.[5] Mr. Golyadkin Jun/ior/ fought in his stead.

Into *Golyadkin*

Elie de Beaumont.[6] The next day he took him by the ear: "You and I are learned folks, Yakov Petrovich, Elie de Beaumont."

Mr. Golyadkin looked with hatred at *Junior,* at how he snorted while splashing at the washstand.

Petrushka's crude remarks about the washstand; Mr. Golyadkin is ashamed that he doesn't have a good washstand.

Mr. Golyadkin and the cabman: Tears flow for the sake of gold. The cabman says: If he's a good man, then you see it right away. *The other day they carried off Zakharka's cow.*

Petrushka's snorting (develop this).

Golyadkin to Petrushka about Junior: "He's repenting." Again there is snorting.

How he snorted and splashed in the washstand. It seemed to him that he was /in vain/ deliberately snorting in order to offend him.

NB From the juridical point of view the authorities act only according to the law. This is only crude subordination and obedience to authority. But if one takes the authorities as a father, then this means familiality, this means the subordination of one's entire self and all of one's family instead of an authoritarian relationship. The principle of the child's relationship to the father. *The childish prattle of innocence, and this is more pleasing to the authorities.*

This is *Junior*'s theory. Junior is the personification of baseness.

The innermost secrets of the bureaucratic soul in the manner of Tolstoy.[7]

Into *Golyadkin*
Their Dreams

Golyadkin on the eve of the duel. Junior, the second, took to his heels early in the morning. Underhandedly duped him. The second fought in place of the duelist.

Petits jeux at Klara Olsufyevna's. Golyadkin taken for a fool. Thereupon the challenge of the lieutenant.

Alone with *Junior*. Dreams of becoming Napoleon, Pericles, the marshal of the Russian revolt. Liberalism and revolution restoring Louis XVI with tears and obeying him (out of goodness).

Mr. Golyadkin Junior reproaches Senior for hiding bits of dinner from him.

Junior tells in company about Senior all those little things (secret and innermost, which everyone has and everyone hides, as secrets, from everyone), comical trifles which Golyadk/in/ Senior was jealously hiding from Junior and was absolutely sure that Junior would not find out; but Junior did find out. Mr. Golyadk/in/ *Junior* knows everything about Senior and finds out everything. Supernatural power.

Junior, it turns out, knows all of Senior's secrets, as if he were the embodiment of Senior's conscience.

Into *Golyadkin*, a big and *most fundamental* scene:

Junior decides to help Senior concerning Klara Olsufyevna. *Petits jeux innocents*; they are taken as *a freak of nature*. Mr. Golyadkin dimly perceives that he will be accepted into society as *a freak of nature*, and does not want this. He sees that Junior too *is babbling* that they are being invited as *a freak of nature*, but he says nothing because of the herd instinct.

Before the *petits jeux* Junior worms out of Senior a confession of love for Klara Olsufyevna (Junior already knows it without Senior's confession of it). He begins to teach Senior how to conquer Klara Olsufyevna; he coaches him in being casual; the theory of how *idle hands just seem to stick out in an odd manner*.[8] Of the need to make a *bon mot*; they try to find out what kind of a *bon mot* to make. They invent puns in the style of Kozma

290

Prutkov.[9] They found a *bon mot.* At the party Mr. Golyadkin Senior (dimly perceives that he is like a freak of nature and that when he starts to speak everyone stops talking, but they whisper, laughing and waiting for him to say something stupid) tries to put in his *bon mot,* but doesn't know how to. Junior helps him, but /it's as if/ in actuality he interferes with Senior's performance; it just does not come off.

Finally, Junior cruelly tells all and relates how they tried to find a *bon mot,* how they wanted to captivate the maiden, etc., in a word, everything that happened at Golyadkin's, even the washstand and Petrushka. Guffaws. *Elie de Beaumont* and so forth.

Mr. Golyadkin's pathetic tirade. He flees. At home: his entire morning coat is studded with candy wrappers.

And then comes the *pathetic* letter. *To Junior.* The duel with the lieutenant and *the final degradation, i.e., the madhouse.*

NB "When you (in Chapter 1) invited /Golyad/ Klara Olsufyevna *to dance the polka,* you revolted against society," says Junior to Senior, pathetically consoling him.

Senior's dreams: we would have lived as twins, in friendship; society would have looked upon us tenderly, and we would have died, our graves side by side.

"We could even have been in one coffin," Junior notes *casually.*

"Why did you note that *casually?*" Senior asks captiously.

NB A poor, a very poor lame German woman, renting out rooms, who at one time used to help Golyadkin and whom Junior spied on, whom Senior is afraid to acknowledge. His and her story pathetically recounted to Junior, who betrays him and tells it.

Notebook No. 2   1862-64

Golyadkin. The doors at the office, their awful bang and noise would always depress Mr. Golyadkin and turn him into a rag.

Mr. Golyadkin was *bashful.*

Mr. Golyadkin asks the Director to be his second.

A project concerning the prosperity of Russia, created by Mr. Golyadkin.

Mr. Golyadkin assumes close ties with the soil[10] at the copyists'.

The Director on the Nevsky at night. Galoshes, a fantastic scene.

The handsome lieutenant.

Mr. Golyadkin is accused of being Garibaldi.

Mr. Golyadkin at the countess's in high society.

Mr. Golyadkin joins the progressists. Oxygen and hydrogen.

Mr. Golyadkin eavesdrops and behind the partition hears stories about quail (at Lomovsky's).[11]

Kittens.

Mr. Golyadkin at /Petrashevsky's/.

Junior gives speeches. Timkovsky[12] as one who has come from out of town. Fourier's system. Noble tears. They embrace one another. Oh, he will inform.

The Double

The next day Mr. Golyadkin goes to /Petrashevsky's and/ finds the latter reading Fourier's system to the yard keeper and to his peasants, and notifies him that *the other one* will inform.

"I don't understand."

"Why, there are two of us."

"Protest."

"But how can I protest?"

"Well, for instance, they flog boys at school with birches."[13]

"Yes, but none of this is an answer to the question."

"Well, sir, I'll tell you: all of this will change when new economic relations come into being, but I won't say anything more."

(P/etrashevs/ky has already been warned by Junior that this one will inform, and he says: "It's you who are the informer.")

The most important psychological incident in the poem:

It is remarkable that Mr. Golyadkin-Senior at all his horrifying moments and in all his difficult circumstances ends up by /unfail/ always resorting to the advice and, if possible, to the protection of *Junior,* while at the same time intriguing against him. Thus the meetings (he even sets the meetings up in advance: at the pastry shop, at the German woman's, etc.)

Finally, *Junior's* last piece of advice:

"Ask forgiveness."

(The stunning news, 1st) about Garibaldi, and 2nd, about oxygen and hydrogen. Oxygen and hydrogen make his head whirl. There is no longer a Supreme Being. What will happen to the ministry and to his superiors? *The dream.* Everything has been abolished. People are free. They all *beat one another* openly on the street. *They provide for themselves* (save their kopeks).

The continuation of Golyadk/in/. 24 July. /One indecipherable word/

Golyadk/in/: "May I ask what all this means? I keep trying—I'd like to have even just an inkling of what it all means."

Junior: "Why do you keep trying? Keep calm, and everything will be fine."

"I'd like to have even just an inkling."

"But why? And what's more, perhaps it doesn't mean anything at all."

"What, sir?"

"Yes, sir. Anything can happen and mean nothing at all."

About the appearance in the town of the famous robber Garibaldi.

In Golyadkin one can see how a person becomes confused because, except for the administrators, nobody knows anything.

(So what, now here's Garibaldi, but I don't know anything about him.)

He checks on Garibaldi in various ministries. It's a secret, sir. For a ten-kopek piece he gets the address: State Councilor, retired, in Kirpichny Lane, No. 31.

Goes to Kirpichny Lane and waits. The footman shows him out. (I am at Gayburksky's.)[14]

Then the chapter night, dawn, corpses.

Mr. Golyadkin thinks: "How can one be without a father? I can't be without having someone who is like a father to me."

We are not society. The simple people are society, while we are the public (into the project).

Mr. Golyadkin /having challenged/ has challenged to a duel, talks with Petrushka about the rules of honor and instructs him (I struck first—my initiative). But Petrushka, out of self-esteem, interrupts him, won't let him have his say and instructs him in the rules of honor.

Notes

1. This translation has been made from the fragments which appear in *Neizdannyi Dostoevsky,* pp. 136-40, 178-79.

2. Dostoevsky was very friendly with the Beketov brothers in the 1840s (*Neizdannyi Dostoevsky,* p. 162). Alexei Beketov studied at the Academy of Engineers with Dostoevsky, graduating in 1844 (*PSS,* vol. 1, p. 496). From October 1846 through spring 1847 Dostoevsky shared an apartment with the brothers (*PSS,* vol. 1, p. 496). In 1877 Nikolai Beketov wrote to Dostoevsky: "I have not forgotten you, even though I was only nineteen when I said goodbye to you. Since then you have ever continued your indefatigable labor of studying the human soul. Reading your works is a conversation with one's own conscience—to such a degree do they have universal meaning, for all mankind..." (*Neizdannyi Dostoevsky,* p. 162).

3. Apparently Dostoevsky intended to use autobiographical material here relating to the deterioration in his relations with the group affiliated with the journal *The Contemporary.* The situation was exacerbated by the fact that the writers I. S. Turgenev and N. A. Nekrasov had written an epigram against Dostoevsky. When Dostoevsky then saw Turgenev, he "gave full vent to his smoldering anger," after which he broke once and for all with Belinsky's circle. "Witticisms and biting epigrams came showering down on him; he was accused of monstrous pride and jealousy of Gogol, at whose feet he should have made obeisance..." (*PSS,* p. 497).

4. At the end of chapter 2 of *Dead Souls,* when Chichikov has departed from Manilov's estate, the latter, a saccharine landowner happily married to the point of silliness, imagines how "the Emperor, on finding out about this friendship of theirs, bestowed on them the rank of general" (see also *PSS,* p. 497).

5. A place near Petersburg where Dostoevsky lived in the summer of 1847 (*PSS,* p. 497).

6. Jean Baptiste Armand (a geologist) and Jean Baptiste Jacques (a lawyer). Golyadkin Junior's reference to them seems to be part of the "double" motif (*PSS,* p. 497).

7. A reference to L. N. Tolstoy's talent for minute psychological analysis, which was evident beginning with his first novel *Childhood*.

8. A line from Nekrasov's poem "Shyness" (1852) (*Neizdannyi Dostoevsky*, p. 164).

9. K. Prutkov was a fictitious poet invented by the poet A. K. Tolstoy and his cousins, the Zhemchuzhnikov brothers.

10. The idea that the Russian educated classes needed to renew contact with the people (the soil), from whom they had become alienated.

11. In 1834-35 Dostoevsky and his brother, Mikhail, were pupils at Chermak's Boarding School in Moscow; Lomovsky was Dostoevsky's mathematics teacher there (*PSS*, p. 429; *Neizdannyi Dostoevsky*, p. 193).

12. K. I. Timkovsky was a retired naval officer. He lived in Revel and attended Petrashevsky's gatherings on the rare occasions when he came to Petersburg (*PSS*, p. 499).

13. A reflection of the polemics appearing in journals then as a result of N. A. Dobrolyubov's articles "Pan-Russian Illusions Destroyed by Birching" (1860) and "Out of the Rain and into the Water" (1861), which were directed against the pedagogue, N. I. Pirogov, because of his inconsistent position on the issue of birching in school (*PSS*, p. 499).

14. The identity of this person has not been ascertained (*PSS*, p. 499).